Toni couldn't understand. How could he do this to her? She thought he loved her as much as she loved him...

"You—You bastard!" Toni shouted as she hurried over to him. "To think, all along I was feeling so sorry for you and—and it was your fault all the time. You used me, you bastard!"

"Toni, what are you talking about?" Mike pleaded as she quickly closed the distance between them.

"Don't play stupid. You know—"

"Wait a minute, will you?" Mike said, cutting her off. "I don't know what you're talking about. Did Doctor Ryan get the results back, is that why you're acting so...so irrational?"

"Irrational." Toni slapped him hard across the face. "Yeah, Doctor Ryan called, but he only talked to me when he couldn't get in touch with you. Seems he was more interested in telling you first!" she shouted.

She watched in renewed anger as Mike rubbed his cheek with the phony hurt look of the innocent on his face. She wanted to slap that look off his face but thought better of it.

The message she carried would be revenge enough, she vindictively decided.

Mike started to mouth a question, but Toni beat him to the punch.

"I asked Doctor Ryan why he couldn't tell me, since we were in this together. At first, he said it was a private matter and he couldn't share privileged patient information with anyone. After I cussed him out and told him we were both affected with his news, he changed his mind and told me."

"Told you what, that I also have the HIV virus?" Mike asked with amazing calm.

The unemotional tone of his voice impressed her. The fear of those three initials had caused her to cry so much over the last few days that she had to go to the drug store and purchase eye drops to stop the burning. Here Mike stood as if he had said ABC and not *HIV. Well, let's see if he can shake these other letters off so easily.* "You don't have HIV, Mike, but don't rejoice too much. The doctor said you've tested—positive—for—for—" Toni said, spitefully dragging it out, "—AIDS!"

What do you do when you finally find *that* person—the one who reaches so deep into your soul you fear the loss of your own identity? And once you've found each other is there any outside influence that can possibly come between two people who love so deeply? Mike and Toni didn't believe anything could destroy their happiness, until something unexpected caused such an upheaval that she ran off to Florida in anger, and he became so depressed he chose to drown himself in a bottle. What could have happened to tear apart their nirvana, another man or another woman? No. Not even that could separate them. But can *any* relationship, even one that runs so deep and true, survive the terrible curse of AIDS?

KUDOS for *Unbroken Blue Light*

In *Unbroken Blue Light* by E Lessly Taylor, Toni and Mike are soul mates who have finally found each other. Both have had disastrous relationships in the past and are extremely thankful for the love they have found. The only "fly in their ointment" is that they want the same happiness for their two best friends who don't seem to be as much in love. That is, until AIDS raises its ugly head and Mike and Toni's relationship is destroyed. How will their love survive? Heartbreaking, timely, and poignant, this is a story you won't soon forget. ~ *Taylor Jones, The Review Team of Taylor Jones & Regan Murphy*

Unbroken Blue Light by E Lessly Taylor is the story of two disillusioned people who finally find true love with each other and begin to plan their future together, only to be torn apart by AIDS. While the story mainly focuses on the two lovers, it also touches on racism, bigotry, and the sacrifices people make for those they love. A truly moving and poignant story, *Unbroken Blue Light* offers hope in the face of hopelessness. It will warm your heart while breaking it. It's a book everyone should read. ~ *Regan Murphy, The Review Team of Taylor Jones & Regan Murphy*

ACKNOWLEDGMENTS

Thanks to both family and friends who have encouraged me to continue publishing another of the fourteen novels I've written over the years. From scribbling notes on the back of whatever scrap paper I could find or gum wrappers; in the few minutes available while fixing the many problems with starting up a new galvanizing steel coating mill; to sitting at my computer in the wee hours of the night, allowing the characters in my mind to tell their stories, it has become a wonderful journey.

Kudos to those patient editors at Black Opal Books who have endured my many mistakes and typos helping me construct my stories in a legible manner.

UNBROKEN BLUE LIGHT

E. LESSLY TAYLOR

A Black Opal Books Publication

GENRE: ROMANCE/FAMILY DRAMA/WOMEN'S FICTION

This is a work of fiction. Names, places, characters and incidents are either the product of the author's imagination or are used fictitiously, and any resemblance to any actual persons, living or dead, businesses, organizations, events or locales is entirely coincidental. All trademarks, service marks, registered trademarks, and registered service marks are the property of their respective owners and are used herein for identification purposes only. The publisher does not have any control over or assume any responsibility for author or third-party websites or their contents.

UNBROKEN
BLUE
LIGHT

CHAPTER 1

Again, as the roar of the jet engines increased, she found herself staring blankly out the window as words of regret painted a bleak picture of her future. Once, it was the foolishness of youth that led her to trust in her feelings. To find justification in giving herself to a stranger whose music touched her hidden places. That wasn't uncommon. Young girls often fell victim to those awakening vibrations.

But how could she let that happen—again? How could she not see she was being used this time? The days of new explorations where a forgotten memory, weren't they? Didn't the title of woman signify she could no longer be so easily deceived? That first time…

As her thoughts drifted into the past, she peered out the window. That first time should have been the last time…

ↄ

The solitude they once passionately embraced now felt like an unwanted friend—like when you desperately sought to be alone with a special him or her and the third person never caught your hint and hit the road. They had finally found that solitude as large trees spread their branches overhead, adding shadows to their intimacy. No cars had driven past where they parked, but that was to be expected here. It was a first-come secluded place for those seeking the dark shadows without previous reservations. But something else was now present between them.

An hour ago, they were surrounded by loud music, and a wild laser light show as his rock band played in a room packed with rowdy young people dancing, drinking, smoking, and a few locked in the shadows exchanging bodily fluids. In a spontaneous act, the musician and the music lover secretly fled that insanity and now found their own solitude.

The deed done, the silence between them now made her feel uncomfortable. Add to that being surrounded by opaque car windows weeping from the steaming effort moments ago that encapsulated the silence.

Now was the moment when good girls saw through the haze and regretted their often-impulsive actions. Toni DiNardo, the young woman lying in the shadows of a back seat, became another one. She closed her eyes and tried to ignore what she had done. Maybe if she had found something in the deed worth having degraded herself for—but, no, she only felt used. There was little hurry to start searching for her underwear when noticing her partner in this crime now sitting up with his head back, eyes closed, and taking long drags on a twisted brown cigarette, with his shirt off, his pants down around his ankles, yet seemingly oblivious to her.

Toni was lying on her side with her knees up to her chest, her blouse off with her bra covering one breast and the other cup around her neck. Other than the one arm, he never gave her the chance to completely remove her bra. The expensive dark brown leather skirt, she excitedly purchased for the concert, lay bunched up around her waist, and one of her shoes was missing she noticed when she moved her toes. As she started to panic, another thought crossed her mind. She finally spotted her black beaded clutch bag, she had borrowed from Katie, lying on the floor partially covered by his pants.

Toni thought about sitting up and getting dressed before someone came along, adding to her embarrassment, when she took a deep breath and came to a more important decision. This would be her last time in the back of a four-wheeled motel. His disdain for herself afterward was copacetic. In her own words to her girlfriends, '*Anyone lying in a pigsty, is also a pig, whether they go oink or not.*' And he was giving her all the respect, or disrespect, she deserved.

When she did sit up, he ignored her and kept his head back, and his eyes closed, smoking as if it was his reward and not the free milk he received from the cow. She sighed deeply, raised her hips, and pulled her black leather miniskirt down over her bare ass. That free breast he'd been sucking on came next as she covered it with her bra. Even as she picked up and put on her blouse, the nameless drummer of the band Black Rain, who suggested they get away from the madness and smoke some weed after their last gig, never bothered to open his eyes and acknowledge her presence or cover up the little pink thing between his legs.

It's the hypnotizing beat of the drums, she conceded as she found the missing shoe but not her red thong panties, *that turns me on*. The hard rock music scene, and the ever present cloud of weed in the room, was what started her dreaming—and dreaming too much was Ms. Toni DiNardo's crutch. Someday, she envisioned, she would find her Mr. Wonderful, and he would be playing his heart out in a hard rock band. Being passionately into the music of her time, she believed the love of her life existed somewhere in that venue.

This was the third member of a visiting band the eighteen-year-old gave her...ah, milk...to this summer. Funny thing was each was the band's drummer. Not the hot lead singer, with the tight leather pants and flowing long blond hair that all the other groupies wanted, or the hunk usually on lead guitar and dazzling everyone with his talented fingers. No, it was the drummer that made her...moist. Something about the pounding of the drums that stirred the beat between her legs—at least that was her claim.

Toni would be dancing on the crowed floor with a nice looking guy, and the jungle-like pounding of the drums would beckon. Inevitably, she would find herself standing near the stage rocking to the beat as she stared at the drummer with her mouth open, breathing deeply with that "look" in her eyes every band member knew and relished.

She loved listening to both country and soul music, but dancing to the harsh rhythm of hard rock was so seductive she would only allow herself that pleasure on rare occasions and never with her best friends Brenda or Katie around because that was her enigmatic world. Her time to allow her demons out—in private.

Unfortunately, the powerful beat the talented drummers flawlessly played on the fake animal skins never carried over to their ability to skillfully milk the cow. After five or ten drum beats, this drummer was lighting up a hand-rolled cigarette before the cow could empty her...udders.

Sadly, again this night, she never came close—and these damn "dairy farmers" also never seemed to have protection.

"That was great, baby," the farmer finally acknowledged her when she started to get out of his car. "Hey, where ya going? Close the door. Let's just chill for a minute, and we can go again."

Toni took a deep breath and then slowly turned and looked at him. He wasn't very attractive, she noticed, and other than the myriad of tattoos, there was nothing physically remarkable about him either. Adding weight to the demeaning question of why, that she now asked herself, was the tattoo of a woman giving fellatio she spotted etched on the center of his pale white chest. *Classy*, she thought as she frowned, wondering how she missed seeing that and forgetting her eyes were mostly closed and her mouth open, sucking tongue.

"Like it," he asked seeing the object of her attention. "That's the image of the perfect woman. Interested?"

The grinning idiot proved one thing. It was the music that caused her to lose her panties, not this Ringo Starr imitation. He had the long hair of most rockers and a beard that rubbed against her skin. Sulking at that painful memory, she shook her head no.

"Come on, babe, that wasn't my best effort," he said as he started to become aroused.

"Maybe not," Toni answered, also noticing the feeble resurrection, "but it was your last—with me, anyway."

"Okay, beautiful, but…well, let me drive you back to the club."

"Why?" she asked, seeing the stupid grin on his face and then noticed he was unashamedly stroking himself.

"Well, I promised the other guys to give them a turn with the prettiest girl there. And you were the prettiest in the building, babe."

"A turn, huh?"

"Yeah, don't tell me you don't go for it, I saw that look in your eyes. You like to party, I can tell."

Toni wanted to cuss him out, but she had pigsty shit on her as well. Fighting back her emotions, she climbed out of the car and started walking. It didn't surprise her when moments later, after tramping through some overgrown weeds before reaching the street, his car pulled up beside her.

"Look, ah...girl...get in." He lowered his window and shouted at the nameless female. "I'll drop you off wherever you want. Hey, don't be a bitch," he added when she ignored him and continued walking, the rolling of her eyes signaling her intentions. "Well, screw you then!"

Toni watched as he raced off with tires squealing. She'd considered getting back in his car until he called her a bitch. She wasn't afraid to walk home from the local park. Actually, she was only a few blocks from her home and chose to stop here and smoke for that reason.

"Okay, Toni, it's time to draw a line in the sand," she said as she looked around, anxious that angry drummer might return. "Here you are walking home alone after having given it up again in the back seat of an expensive car with a cheap asshole." She looked around again, making sure she was walking alone. "He was a low life, but what does that make you? Hell, he didn't even value you enough to take you to his hotel room."

The next few steps were quietly given over to the tears leaking down her face. "Time to look elsewhere," she said as she walked out of the park and onto her street, "for the love of my life. Or...or stop looking altogether and let it happen like Brenda and Katie are always saying."

The girl—who was popular and dated frequently in high school, never allowed guys, other than these musical icons, to get past second base—made another vow as she spotted her house in the distance.

℘∽℘∽

What happened? David wondered as he drove over to Mike's apartment. How had things gone so bad—so quickly? Mike was very ill, Toni flying away to...somewhere, Brenda was angry with everyone, and none of his three friends were talking with each other. Mike and Toni, once so close he was privately envious of their passionate relationship, were now miles apart—literally and figuratively. How could you love someone that much and allow anything to come between you? he questioned.

David slowed as traffic came to a halt on Fifth Avenue. Usually, the variety of nice-looking girls, walking in every direction in this college section of Pittsburgh, proved a worthy distraction when waiting for the always congested traffic to start moving again. But that pleasing diversion failed to last. Again, the painful split up of his once-very-happy best friend Mike, and Toni, the beautiful girl Mike fell deeply in love with, returned to weigh heavily on his spirit. What could have possibly happened to break them up—again? David wondered. They survived one break up over a misunderstanding and seemed to have grown even closer. Could Mike have, no…he was too infatuated with Toni to be fooling around on her, David was sure of that.

"I thought the two of you had found your perfect match," David whispered, talking to himself as he waited for the traffic to start moving. "Everything was working out great for the two of you. Yeah, Brenda and I were lovers a few times but the two of you…wow. Your loving relationship was the nirvana she and I were reaching for and now…"

David shook his head as he turned onto Mike's street. It was the last place he wanted to be fearing that seeing his broken-hearted friend again might strain their friendship. He pulled up to Mike's apartment, turned off his car, and—and sat there. A smile formed on his face when a treasured memory floated across his thoughts. It was the same broken-hearted guy, hiding up in his apartment, that had once made him laugh so hard tears leaked out his eyes when he was also at his wit's end…

છ∕૭છ∕૭

After the flight attendants had performed their monotone discussion about the exits, and as the plane climbed to its scheduled height, the dark-haired young woman sitting in seat 22A stared out the window as Pittsburgh shrunk from view. Only her anger kept the tears away because of the reason for this hurried departure. *Funny*, she thought, remembering another time about four years ago when she made a similar decision to change the direction of her life. At least this time she was wearing panties—also red, she realized. That mundane thought elicited a sneer no one on the plane could see.

Panty-less, that decision made partly from embarrassment. But this time, as she closed her eyes to keep her emotions at bay. It was because she was a fool—a fool with a very dim future that suddenly made her reaching thirty years of age...a retirement plan.

CHAPTER 2

Finally, he was headed for that cup of hot coffee in his very cold air-conditioned office that he'd craved for the last three hours. There were numerous sounds in a galvanizing plant but only certain ones that superseded every other. The man, stopping when he heard something, was already soaked with sweat from a relatively busy day in the stiflingly hot plant—*Yes, it's another hot and humid day, like every day the summer of 1987 in Pittsburgh*—when he heard something that would rob him of the air-conditioned office and that coffee.

The piercingly loud metallic sound took his attention away from his sticking uniform and the hot, humid day, causing him to turn around. There was certainly no mistaking the sound's origin, as it cascaded above the normal high-pitched clamor of a busy steel coating plant. Everyone working there quickly identified the source. Heads turned, and shoulders slumped in unison toward the exit section of the line as the metallic resonance increased in volume. The crash of hundreds of feet of sheet metal thunderously falling over eighty feet to the cement floor became the center of attention as it startled the unfamiliar, and frustrated those most familiar.

Team Leader David Jackson leaned against the cold hard metal of the huge temper mill housing. Taking a deep breath, he closed his eyes and lowered his head—the picture of the steel strip crashing to the floor still visible, even in that dark realm. It was something that happened too often lately as they learned how to coat the thin-gauge steel used on this very new zinc coiling line. The only difference this time was that he was already exhausted.

"My legs feel like they weigh a ton," he mumbled to himself as he leaned over and massaged his calves. He tried to move, but his tired muscles ached in rebellion. He was quickly losing the battle to keep his cool and wanted to hit something and vent the growing frustrations that were starting to try his patience. This was more than just another setback. Somehow, these failures were starting to become personal.

The promotions he had earned were because of his ability to find quick solutions to problems, and not his advanced education, as he had none. He was a people person and gifted at motivating others beyond what they thought they could perform. Starting a very difficult light gauge galvanizing line from scratch would one day need the very educated to ramp it up until it was a money maker, but not at start up. The financial investors of this new venture knew that it would take people with the stubborn will to succeed, despite equipment that never seemed to function as advertised, and would persevere until adjustments could be made to make a silk purse out of a sow's ear.

David opened his eyes and looked around knowing he only had a moment before his crew would stop whatever they were doing, as they were trained by him, and drag themselves toward the latest strip break. He took that momentary respite to try and energize himself and put on his fading mask of confidence and the, heavier by the minute, mantle of A-Crew Team Leader.

❦❦❦

"Damnit!" Zack Cates looked at fellow material handlers Donna Winger and a swearing Mike Buffer. "Another damn strip break," Zack added. "Shit, let our team leader thread it by himself, this time."

The three material handlers turned in unison when a fourth worker opened the door to the shipping office and stood there.

"Come on, guys!" Jon Carter shouted at them. "Don't tell me you didn't hear the line going down. If you guys don't want David's foot up your ass, you better get moving."

Mike Buffer was about to say "F-him" but thought better of it when both Donna Winger and Zack Cates stood up and started out the door. He swore under his breath when a grinning Carter held the door open for him and then followed the others out the door.

"All right," David shouted to his crew as they slowly approached piecemeal, "let's start threading that damn strip again."

The brusque tone of his voice echoed their frustrations as well. They more than understood the souring mood of their team leader. They often wondered among themselves when he would finally lose that gung-ho attitude altogether. It had taken the third time the strip tracked off and tore in half and shut down the line this turn to provoke him.

July was a very hot and humid month, and inside the former Westinghouse transformer storage building just outside of Pittsburgh, Pennsylvania, and this week, it seemed to peak. Having to re-thread the line repeatedly, in this heat and humility, had taken its toll on nearly everyone. A group of sore arms and tired legs grudgingly fell in line and played another round of follow-their-team-leader.

This plant, "Zinc Coater," was the second galvanizing mill opened by three former big steel company executives. Their first mill called "Steel Coater," located on Third Avenue in Pittsburgh, was the original business venture for this newly formed partnership. They had purchased a closed galvanizing plant six years earlier, retooled, and converted it into a non-union work force. Within three years, they were paying bonuses and great profit sharing checks to all the employees.

Buoyed by the success of their first venture, they saw a new market for a lighter gauge—thinner sheet—galvanizing line. Steel coater was a strong player in the .020 to .130 thickness gauge sheet market. At that time, no domestic galvanizing plant was competing with the overseas producers of light gauges in the .006 to .020 ranges. The zinc coater plant was designed to break open that market in the states and compete with the imports. There was only one small problem. No one in this country had any real experience producing galvanized steel sheets that thin. And nowhere was that fact more obvious than to the tired men and women threading the line for the third time today.

David Gary Jackson was the team leader—turned foreman—for A-Crew. There were presently three crews—A, B, C—that consisted of a team leader, pot operator, exit and entry end operators, four material handlers and two maintenance techs per turn. The pot operators were in charge of running the galvanizing process. The exit operator wrapped up the finished zinc coated coils and decided if the coil meets customers' requirements. The entry end operator welded on the raw or bare steel coils, and the material handlers packaged, stored, shipped, received, and loaded and unloaded coils. The maintenance techs were empowered with keeping the many motors and generators running smoothly. The team leader had the responsibility to see that all these diverse parts function smoothly and when they didn't, the buck stopped there.

There was nothing smooth about the last five hours. First, the paper-thin metal strip tracked off the rolls and tore in half in the entry accumulator an hour and a half into the turn. The accumulators were five-story-high towers that held rows of steel in vertical loops. The bottom section moved up or down to fill or empty the accumulator of steel. This occurred when that section of the line stopped to either weld the head end of the next coil to the tail end of the one running or to remove a finished coil.

After forty minutes of re-threading the entry accumulator on the first line stop, the line started up and ran smoothly for two hours before it suddenly tracked off at the zinc pot and started tearing. Before the shocked pot operator could stop the line, the strip ripped apart and fell out of the cooling tower. One end fell onto the water quench tank, and the other half fell into the molten metal zinc bath splattering hot, liquid zinc over the floor area around the pot. Thankfully, no one was in the area because molten zinc can cause very deep burns.

The cooling tower was a four-story tower that had four plenums—air blowers—to cool the hot zinc-coated steel strip as it passes through them. One hour later, they had pulled the strip back up and through the cooling tower and stitched it together again.

Two coils after starting up from this latest fiasco, it occurred again when the strip moved too far to one side of the melted zinc pot and started tearing along that edge. The pot operator was able to quickly turn up his furnace tensions and slow the line down to get the strip to move back toward the center. However, the already-damaged edge of the strip continued through the line until it reached the exit accumulator. At that point, one of the damaged edges caught on a roll, or something, and started to rip apart. Before the pot operator could spot the trouble, the strip tore apart and fell out of the exit end accumulator onto the floor narrowly missing a maintenance man greasing a bridle motor.

David led his group of disgruntled workers to the exit end of the line to remove the damaged strip and stitch it together again. Over a hundred feet of mangled galvanized paper thin steel lay on the floor in a twisted pile at the entry side of the tall accumulator tower. The remaining end of the torn strip was hanging down from the bottom carriage, suspended sixty feet above their heads.

Pot operator Frank Sanders assisted the exit operator Eric Williams and two of the material handlers, Bob Carter and Donna Winger, as ordered, cutting up the steel on the floor in manageable-sized pieces and dragging them out of the way. Team leader David Jackson assigned material handlers Mike Buffer and Zack Cates to accompany him up the steps to the top of the five-story accumulator.

Buffer waited until David's back was turned to give him the finger for being picked for, if not the hardest then surely the hottest, part of the job.

At each of the five levels they climbed, they could feel the temperature in the large building raise another five to ten degrees. By the time they walked up the ninety-six steps to the top level, they were all soaked to the skin as the temperature reached above hundred and twenty degrees at the top level of the accumulator. They had to wear their gloves when touching the metal safety railings as they climbed, or it would have burned the skin of their hands.

David was one of four employees of the original Steel Coater plant assigned to teach the new hires the galvanizing process. He was a six-year veteran of galvanizing and helped start up the parent, Steel Coater mill. When things went wrong, which they had been doing on a regular basis since starting up the new plant, the crew looked to him for direction and encouragement. David had only six years' experience, but that was six years more than the two men standing beside him trying to catch their breath at the top level of the accumulator.

The men on the floor cut up and disposed of the damaged galvanized strip and were attaching the rope to a good section of the strip when Mac and David came down the steps. David watched them as they went about the task of tying the rope to the strip. This was the third threading today for his crew and the fifteenth in the last month.

They weren't the same exuberant collection of people excited about passing the written tests and their physicals to get this job. The sweaty, scruffy men and women who were going about the job of readying the line to run again were inexperienced at making galvanized steel, but they were quickly learning the many different ways of threading it.

Twenty minutes later, they had pulled the strip up and through the accumulator and down to the exit end. Eric Williams, the exit end operator, had taken off the threading rope, jogged the strip down to the coiling reel, and announced he was ready at his end. Brad Zinger was on his way back to the entry end to give his section of the line a final once over. David followed his pot operator into the control room. Once the entry and exit ends checked their equipment, Frank would be ready to start up the line.

"Ready to fire her up again, David," Frank told his suddenly quiet team leader as he put down the phone after getting an all clear from both the entry and exit ends.

David gave him an I-hope-it-works look and pushed the plant buzzer twice. That was the line run signal to stand clear of all rolls and pinch points in the plant. There was a loud shrill as the pot operator turned up the air to his zinc blow-off air knives. He then pushed the furnace tension button on and off, trying to tighten up the strip in the furnace without tearing it. Having thin steel sitting in an atmosphere of eighteen-to-twenty-two-hundred degrees tended to weaken steel by making it very brittle. Over half of the re-threads this month were from starting back up after a line stop and pulling the strip apart from the excessive heat of the furnace.

Satisfied that the strip was tight, Frank pushed the tension-on button and observed his furnace tension read-out. If it was under one hundred-PSI, the strip probably had pulled apart in the furnace again while they were busy threading the accumulator. The PSI numbers rose up to three hundred and sixty. The strip was tight.

"Here goes nothing," Frank said over the intercom.

Regardless of what the other nine crew members were doing,

each heard and understood the skepticism in his voice.

Frank, with David standing behind him, stared at the length of dull silver strip that reached from the molten zinc bath up into the ceiling thirty feet over their heads. There was something menacing about that man-made collection of molecules. It seemed to carry an aura of malevolence today. It was clearly an inanimate object, yet it effected the emotions of so many people. That was usually the spot where everyone could watch and see if the line actually started moving. Frank held his breath for a moment and then pushed the line-run button. For one excruciating second, nothing happened. After a period, seemingly too long to be momentary, the strip started to move slowly upward toward the cooling tower. David held his breath.

The first few seconds of movement would reveal if the strip was strong enough to survive the necessary furnace tension. It was this tension, or drag on the strip, that was designed to prevent the strip from walking too far to either side and tearing against the annealing furnace wall. The same furnace tension, or pull, on the strip could, and often did, pull the over-oxidized or brittle strip apart.

The galvanized strip started inching its way upward.

It seemed like hours passed before David could breathe again. He took silent notice of the sound of another pair of lungs expelling air moments after him.

Frank turned around and smiled weakly at David, then he checked the furnace temperatures behind him. *So far so good*, he allowed himself to think. The next few minutes, he knew, were equally as important. The strip that sat in the furnace during the line stop might have held together but was badly burned by remaining stationary in temperatures it was designed to move through at speeds of 400 to 500 feet per minute. Remaining stationary usually warped the shape of the strip in the furnace and could cause it to track off again when that damaged section came out of the liquid zinc bath.

The galvanizing gods were smiling on A-Crew this time. The oxidized section of the strip came up out of the pot without tracking off the pot roll. It did move very close to the edge, causing two very nervous and tired members of the crew who were observing the start up from the pot control enclosure, to silently pray that it would start moving back to center before it tore—again.

Within twenty minutes, operator Frank Sanders had the line running fast enough to make a prime coil. The exit end operator had stopped and removed the reject coil wrapping on his mandrel and started a new one. The line was running at hundred-feet-below scheduled line speed but was producing one of the few sell-able coils of the day.

Frank looked over at David as he stood near the door with his back to him watching the strip moving smoothly out of the zinc bath. There wasn't much to say. There was no way of telling when, or if, the strip would track off and tear again or if something mechanical would go wrong that would shut the line down. Frank remembered an old mill adage to never verbally mention that possibility, or it would surely happen. He failed to take in account that mentioned or not, it had already occurred three times today.

Frank grabbed his face shield and headed out the control house to scoop out any dross on the zinc bath surface. After every start-up, it was necessary to skim the dross and strip-scale off the top of the 875 degree temperature liquid zinc bath or it would stick to the strip, causing defects on the surface. When he opened the door to leave, the sudden, ear-piercing sound of the air-knives broke through David's tired stupor. There were reports to fill out on the last strip break, so he put in his ear plugs, followed Frank out the door, and walked slowly to the team leader's office.

The wave of cool air, that washed over David when he opened the door to his office, was refreshing. The plant was hot and muggy, but at least his office was cool. Even so, the sweat rolled freely down his face as he sat at his desk, trying to catch up in the daily log each team leader was required to maintain. On days like today, when very little went right, he found it difficult to keep up with recording all of the many problems, big and small, occurring each turn. Experience had taught him that if you put off the paperwork, it would come back to smother you under its growing redundant weight.

With pen in hand, David stared down at the logbook. His thoughts raced by in so many different directions it was a battle to single out the facts in a coherent fashion. One of his strong suits was his innate ability to find the right words to express himself.

He grew up the strong, quiet type but with a burning need to tell everyone what his opinions were. The shyness of his youth turned into a young man's determination not to take any "shit" from anyone. Years later, he was the most verbal of the three team leaders—not abusive, just resolute to never let some verbose person tell a lie, look him directly in the eye, and say it was the truth. Dog shit wasn't a chocolate bar, even if the CEO of the company said it was.

David was a man envied for his ability to stand in front of any congregation of people and relate to them. That virtue was almost lost on this weary summer day in the humid Coil Coater galvaniz-ing plant. During his second attempt at writing the reasons for the last line stop, David heard the door to his office open. Looking up, he saw Mike Buffer, one of his material handlers, enter, and look over at him. Groaning, David put his pen down, waiting for a request for something or a report on another problem that had popped up. Buffer was a very good worker but complained about everything.

But Mike just smiled at him as he shut the door and walked toward the coffee pot in the adjoining office. The last line stop had summoned David just as he was about to pour the last cup for himself. Mike's quest for the same was greeted by a glass coffee pot that was on the brink of burning.

"Great," Mike said to himself as he removed the black bot-tomed pot from the eye and placed the pot under the distilled hot water tap next to the coffee stand. Only enough water dripped out to wet the burnt coffee staining the bottom of the coffee pot.

"Great!" he said loud enough this time for David to hear.

Now, what is he bitching about? David wondered. Then he remembered something. "There's a fresh jug of water in the cor-ner," he shouted to Mike when he figured out what prompted his outburst. "I didn't have time to change it today, for obvious rea-sons."

"I hear that," Mike answered, looking around and spotting the five-gallon plastic water bottle sitting in the corner near the door.

David leaned over his desk and watched as Mike put down the coffee pot and removed the empty water jug from on top of the dispenser, unsure if Mike had ever changed a heavy five-gallon bottle of distilled water. The near fiasco of David's own first attempt was fresh on his mind as he watched Mike lug the bottle over to the dispenser.

Mike carried the plastic water bottle in both arms as he walked across the room. He had just reached the middle of the room when the bottle slipped out of his sweaty hands and crashed to the floor. David looked on in shock as the bottle hit the floor, burst open, and waves of distilled water washed across the tiled floor. Their eyes met, and the surprise of the accident caused both of their mouths to drop open.

David fought the urge to laugh. After all, he was Mike's team leader, his example. He looked down at what appeared to be inches of water at Mike's feet. The final straw was when he looked up at Mike, expecting to see his face colored with the obvious brush of embarrassment, and was stunned when all he did was mouth the word "Oops."

Laughter rolled up from David's stomach and rushed out his mouth. The silly reaction of Mike freed David from any normal restraints one tried to show at the misfortune of others. He placed his face in his hands and just let go. Tears streamed down his face as the laughter rolled from him in great heaves. When he tried to stop, the shocked look on Mike's face, after he realized what he did, came flashing back to David freeing up another burst of laughter. All the frustrations of the day melted off David's broad shoulders as he yielded to the humor of the slapstick-like misfortune of one of his co-workers. Seeking control, David finally wiped his eyes with the back of his hand, took a deep breath, and looked up from his desk again, only to see Mike now lying on his back in the water doing the backstroke. What little control, David had regained vanished as he watched a man, he only knew from working with him a few months, act a complete fool. David pounded on his desk hysterically as Mike's foolishness found his L-spot. Their laughter turned into howling as they dined on Mike's misfortune.

The shock of what happened had surprised Mike at first, as he watched the water roll over his shoes. He'd walked into the team leader's office to get a cup of coffee and work up the nerve to tell David that he was quitting. Standing at the top of that accumulator, sweating like a pig during that last line stop, had convinced Mike to look for work elsewhere. He had lost what little faith he had in this place becoming successful. When the water bottle slipped from his hands and exploded, it was the signature on his pink slip, leaving no reason to hold back now.

Mike looked over at his team leader and saw the shock written across his face. The urge to do something crazy found root in his decision to quit and found release when he said an exaggerated, "Oops." The laughter he heard urged him on. The backstroke idea was one he had seen on TV somewhere and decided it would be a final act of lunacy.

When they regained their composure, a friendship was born. David helped Mike clean up the mess, although they stopped more than once as laughter broke out anew. For Mike, the incident changed his mind about quitting, and David found the simple humor a cleansing shower that removed his exhaustion and the day's tension. As their friendship grew, he would come to welcome Mike's odd sense of humor as a means of releasing his frustrations and disappointments.

Months later, as they were sitting in David's living room with a couple of dates that were bored watching them more interested in a Steeler football game, he asked Mike if he dropped the water bottle on purpose and never received an answer that settled his curiosity.

"It will be like Frenchy Fuqua and the Immaculate Reception," Mike told David. "I'll take the truth to my grave."

David thought for a minute about how to answer his buddy's boast. He knew if he said what was on his mind, the evening's somber mood would be shattered into little pieces. *What the hell*, he decided as the fourth beer loosened his tongue. "Speaking of 'graves' my good man," he said loud enough to get Mike's date, Mary's, attention, "could you please get that tramp, Donna Graves, to quit calling here for you. I thought it was over between you."

The look on Mike's face told him two things. One, he had accomplished his goal in pulling Mike's chain, and two, he would soon be alone with his boring blind date, the homely but possessor of a very sexy body, Shirley...Something.

Between the words "Are you seeing that grave-digger again" and "Take me home," was twenty minutes of an angry Mary Thomas putting her finger in Mike's face and telling him if he was fooling around with her again, he could kiss her pretty ass goodbye.

"Come on, let's leave these lovebirds alone," a snickering David stood and suggested to Shirley "something-or-another" under the guise of letting them work out their differences.

"Great idea," Shirley admitted as she let him take her hand and lead her to his bedroom.

David sat her down on his bed and leaned close to kiss her.

The twenty-minute argument was just enough time for his "homely" date to surprise him by whispering in his ear and suggesting they hurry and consummate their new friendship.

When Mike returned from taking both girls home, David tried to apologize for ruining the evening. Mike affably accepted his apology. Only after ten minutes of watching him through the corner of his eye did David finally accept the fact that Mike wasn't planning any reprisals, at least not tonight.

David never told Mike about the tryst he had with Shirley "what's-her-name." The truth was he wanted to kiss-and-tell very much, but he didn't think Mike would believe him anyway. David had a hard time believing what had happened himself. He only intended to get her alone for some K and H—Kisses and Hugs. After the first kiss, she pushed him down on the bed. By the third, she had removed most of his clothes.

Until they finally called a truce, David and Mike each had lost two girlfriends to the practical jokes they pulled on each other.

CHAPTER 3

"Toni DiNardo, I dare you," a smug Brenda Joy McShane railed, teasing her best friend as she posed in front of her bedroom mirror. "Your dad would die if he saw you in that."

The outfit she had chosen to wear left little to the imagination. Toni turned in the mirror, admiring the sculptured figure God gave to girls who worked at it in their youth and choose salads, diet pop, or water on occasion over a Big-Mac, fries, and a milk shake. She knew that reflection was the image she wanted to portray. Show enough to tantalize was her motto, but not enough to falsely advertise.

"But he won't see my new half T-shirt and these tight shorts, now will he? That is, if we hurry up and get out of here before he gets home. Besides," Toni said, while mimicking her I'm-an-innocent-little-girl look, "my daddy trusts me."

"Sure, he does, Tone," Brenda teased, taking her turn standing in front of the door length mirror, "that's why you're rushing me out your house."

"Smart ass," Toni countered, as she pushed Brenda away from the mirror, "there's nothing wrong with showing a little skin. It's just that my dad is such a prude. By the way, Miss Lady, you're basically wearing the same thing I am." They posed together in the mirror as sensual as they could. "Let's get to Kennywood Park before all the good-looking boys are taken."

"It won't matter, Miss Thing," Brenda said as she stuck her rear end out at Toni. "We'll just pull these shorts up tighter and take them away from the poor girls."

Toni laughed at Brenda's attempt at imitating the missing third part of their triangle. Miss Thing was what Katie Thomson used to call Toni. Katie was a vivacious Black girl they hung out with before she went off to college in California. The three of them had grown very close during their junior and senior years at Washington High School.

They had a final sleepover—screwdrivers drinking party—before Katie left for college on a weekend Toni's dad was on one of his weekend fishing trips. They first thought about throwing a beer party for all their friends but vetoed that after recalling it took all their savings to replace the things broken by the hormone-driven guys showing off at the last party they threw.

This sleepover was a two-fold celebration. One to mark Katie's acceptance to UCLA and two, her finally breaking it off with her long-time boyfriend, Darwyn. Knowing Katie had always planned to go to school on the west coast to be near her sister who lived out there, his demanding that she go to school at home—so they could be together or else—became the final breaking point.

"I couldn't believe he got in my face and demanded I go to school here," an intoxicated UCLA freshman voiced. "You guy know I always planned to enroll in a So Cal school. See? I should have never given him a taste of honey. It was too sweet for him to handle."

"Please, girl, you weren't that good-looking boy's first time," Toni added.

"But his first with a real woman," Katie boasted.

"There ya go," Brenda said. "Some men can't handle a real woman like us."

That prompted stories about the men in their lives, as the consumption of alcohol loosened their tongues, and they reflected on a few guys they really would have like to have dated.

"Promise me you two will come visit me in LA."

Brenda was about to get another drink, and Toni was trying to delay getting up from her bed where they were all sitting and walk all the way—ten feet—to her bathroom to pee when Katie asked. Both Brenda and Toni turned and looked at the young woman sitting between them.

Not waiting for a comment from her inebriated best friends, Katie added. "Because here we are the three best-looking girls at school. Out there, I don't know, I might need your help to get a new boyfriend."

"With your shapely ass, I don't think that will be a problem. It never was, right?"

Brenda nodded in agreement at Toni's analysis after reaching for the nearly empty pitcher of refreshment and pouring the last of the vodka and orange juice in each of their glasses. Sweet Katie did have a figure that made all the boys stare. Then Brenda asked, "Katie, who—no, why are...ah, men are like...ah, vacations?"

"What?" Katie asked, already laughing at the funny face her buzzed companion was making as she tried to talk.

"Why are...ah, the men in my life like...vacations?"

"We don't know," Toni volunteered after Katie just laughed at Brenda and failed to answer.

"Like vacations, they...never seem to last long enough. Haawwww," Brenda laughed.

She was joined by the two other giggling drunks.

That started the man jokes.

"Yeah, yeah, yeah, wait, wait—and like vacations, they are always over before you're ready," Katie chimed in, tears running down her coffee-colored face. "Wait—wait, my turn," she managed to say. "Why are men like...like hor-dor-scopes...horoscopes, yes?" Having screwed up the line, she spurted out the answer before they could. "They think they can read you...and are usually wrong."

Toni spilled the last of her drink on her chest as she laughed. Brenda gave up and placed her drink on the bed headboard and her face in a pillow. In their friendship-inspired stupor, tonight quoting the alphabet would have seemed funny.

"Okay, okay, I remember another one," Katie recounted, after the laughter died down. "Men are like fine wine. They start out as grapes, and it's our job to stomp on them and keep them in the dark until they mature into something you want to have for dinner."

When the chorus died down, a horny Brenda added a different spin to the commentaries. "Men are like cement. After getting laid, they take a long time to get hard."

Katie fell backward, laughing, and hit her head on the headboard, spilling some of Brenda's drink as the answer took her by surprise.

Toni, after seeing that Katie was unhurt, stood up in bed, holding herself.

Brenda was on a roll. "Men are like a laxative. They irritate the shit out of you."

"Stop," Toni begged. "I have to pee."

"Wait—wait," Katie pleaded as Brenda, ready to give another, and Toni, who had jumped off the bed and was standing with her legs twisted together trying to hold back the flood. "I remember another one. Why are men like snowstorms?"

"No," Toni screamed and ran into the bathroom, laughing.

Brenda fell back on the bed, laughing, before Katie gave the answer that she, like Toni, also remembered.

Katie lost half her audience but continued anyway. "Men are like snowstorms because you never know how many inches you are going to get and—and—" She tried to continue as the tears ran down her face. "—how long they will last, haaaaawwwww."

One young woman was laughing in the bathroom as she kicked away her wet underpants and PJ bottoms; the other was lying on her back in bed, wiping the tears from her eyes; and the third lay face down, laughing in her pillow. An hour later, the three drunks were fast asleep in each other's arms.

When they neared their last months of high school, Katie's aspiration was to further her education some place hot with nice beaches, but Toni and Brenda wanted to make an immediate impact in the world of concert promotions. Waiting four years to take up the challenge was a waste of time, they believed. Brenda's plans were sidetracked when her parents insisted she also go to a school. Relenting, she chose a two-year nursing program at the local community college. Three years later, they were just beginning to carve out a small piece of the local concert pie.

Brenda Joy McShane was Toni DiNardo's alter ego. They were friends since they sat together in Mrs. Viccola first grade class. Brenda, with her long carrot red hair, seemingly always in a different style of ponytail, and Toni with her short cut curly black hair, were opposites that grew up liking the same things, just approaching them from different angles. Brenda's smile got her in the few places her good looks and long legs couldn't. Toni, an inch or two shorter and not quite as pretty, just talked her way into the same doors. She was a strong believer in her father's motto, "Dazzle them with bullshit." As was always the case, they both envied the other methods.

Both girls matured into confident, assertive young women. Add to that two strong personalities that weren't afraid to take what they wanted, and you had Brenda Joy McShane and Toni DiNardo.

Today, they were celebrating the signing one of the better local rock groups to play at a concert they were arranging for later this summer. They didn't have signatures on paper yet but were assured they would, as soon as the group's manager came to town the middle of next month. The doors to promoting were slowly opening for them.

CHAPTER 4

From the hilly parking lots across the street, the crowds of picnickers flowed down to the entrance of the amusement park. After paying their way in and getting a color-coded paper band placed on their right wrist and with the word "ride" stamped on their hand, they moved quickly down into the tunnel that led into the park. A smorgasbord of humanity in all ages, sizes, shapes, colors, and different modes of dress exited the tunnel to the sounds of harpsichords and the colorful spectacle that is Kennywood Park.

For many, this was a yearly family tradition that dated back as far as they could remember. Back to a time when they were carried into the park in the arms of parents, some long since departed—good memories of simpler times, kinder people, and fun days that excited the kids like almost no other. The first visit to Kennywood Park was the summer's equivalent of Christmas. It was a May/June reward for the end of a long school year and, on Labor Day, a final farewell to their summer vacation.

The park dated back to 1898 when, as a trolley park, it catered to local industrial workers and their families. It became a popular attraction and started making more revenue than the street trolleys. Purchased in 1906, it became the wonderful amusement park we knew today.

The many songs, emanating from almost every ride, complimented each other in the time-honored tradition of the older amusement parks. Kennywood Park was able to keep most of the old and flavor it with some of the newest rides on the market. Continually voted in the top three amusement parks of its type in the country, that high-wire act returned the same friendly people year after year.

The throng of picnickers moved along the crowed avenues in

wild patterns that were a tolerated nuisance to nearly everyone in the park. Some thought that you should always stay to your right when walking like one would drive on the roads. Others, equally convinced, thought that you should just weave your way through the aimless mob the best you could. The conflict fed the confusion. Then there were the observers, people who were happy to just stand wherever they decided to stop, and just look around at the diversity of the crowd. Two such on-lookers were standing off to the side near the rifle target shooting booth.

Michael Buffer and David Jackson were pre-occupied with judging the quality and quantity of the young ladies in the park. They knew there were days when the park was packed, but the available females were plain, dumpy, pimple-faced girls. Then on other days when the park was less crowed, either from poor weather or being early in the week, and they were surprised by the abundance of amazing-looking young ladies. There was no pattern to follow, they quickly surmised, just blind luck. So far, today held promise, as a variety of attractive young women, in singles, doubles, and groups paraded past the two men, unaware they were competing in a beauty contest, though many of the young ladies were dressed as if they came prepared for such a contingency.

"Well, what now?"

"I don't know, Mike. I think we paid our dues," David answered after had they walked away from the company sponsored picnic shelters. "We stayed at the annual company function long enough to impress the owners. This was a great place for a picnic, though."

"Yeah." Mike gave his usual one word comment and nodded in agreement as he watched a pretty coffee-colored girl, of possible legal age, saunter past him, totally unaware he existed. Her enthusiasm was directed at getting on a certain ride she liked before the line got too long, never noticing she was the object of his interest as she brushed past.

"The food was great, and we didn't win any, but they gave out some great prizes."

"Yeah," Mike added.

"Unfortunately, our company is a great place to work, but most of the women are married or married with kids. We single guys are as welcome as a woman's monthly—never mind."

"Yeah."

David was right, Mike decided, while watching the owner of a pair of shapely white-jeaned shorts appear and then disappear in the flowing river of people, *this is a great idea to have the company picnic at Kennywood Park this year*. Having it at the South Park picnic grounds year after year had grown somewhat stale. There were only so much bingo and pick-up games of softball you could stand before it lost its appeal as, unfortunately, the poor attendance last year proved. Today, there was many times the usual company workers in the picnic crowd, all appearing to be having a great time with their families.

David winced as Mike elbowed him in the side and then slyly pointed at a very attractive dark-haired girl in her early twenties that was carrying a plate of cheese-fries with an equally pretty, taller redhead. Mike whistled under his breath as they walked past them and stopped a few feet away to eat their food at one of the few unoccupied shaded tables lining Kennywood Park Lake. From where the two men stood, they had an unobstructed view of the feeding females.

"I like the dark haired one," Mike confessed, after exhaling like he was blowing out a birthday cake. "She's a knock-out. Damn, she's beautiful."

"They both are, Mike. Let's go over and introduce ourselves."

"No! Not while they're eating, Davey. That would be rude, dude."

After thinking about it for a moment, David reluctantly agreed. He turned so he could watch the dark-haired girl more closely, using Mike as a shield. *She is pleasing to look at*, David conceded. Her short black hair gave her a very neat appearance, despite the gusting, and very welcomed, refreshing summer breeze blowing through the park. Her face was small and evenly proportioned with a small nose and perfect lips. Stealing a few glances, he had to agree with Mike, he couldn't find anything wrong with the way she looked. When she turned toward the lake, that gave David an opportunity to observe her profile. He noticed that her thick eyebrows accentuated her face like that girl in the movie, Blue Lagoon. He spent a minute, trying to recall her name, then gave up.

He continued watching them as he pretended to point something out to Mike on the other side of the lake. David noticed the dark-haired girl was wearing a white T-shirt with a picture, he couldn't quite make out, printed on the front. As she moved, he thought it looked like a couple of birds. The shirt was cut off a few inches above her belly button, revealing her narrow waist and taunt stomach muscles. The V-neck was cut just low enough to...*Mmm*, David thought. A pair of tight jean shorts that accentuated her round hips completed her outfit. It was common park attire that took nothing away from what nature had created. It was her legs that held his attention. She had to have been into sports of some kind, maybe like a runner, tennis player, or into something that required lots of exercise because her legs were tanned, toned, and shapely. Not manly looking but chiseled. David whistled softly when she struck a pose while chatting with her girlfriend.

The red-haired beauty with her was about two inches taller than her fry-eating accomplice and richly tanned. She was dressed in a white-and-yellow-print blouse tied at the waist and blue jean shorts with cuffs. What first caught his attention when he looked at her was her thick red hair that reached down her back and her long, shapely legs. From where he stood, she was impressive looking. She was also into something physical he guessed, like dance maybe, judging from the shapely cut of her calves.

From the side, David noticed Mike's favorite female features were very evident, and more so in their thin shirts. Neither girl was busty. But both had enough to make you notice and appreciate.

The dark-haired girl turned around twice, briefly looking David in the eye in passing. The third time they made eye contact, neither looked away until their partners interrupted. Every time they picked up a fry and placed it in their mouths Mike would groan. David shook his head at his buddy and pulled on his arm. "Let's move around and check out the rest of the park," he suggested as he walked away from Mike. When David turned around and noticed Mike watching the girls eat, he walked back to implore him more emphatically and was surprised when the dark-haired girl smiled over at them and nodded.

The mating ritual between men and women must be the strangest in the animal kingdom. As long as they ignored Mike, he acted like he wanted to run over, grab one of them in his arms and have his way with her. As soon as they acknowledged his interest, gave a friendly indication that they were also curious, he bolted past David like his ass was on fire.

David watched his friend move off quickly into the festive crowd. Chuckling to himself at Mike's strange behavior, David turned to see if the two women had noticed his partner's hasty retreat. They had. David looked into the confused faces of the two women, also surprised by his friend's reaction. Smiling his best little boy smile, he shrugged his shoulders at his buddy's quick departure. Before leaving, he mouthed "See you later, I hope."

They nudged each other, laughed, and then both ladies signaled a thumbs-up. David copied their actions with both thumps, mouthed an ecstatic "Yes" in return, and went in search of his partner.

"They both were cute," Brenda said, while reaching for a few of the last fries on the plate.

"Yes, they were, but I think I might have shaken up the fair-haired one."

"Why, Miss Toni," Brenda mouthed in her heaviest southern draw, "I *think* you just may *have*. Did you see how quickly that there boy ran off when you flirted with him? He was captivated by your southern charm—or, or was it that tiny T-shirt?"

Toni stuck her chest out, and both young women laughed.

"I'll tell you what I'm going to do, Miss Toni," Brenda informed her as she slowly slipped a fry into her mouth for effect, "since that little colored gal Katie isn't he-ya, um-a-gonna swallow my family pride anna take the brown one—in her honor. Just in her honor, mind you. I would ask you to, but I wouldn't want you to ruin your saintly, virginal reputation," Brenda said, tongue-in-cheek, in her poor southern belle accent.

"What a neighborly sacrifice, Missy Brenda, that's mighty big oh you. Or is that because he is mighty big?"

The obvious dig caused Brenda to gag on the last of the food in her mouth. Both women laughed so hard people began to look at them with more than the usual curiosity pretty girls gleaned.

David caught up with Mike near the entrance to the Jackrabbit roller-coaster, his obvious embarrassment still evident on his wide-eyed, flushed face.

"Wait, Mike, where are you going?"

"I'm out of here! Did you see what I did? She smiled at me, and I acted like a complete idiot," Mike blabbered. They both stopped and looked around to see if their shouting caused a distraction.

"What are you talking about?" David asked?

"Don't play dumb, David. What little chance we may have had to pick up those two fabulous chicks died when I choked. I can't believe I choked."

"Mike, you didn't choke. Women like that little bit of shyness you displayed. It makes you seem innocent and trusting. And remember what I told you, if a woman trusts you, you're half way there. If she doesn't, you're just spinning your wheels."

"Yeah, well, I spun my wheels so fast I flew out of there. I can't believe I acted so corn-ballish around a woman," Mike lamented. "Hey, buddy, I'm leaving. I'm so screwed up you would have better luck on your own today."

"Wait, Mike, see, you're wrong again," David said as he watched Mike walk away and take another few steps before stopping.

"What do you mean?" Mike asked without turning around, as his shoulders slumped.

It was a good thing because he never saw the smirk on David's face. David knew Mike's curiosity would get the best of him.

Not getting an answer Mike turned around. "Well?"

David had dangled that hook in the water and snickered when the blowfish bit on it. "What I'm saying—" He walked up to him. "—is that after you left, the two ladies walked over and asked me who you were. The tall red head said you looked very familiar," David said, lying through his teeth.

"What?" a shocked Mike asked while stepping back and excusing himself for bumping into two mean biker-looking dudes behind him. "They don't know me, David, that's bull."

"Exactly, my friend. It's just their way of breaking the ice. I say we hunt down those ladies and see if they meant business or are just out ball-busting. What have we got to lose, remember?" David said, quoting one of Mike's favorite lines for talking to women.

Mike was very hesitant, weighing the fear of further humiliation and embarrassment against the need to find someone of the opposite sex to start a meaningful relationship. He had yet to express how important that goal had become to his best friend, fearing he might think him silly for wanting to settle down and love one woman. Their past history of picking up one-nighters seemed to belie that noble goal.

David searched Mike's eyes for that usual gleam of overconfidence he got when he decided to go for it. He found it, but barely.

"Okay, partner," Mike said, unconvinced. "What have we got to lose?"

"All right! Now you're talking," David declared and patted him on his back. "Here's what we'll do, buddy," he continued as he put his arm around Mike's shoulders and pointed at the crowd, "we'll just filter through the park and, if it's meant for us to find them, we will. If not, we take what we can get, okay?"

David's enthusiasm sparked the coals in Mike's furnace. He began to feel the old confidence that strange, black-haired girl had somehow stolen from him. He began to walk with that strut he picked up when he and David became friends. Why white guys thought most black guys really walked like that David didn't know. He hated it, but would never tell Mike. He had on many occasions hinted that he couldn't stand it when people tried to be something they were not. The only response he got from Mike was, "That's right bro, give me five."

Today was different. David felt better when Mike resorted to trying to walk "cool" again. That meant his confidence had returned. Soon, the fun-loving guy he had grown to love and admire would surface and take on all comers.

As they passed, single-file through a crowed section of the park, David couldn't help wondering what had really happened to Mike when those girls smiled at them. With all the other women they were successful with or failed miserably, Mike's keen sense of humor had always saved them from complete embarrassment or opened a door David thought closed shut. This time, he ran away. *Hummmmm*, David wondered as he slipped between two rather large women in an effort to keep up with his friend, *he must feel something special for that girl.*

David was one of those people, and there were probably many others around the world, who believed things happened for a reason—that odd occurrences were not just random acts, but carefully integrated parts of a puzzle. He was sure Mike's strange reaction to this girl would lead to something. Because of his faith in that theory, he resolved to set the wheels in motion *when,* and if, they next met.

An hour later, they had no luck in finding them, and neither noticed that the other available girls seemed to have lost their allure. With it, went the opportunity to carve out some potential amusement park companionships as they walked past and missed signals from a few interested young ladies. It was like looking at the sun too long, and now everything had spots on it.

With the very large crowd that this hot and sunny, ninety-five-degree late July day had lured out to the park, it was very possible that they had walked right past them. They could have been seated watching one of the stage shows or be on one of the many rides as they sauntered past, Mike and David came to realize. Thus the decision was made to have fun and, if they met them, good, if not, oh well.

Three rides later, they were standing by the Thunderbolt, one of the fastest roller coasters in the country at that time. The usual crowd of pre-riders slowly moved up the ramp past them with different degrees of anticipation as their turn to be shaken, tossed, and brutally whipped in their seats approached. Every few minutes, a couple dozen shaken, laughing, riders would walk down the exit ramp past those in line, exaggerating the ferocity of the ride, in hopes that it would add to the anxiety of the people waiting next. It had become a kind of park tradition to try scaring the people waiting to ride the ride you just finished.

Mike was trying to persuade David to ignore the long line and ride the Thunderbolt, when they spotted some kind of commotion going on near the exit gate from the ride. A young Black woman was agitated about something. She was looking under the wooden columns of the roller coaster as if she had dropped something. *She must have lost her hat while on the* ride, David assumed, because she had run down the ramp holding her hand over her—

David's mouth dropped. He took a step back when he noticed the girl's head covered in tiny little one-inch high braids. He felt embarrassed for her and, at the same time, fought the urge to add to her humiliation by laughing out loud at her plight.

She ran under the wooden support beams of the roller coaster followed by two frantic girlfriends and three employees of the park looking for a hat or...whatever she had lost. Then it occurred to David what must have happened. Now the urge to laugh at her dilemma mushroomed until he had to fight hard to hold it in.

He could picture that roller coaster careening around one of the sharp bends and then hurtling over one of the many dips in the ride, her wig suspended in the air like in a cartoon, as her head slipped out from underneath it. *That poor girl was having the time of her life*, he surmised, *until that last dip popped that wig off her head like a cork out of a bottle.* David's eyes started to water.

"For lack of a hair pin," he recited to himself, "a wig was lost."

David knew he dared not look at Michael now. Any kind of odd facial expression from him would snap the thin wire of restraint that held David's lips tight, freeing a howl of laughter toward the embarrassed girl.

He watched as the park attendants searched in vain for the wig. The poor girl gave up trying to cover her head. Those little braids stuck up on her scalp like little ears of corn in a garden. That thought caused him to close his eyes, in hopes of gaining some of the composure he was quickly losing. He almost made it. David turned away from the girl, lest he make a fool of himself. As he turned around, he came face to face with a tall, burly, park policeman. The strained look on his face caused David to hope the cop hadn't seen the smirk on his. Too late, the cop frowned at him for a long minute, and then he burst into laughter. That was all David needed to free his own inhibitions. He started laughing so hard he had to lean against the wall. The park cop staggered over to him and did likewise. While the two of them cavorted shamelessly out of sight of the search party, Mike, ignorant about the search going on and the comedians behind him, nearly panicked when he spotted the two fry-eating young women heading their way.

"Come on, David, let's go," Mike said as he pulled him away from the hysterical cop.

David, wiping his eyes, didn't resist Mike's insistent tugging. "Okay, Buff, I'm—coming," he answered between laughs.

Mike nervously looked around for the girls as he led David quickly away from the Thunderbolt ride. He last spotted them by the cotton-candy booth, surrounded by six or seven guys. Mike used that shield of spastic walking hormones to lead David away unseen.

Kennywood Park was jam packed as the afternoon heat drew kids from everywhere. The sounds of laughter, screams of delight and merriment, mixed together with a crying child somewhere to create the park experience. The smells of hot dogs, greasy fries, buttered popcorn, and the sight of multi-colored cotton candy incited the chaotic rush of people in every direction seeking to fill their hunger, thirst, and cravings. Into this mass of confusion walked Mike and David. Their passage was slowed by a large group of teenagers that were hamming it up in front of them. By the time they had expedited themselves from the pimple-faced army, Mike had lost sight of the two young women. He looked at David to offer a viable explanation for his actions but noticed he was still laughing about whatever he had seen near the Thunderbolt ride. Mike would have to ask him about that, making a mental note to do so.

One of the traits he liked about David was that he truly enjoyed a good laugh. Sometimes they would carry on for hours about something they found funny. Mike fondly remembered when they would laugh themselves to tears at times. It didn't bother Mike to be out of the loop this time. It always felt great just to watch his best friend enjoying himself.

Their friendship had grown much deeper than either of them had ever expected. They never discussed that fact, men rarely do, it's not considered masculine. Strong, emotional feelings are something either felt by women, or by men toward women. The brown guy, standing in front of the Noah's Ark ride shaking his head and giggling to himself, was the only person Mike had ever permitted to get that close to him.

"Hey, knucklehead, where to now?"

David just grinned at him.

Now Mike was starting to get a little annoyed. He had acted a fool in front of two of the nicest-looking girls he had ever met, and his buddy was acting like nothing had happened.

David realized something was wrong with Mike for the first time when he saw the irked look on his face. Maybe he didn't see the girl with the brussel sprouts on her head. That did it. That picture started him giggling again. Only the stern look on Mike's face held back another outburst. "Let's see...yeah, okay, I know, let's go over by the arcade," David said, pointing. "That's where we met most of the ladies who're on the prowl."

"Right," Mike answered, looking over the lake toward the penny arcade building. For some unexplainable reason, that was where they had been most successful meeting girls in the past. Maybe it was because that was also where most of the people entered and left the park, he once confessed to David. There, they would be first in line to meet any pretty new arrivals or those leaving and still looking for a Mr. Right-now, he told himself, trying to sound confident.

They filtered through the crowd of diverse picnickers, doing the same things young men have been doing for years. They watched the prettiest of the opposite sex go by, trying to convince themselves they had a chance with them.

The hot day produced a girl watcher's feast. The outfits they modeled did nothing but amplify the beauty of the wearer. Add the outrageous clothing of some of the larger women, and they had plenty of visual entertainment.

"It must be the same everywhere," David suggested to Mike when they got in line for something cold to drink, "people either dress to draw attention or just don't give a damn. There are the very dark people who wear very dark clothing that hides their beauty in the shadows and the very pale people in pale, colorless outfits that only highlight their lack of highlights."

"What about the people," Mike answered, "who wear outfits that were too small for them *before* they gained fifty pounds? From a guy's point of view, those tight outfits should be reserved for those women whose figures rate an eight or better, not point eight."

"Ha, ha, yeah," David countered. "And what about those women, blessed or cursed with very large posteriors? They wear bright spandex clothing that only draws attention to their extra dimensions. These are the same women who catch you staring at their ass-vertizement with your mouth open in shock that ask, 'What are you looking at?'"

It took them twice as long to reach the arcade pavilion as they spent some of the time stopping to rank the girls they saw by number. Each guy judged them differently. David, a self-professed leg man, said a "ten" in his book had to have great-looking legs. Those he chose were dressed in a variety of cut-off jeans, short-shorts, and a few miniskirts. There was a variety to choose from as they made their way through the crowd.

Mike shook his head in obvious disagreement. "If she doesn't have ample breast," he explained to his ignorant friend, "she can't qualify as a 'ten.'" He shrewdly pointed out numerous contestants for his top ten and a few who just fell "flat" of making his list. David found it hard to repudiate Mike's choices of "tens." Three or four of them had nice legs that also qualified them on his list. The game continued as they reached the penny arcade and scanned the passing crowd. It only came to a halt when two contestants that more than qualified in the eyes of both judges headed their way.

The boys had found an elevated corner of the arcade building that offered them a great view of everyone walking by. It also, they failed to consider, offered a good view of their quarry. The two "tens" had spotted them first and were weaving their way through the crowd in their direction.

Mike, distracted watching the games of chance people were playing in the arcade, turned and wondered what was David staring at. Following his line of sight, he lost his breath when he saw two certain young women walking directly toward them. Mike suddenly felt like he was the prey and they were the hunters. He felt trapped! He could swear his stomach had broken free, moved up his chest, and was now situated in his throat. A cold drop of sweat ran the gauntlet down his back. Could they be the reason, his panic asked, that he was suddenly felt paralyzed? Add to that the sudden appearance of his underwear stuck between his ass cheeks…maybe?

David smiled in anticipation when he spied them heading their way. He was going to suggest to Mike they make another tour of the park and then call it a day. Turning to point them out he realized Mike had also spotted them and was near panic. Oh, well, he couldn't run away this time, David had him blocked. "Come on, Mike," he tried sending his buddy some good vibes, "you can do this. Hi, ladies," David said exuberantly as he stepped forward to greet them.

Mike stood transfixed as he looked into the stunning eyes of the dark-haired beauty standing only a few feet in front of him.

"Hi, yourself, we wondered where you guys were hiding," the dark-haired "ten" said in a teasing voice.

"Hiding? That's funny. We were searching all over this park for the two of you," David quickly answered, trying to hide that obvious lie in the brightness of his smile. "You won't believe this," he added, looking from pretty girl to pretty girl, "there were some great-looking young ladies here that were attempting to get us sidetracked. It was tough turning them down," he animated by shaking his finger back and forth, "but we had to. Because you know—" He looked down before raising his head. "—sometimes you just can't settle for second best."

"I know what you mean." The leggy red head smiled as she walked up and stood directly in front of David. Their eyes revealing things yet spoken. "You should have seen all those poor guys who walked away crushed when we turned them down. It was so sad, we were heartbroken. But you know what?" The brash young woman moved even closer to him and copied the finger waving thing. "Sometimes you just can't settle for second best."

The handsome brown guy surprised Brenda by holding his ground when she stepped in his face. Usually, a guy either grinned like a Cheshire cat, mumbled like they were having a stroke—she liked that one—or backed off. This guy's eyes remained fixed on hers, and she loved that. They made eye contact, brown and green. In that moment, unspoken words passed between them, and in that moment—clarity.

"My name is David, the quiet one is my buddy, Mike. What's your name?" he asked, never taking his eyes off the red haired fox in front of him.

"I'm Brenda," red said, "and this is my best girlfriend, Toni. That's Toni with an I."

"Toni with an I" looked up at Mike and smiled a warm hello that he acknowledged by nodding.

There was a long silence as the four people found it both difficult and intriguing staring at the person in front of them amidst the talking and laughing throng that passed by, between, and around them.

"Look, girls," David said, breaking the silence, "the park is already too crowded to ride anything. The lines to all the best rides are so long it would take an hour just to get on."

The girls nodded in agreement but said nothing. Brenda gave him a look that made it plain that she was open to suggestions.

Taking the initiative, David continued. "Would you ladies want to hang out at the park and get to know each other or leave and get something to eat? We can come back later tonight after the crowd leaves if you still want to ride."

"I'm open to anything," a smiling Brenda said, passing the buck to Toni.

Toni was a little surprised by Brenda's answer. But it was her way of saying she liked the guy in front of her and, if it was okay with Toni, she wanted to pursue it a little further. They used little phrases to convey their intentions to each other without seeming obvious—unless they wanted to be obvious.

David understood the game the two girls were playing. It was an important ritual in the dating game. It would give direction to the evening, or stop it cold.

Mike, on the other hand, was dying. He was having trouble talking to these two pretty girls in a park full of people. David was going crazy trying to get them alone. What the hell was Mike going to say to them if they *did* get them alone?

"Mike, Toni with an I,—any suggestions?" David asked, never taking his eyes off Brenda. He didn't care what they did, as long as she was a part of it.

"Well, Mike?" Toni asked softly, "what do *you* have in mind?"

Ooooh, David thought, *did she ever put him on the hot seat.* This was one of those times he was glad it was the other guy in dutch. *Come on, buddy*, David silently pleaded, *please give her the right answer*. Everyone could sense the whole evening was hanging in the balance.

Mike swallowed hard. He looked from his buddy to the very pretty girl still looking at him with her powder-soft blue eyes. She easily was one of the most attractive girls he had ever met, and he hoped that whatever he suggested wouldn't ruin it for everyone. *She's so beautiful*, he thought, stalling for time.

"Let's party here for a while," he said, taking a deep breath and trying to read the reactions of the threesome, "and if it works, out we can take the party with us. We don't have to ride to have a good time, right? We can just walk around and, like David suggested, get to know each other."

Mike looked up from those stunning blue eyes to David standing beside him. The expression on David's face when he finally looked away from the redhead said, *Great answer*.

"Hey, that sounds cool to me," David said, finally coming to the rescue of his sweating buddy, and trying to look for any signals from his partner that he really didn't want to be with them. "What do you think, ladies, is my buddy on the right track or what?"

Toni looked at Brenda and nodded. Brenda's wink signaled her intentions to Toni, who then looked up at Mike and innocently smiled.

There was something about him she wanted to get to know, Toni decided on a whim. The black guy with him was very good looking too, but this guy's shyness intrigued her. She found that very attractive for some strange reason. *That's odd*, Toni thought while watching Mike's eyes trying to read hers, *I have never been enamored with the shy, quiet type*. All the guys she had dating were loud and energetic. Well, a few were maybe even spastic, she recalled. "I'm with Brenda. Whatever she wants to do is find with me."

Brenda read from that, maybe Toni was feeling a little reluctant. But the guy in front of her never gave her a chance to think anything negative. He gently put his arm around her bare waist and led her out of the penny arcade into the park.

Toni watched them melt into the crowd but didn't move. *Don't pressure the shy guy*, she told herself. She wanted to laugh as she wondered what shy-guy was thinking as they watched

Brenda and his friend walk away and leave him there with her. *Are you sweating bullets you sweet, handsome hunk?* Standing with her back to him, she was able to hide the grin on her face.

Other than the obvious differences, with Brenda's tan and David light brown complexion, Brenda and David had a lot in common, Toni noticed while waiting on the shy guy to make his move. Brenda's tall and leggy figure fit smoothly in the muscular arms of that tall, handsome brown man. Brenda's white and yellow blouse and cuffed blue-jean shorts matched David's white and gold Steelers jersey and blue-jean shorts. They even walked alike, Toni thought, as the frustrated former ballet dancer in Brenda moved her hips in unison with David's athletic figure.

"Toni," she heard someone call her as her best friend and David disappeared into the crowd.

She turned around and saw Mike's hand extended out toward her. Toni smiled up at him and placed her hand in his. He slowly pulled her into his body and leaned down very close to her face, lips to lip. His surprised action prompted a slight resistance from her. She quickly relaxed as his eyes revealed nothing threatening.

The scent of him that close added to her mood. Their faces were almost touching. Toni started to close her eyes in anticipation of the kiss that was obvious the next step. Usually, there was little chance she would let a guy she just met kiss her, but she was curious, so she started to—

"Shall we go," she heard him say just as she closed her eyes and before their lips met. He didn't wait for her answer as he took her hand and led her out into the surging crowd in the direction David and Brenda had departed. Disappointed, Toni frowned and reluctantly followed his lead. His change in character had caught her completely off guard. *Okay, handsome, the first serve is yours*, she thought smiling up at him as they maneuvered through the crowd, *but now the ball is in my court*. There was excitement in the air, she could feel it. *It's going to be fun getting to know this shy-guy,* she decided.

Toni had first spotted David and Mike when standing in line with Brenda waiting to ride the Ferris Wheel but never thought all this would happen. She had just agreed with her frustrated BFF that they had only seen a few good-looking guys at the park when she saw them. With the slow moving line, she was able to tender a fair evaluation. *Wouldn't mind spending the evening at the park with the two of them*, she thought then, as she watched them drinking something, *but that would be up to Brenda.*

They were casually dressed, she observed, as the line slowly moved forward. The white guy, who turned out to be Mike, wore matching khaki shorts and a short-sleeved shirt. He looked clean and masculine. The tanned "brother," was dressed in jean shorts and a white and gold Steelers knit jersey that fit his broad shoulders like skin. Damn sexy.

Mike, she remembered, appeared to be laughing about something and looked so cute. He had a kind of honesty about him that was easily read. With his strong and handsome features, he stood about six feet tall, or so she guessed, with a head full of wavy brown hair. From the way he moved, he appeared very athletic. She had always loved that in men, Toni admitted as she turned around and took a few steps to catch up in line with her riding mate who was busy fending off an admirer. From the guys' interactions, they appeared to be best friends. Something about the way they related to each other, she garnered, reminded her of Brenda and a missing third girlfriend.

The first half hour in the park and they were approached twice but turned the guys down. It wasn't because they weren't interested. The guys were very nice. It was just that they wanted some time together before having to put up with the constant come-ons of horny guys.

It was while appeasing their hunger pangs that Toni again spotted Mike and David. She had observed them while Brenda ordered their favorite fries with cheese sauce and bacon bits. Intrigued, Toni guided Brenda over to a table near them. As if scripted, Toni chuckled as the two guys pretended not to notice them as they ate. She didn't have to inform Brenda. They had played this game too many times. It did surprise her when the cute guy, now holding her hand, turned and scampered away. Maybe that was why she was so curious about him, she pondered as she spotted Brenda and David up ahead.

Toni liked David. He appeared to be a fun loving guy. He and Brenda were having a good laugh about something, oblivious to any scrutiny they were under. From what she could tell, David was a nice guy and very good looking to boot, but he wasn't her type. He was powerfully built, probably about two hundred and twenty five pounds, and a few inches taller than Mike. His hair was cut close, very neat with waves across the top. *He is the color of coffee with two creams*, Toni thought, giggling to herself. His dark brown eyes seemed to laugh when he talked, and his hands and body moved as if he was acting out his conversation. There was a tough aura about him, Toni sensed, that belied his seemingly amiable nature.

David is a man you wouldn't want to screw with, or would you...mmmm? Toni looked at a very interested Brenda and chuckled to herself at the other meaning of that sentence. Apparently, Brenda was comfortable with him, and, admittedly, there wasn't anything threatening that Toni read in his face. She just felt more comfortable around men who were closer to her physically. She liked them medium sized. *Get your mind out of the bedroom*, Toni snickered as she turned that harmless thought into another sexual innuendo. Running with that naughty line of thinking, she recalled a horny Brenda once saying she liked more of it and color wasn't the most important quality, but how a guy approached the subject. Katie, the missing part of the triad, had quickly agreed.

When the three of them were together, Toni fondly remembered, as Mike led her through the crowd and over where David and Brenda apparently were playing a game, sex always came up for open discussion. Toni remained accessible to new ideas, but her choices were more conservative than her friends.

Then again, Brenda and Katie were more experienced. It had been over two years since Toni last surrendered herself to a man. Her best friends measured that sometimes in months or weeks. It had taken Toni that long to wash off the dirt of that last encounter, she used to say, when she felt the need to defend her chosen celibacy.

"There the two of you are," Brenda said as Mike led Toni up to them. "We were about to go looking for you."

From the look on her best friend's face, Toni seemed comfortable with the two guys, and that made Brenda relax. Even though she enjoyed David's company, if Toni wanted out—they were gone.

"Well, we—"

"Toni with an I is in good hands," Mike said, cutting off Toni.
Her smile at him signaled she agreed.

"Let's try playing some of the games," David suggested.

They came to a booth where you tossed dimes in floating cups trying to win some CDs.

"Let's try this one," Mike suggested.

"Mike and me against the two of you."

Brenda smiled at her BFF but didn't say anything.

After that, every time they came to a booth of chance, it became a bragging contest between couples. David and Brenda quickly established their dominance. A lot of laughs later, Brenda was carrying a half dozen small, cheap, and useless stuffed animals of every possible shape and color. Finally, after winning a small brown bear, she walked over and gave the remaining ones to some little kids.

"What about the bear," Toni teased, guessing the answer from the snicker on the redhead's face.

"I'm keeping the bear," Brenda told the threesome, "because it reminds me of David." She named the bear Davey, prompting a huge smile from its namesake and a sparkle in his big brown eyes.

Toni just shook her head as she watched Brenda play David like a cheap violin. *Guys*, she thought as she watched Brenda performing her magic, *drop-like-a-rock for those emerald green eyes every time*.

As the evening turned into night, they made one last trip around the park and approached the Ferris Wheel.

"Are you guys sure you want to ride the Ferris Wheel? It's kind of boring."

"True," Brenda added before anyone else could question Mike's affirmation. "But the mood is too mellow," she suggested to the group as she held David's arm, "to go whipping up and down on one of the coasters."

Everyone agreed but their reasons varied. The slow ride skyward gave the shy guy a chance to cuddle with the amazing woman holding his arm and his buddy, in the next car, quite a few deep kisses as they circled.

Mike and Toni hit it off after that shaky start. They were playing all the little sickening games lovers played when infatuated with each other. She stared up at him as if his words spoke the worlds into existence. Wasn't that another God?

He walked with his chest out so far, it was a wonder he didn't fall over face-first. Brenda was so happy for Toni that she had trouble keeping her eyes off them. She knew Toni's last serious lover had hurt her so deeply she wouldn't even talk about it with her. But this Mike, much to her surprise, was the first guy to make her swoon again. Brenda knew Toni only tolerated the other guys she dated. They were useful for dating, buying her things, and having fun outings with, but she wasn't about to let them in, not for a moment. Mike's smile seems to have broken the chains around her heart.

When Toni offered to share a Coke with him, saying she just wanted a few sips, Brenda was both shocked and pleased. Miss Toni never drank behind anyone but her or Katie, and never a strange guy. "I don't know where his mouth's been," being the reason most often quoted.

The two of them were walking in front of David and Brenda, but in a world of their own, when Brenda tugged on David's arm. "Does it seem like we are being completely ignored by our best friends?" she asked David.

David snickered in agreement and whispered something in Brenda's ear.

When they reached Noah's Ark, Mike turned to ask if they were ready to try the Ark now that the lines weren't as long. It was then that he noticed for the first time they were alone.

"Where did they go, do you see them?"

"No, I don't, Mike," Toni answered, as she carefully scanned the faces around them.

"Well, should we go looking for them?"

Toni weighed her answer. It wasn't like Brenda to just take off like that unless—

"Hey, if they want to be alone, that's their loss. Maybe we will bump into them later."

"You're right, let's go."

Both Toni and Mike continued to occasionally look for them as they walked. After ten o'clock, most people had left or were leaving the park. If Brenda and David were nearby, Toni and Mike would have easily spotted them. They gave up the search and continued walking around the park, holding hands, making small talk, oblivious to everyone around them.

Mike felt the difference—unsure why, but he felt the difference. He didn't delude himself into thinking that the sexy woman walking with him felt the same way. He had gained enough experience to realize men and women saw and felt things on separate levels. Then again, he wasn't all that sure yet about the depth of his feeling for her either. Seeking some simple reassurance, he softly squeezed her hand in his as they walked. She returned the gesture, indicating she was conscious of him also—at least that was how he interpreted her reaction.

Gawd, she feels so good, Mike thought when he stood behind her putting his arms around her shoulder. They had stopped to watch some kids trying to roll plastic balls into the correct colored glasses at one of the few booths of chance still open. Mike felt her lean back against him. He placed his face against her hair and inhaled its clean scent closing his eyes for a few seconds to forever stamp the moment in his memory, the sounds and smells of the park a background to that vivid memory.

"Mmmm," Toni moaned under her breath when Mike hugged her from behind. His strong arms felt great. She liked him, she admitted to herself as they watched the balls rolling haphazardly across the glasses, just missing falling in the winning colored ones, and hoped there was nothing weird with her shy-guy. Past boyfriends drifted through her consciousness. Names and faces that were both good and bad memories. Experiences she knew were a part of growing up, a part of finding your place in the world. Good or bad wasn't as important as having lived the experience, or in some cases, surviving—but always learning from them.

The gentle rocking of the man wrapped around her brought her back from her past to the present. Toni pushed back against Mike, as if trying to lose herself in him. She felt him softly grinding his hips against her and smiled at his obvious over-reaction to her cuddling. She had forgotten how single-minded men's minds were.

Toni never had any problems relating to guys. She held all the cards and understood that. Never overconfident, she just understood the rules and played by them. God had given women something the physically stronger sex couldn't live without. If women were smart, she believed, they should use it, or the unspoken promise of it, to make their lives better. "Why buy your own drinks when that big, strong, horny guy at the end of the bar," she often told her girlfriends, "is hell bent on buying it for you? Of course," she said as she continued to explain the bar rules to them, "don't give him more than a weak thank you or you will be stuck with more drinks than you want. And unfortunately, more of him than you may want."

Earlier, as Mike and Toni followed Brenda and David around the park, the fear that had erupted in him at the sight of her quickly diminished. The more he relaxed and acted himself, the more he sensed Toni felt at ease with him. He felt certain she was enjoying herself. Add sassy Brenda and David's ability to fill in the dead spots when the conversation lagged, and the evening went quickly.

Mike walked proudly as he held her hand. The glances they repeatedly got from guy and girl alike only heightened his enjoyment. He never took dating seriously, he realized the more he thought about his past, until he was smitten by a certain woman's smile. *It wasn't her great body that first enamored me or her knock-dead good looks, but her smile*, he tried convincing himself.

By not taking dating seriously, Mike's philosophy freed him from experiencing the one thing that men feared the most when approaching a beautiful woman—rejection. If he didn't expect much, his reasoning was, then he had nothing to lose if he was rejected. Strangely, that was something he rarely had to face. Women found him very warm and friendly, with an endearing sense of humor. He was easy to talk to and was never bored, or acted like he was, when they talked. He was very handsome but didn't seem to realize it or strut like guys did when they discovered women thought them attractive.

One of the reasons he had hit it off so quickly with David was that they enjoyed each other's company and didn't let any other considerations or people's opinions interfere with the natural growth of that friendship. They quickly established a trust they both believed unbreakable and enduring.

Toni was the first woman to make Mike feel she was worth

the gamble. He wasn't aware that since Adam, men were the last to recognize when that pudgy flying archer shot them in the ass and changed everything.

The rides started closing as it neared eleven o'clock. Toni and Mike had made a dozen half-hearted efforts to look for their friends as they made a final tour of the park. Only once did they think they saw them, but by the time they reached that spot, if it was them, they were gone.

"Look, Toni," Mike said, stopping, "do you think they took off together? Maybe they grew bored with—" He looked into her eyes and lost track of what he wanted to say. She smiled, and his thoughts returned. "—with watching us moon over each other or something and left."

His candor is refreshing, she thought. *Does he feel the same way about me?* she wondered while smiling up at him. Toni reluctantly acknowledged being captivated with him and that it felt so good that she didn't want the night to end. "I don't know, Mike. Usually, Brenda will signal me when she wants to leave with a guy. But you know what? She drove today. If her car is still here, then she is too, because I don't have keys for it, and she wouldn't leave it here. She loves that car."

Mike nodded. "Okay, let's walk out to the parking lot and check. Even if they're hiding from us, they'll have to leave the park. It's closing soon."

"Mike, could we grab a snack on the way? I'm hungry. I could go for something sweet like a cookie or something."

"Me too," Mike agreed. "There are a lot of stands by the arcade building if they're still open. We'll stop there and see on our way out."

They headed toward the penny arcade main exit all the while looking around for their friends and a snack stand.

The late evening crowd was very different from the carefree picnickers who came early to the park to ride, eat, ride, enjoy the sun, ride, get away from home, and ride. After dark, the young hunters came out, looking for fair, and slightly less-than-fair, game. The large groups and families were replaced by sets of twos. Now there might be ten or more sets of twos walking together, but if divided, they would mostly separate into pairs.

An evening at Kennywood belonged to young lovers and

those not so young seeking the same. The tempo at the park slowed from little kids, running into you as they raced from ride to ride with dripping ice cream cones and sticky fingers, to the racing heart of a young person maybe on their first date. The ancient wooden boats of the Old Mill ride earlier carried candy eating, boat rocking, and water tossing loud adolescents. The same boats drifted quietly now on the water and more smoothly, the new occupants more interested in the lips of the one seated beside them than the old peeling statues and flaking figurines set up to amuse the ticket holders. At night, the couplings of the young and not so young became the most popular riders. The last few hours in the park were for lovers.

Two of those were walking in the exit tunnel when the young man stopped. The young woman holding his hand also stopped, the chocolate chip cookies earlier consumed as they wandered toward the parking lot. Now Mike wanted to toast an exciting evening by kissing the woman who had made it so.

Who knew what awaited them should they catch up with Brenda and David? he worried as they walked. Maybe they had a falling out and were angrily sitting on one of the benches at the gate, waiting for him and Toni to come out of the park. If so, that would be a bad time to toast the evening.

So when he stopped in the middle of the tunnel leading out of the park, Mike pulled Toni into his arms. He caught her completely off-guard as he looked deeply into her beguiling eyes. Everything he saw in them said she wanted him also. There was no mistaken their message. He knew he had earlier missed the same signal a couple of times tonight. Once when they were in the arcade, for sure when riding the Ferris Wheel, and a couple of times when they stopped to hold each other. *No, not this time*, Mike thought. Slowly he lowered his head, never taking his eyes off the soft woman in his arms. Just as their lips touched, her lips opened and her eyes closed.

Toni liked to close her eyes when she kissed. That made it easy to erase everyone and everything that could distract her from the pleasure. She moaned as his mouth remained open on hers and their tongues danced. She hated men who kissed her like she was their sister. The DiNardos were kissers, all of them. Uncles, aunts, and grandparents, all kissed each other and every *unlucky* child in the room on the mouth. Having been very slow to learn to stay out of the room when her relatives came to visit, Toni had plenty of experience with kisses.

Turned on by his experienced mouth, she pushed against his chest. An involuntary reaction to the pleasure she was receiving. When his tongue started to move in and out of her mouth, she lost track of where they were, wrapped her leg around one of his, and squeezed. His reaction to that would be the subject later of many laughs between her and Brenda, and a snicker on Brenda's face for weeks afterward, every time she saw Mike.

Toni described it later as if she had stepped on the petal of her kitchen garbage can and the lid popped up, because when she squeezed Mike's leg, his tongue shot into her mouth so quickly it startled her. Only the giggling of a scattering of on-lookers, as they were leaving the park, stopped her from taking their embrace to the next level. It felt that good. Slowly, she pushed away from him, signaling a truce to the lovemaking. Not a halt to it, her dancing eyes told Mike's, just a truce until later.

As she walked with him, Toni realized she was more turned on from his kisses than that night she lost her panties. She squeezed his hand and smiled when he looked at her.

It took them a while to find the spot where Brenda parked. The parking lot at night was a different world than it was when they arrived. Toni remembered they parked directly across from this big white Ford truck, but now every vehicle in their row was gone.

"Well, that settles it, I guess," Toni said to a surprised Mike. "This is about where we parked, and I don't see her car any- where. It's not like Brenda to leave like this. You don't think something is wrong, do you, Mike?"

He hid any concern he might be feeling from her and hoped David knew what he was doing. Mike considered the alternatives before answering. "You mean between David and Brenda?" he asked, wondering if she was thinking what he thought. Mike held her at arms' length and tried to be as reassuring as he could. "Look, this much I can guarantee you. Brenda has nothing to worry about from David. He's not a taker. We have double dated before, and he is the last to act improperly. Not...not meaning I'm the first...well, you know what I..."

Toni looked apprehensively into Mike's eyes for a while before taking a deep breath. She trusted him, hell, she also trusted David. There was nothing in their mannerisms that suggested otherwise. That was one reason why, when she watched Brenda and David "sneaking" away, she didn't alert Mike. If Brenda wanted to be alone with David, that was all right with Toni. It didn't happen very often that they split up after arriving somewhere together. Usually, only after both felt comfortable with the people they were with. Only once did they regret it, and that time because they ended up being more bored with their dates than threatened.

"Let's walk over to my car," Mike suggested. "I'm parked over the hill far from the main exit. All these parking spaces were filled when we arrived," Mike explained as they reached the crest of the parking lot.

They cleared the hill, and Mike quickly spotted his red Cavalier parked about ten spaces from a lone black pickup that was driving away. It was a space, he explained to Toni, that he had to squeeze into when they first arrived. There was no sign of David or Brenda. Mike took a long look back toward the park and saw a few people still leaving. None were headed in their direction or resembled David or Brenda.

"Come on, Toni," Mike said, starting to enjoy playing detective, "we can drive around the parking lot and see if we can spot them."

They walked quietly down the hill to his car. Both had different thoughts as to what had happened and neither wanted to risk damaging the rapport they had developed between them by speculating. It was Toni who spotted the piece of paper under his windshield wipers. Mike leaned over and slipped out a card. It was David's Zinc Coater business card.

"There's nothing written on it," he told an anxious Toni after flipping it over and examining it carefully. "Maybe they didn't have a pen to write with."

For some reason that made sense to both. Maybe they just wanted to believe they knew their friends well enough not to be surprised they would find themselves with paper and no way of writing on it. "Anyway, finding David's business card indicates he was here and left. Brenda's car is gone. I think they decided not to wait for us, Toni."

"Well, that's their loss," she said while grabbing his arm and hugging it. "If they don't want to be with us, so be it. Take me home, James."

Mike's shoulders slumped, and he looked dejectedly into her eyes. His mouth formed a word that he couldn't find the strength to say. It only took Toni a brief moment to recognize his disappointment.

"Okay, driver," she said to those sad eyes and kissed him lightly on the lips, "take me to your home first. I'd like to try a glass of that super delicious punch mix of yours you were bragging about. Then, sweet man, you are taking me home, right?"

"Youse got it, Miss Daisy, let me get dat dare doe fo ya."

Miss Daisy waited until he opened her door before nodding to him and climbing into the car. Mike enjoyed their play acting as he ran around the front of the car, hoping that last batch of punch he made tasted as good as his boast. *Of all times to forget to sample my creation first*, he thought grimacing out of view of his passenger, *today would be the day*. While buckling up, he replayed every ingredient he added and the right proportions of orange juice, vodka, rum, lemons, and the fruit juice concoction.

"Are we waiting for the light to change?"

"What? Oh—sorry."

Miss Daisy's embarrassed driver finally put his car in gear, and they made an unsuccessful tour of the emptying parking lots.

Toni looked out her window as they drove away from the park. She felt safe with Mike and hoped Brenda was likewise. She then turned her full attention to her good-looking driver.

CHAPTER 5

After watching the K and R Company tractor-trailer driver finally succeed on his third attempt at backing his eighteen wheeler into the plant truck doors, Mike walked with the overhead crane into the coil field to pick up the driver's load of coils. The Zinc Coater building was one of the toughest plants to back into because of the short driveways in front of the shipping/receiving doors. Because of the limited parking lot between the buildings, every truck had to back in at an angle and then straighten up after the trailer was in the building. Some of the older truckers had little problems backing in. The younger drivers dreaded loading here.

Mike heard the truck driver mumbling something under his breath as he approached his truck bed with the crane and the second of the three coils he was scheduled to receive. He, like all of the material handlers, had grown accustomed to the grumbling of the drivers, who always seem to complain about being in a hurry. Mike stopped beside the trailer bed and guided the crane C-hook with a coil on it over the trailer bed.

For safety, he motioned for the impatient driver to move to the end of the trailer. The driver walked a few feet, stopped, gave Mike a look that could kill, and then waited for him to bring the coil closer. Mike stopped and with the crane control box belted around his waist, returned the driver's stare. The trucker swore something under his breath and stomped off toward the end of the truck bed.

"Which coil is that?" the tired driver asked.

His wait had been only an hour since he arrived, but he was already running behind schedule when he pulled up to the plant. As his luck would have it lately, there were ten trucks ahead of him when he arrived.

"This is the nine-thousand-five-hundred-pound coil," Mike shouted over to him.

"Put it in the middle," he demanded.

Mike stared at the trucker for a moment. They had already decided the positioning of the three coils he was going to receive. The 11,000 pound coil was already placed on the front of the trailer bed, the 9,500-pound coil on the C-hook would be placed in the middle, and the 12,500 pound coil would then be placed at the rear of the trailer. *This isn't brain surgery*, Mike thought as the trucker pointed to the empty coil racks.

Mike maneuvered the coil over the beveled lumber and coil racks in the center of the trailer and pressed down slowly on the second lever on the remote-control overhead crane box around his waist. The coil slowly dropped down toward the coil racks on the trailer. The flat-bed trailer rocked a little as the weight of the heavy coil settled into the rack. Mike backed the C-hook out of the coil and raised it up and away from the truck.

One more coil for this truck and I'm taking a break, he decided.

David, walking along the furnace platform about twelve feet above the loading docks, heard the crane approaching. Looking down, he noticed it was Mike, of the four material handlers on the crew, loading trucks. David stopped a minute to watch his friend from the furnace level platform. He was in the middle of performing his routine furnace pilot-burner check when he heard the heavy crane rattle overhead as it approached. All morning he tried to catch up with Mike to ask how his evening went with the other girl they had met at Kennywood Park last night. Meetings, problems, and the busy truck traffic had prevented them from crossing paths.

David watched as the paper wrapped galvanized coil was placed on the flat bed, and the now empty C-hook was raised up and moved away from the truck. He then turned and studied the busy driver to see if he was properly chaining down his coils. The only thing unusual was that the trucker's grimy pants actually fit him. That, David knew, was an oddity. After years of loading trucks himself and watching numerous truckers bending over and showing their butt cracks, seeing one with pants that fit—now, that was unusual.

David chuckled at that sick thought, turned, and continued his inspection of the furnace pilots.

David would catch up with Mike later. His crew had made plans last week to stop at Vinnie's Pizza parlor after work tonight and have pizza and beer to celebrate John Walter's retirement from Zinc Coaters at the end of the month. *If we don't cross paths before then*, David thought while checking the furnace, *I'll corner Mike there.*

ℯↄℯↄ

A family of five stepped through the weather-beaten screen door of Vinnie's and looked around for an empty table. As usual, it was packed with the faithful pizza and beer lovers. The smell of pepperoni, tomato sauce, and sausage stirred the appetite of anyone walking through the old wooden door. Vinnie's was one of the favorite eating places along this section of Route 30, was a throwback to the old Pizza Parlors of the 1960s with sawdust on the floors.

The laughter echoing above the drone of something loud playing on the jukebox had increased in direct proportions to the amount of beer being consumed. Vinnie's being crowded was usual for a Saturday evening. The back room was usually reserved for a party, and that seemed to be the source of most of the festivities, the newcomers noticed. They looked for a table as far away from that as they could find.

"Well, tell me," David asked, leaning over and trying to talk above the din of the party.

"Tell you what? There's not a lot to tell," Mike explained after David's frown clearly clarified his meaning. "I took her home—"

"To her house?" David asked interrupting.

"To my apartment," Mike said. He knew that comment would tantalize his friend into asking more.

"Whoa, you lucky dog, did you..." was all Mike heard as David's words were drowned out by loud cat calls for either their overly endowed waitress who had returned, or for the three pitchers of chilled beer she carried.

From what Mike could read on David's lips, he was asking

him if he got lucky. The momentary respite gave him time to ponder his answer. A yes would gain him David's respect because Toni was an awesome-looking woman who probably stirred the animated imagination of every man she met. *Getting in her pants on a chance date,* Mike thought, expressing his own lusty verbalism, *is bad!* Great, amazing, awesome.

Mike looked into the smiling brown face on the man seated next to him. "No!"

The confused expression on David's face said, what in the world are you talking about?

"No, what?" David asked, as nine men stopped shouting for a moment after toasting the retiree and guzzling down a tasty glass of the cold beer.

Mike just shook his head. "Nothing."

CHAPTER 6

Brenda reluctantly got up and walked into the kitchen to check on her favorite snack. The buttery aroma emanating from the microwave had drifted into her living room, playing havoc with her concentration. She knew better then to leave the kitchen while it was cooking, but she couldn't tear herself away from Toni's rendition of her date last night. Brenda had set the microwave timer for two minutes and rushed back to her grinning friend. That would guarantee the popcorn wouldn't burn but would also limit the amount that would pop. She would never admit she liked it that way because the less popcorn in the bag, she came to realize, the butterier it became.

"Okay, tell me more about that handsome Mike person," Brenda said, setting the hot bowl of deliciously smelling popcorn down on the coffee table and grabbing a seat on the couch next to Toni.

A big grin erupted on Toni's face. She had that cute-little-girl look, Brenda noticed, that she got when she was excited about something.

"Like I said, he seemed like a nice guy when we met him. He was very polite all night. When we went over to his apartment, I thought for sure he would try to hit on me a little, but he didn't. And, Brenda, he's so cute when he's embarrassed. When we walked into his place, I saw his underwear on the couch. Obviously, they were clean and neatly folded, but I made a face anyway when I saw them. I thought he was going to die when he realized what I was looking at. He grabbed those BVDs and made a hasty retreat into his bedroom. He returned red faced and apologizing. The poor boy didn't catch on to me until I asked him if the couch was clean enough to sit on now. After that, he joined in with gusto. We were teasing each other about everything. Brenda, would you believe I had the nerve to ask him if that lump in his throat was because he was glad to see me. He made a surprised face then asked me, laughing between his words, 'Is it *that* cold in here or are you *that* glad to see me?'"

Four or five kernels of popcorn fell out of Brenda's open mouth.

"Brenda," Toni said, acting out the surprise she felt then, "I was blushing with embarrassment. Me embarrassed, can you believe that? I tried to ignore him, but I just had to cross my arms. But that's as common as we got. After trying a couple glasses of his 'Home Brew,' he took me home, kissed me at my door, and left."

Brenda managed to quickly chew the hand full of popcorn she had shoved into her mouth, not expecting Toni to finish talking so quickly. "That sounds kind of like a boring date," she finally was able to say.

"No, it wasn't, Bren. I enjoyed talking with Mike. He has a great sense of humor and kept me laughing all night. We were so relaxed together I kicked off my shoes and had fun chatting with him, know what I mean? I think he's the kind of guy I need right now."

"Laughing all night, huh?" Brenda said with a look of sarcasm on her face. "Anyway, do you plan on seeing him again?"

Toni wanted to say yes, but she didn't. Brenda's teasing had made her take a second look at her feelings for Mike. Instead of answering, she reached for her first taste of the quickly disappearing popcorn. Brenda joined her as both put a fist full of popcorn into their mouths.

Toni enjoyed the simple repast and the pause. "I would love to see him again," she finally said. "I gave him my number. Now, let's see if he's serious."

"Good," Brenda said, finally voicing her opinion.

"What do you mean —good?"

"Honey, he's a nice-looking man, and I think you two were good for each other, that's all. The way he looked at you, girl— the guy was smitten with little Toni. Who knows? He might be the one."

Toni couldn't get over the change in her closest friend. The Brenda McShane she knew had sworn there is no such creature as "the one." Toni, caught off guard, looked down at her hands trying to hide that from her.

Brenda grinned teasingly at her. "Don't pitch a fit. If you don't want him, I'll take him."

Toni frowned good-naturedly and threw a couch pillow at Brenda with her non popcorn hand.

"Okay, what about you, girlfriend? How did you and that hunk of chocolate that you *snuck* away with make out?"

"Unfortunately, nothing happened between us either. And we didn't sneak away. The two of you were so enamored with each other you never noticed when we made a wrong turn, is all."

"Wrong turn, my perfect ass. Now tell me what happened. Mmmmm, that's great popcorn."

Brenda debated lying to Toni about her evening with David. The reason why escaped her, but the thought remained. Later she would debate why.

"We were sitting here on my couch," Brenda said, putting the bowl of old maids on the table after picking out the last edible kernels, "about where you're sitting. We were kissing heavily, and his hands all over me and my hands were all over him—"

"Wait, wait, wait a minute," Toni said with a questioning sneer on her face, "I thought nothing happened. Seems to me a lot was going on." She had forgotten they judged the success of a date differently.

Brenda moaned softly as her skin tingled in remembrance. Gaining control, she shook the mental picture of last evening's events and then frowned at Toni. "Like I was saying before I was so rudely interrupted, he was holding me in his strong arms while his hand slipped under my shirt."

Toni's eyes and mouth opened wide as her interest quickened. With the small shirts they were both wearing, he didn't have far to travel.

"His tongue danced in my mouth without choking me like most men do and think you *looove* that. You know what I mean, Toni? It was great, and he smelled soooooo good. I was so turned on, and when he slipped his large hand over my breast and gently kneaded my nipple, I was so hot. It was all I could not to strip right there. And, Toni, I was dying to see that powerful man naked. I wanted to see all of him, know what I mean? It seemed like my bedroom was the obvious next step, but we never made it. It was as if he was waiting on me to say or do something, and I guess I was waiting for him."

Toni was speechless. She had forgotten how easily Brenda could discuss intimacy.

"We stopped kissing and caught our breath," Brenda continued. "I turned toward him and started to tell him how much I wanted to make love to him, but all I could do was swoon over him like a stupid school girl. As I looked in his dark, sexy eyes, I think the realization became clear to both of us that we were just horny and, being strangers, it wasn't quite enough to rush into and get intimate over. You and Mike, you guys had a look of love in your eyes when you were together. It's obvious that there was something deep happening between the two of you. David and I," Brenda looked up at the ceiling and shook her head, "we just wanted to screw each other's eyes out."

"Brenda, when has that ever stopped you? I mean neither of us are prudes."

"I know, Toni, I know, that's what's so weird. Hell, I still get weak when I think about him. Oh, girl, his arms are sooo strong, I know it would have been fantastic."

"Well then," Toni asked, trying to understand how her openly sexual girlfriend and that hunk of a man got that far and stopped. "How were you able to, I mean, most guys—"

"That's the point, Ton, he's unlike any guy I've ever met," Brenda continued as she started rubbing her hands up and down her arms. "I mean he was ready to rip my clothes off, but still in control, I liked that. But I think he knew we weren't ready to commit to each other." Yes, she had always said she wasn't into commitments, Brenda was going to admit as she watched Toni questioning her with her eyes. She knew her friend would have to ask "the question."

"What commitment? Are you telling me you're ready to—is the most popular girl at Washington High ready to settle down?"

"I don't know, Toni. It's just with him I sensed it wasn't going to be just a one nighter, know what I mean? There's something more than that brewing between us. He seemed to sense it also I think. We did make a date for next Saturday night, but I don't think we'll ever be more than good friends."

"Really, after getting that close?"

"Yeah. Weird, huh?

"Well," Toni told Brenda as she touched her hands, "there's no law that you have to fall for every person you meet."

"But that's the strange thing, Ton, I could easily fall for him. There's just something missing, something that's lacking. It's nothing to do with our obvious differences. I was thinking about that last night in bed—alone," Brenda said, closing her eyes for a moment and shaking her head. "It's, it's more like we are too much alike. Do you know what I mean? We had just met that day, but it's like we knew each other too well. Like we both knew just where the other's buttons are and were a little leery about trusting that power to a stranger yet. Does that make sense?"

"It doesn't have to make sense, Brenda," Toni injected. "Physically, you two are attracted to each other, that's why you were almost raping him. That's one thing. But it's separate from what you feel in your heart. You like David, you're just not in love with him, and that's okay."

Brenda's green eyes shone with acceptance. She got out of Toni's explanation what she wanted to hear. It was all right, according to her best friend, to want him without being madly in love with him. And, after all, that was what she had wanted to do anyway.

Over the next few months, Brenda and David spent time double dating with Toni and Mike. As a foursome, they went out to dinners, back to Kennywood…twice, and spent time huddled up at their apartments playing cards or just chatting. Everything was light and friendly lacking passion. When they were out alone together, Brenda and David had a ball. They had like interests. He invited her to sporting events, she took him to Broadway stage plays downtown, and they went to first run movies together. In doing so, they became very close friends. Nothing romantically special developed between them, but they did fool around some. But on their seventh "date," they made love. Well, making love was a play on words, what they found was fantastic sex. For most, having great sex was enough, but what they craved, when the smoke cleared, was a deeper relationship.

"I'm kind of glad the theater was sold out, Davey."

"I'm not. They promised to hold two tickets in my name. It's a good thing I called. If it was just for Mike and me, I would have made them find some seats. But dinner with you was great, and you look so good walking into that restaurant, I've calmed down and mellowed out. I really enjoyed showing you off to the rich and upper-crust that dine at Christopher's. Did you see the looks we got?"

"So, you enjoyed my being your ah...trophy...date for to-night?"

David thought about his answer and the possible angry repercussions. The way Brenda looked in that red dress that hugged her like skin, any negative repercussion could ruin the rest of the evening.

They were in his car, driving toward the house she shared with Toni. David had asked her out with the plan to see *Superstar* playing on stage at the Benedum Theater downtown, and then an intimate dinner at Christopher's Restaurant on Mt. Washington. They were both dressed to impress, with Brenda wearing a stunning red cocktail dress that accented her shapely figure. Her hair was beautifully styled and not the long and straight way she usually wore it down her back. Add the coral color of her lips, and she impressed David.

"I admit I did, Brenda" David grinned at her an admitted. "Damn, you look that good, girl. I was proud to be seen with you."

Right answer, Brenda thought as she smiled at him, *right answer*. "Davey, it's early yet, and I don't want to walk in on Mike and Toni in our tiny apartment. She said he was coming over later, and I'm sure they don't expect me home any time soon. Where else can we go tonight?"

David had a suggestion that was prompted by the leggy lass sitting beside him. "It's too late for a movie, but we could go to a club and dance."

"No, not in these high heels. I should have worn some—"

"Noooo, your legs look great in them."

"Thank you, but they are lousy to dance in."

David slowed at an intersection for a red light. He would have to turn left at the next intersection to take her home. Fueled by that, he decided to ask? "We could chill at my place for a drink after that big dinner we had."

"I'm full, but that drink sounds amazing. Do you have any more of that concoction you made for Toni and me the other day?"

"No, but I can make it in a few minutes. I have all the ingredients."

"Great, let's skip dancing and have a few drinks. Wait, what's with the pouting face?"

"I admit I was looking forward to showing off my trophy date at a club."

"Another time, I'll even wear something more revealing. How's that?"

The driver looked at the beautiful woman sitting close to him with her legs crossed and her short dress a major distraction and happily turned right at the green light. "You're on!"

This was the second time she was at his place. The last time was with Toni when Mike was called in to work at the last minute and had to cancel coming to the cook-out as planned. They decided to come without him. David, thinking the evening was also canceled, didn't pull out the steaks he planned to cook for them. Instead, he put on a white wife-beater, black running shorts, and when the doorbell rang, it was a pleasant surprise. When he explained the canceled dinner arrangements, they apologized for not calling first and decided ordering pizza would be just great.

His two-bedroom apartment was similar to Mike's, but on the first floor, with a nice back yard. It had a large living room with the biggest TV Brenda had ever seen and sliding glass doors onto a paved patio. His building was at the end of the street and offered privacy. Brenda thought it was nicely furnished for a guy, and clean. David converted the smaller bedroom into a weight room and extra storage space. That explained a lot, Brenda thought, as he gave them the tour of his apartment.

They spent most of the time there that day just sitting out in the sunshine on his patio, eating a delicious pizza and drinking too much of a delicious fruity drink he got from Mike, made with rum and vodka. Maybe it was the alcohol, but David's chiseled features looked so good in that plain outfit that day, Brenda considered sending Toni home alone and spending the night, but couldn't do that to Toni. Tonight, there's no Toni.

It was a thought born when she opened her door tonight and

saw this handsome guy standing there. David looked dreamy in tan pants and a tight-fitting white V-necked short sleeved sweater. His Nautica cologne, when she hugged him, gave her ideas for a different evening's entertainment, but she had spent hours getting pretty and wanted to bedazzle the man staring at her with his mouth open.

When she turned and looked at Toni that evening, after David excused himself to make more of the fruity concoction, the snicker on Toni's face said she had felt those same vibes.

"Do you want me to leave?"

"Yes!"

Toni laughed.

"No, Ton, but doesn't he look hot?"

Toni nodded.

Brenda had little doubt that if she suggested what was on her mind that day, the broad-shouldered man pouring Toni another drink would have voted hell, yes!

As they drove, and she snuggled close to him, those vibes returned. They both look great, had fun at dinner, and now she felt the desire for him building again. His eyes had made it plain all evening that he found her very desirable. The leg show, as she crossed them twice in the little red dress, worked and she caught him looking out of the corner of his eye. That only enhanced the game she was playing. Maybe, if the drive was a few minutes shorter, she would have followed through with her plan to seduce her handsome driver. But when he parked and opened her car door for her, with that contented look on his face, she decided to relax and just have fun like they usually did when together. She put her arm in his as they walked to his apartment door.

Maybe it was because of the very dark apartment they entered after closing the door, but when David felt around for the light switch on the wall, he bumped into her. He was about to apologize when she put her arms around him and kissed him hard on the mouth. Both then became instantly aroused and went at each other as if they were starving for love.

David held her head in both his hands as his tongue explored her tasty mouth. Brenda groaned, released the sweater grasped tightly in her fingers, and started to unbuckle his belt. He stopped kissing and looked at her in the dark. The question was out there.

The answer, as she next unsnapped his pants, nearly took his breath away.

"Make love to me, David," she whispered to the shadow standing over her.

"I would love to, beautiful lady."

She allowed him to take her hand and lead her toward his bedroom in the dark and undress her with experienced hands. And in that darkness, they lost their identities and became just a man and a woman. And that's how they both wanted the experience.

Like she desired, he took control. David liked to visit everything worth seeing when he was the driver. There was no racing up the highway in a spastic hurry to get there and risk missing some important locations along the way. He would often pull over someplace special, leave the vehicle running, and take the time to relish, taste, and touch the beauty…of nature. He knew he had plenty of gas in his tank, so there was little fear he would run out before reaching their ah…destination. It was a scenic road he'd successfully traveled many times and knew where the best spots were. The joy she displayed each time she arrived made the effort worthwhile.

Every place he kissed and touched was soft and delicious. Her verbal response answered any questions and left no doubts she was enjoying the trip. After the third time she screamed out his name, he kissed his way up her damp body. His kisses finally arriving at her lips signaled it was time to blend their bodies together until they either screamed names or…something.

Brenda, thinking she could now offer him what she had found numerous times while his tongue explored her, was surprised when it was she who succumbed first and second to their dance under the sheets. But only minutes afterward, she grabbed hold of him and locked her body tightly around his until he also found release.

After they lay in each other's arms, catching their breath and reveling in the high they found, she got behind the wheel, and, as was her style, led him on a race as she floored the gas pedal. He also liked speed—sometimes, and he quickly learned there was nothing to fear with her in control. His passionate driver was very adept at racing in the fast lane. But with her driving, there was little time to enjoy everything to the fullest, some places they just whizzed by. But having a quick taste of different things, a smorgasbord if you will, could be a delightful treat. She did have to slam on the brakes when they suddenly arrived, but he did thoroughly enjoy the trip. Exhausted, they parked the vehicles and spooned until they fell asleep.

The bright morning sunlight shining in his bedroom window awakened them almost simultaneously. Brenda rolled over, and, when she did, he opened his eyes. She almost said those dangerous but delightful three words—almost. He smiled and gently kissed her. That was followed by her smile, and a much longer kiss. This time, she pushed him on his back, and her soft lips awakened his ardor.

At Kennywood Amusement Park in Pittsburgh, they had a popular Bumper Car ride. You climbed into these electric cars and, when the power was turned on you tried to smash into each other—going forward, or in reverse, or sometimes sideways—as hard and as violently as you could. That would clearly offer a more vivid and graphic explanation about what happened next in his bed. Once the kissing turned on the electricity, they tried to bump into each other as violently and as hard as they could. His trip ended in one explosive hit before his bumper car ride was over. But she was the winner. She hit hard over and over during that ride—and maybe an additional over.

Their partner was everything they hoped and thought they would be. Neither was at all disappointed. Brenda always craved a physically powerful lover with great equipment that could maintain control and knew what to do with his…blessing. She delightfully discovered David was all that and more.

David desired a woman who liked diversity and was open to new things. Brenda proved she was more than willing to try different things, it pleased him to find out. Even though they were physically sated, yet each still was searching for something. For Brenda and David, it was like having turkey without stuffing, or pie-ala-mode without the ice cream. Each wanted more from the relationship. Their bodies were satiated, but they both felt, deep down in their spirit, that there was something deeper for them, something they were missing as a couple.

The passion they generated together was wonderful and unique. David affectionate and considerate, Brenda adventurous and spontaneous. Both were near perfect matches between the sheets but what they were lacking was an emotional copulation. They both hungered for that special caring that fueled the fire of passion in lovers and remained long after the desire was appeased. What you saw in the other when you woke up and saw them with dry spittle on their cheek or bed-head and it didn't change one bit what you thought of them. Hell, you didn't even notice.

At the same time, Mike and Toni were inseparable and made a commitment to each other a few months later. The strength of their relationship was the fun they had doing anything and everything together. Their passion started slowly. Kissing and holding each other was satisfying enough in the beginning of their relationship. The excitement of getting to know each other was a stronger sedative than the fire of just their physical attraction.

The slow pace of the relationship was the aspirin that Toni needed to remove the painful memories of losing her self-respect in the popular de-flowering bed—the back seat of cars. It had taken her years to find her pride but only minutes for the shy-guy she met at a park to stir her juices again.

She was, to Mike, a pillar he could depend on, and each day he relied on her more. That need was stronger than his normal physical wants, and if anything, was the basis for them. Relaxed and more self-assured, he opened up and expressed his feelings more confidently—both the things that touched him and, more importantly, the things that did not.

The time they took to get to know each other gave them the opportunity to get a sense for where they were headed and a faith in the stability of their relationship. Being clear on what they felt made it easier to relate to the needs of the other. In essence, they were able to easily communicate what they were thinking. Simple concept, yes, but common—no. Actually, they were so compatible, they worried about the ease in which they were growing close.

They would be together almost eight months before they took their love to the final level…

CHAPTER 7

So far, dinner tonight was everything Mike had hoped it would be. Toni had arrived on time, as usual, alleviating the tension that threatened to wreck his nervous stomach. She looked boss and smelled even better when she walked past him into his apartment dressed in an olive green silk blouse, cut low enough to attract his attention, and loose fitting dark green silk pants. Even though she looked great, he was a little disappointed in her attire and was smart enough to keep that to himself. He wanted her to wear that sexy cream-colored silk cocktail dress that she wore to the company Christmas party downtown at the Hilton Hotel Ballroom. No, that would be too formal, he reluctantly admitted. Damn, did she look great that night or what?

He remembered all the stares they were getting from the guys who were there, and the "she looked nice at the party, but her dress was too short for me to wear" comments he overheard that next Monday when walking past the office lunch room, confirming his biased evaluation. Mike chuckled, remembering the music seemed to stop when the foursome walked into the ballroom looking like royalty. Even the millionaire owner's wives paled in comparison to Toni and David's date, Brenda.

Toni had the kind of hour-glass figure that made pants look sexier than a negligee, Mike concluded after she walked past him. He had to admit, as his hormones settled down, she looked great in everything.

He was dressed in black from shoes to T-shirt, the open golden silk shirt over the T being the only color deviation. Her saying he looked great in dark colors having *"nothing"* to do with his choice of dinner attire. Right.

Toni was different from the girls he had dated in many ways. One, she really loved to eat. No pretending to survive on celery sticks with this girl. She was a meat eater. The Delmonico steaks he had cooked were as tender as David promised they would be when he dropped them off. Sautéed and tender, he promised, or your money back. Mike would never admit that to him, having already decided to complain about how tough the steaks were.

"I love the salad, Mikey, but this tender steak is amazing. Mmmm, I love a great steak. You are a great cook."

The way the pretty blue-eyed woman looked at him sealed the deal. They were half way through the meal, and he reluctantly admitted that David's recipe for sautéing the meat was everything he vowed it would be. As Toni praised his culinary abilities, Mike relented and decided to thank his buddy.

The soft music and dimmed lights created a romantic atmosphere as they sat on his couch talking and sipping a chilled red wine after dinner. With Kenny G's sax hitting those unbelievable mellow notes, she was as lost in the music as she was in him.

Toni kicked her shoes off and pulled her legs up under her. *Careful girl*, she warned herself, *the wine, the music, and the man are getting to you tonight*. The beauty of the mood, and the man, erased that warning moments later when he sat beside her and started rubbing her feet. Toni closed her eyes and lay back on the couch. The music was like cloud-hands lifting her softly above herself.

Mike watched as her body moved in step with the notes of the song. With her eyes closed, he took visual liberties and fed upon the lithe figure rocking to the soulful beat. Carefully reaching over, he took her glass of wine out of her hand and placed it on the coffee table.

What? Oh, mmmm. What do you have in mind there, mister? Toni wondered after opening her eyes when she felt Mike take her glass. The change in the evening's entertainment was noted and devilishly welcomed by Toni. Her shy-guy wanted more than the mellow music and foot rub, she realized, while trying to hide her rising anticipation in the "what are you up to" look she had on her face.

Mike put his hands around Toni's waist and, as he lay back on the couch, lifted her up on top of him.

Toni helped him by sliding up between his legs. "What do you have in mind mister?"

He smiled and then gave her his answer with his lips. The mood fired up their passions as each kiss became deeper, wetter, and more probing. Toni lifted up on her elbows and looked into his eyes. With her finger softly touching his lips, she made a decision. It didn't come from anything she felt she owed him, it was just...time. There were other times when the passion they shared burned hot, but the vibes didn't feel quite right. If either had pushed a little harder, the other would have readily joined in, but it didn't happen.

Mike, so caught up in the gorgeous woman laying on him, just relished the moment and didn't look beyond that missing the message in her eyes. But that was his way, enjoy the moment.

Toni placed her hand on his chest, deftly tugged his shirt out of his pants, and ran her hand up his bare chest, raising the tempo another notch. In the eight months that they dated, touching was the extent of their exploration. Each harbored secret fears that the next level of passion might ruin the beauty and fragile tenderness that they had carefully nurtured. That unwarranted fear, a creation not from the person nearest them but of past failures, marred the present.

What Mike felt for Toni, and she for him, was by far deeper than either had ever felt emotionally before. Every time they were together, they seemed to find a way to draw closer. Their love blossomed brighter each day as they truly enjoyed each other's company. Mike, just happy being with her, never really tried to search out the limits of their intimacy. Toni, feeling content with the good times they were having, didn't label their relationship until Brenda asked her how good a lover Mike was. Now, their needs seemed to reach out for more, together.

Tonight is the night, Toni told Mike. Not verbally, but with the feel of her soft lips, the searching of her small hands, and with the gentle grinding motion of her silk covered body. Do *you want me, baby*? she thought as he pulled her blouse out of her pants.

He answered that as he slid his hands under her blouse and touched the smooth, soft skin of her back.

They had taken their love making beyond this point on a few other occasions and always found a way to put on the brakes. Once because of nature's poor "timing." Another time the copious amount of alcohol they had consumed unknowingly put both to sleep—half dressed. But each sensed that those same brakes wouldn't stop them this time. The hill they were racing down tonight was too long and the road far too wet. There was a much stronger need calling out to both. Toni could feel it, as she squeezed the hard muscles in his back.

While their tongues danced, his fingers brushed over her bra strap, and he mulled over risking her wrath by unsnapping it. The increased grinding of the hips of the scintillating woman in his arms answered that question. As her bra unsnapped, Toni's passion seemed to break as free as her breast now were. She needed his hands on them, she told herself as she turned on her side. Mike read her hunger and pulled his left hand from around her back and very slowly slipped his fingers up under her loose bra cup. The deliberate movement of his fingertips was such a turn on she wanted to stop kissing and urge him to hurry. When his fingertips touched the curve of her breast, and they moaned together—she, from the excitement built up from expectation, he, from her nails digging into his chest. As Mike buried his face in the softness of her neck, kissing up the side of her face, his hand moved up and around to the fullness of her breast feeling the weight of it. She arched her back, thrusting her chest farther into his hand.

"I love you, Toni," he said when his lips reached her ear.

She answered him by pulling his head around and kissing him hard on the mouth. What happened next would depend on your point view. Mike either found it, if that was how you saw things, or lost it. He flipped over on his right side, pinning Toni on her side between him and the back of the couch. Unsnapping her pants, he slid his hand down the front of them. It wasn't the first time, but the fervency of his actions surprised and pleased her. Toni's stomach involuntarily tightened giving him an unhindered path. To touch her there this time meant far more than it had in the past. She groaned as his fingers slipped into her wetness.

His action prompted a reaction. Toni pulled down the zipper of his pants, not bothering to struggle with his belt, and thrust her hand in grasping hold of what she sought.

Up until now, that next door had been locked shut, and neither had the combination to open it. But tonight, the urgency was too strong to be so easily reasoned away. Tonight, they would find a way to kick open that door if they had too.

They continued touching each other until, like a kettle of water heating on the stove, they reached the boiling point. Toni released her hold on Mike and pulled his arm up, causing him to dejectedly withdraw his hand. Had he gone too far this time? Mike wondered, while reluctantly searching her face for an answer.

Toni stood up and looked around his apartment. She didn't realize the music was still playing and, for a moment, forgot the direction of everything after being in the powerful throes of their foreplay. Quickly she got her bearings and then looked down at Mike lying on the couch with the perplexed look of a confused teenager on his face. Toni smiled down at him. She answered the question on his lips by letting her pants, which she held bunched up in her hand, drop slowly to her feet. When Mike's eyes followed them to the floor, her surprise was complete. Toni stepped nimbly out of them. She was moved by the palpable want in his eyes as she watched him visually exploring her body. She used it to fan her own desires.

His eyes did travel from the bunched up green pants on the floor up the curve of her legs until he looked at the curious expression on her face. He was about to ask—

But she didn't disappoint him. Toni, as seductively as an inexperienced stripper could be, let her blouse and bra slip down her arms and onto the floor. She stood before him, looking demure in only her laced green thong panties. Her every curve exceeded what his imagination had often created. The next move was clear, even to the gawking man lying on the couch with his pants and mouth open.

Mike surprised her, not by standing up, but by adroitly picking her up in his arms, unbuckling his pants an effortlessly stepping out of them as he held her. He kissed her again in his arms and then carried her into his bedroom, careful not to bump her head against the wall. When he laid her down at the foot of his bed, Toni sat up, gave him a wide grin, and then crawled backward on her hands away from him.

She giggled a little as she propped up his bed pillows and lay back against them. Taunting, she slid her hands down from her mouth and slowly outlined the curve of her breast.

Mike watched as Toni then trailed her fingers farther until they reached the waistband of her panties. She slipped a couple of fingers in and out of them. Mike thought she was debating whether to make that light-year jump from caressing to intimacy. He was watching the wrong channel. That became abundantly clear when she suddenly pulled her panties up over her belly button like granny panties and started laughing.

Mike shook his head as she grinned at him in the semi-dark room. He finally understood the game she was playing. He snatched her by the ankles before she could move and pulled her toward him. She feigned her objection to his cave-manly behavior by trying to twist her legs free from his grasp—weakly. Toni enjoyed this change in Mike's personality. Her provocative taunting had induced the man out of the boy, and she loved the change.

Mike knew she was in control, even as he easily pulled her to him, but he couldn't resist her. Her shapely body was provocative, and even more so when she pretended she didn't want him. Just that little act of resistance that suggested, *"no, maybe I've changed my mind,"* was powerfully erotic. *Yeah*, he thought as he let her dictate the evening's entertainment, *the weaker sex is in complete control.*

When he pulled her ankles close, a thin band of light from the dimmed lamp in the living room painted a line across her, revealing the smirk on her face. Mike saw her devilish grin. In that same faint light reflecting into the room, Toni could see his silhouette. He was a living shadow standing at the foot of the bed, motionless. She put one of her fingers to her lips and gave him a coy, alluring look. The shadow removed his shirt, put his hands on the top of his underwear, and started pulling them down. She watched as her aroused shadow kicked them away and moved toward her. As the shadowy figure kissed its way up her calves, Toni bit down on her lip. The need she felt was growing faster than the pace of the seduction. It had been a long time since she had a man in her, and she needed to feel that *now! But* the lips and tongue of the dark figure slowly kissing up her leg stirred up some strange, strong, and new appetites. She would give him a moment more, resisting the growing panic, before taking over. Relieved of that important decision, she lay back on the pillows and closed her eyes. She tried to relax and enjoy his kisses, but the need quickened her anew, and she sat up, her panting breaths matching the pounding in her chest, and then reached for him.

Mike knew what she wanted when he climbed up on the bed. As bad as he wanted to ride her as long as he could, he refrained. There was more he wanted to give her than just that. He looked up at her face, as his tongue tasted the smoothness of her thigh. There was intensity in those eyes. They were shouting something at him, and he wanted more than anything to know exactly what they were saying. Then he understood and read her expectancy when she reached out for him. That next move was halted when she suddenly leaned back, tossed the pillows under her head on the floor, and close her eyes. The message was clear. He reached up and gently grabbed at her panties, with her help, and pulled them over her hips and down her legs.

Toni's sexual résumé consisted of five dives in the back seat of three different boy's cars. Two quickies in the moonlight overlooking the city—during her moonlight-is-very-romantic-to-make-love-under period—and one very disappointing trip to the Scenic View Motel with a drunk, almost comatose, drummer from the rock band New Chaos. A grand total of eight sexual encounters that took from her far more than they gave. And the swiftness of those adventures discolored her conception of having sex. It was both fun, she learned, and at times very disappointing.

Sure, Brenda had told her about some of her bawdy, wonderful times, but Toni thought she was just boasting. Her favorite person on Earth was known to spice up a story. Toni and Katie often laughed and teased her about that.

The lovers Toni had given herself to crudely thrust themselves into her as quickly as they could, taking little thought for her needs. Foreplay was almost choking her with their tongue down her throat and roughly grabbing her tits. They were, she began to realize as Mike's arousing and wondrously slow sojourn up her legs revealed, as inexperienced as she.

The question of what to do if he continued flashed across her mind. *Hell, what do you do if he stops?* was her quirky answer. She almost laughed at that thought, but the power of her body's response to his lips and tongue's exploration prevented such a glib display.

The man and the coming act were new to her. It was something her two girlfriends had discussed with her often, boasting
about the intense power of it when their boyfriends were there.
Toni never said anything during their naughty conversations, but
she secretly had thought it disgusting and unsanitary. She was
glad that none of her boyfriends had asked her if they could or if
she would. Now Mike, a man she had taken the time to con-
sciously get to know and grew to love more than any man she had
ever met, had almost kissed his way there. As he grew closer,
disgusting and unsanitary suddenly lost their bite.

Toni closed her eyes and took a deep breath. Her whole body
tensed, as one might await the doctor's needle in your arm. Voices in her mind questioned her judgment and willingness to submit
to Mike's advances. Their complaints were quickly drowned out
by the pounding in her chest. The powerful fingers of guilt
couldn't dirty this moment as she dug her trembling fingernails
hard into the bedspread. There was a growing excitement in her
loins that reached out to every part of her being. She felt virginal
again in the hands of her lover. They were about to share
someth—

She suddenly grasped the bed linen in a failed effort to try and
stop the trembling.

She had always liked the physical, touching part of sex. The
wild, spontaneous, tugging, and grabbing race to enter and be
entered—unfortunately, and too often, followed by the failed race
to the "finish line." This time it was different. Not just a different
guy, but she felt different. There was none of the adolescent
bumbling of past excursions. His deliberate lovemaking had giv-
en her time to tune into her passions and their effects on her.
There was a beauty to "stopping and smelling the roses," she realized. What made it so beautiful for Toni was the person who was
giving her such gratification was her Mike.

A surge of pleasure shot up her legs, signaling the beginning
of what she hoped was an orgasm. She had traveled that road before in the back seat of cars, only to be side tracked by a sudden
"oil leak," followed quickly by a "flat tire." Not this time, she
realized, as she felt it barreling down her road. It was much
stronger than she had imagined and the speed with which it was
approaching frightened her a little. She was losing control and

realized, in those frantic milliseconds, that she didn't give a damn. Toni's body suddenly tensed up, and it arrived abruptly, racing over her, unleashing what little restraint she had left. Her body betrayed her as it flailed about on his bed as if he wasn't giving her pleasure but exorcising her demons. She made guttural sounds that came from her soul and muttered words that had no meaning. And when the demon was exorcized, her body slowly stopped spazzing.

Mike let her slowly ride the elevator down from wherever floor she was on. Gently, he kissed her there as her heavy breathing waned. He wanted to take her there again, but his own desires prevented him. He had to have her, and now.

Toni, taking his head in her hands, had the same need and pulled him up over her. As their lips met, she wrapped her legs around his waist, awaiting him. She got her wish as he carefully moved deep inside her. She clenched her teeth as the rampant pleasures, radiating out from the tingling nerves enveloping him, threatened to make her scream.

Again, the fire stirred up in her as she accepted him. He was experienced enough, she realized, to give her body a moment to adjust to his intrusion. Toni was alive with the way she was feeling while making love to him.

Oh, this feels so good, Mike thought, delighting in the pleasure and from whom. None of the other women he had been with came to mind. Being in her arms was wonderfully virginal and special. It was a place he never wanted to leave.

Mutually, they found their pace and rode it to fulfillment. Their love maintained the fire, even as they gasped for breath. Soft, innocent kisses later re-ignited the fumes of their appetites and lasted again into the earlier hours of the morning.

The almost a year of feeling their way through the relationship was topped by the evening's entertainment. Toni felt she knew the man who lay snuggled against her back, breathing softly in her hair. She searched for that old feeling of being used that always seemed to accompany her after the other experiences. There was none. She only felt a powerful sense of fulfillment.

This guy was different, she was quick to realize—or was it her? Still wide awake an hour later, she replayed the movie that was her life on the dark walls of his bedroom. She remembered each face, each act, and how she had settled for less. Why she thought her future was in the arms of hard rockers remained unanswered. Comparing that to the feeling she was enjoying afterward, she struggled to resist thinking that she had been used in the past.

Mike, before he fell asleep, felt their lovemaking a natural act born of two people who cherished each other. She wasn't a notch on his gun as others might have been, she *was* his gun. Never before had he felt so manly, so masculine, and so real. This woman, Mike thought, dared him to be all that he could be. Mike had to turn away from her, lest she see the stupid grin on his face as he remembered where he first heard that over-used axiom.

They slept in each other's arms without questioning their future. The future was theirs, they believed, together.

CHAPTER 8

Over the next two years, Mike and Toni continued to let their relationship evolve naturally. The depth of their caring enabled them to freely express those private idiosyncrasies that they each held so dear. Those private expressions and beliefs that were the root of their individuality and were so fragile it could take years of trusting someone before they could begin to reveal them. Because of the slow evolution of their relationship, they were able to learn to read the other quickly and to give value to each other's opinions.

Mike was first to introduce his parents. They were as taken with Toni as he was. His mom even hinted about marriage before dinner was over. Mike saw a gleam of pride in his dad's eyes as his dark-haired beauty talked about her dreams for the future. She was so friendly and, with those amiable eyes, it was hard not to warm up to her. Dad, Mike was quick to notice, was captivated with little Miss DiNardo. Mike hadn't seen that look since he hit the championship game winning home run in his last little league game. Dad approved.

Now, Toni's dad was more suspicious, as dads usually were of their daughters' choices. Having lost his wife, Toni was the love of his life. But Mike's free spirit quickly erased any concerns he had about the guy his daughter was fawning over. This Mike was easy to chat with and had his own opinion on lots of things.

He was quick to disagree with Toni if his opinion differed with hers, something her dad never saw in her other "friends." She was obviously more smitten with him than any of her previous beaus, her dad thought, laughing, because she allowed him to have an opinion. The others—much to his chagrin, she gave them theirs.

Toni and Mike's mutual love of sports was just another link in the chain that inevitably led them to make a commitment to each other. They went to football, baseball, basketball, and hockey games together. The key word in their having a good time was together.

The only time they had a serious disagreement was about a month ago when Toni's dad asked Mike if he would like to go up to Lake Erie for the weekend on a fishing trip with him and a few of the guys.

"Do you like fishing, Mike?" Mr. DiNardo asked as they sat out on the deck after a grilled steak and corn-on-the-cob dinner. "Some of the guys drive up to Lake Erie one weekend a month and fish. We have a cabin up there we use if the weather is bad."

"Hey, that would be a great idea, Mr. DiNardo. I love fishing. Thanks for inviting Toni and me."

The frown on both Toni and her father's face caught Mike off guard. He looked questioningly between the love of his life and her dad. Toni rolled her eyes, got up, and walked into the house. Mike looked at her father for an explanation and received only a shrug.

"I don't fish," Toni finally told him when he found her in the kitchen making coffee. "My dad tried to teach me, but I don't care for slimy fish or worms. I don't think he ever forgave me for not being a tomboy."

"I forgive you," Mike said, walking up behind her and pulling her close. "Well, you don't mind if I go with him, do you?" Mike asked, thinking he was doing the right thing in getting to know her father.

"Of course not, honey," Toni said after turning around and placing her hand on his face. "You can spend the weekend up in Erie. I'll just stay home and work on my tan. With my dad gone, I can finally wear that tiny yellow string bikini I bought—or noth-ing—all weekend."

Mike apologized to Mr. DiNardo for being unable to make it this weekend. The look he received said more than Mike wanted to see. Yes, he had to admit, his nose was wide open, and the beautiful lady in the kitchen already had a ring in it. That disgust-ed look on her father's face was a painful shot to his masculinity, Mike realized as he walked to his car. But the thought of being alone with Ms. Toni as she walked around in that almost nothing bikini all weekend was just the aspirin his crushed ego needed to heal.

David and Brenda filtered in and out of Mike and Toni's lives, always remaining close friends. The foursome often partied together. Each time Toni thought an emotional bond was developing between Bren and Davey, they seemed to back off. As Toni became more involved with Mike, Brenda with her nursing career, and David working overtime at work, they were seeing less and less of each other.

When Brenda had asked Toni to get a larger apartment together, but closer to her new job at West Penn Hospital, the door opened to get the four of them together more often. Toni agreed to because she wanted Brenda to settle down and experience what she had with Mike, and David was her first choice. There was no mistaking what she had seen in the eyes of their best friends when they were together. When they went out, she noticed they only had eyes for each other. And when they partied at Mike's or David's place, the laughter and fun they generated when together was contagious. Onlookers misinterpreted how free the two of them were with each other. Most figured, incorrectly, that they were intimate back then, as openly affectionate as they were. But that came later. Brenda and David were like kids at Christmas when they were together. The only thing missing was a commitment, and Toni, the determined matchmaker, laid her trap and would soon have the perfect bait.

ѕ/ѕ

David held on to the end of the couch as Mike stepped carefully down from the back of the rental truck. "Hold on a minute, Mike."

Mike held on to the other end of the couch as David turned around while still lifting up his end of the couch until he was facing forward. Carrying it this way permitted him to see where he was going. He hated carrying things while walking backward.

The couch was the last piece of furniture they had to move. The girls had carried all the boxes and clothes into their apartment. Mike and David, because Brenda's new "friend" didn't bother to show up, had to move all the heavy furniture themselves.

"They're almost finished," Toni said, looking out the window. "Our couch is the last piece on the truck."

"Good," Brenda fell back on the bed and groaned, "I'm almost out of gas, girl."

"I know, but we have put everything away. Now, all we have to do is get the boys to move the furniture around like we want. Hey, I thought Jeffery was coming by to help." Toni turned around and looked at Brenda lying on her bed. From the grin on her face, Toni knew something was up.

"I told the boys that to make someone we both know and love jealous. There is no way I want the two of them in the same room."

Toni just shook her head at her conniving BFF. *Must be hard to love someone from afar*, she thought when Brenda turned over and looked the other way. *You must really ache for him, don't you, girl?* "Well, I agree. But I thought for sure you would love to see those two come to blows over pretty little Brenda."

The devilish look she got from her, when she thought about that interesting scenario and turned around, answered that question.

Brenda and Toni were spastic over their new place. A duplex on Friendship Ave only three blocks from West Penn Hospital where Brenda worked as a nurse. The building was old enough to have its own atmosphere yet still solidly built. Their duplex had two large upstairs bedrooms, which offered each of them some privacy, separated by a large four piece bathroom. The large bright kitchen had a built-in breakfast nook. The cozy living room was done up in warm tan shades that made it feel comfortable. The basement had been renovated by its previous owner into a nice family room, small laundry, and a half bath.

The girls envisioned entertaining in the family room, and with the bedrooms two floors above, they could also escape when they wanted to and find quiet solitude or privacy. It was that last fact that sold them on the duplex.

"Try it over there…again."

David walked over to the spot Toni had indicated and set his end of the couch down. Mike followed suit. Both men slumped down on the sofa they had just carried into the house, exhausted.

"What do you think, Brenda?"

"I think they should move it at least three more times."

"Yeah. Well, I like it best there."

"That's where it was three moves ago."

"Yeah, we know, Davey," Toni said.

We just wanted to watch you flex your muscles," Brenda teased.

Both men gave the finger to the two women who laughed and ran up the stairs.

While the girls were upstairs putting away clothes and stuff, the men sat quietly, listening to them laughing and talking. Earlier suggestions, by the then-energetic moving men, to break in the new beds were ignored as the two beasts-of-burden struggled to move the heavy furniture.

"Let's get a cold beer and see what they're up to," Mike said, looking over at David.

He nodded in agreement and moaned, as his sore muscles revolted when he stood up to follow Mike into the kitchen.

They had drunk half the beer before they climbed the stairs to the bedrooms. David led the way and stopped at the top of the steps. Mike, noticing him staring at something, walked around him to see what caught his attention and also stopped and stared. The two women were lying on their stomachs across a bed in one of the bedrooms laughing at something in a magazine. Whatever they were laughing about was hidden from the men. It wouldn't have mattered anyway because the men were staring at something else on the bed.

The hard work of moving boxes, clothes, and heavy furniture had stolen the usual fun they normally had together. Listening to them laugh was a wonderful sound to the tired men. Mike elbowed David and indicated with a nod of his head to follow him. Mike put his beer down and crept up closer to the bedroom door followed by his curious buddy. Without saying a word, Mike ran and jumped on Toni's back. David thought, what the hell, and followed his lead.

"Hey!" Toni said, laughing, as Mike wrapped himself around her.

"Mmmm, me so horny," he said as they bounced on the bed.

The bed bounced a second time as David landed on top of Brenda. Both women fought off their attackers, laughing hysterically. The fun had returned to the foursome. A couple of well-placed and unfair punches and kicks ended the free-for-all. While the men grabbed their injured members, the women ran downstairs to safety.

"Great plan there, Mikey," David said from the floor where Brenda had thrown him.

"I don't know, buddy, I thought I saw you grabbing a hand full of pretty little Brenda before she bounced you on your butt," Mike fired back at him. No answer. "You still have a thing for her, don't you, David?" Mike questioned his mute partner as he lay back on the bed. "I won't go there," Mike continued, "if it bothers you."

"No, buddy, I'm cool with it."

But it did bother him, David realized, but unsure of why? He always enjoyed being around Brenda, he thought, after putting his hands under his head while lying on the floor. It was just that he didn't know if he could deal with the problems there might be if they were a couple.

David understood that it wasn't just him. It was a question that thousands of people faced every day. A question that people of different color, religions, ages, national origins, and some with a different status in life than the ones they desired, had to face when they fell in love with someone opposite or different. He wasn't sure if he could handle the prejudice he envisioned would certainly accompany their relationship. He had seen it firsthand from black as well as white. His mother was as biased against whites as the worse pillowcase-wearing fool. And with a woman as attractive as Brenda, there was sure to be some bias.

Dealing with ignorant people was one of the few character flaws David had trouble overcoming. He was quick to anger when someone gave him a smart-ass comment or even a snide look. Subjecting sweet Brenda to that was the brake that held back his emotions. David more than understood it, but couldn't explain his misgivings to his friends.

Who am I fooling? he asked himself as he sat up and put his back against the bed. Why would she want more from a relationship with him other than just being good friends? David sighed deeply as the stubborn battle to get green-eyes out from under his skin took another turn for the worse.

It had been months since they shared more than a friendly kiss. That night she had asked him to take her home from a gala hospital party the four of them attended when Mike and Toni had to leave early because he had to be at work early the next morning. A thank you kiss quickly turned into...

"Guys, we're leaving soon. Mike has to get up early tomorrow for work," Toni announced when they sat down at their table after dancing another dance.

"Yes, I do," Mike said and stared at David.

"Look, buddy, you volunteered to work if the morning crew was shorthanded."

"Yes, but do you see how good my date looks?"

Toni, who did look great in a light blue off the shoulder dress, frowned at David, as if it was his fault.

"Wait a minute there, girlfriend," he said to those judgmental blue eyes, "you have to be home before midnight anyway, or you'll turn into an old hag and lose your ruby slippers."

"Wrong colored shoes, oh mighty wizard."

"Oh, yeah, your blue slippers."

"Brenda." Toni rolled her eyes at David. "I'm staying at Mike's tonight so don't worry about me."

They traded winks that the guys missed.

"Ready to go, babe?"

The four stood and traded hugs and kisses.

"Drive safely, guys."

"We will, bye, Brenda, David."

"Well, I guess you are stuck with just me."

"Yes, beautiful, I'm stuck with you. Shall we dance one more time?"

The woman David led to the dance floor was easily the most impressive girl at that party, even though Toni was a close second. David smiled when he thought about how the redhead could change, as if she was Cinderella. He once checked, in jest, to see if she was also wearing glass slippers and to admire her gams. Brenda was naturally great looking, but when she put on the Ritz, she was dazzling. It was as if she changed from commoner to royalty, from a McShane to a Kennedy or Rockefeller.

Being with her was both very satisfying and sometime troublesome, to David anyway, because this honey attracted every bee in the hive. She was a working-class woman as a nurse, but after putting on the Ritz, everyone looked upon her as if she owned the place—wherever they went. She carried herself with that much aplomb. One would never guess just how down to earth the long-legged centerfold was when she was out of the limelight. He would never admit it but, when she made him the center of her attention, David relished in the jealous looks he garnered.

Most of the night their table was surrounded by doctor types all wanting to ah...examine her. Brenda would stop whatever the four of them were talking about and introduce the latest intruder. The longer their title, the more cocky the intruder, David noticed, but he was overly friendly, even after they ignored him. Brenda gave each a polite few minutes and then ignored them and returned to the foursome. A few guys pulled up chairs to their table, grinning, until it became obvious they were a fifth wheel.

After Mike and Toni had to leave, it became worse. Some testosterone-driven A-type personalities thought they could just walk over and talk their way into leaving with the gorgeous redhead. David didn't take offense at their efforts because Brenda did look stunning in a slinky short white dress that even had the other women there were staring at her when she walked past or danced.

"Look, beautiful," David said when they had a few minutes alone, "these are the people you work with. I appreciate you giving me your undivided attention, but it's not necessary. I'm going to walk around and be sociable, and I think you should also."

"Davey, we came together."

"I know that, and I hope we can leave together. But some of these important people can make it hard on the career of a nurse at your hospital."

"Screw them."

"No!" he mockingly asserted, "don't be that friendly." David laughed at the prettiest woman in the room who made a funny face and stuck her tongue out at him.

When David walked over to the bar for drinks, the male table watchers descended on her like flies to—

Brenda handled the bursting male egos with class and ease.

David found himself the interest of some of the other ladies there, both single and very married. Being the escort of *numero uno* had other enticing benefits he learned from their walking up to him and flirting. He spent time dancing with some of the more demanding ladies, but still traded longing looks from across the room with Brenda most of the night.

Brenda cemented his feeling for her by excusing herself from a group of big shots from the hospital, walking across the room where three young women had David cornered, and drawing the attention of most of the people still at the party. Some sensing a possible cat-fight.

"Are you ready to take me home now, handsome?" she asked, slipping her arm into his.

The looks from two of the three ladies could kill. The other just turned and walked away.

"Yes, I am, beautiful. Excuse me, ladies."

Arm in arm, they headed for the exit. Having maintained his decorum, as repeated males in heat ignored him and attempted to seduce his date, David took those few minutes to give an up-yours sneer to all his offenders.

"You know we will be the talk of the hospital tomorrow," Brenda said as they drove out of the parking garage.

"As good as you looked in that little white dress, I'm sure of that."

"Why thank you, sir. I didn't think you noticed."

"Yeah, right, so you didn't see me drooling all night Little White Riding Hood?"

LWRH laughed and re-crossed her legs when they stopped at a red light. David didn't bother hiding the effect it had on him.

Walking her to her door, David shared something with her. "Thank you for inviting me to your hospital gala, Bren, I had a ball."

She smiled at him and handed him her keys. David unlocked her door and handed them back to her.

"There isn't a man I would have rather gone with."

"Liar."

"Well, yes, but Tom Cruise turned me down."

"Well, that proves the rumors about him are true."

"How sweet." With that, she kissed David.

What started out as just a kiss continued as neither resisted. Of course, David was first to express his interest in the attractive woman by pulling her closer. Brenda put her arms around his neck and slowly opened her mouth. That might have been the extent of the passion had she not slipped her leg between his, as she often liked to do, and felt his growing interest. She whimpered—and he groaned.

They both later associated her pulling him into her house, kicking off her high heels, and their racing into her bedroom and the acts performed a few times that night, more with the amount of alcohol they consumed than anything special they felt for each other. At least that was what they told their cynical friends later that week over dinner. And to prove it, Mike sarcastically answered him the next time he used that as an excuse, they both started dating people they didn't really care for. The truth of that statement left David speechless.

Mike and David got up, picked up what remained of the beer, and headed downstairs after they heard voices calling them.

It was about seven that night before they finished moving everything around until the girls were satisfied. They placed the couch in the far corner, for the third time, and the stereo unit directly across from it. The girls had decided to place the TV downstairs in the family room and use the living room for more mellow occasions.

Mike and David suddenly felt left out when the girls, standing off in a corner of the living room, looked at each other and started snickering. They had something up their sleeves, it seemed obvious to the guys, and they hoped it had something to do with them.

Toni walked over and whispered something in Mike's ear. The Gomer-Pile-sized grin on his face told David all he needed to know. Once again, he felt apart from what was going on with his close friends. More and more, he sensed they were starting to go their separate ways, and it bothered the hell out of him.

"Hey, guys, I've got to be going," David injected into the quiet that developed. He felt that would relieve everyone of an awkward moment and started walking toward the door.

"Oh, no, you're not!" Toni abruptly added. Her sudden change in demeanor caught them all off guard and David more so when she walked over and put her finger in his face. "I know you don't have to work tomorrow. I've already started cooking dinner for all of us tonight. You're staying here tonight, mister, and I won't take no for an answer. Even if I have to tie you up, you're staying."

David, flabbergasted at the fire in her voice, looked at Mike. He was still wearing the Gomer mask on his face so David knew he would be no help. He looked back at Toni to protest and watched, dumbfounded, as she placed her hands on her hips and rolled her eyes at him. When she raised her eyebrows, David knew what that meant—

"All right."

There was always something about that stubborn woman with her hands on her hips and blocking his exit that made David feel helpless. She was more than the little sister he never had. She always took the time to show her love and appreciation for him, no matter how busy or whatever they were doing, and he sincerely loved her for that. He knew, even if she didn't, there was nothing he wouldn't do for her if she asked.

Toni then smiled up at her stunned "brother," grabbed Mike's arm, and pulled him toward the kitchen. "Come on, Mike. I need your help with the salads."

Brenda, David wondered, as he watched the two of them turn the corner into the kitchen, *what does she think of all this?* When he turned around to face her, Brenda lowered her head and wouldn't look him in the eye. There was something about the fact that bold Brenda wouldn't look at him that really blew him away.

Aaaah, shit! David thought, walking over to her. "Okay, what's going on here, Brenda?" he said, just low enough not to be overheard by the dark-haired indignant overlord in the kitchen.

She smiled coyly but didn't look up or answer him. David's mouth felt very dry. The girls were cooking up something and he started to realize he was the turkey.

"Are you staying?" he asked her.

"David, don't you remember?" she said as she looked up at him, "I live here now."

"Yeah, that's right, sorry. It's just I don't want to put you in a tight spot."

"Listen, David," she said as those sparkling green eyes came alive. "No one makes me do anything I don't want to do," she answered with a sharp, unmistakably clear tone, looking directly in his eyes.

David knew he had stepped on her toes a little. That was confirmed a moment later.

"What did you have in mind anyway?" The look on her face clearly indicated she was now ready to spar with him about what he insinuated.

"Ah, nothing, Bren, you—you know Toni," he answered in an apologetic voice that said more than just words. "She's always trying to put us together. I've told her that if we are meant to be together…you know."

The softness returned to her face, and she smiled, easing David's fears somewhat. "Davey," she said sympathetically, those green eyes regaining their sparkle, "Toni loves us with all her heart, and I can't get angry with her for that. Let her have her evening, even if she tries to push us together." Brenda drew closer to him and whispered in his ear. "The poor thing, she doesn't realize that there's no way you would want to make love to me tonight. I'm sweaty—all over."

David watched her as she winked then turned and walked provocatively toward the kitchen. He was very grateful she didn't turn around and see the stupid look on his face and where he was staring. It took a while, but his mouth finally closed as did the vision of her clothed in only sweat.

He knew of the delightful pleasures that encompassed the red-haired vixen who sashayed out of the room, leaving little mental reminders with each curvaceous step. The sweetness of her he had tried to, but never could, completely erase from his heart and mind. The fact that Brenda was stunning looking, most would write down on the bottom line as the reason he, like most men, was infatuated with her. They would be right—and wrong.

What made her special to David was that she was the only woman, other than Toni, to open up and allow him to see the real woman underneath. Maybe she was open to everyone, but few took the time to look past the obvious. He had, and that was one reason he would always have a key to the door to her heart. They loved each other. That much was obvious. But—and it was the fact that there was a but—was what stood between them.

David thought about that for a moment. The answer was that

she was a flower he considered too precious to pick. Brenda, he reasoned while pondering their relationship, was the kind of woman who left a lasting impression on you. She was spirited and funny, unassuming and down-to-earth, as at home in cut-offs as in an expensive Paris evening gown. Physically, she was perfect...well, perfect as he judged perfection. Her skin was flawless and lighter than Toni's, with Brenda's Irish heritage and red hair. Only a few freckles remained on a face that he'd seen from pictures of her youth that had been covered with them. She had a centerfold's figure—ample where she needed to be, in his judgment, and shapely where he though a woman should be.

He found Brenda to be very intelligent and opinionated on a variety of subjects, competitive, sensitive, and very perceptive. No matter how many times he challenged her, she stood her ground and fought back, many times beating him at his own game. She was a pistol, he reminded himself.

Many were the guys who looked at him with envy when she made it clear to everyone that he was the only flower this red-haired honey-bee would be with tonight. When she dressed up, few women could complete with her grace and beauty. In high heels, her legs were distractingly awesome. Everything she wore just accentuated her shapely figure. Then there was that glowing mane of red hair that seemed alive as it hugged her shoulders. Hell, not even Toni, who was herself awesome, could compete with Brenda when she turned on the charm.

Another reason he loved her was that, no matter their confusing relationship, Brenda never let anyone that they met at parties or places they all went to as a group, or anything that the two of them were involved with, cause him to feel second when he was with her. With a woman as striking looking as she, David greatly appreciated that because she inevitably drew men to her—some believing they could entice her away from him with their looks, money, or position in life. If she desired them, she never let it be known as long as she was with him. Her first refusals were polite—the next brutal. You didn't want to be the idiot that pissed off the prettiest woman in the room. That was all anyone could ask of a relationship from friends with occasional benefits—and not lovers.

When she laughs at something, David amusingly recalled,

something that may not be funny, you find yourself laughing with her anyway. And does she love to laugh. With those close to her she could act very silly and then put on a serious face to anyone trying to butt into their small circle. When she offered you a kiss or hug, you wanted that sweet offer to last forever. Brenda was the type of woman that melted in your arms and felt almost weightless. She was the most—

"David! We could use your help in here," he heard Toni-the-Tiger shout from the kitchen, ending his evaluation of the red-head.

"Huh? Be right there, boss," he answered. "I need another minute more to put my tongue back in my mouth," he whispered to himself. Just when he thought he had come to grips with that part of his life, he was still seeing…red.

"Okay, I'm giving the toast," Toni said, standing up at the table.

❡❦❡

They had stuffed themselves on spaghetti, tossed salad, hot buttered toasted garlic bread, and a tart red wine. The dinner, the wine, and the hard work had put them in a warm mellow mood. That was the impetus that prompted Toni to take center stage.

"Brenda and I would like to thank our guests for their invaluable help in moving us into our new home. We finally have room to breathe here, and I don't have to listen to Brenda's snoring."

"That wasn't snoring you heard," Brenda teased, prompting laughter.

"Anyway, we hope this meal expresses our thanks to you guys. It was the only way we could think of to say how we feel."

Mike looked at David with an inquisitive smirk. "I can think of other ways of saying thank you," Mike mouthed to David.

David gave him a thumps-up.

Ignoring him, Toni continued, "Monday, I start my new job as a manager at the Horne's downtown store." When her three friends clapped and cheered, she curtsied. "I thought they would never call. It's been a month since they gave me my physical and that, I'm told, only happens right before they hire you. It took me much longer, but that's par for the course." Her fourth glass of

wine had freed Toni's tongue, her friends realized as she ram-
bled. "But tonight, I toast my best friend Brenda, who I have
known and loved since we were little girls."

"I thought there was something queer about the two of you."

"Shut up, Mike. And to the wonderful man in my life who has
taught me how to love and make love—"

David stood up and took a bow, to the howling laughter of
Brenda and Mike. Toni threw the last sip of her wine on him.

"And to the man deservedly wiping wine off his face who,
two years ago, introduced me to the love of my life and is the
other love in my life, I thank you."

Only the three with wine remaining in their glasses tapped
them together. "Cheers."

Many speeches and blurred toasts later, Toni announced,
"Okay, everyone, enough gaiety, enough wine, fun, and food. I'm
going to bed, and not alone."

Mike stood up. "My new name is not alone."

Shaking his head at his drunken friends, David watched them
stagger playfully up the stairs toward the bedrooms and started
cleaning off the table.

"All come on, Davey, let's just put the dishes in the sink until
morning," an equally exhausted and tipsy Brenda pleaded with
him, sitting with her head down on the table as her long mane
completely covered her face. When he didn't answer, she raised
her head, pulled her hair back off her face, and looked at him.

"You go to bed, Bren," David told the disheveled, but still
attractive, woman, "I'll clean up some of this mess. We can't
leave the butter and salad dressing out. Miss Toni will kill us
when she sobers up."

"Then I'll help you," she declared, standing up gingerly and
pulling her hair off her face. "I don't want to face the wrath of
that tyrant either." In twenty minutes or so of laughing, talking,
and fooling around, they had the kitchen looking spotless. "Okay,
Mister Clean," she said as she started walking toward the stairs,
"now I'm going to bed."

"Good night, Brenda," David said, hoping she wouldn't question him further. Wrong.

"Aren't you coming to bed yet? Oh, I'm sorry," Brenda said,
having assumed he understood that a bed was assigned to him. "I

told Toni it would be okay for you to celebrate and drink because you can sleep in my bed with me tonight. As you know from carrying it," she said with a look of innocence, "there's plenty of room."

Her *"as you know,"* only served to fill him with conjecture and that was part of the problem. He didn't know what was expected of him. He bit down on his bottom lip as he weighed the consequences of assuming.

Brenda, growing impatient with him, walked over and looked up with her sleepy eyes, took his hand, and then turned off the light as she led him firmly up the steps to her bedroom. She let him enter and then closed and locked her door.

"Look, mister," she said, after exhaling a long sigh. "I know what Toni is hoping will happen tonight and so do you. Well, sweetie, not tonight. After working last night and moving today, I'm too tired to screw in a light bulb." She walked over and kissed him softly on the lips. "I'm taking a quick shower, jumping in bed, and going to sleep."

She took a couple of steps toward her closet and then had a change of mind. Turning around with a smirk, "You're welcome to join me in the shower, handsome."

Before David could answer, she stepped out of her worn jean shorts, picked them up, and walked toward her closet. With her back to him, she stripped off the rest of her clothes and put all of them in a hamper. Reaching up, she took a very plush looking, long white terry cloth robe off a hook on the back of the closet door.

The innocence of the act caught him by surprise. Yes, they had made love before but with the speed of passion's call, throwing their clothes off in the rush to meet again in proper un-attire. This was different. She was granting him the privilege of watching her undress. Silently scrutinizing the curvaceous model from behind, David wondered if there was some other significance to her actions.

When Brenda finished tying the belt of the robe around her waist, she pulled out the luscious mane of copper-red hair from down her back, and it fell in shimmering waves onto her shoulders. Turning around, she looked surprised and then annoyed at David. He was still dressed.

David didn't know for sure if he was relieved or disappointed when he saw no sign of passion in the eyes of the exhausted stripper. The semi-open, red tinted pupils looking softly up at him had little of the craving he secretly hoped they would. Their only desire, as she had tried explaining to him, was a hot shower and cool sheets. As if to emphasize that point, Brenda put her hand on her hips and stood tapping her foot.

David got the message and started undressing. He might have been confused about what he was feeling toward Brenda, but the unemotional way she disrobed spoke clearly of her intentions.

While he undressed, Brenda searched her closet before finding the extra-large black and red striped robe Toni had given her for him. Naked, David walked quickly up to her before she could turn around and took the robe from her arms. He turned his back to her before putting it on. *This is silly*, he realized, *we're about to take a shower together, and I'm acting modest.*

"Mmmmm, you look nice in that robe," Brenda whispered as she wrapped her arms around his waist from behind him. "Toni bought it for you yesterday. So don't worry, no one else has worn the robe."

When David turned around to face her, he smiled.

"Men," Brenda whispered, shaking her head.

She led him out of her room and down the hall to the bathroom. David closed the door behind them and searched for the lock. He was surprised to find only an old hook-and-eye lock. He took the little hook that was attached to the door and put it into the eyelet that was screwed into the door frame.

Brenda turned on the shower and was busy adjusting the water to a mean temperature that would hopefully please both of them when David finished "locking" the bathroom door. While she ran her hand through the warming water, Brenda had to acknowledge the stirring she was feeling at the thought of David's strong hands washing her sore shoulders and back. She closed her eyes and let that thought take root. After a crazy shift last night at the hospital, and then a long day of moving after getting very little sleep, plus the evening's entertainment, she felt drained.

Brenda turned around to see if David was ready and to read him some of the rules on co-ed showering she had just thought of, and to her surprise there he stood wearing only a smile with a white ball of lint in his hair. He looked so nervous and cute, she forgot about the rules. Brenda walked over to him, reached up, and pulled the little ball of cotton from the right side of his head just above his ear then kissed him gently on the cheek. She looked affectionately into his eyes as she rubbed in the kiss with her fingers. He had a way of touching something in her, she acknowledged, that made her care sooo much for him. There were plenty of great guys in her life, and some she had regrets about, but none touched her the way this brown man could.

Brenda stepped back, smiled meekly at him, and let her robe drop softly to the floor. Her shower-mate's little boy innocent grin as he gazed upon her, endeared a tired woman. *This shower just might be fun*, she told herself.

It was.

Toni listened to the occasional bits of laughter that drifted into her bedroom above the din of the shower. She was laying on her back with Mike already sleeping soundly, his head resting on her shoulder. His slow, deep breaths signaled he was done for the night. Toni felt the heavy fingers of sleep grabbing hold of her eyelids and beginning to pull them down. She resisted, wanting to be sure Brenda and David were all right before she fell asleep. She never had the chance. Hearing them cavorting in the shower softened her resolve until the room, and her consciousness, faded to black.

CHAPTER 9

A song played softly on the radio as the lone occupant of the room listened and pondered the words "Love and happiness," that flowed from the silky voice of Al Green. The lady at the table no longer believed it was possible to have both. Toni stared absentmindedly at the cold food on her plate. After sitting down to dinner alone, she had lost most of her appetite by the second bite of mashed potatoes. While one hand moved her fork around in random patterns in the mashed mountain she'd created, the other twisted her hair around her fingers. Toni, the decision-maker, was reduced to idle daydreaming, haunted by the empty plate and chair across from her.

Brenda, who shared the duplex with her, was scheduled to work the nightshift this week to fill in for two nurses who decided to take last-minute vacations. Toni took Brenda's misfortune as an opportunity to cook a big dinner for Mike because the house would belong to just *them*.

She looked down at the sparklingly clean plate and dinnerware across from her. Their silent reflection spoke volumes about tonight's prospects. She felt just as empty. Toni closed her eyes squeezing back the tears. She swallowed hard because that was the problem. There wasn't going to be any "them" tonight— or any other night. She was *alone again*, she told herself, remembering the lyrics to another song, *naturally*.

The first few times Mike had either canceled a date or later apologized for not calling and saying he couldn't make it, she shrugged it off as "men." Then she painfully remembered, it started taking on a pattern. It took her a while, but she finally grasped what was happening. If they were going somewhere as a group, he would be there, but if it was just the two of them alone, lately he always managed to find an excuse to miss it. Tonight's dinner was the final exam. Three hours into dinner had made it pretty clear to her Mike was studying somewhere else.

Toni got up slowly from the table, feeling a little stiffness in her legs. She wasn't quite sure why, disregarding the hours she had spent sitting at her table wondering how things had gone so wrong, so quickly. The meal she had prepared for them slid off her plate and down into the sink drain. Brenda would enjoy the leftovers, she decided as she washed off the last morsel of food from her plate under the hot water of the sink faucet. Suddenly feeling some vague, nebulous, female intuition that tied in the empty plate in her hand with the future of her relationship with— the plate slipped from her fingers.

است

Mike took a deep breath and exhaled as he put the phone down for the third time. *You can't call her after standing her up again last night*, he scolded himself. *What are you going to tell her this time? Not the truth, that's for sure.* He looked at the phone again, turned, slowly walked over, and sat down on his La-Z-Boy. *How do you explain your latest goof-up? You don't*, he answered himself.

How did this happen? Why me, or better yet, why us? he questioned. *Am I doing the right thing in breaking it off with Toni?* At first, the road he had chosen was clear, and Mike knew just what he had to do. But miles down the road of life the bends became sharper, and it started to get very foggy. Now, the why of his actions weren't as clear as they were when he started on this journey. He was having second thoughts as the realization of what his insensitivity was doing to Toni broke through the self-righteous wall his actions had created. Second-guessing himself, Mike sensed there was probably a better way to have done that. He also resigned himself to the fact it was now too late. The die was cast. He had made that decision with a clear heart and conscience— then. Now he was troubled by his decision and afraid to trust in the judgment of the shaken man sitting in his favorite chair.

Mike found himself staring at the white phone on the end table next to his couch. It had become an evil thing in the last few weeks. Nothing but harsh, hurtful words seemed to emanate from

Bell's invention. The simple ringing of the phone fueled fears of who could be on the other end and why. It wasn't always that way, Mike reminded himself. The hours spent on that phone, usually talking to Toni, but sometimes with other people like David and Brenda, were fond recollections. He could picture the times he was curled up on his couch talking on the phone or while doing the same hanging upside-down with his feet hanging over the back. That picture carried with it sounds of laughter and words of love spoken in unabashed sincerity and genuineness. The man in that picture, on that couch, had no plans of ever hurting the gentle voice on the other end, yet that's exactly what he had done.

"But it was the right thing to do, under the circumstances," Mike whispered to silence the voices of his guilt. "Wasn't it?" His cry for justification met silent applause.

He couldn't stop the bitter pangs of remorse that gripped him tighter and tighter as he succumbed to the truth. His actions seemed to take on a life of their own when he felt his chest tightening up over what he had done. In his bout with self-pity, he couldn't relate that pain to his stress over losing someone dear to him. No, his guilt told him, this was retribution for the cowardly way he ended their relationship. The truth was he battled long into the night with the decision on what he should do with the information he had discovered. This wasn't some haphazard action by a cold-hearted lover, tired of the romantic situation he was in, and not willing to man-up and express that face-to-face. Mike's decision, now genuinely regretted, was made to ease both of them out of their love commitment as painlessly as he could. Of course, there would be pain, of course, there would be hurt, but this was the path of least resistance, he tried convincing himself.

"I could have told her I didn't love her anymore. I could have acted like there was someone else," he said to the silence. But he could never hurt her that way. Letting her make the break, he believed, might save her some self-respect. He could never tell her his secret. The pain he imagined he would see in her eyes, if she ever found out, was more than he could bear.

"I'm a coward, but I am letting her down slowly," he said softly in the quiet apartment. "If I told her the truth, it would crush the life out of her. How could I tell her that? Oh—" Mike groaned, as the ringing phone startling him.

Rrring. Rrring.

There was no way he was going to answer it. He didn't have call waiting, so he couldn't be sure who was on the other end. He would have to eventually face Toni, he knew that. Now, however, wasn't the time.

Rrring. Rrring.

She would ask why he stood her up again. He knew that the spiritless sound of her voice on the phone was born of her disappointment in him. That would hurt more than he could deal with now, so he took the cowardly course and let it ring.

Rrring. Rrring.

Could that be David calling? No, probably not. David was acting a little aloof since Mike told him he had broken it off with Toni. Finally, it stopped.

That was the other side of the dilemma, Mike realized as he tried to focus in on a way out of the hole he had dug for himself. What to do about David? If it came down to losing that friendship, Mike would have to tell him everything.

Mike valued their camaraderie like the brother he never had. Their friendship was as strong as he could imagine two people could possibly achieve. They loved each other and, more than that, respected the other's space. David would never voice his opinion on Mike's personal affairs unless he thought it was harmful to him. Harmful, yes, stupid, no. Even their close friendship didn't grant the other the right to judge. If anything, it gave greater leeway to make bad decisions and still have someone in your corner, regardless of the stupidity of that decision. That was the freedom he gave David concerning Brenda, and Mike expected no less in return from him with Toni.

Mike felt alone for the first time in years as he carried the reason for his actions locked up in his heart. He should have told David, he realized as he replayed the last few weeks, the minute he found out, and gotten his opinion before he tried breaking it off with Toni.

"It was the right thing to do!" he shouted off the white walls of his apartment. His display only intensified the burgeoning headache that had already reached the point that no aspirin would be able to relieve. He sensed the pain in his head was probably an all-nighter, the pain in his soul—that would last much longer.

"It's not my fault this happened," he mumbled, as his temples started dancing to the beat of his heart. *Lie back and try to sleep,* he thought, *that usually helps.* He pulled up on the handle of the La-Z-Boy chair and reclined backward, closing his eyes. "It's not my fault," he repeated. "Anyone would have done the same thing if they were in my shoes."

He knew David would have. Mike stopped and opened his eyes. He wondered what would David have done. Would he have been strong enough to—

Yes, Mike thought, *he would have reacted the same way.* Well, maybe not the same way, but he would have ended it right away, Mike thought as he closed his eyes on the pain in his head—and the truth. *Well, the horse is out of the barn now,* he theorized. No use in wondering if he should have locked the gate. He swallowed twice, trying to keep from saying the words that were bouncing around in his head. As he relaxed in the chair and yielded to the powers of suggestion, he said a prayer. "Toni, please forgive me for hurting you. This is best for you…I think."

They had both recognized the division that now existed between them, but neither fought hard enough to uncover the reason for it or to save the relationship. They had spent the last few years learning how to let go and trust each other, not—as with most relationships today—building walls to protect themselves, just in case things went bad.

As expected, Toni finally made the first move by telling Mike she no longer wanted to date him. She had David tell him she wanted him to call her. Mike finally got the courage to forgo that and instead knocked on her door.

"Hi, Toni."

She turned and walked away from the door without answering.

"Toni, I'm sorry for—"

"Mike, I don't know what went wrong with us," she said, ignoring his plea. "But I can't take this anymore."

"Yes, I know, Toni, and I'm sorry. I should have been more up front with you."

"Yes, you should have. I—" She stopped when she felt the pain returning. "Just go, Mike. It's over, no hard feelings."

"Maybe—"

"No, Mike, it's much too late for that, just go."

"You're right," he said when he saw the emotions swelling up in her blue eyes. A despondent man turned and walked out of her house.

Mike, surprisingly, had started to think differently after actually seeing for the first time how much this was hurting Toni. Then, just as he was going to argue for them to try again, he reversed himself and agreed it was probably the right thing for them to do.

Hurt, confused, and angry, Toni closed her door on Mike, as he walked out of her house, and on that part of her life.

As the empty days and tearful nights would confirm, she found it nearly impossible to get over him. Never again, she vowed, would she let herself love a man like she loved him. Around Brenda and David, she put up a good front, but it was obvious to them she was hurting. When she was alone, it was worse. Eventually, she tried dating again but couldn't stand for any man to touch her, and for a long time, to even try talking to her.

"What the hell is wrong with him, David?" Brenda asked when she called while Toni was in the shower. "Can't he see what he's doing to Toni? I could ring his damn neck."

David took a deep breath and dreaded having to defend a man he agreed was acting like an idiot. When Brenda called, he knew she would eventually turn the conversation in that direction. Hell, he couldn't blame her. Mike's suddenly acting like a dork caught everyone by surprise. Brenda was right, and he knew she was waiting on him to verbalize that. It was bros before hoes, but once you'd held had that redhead in your arms it was hard to—

"I know, Brenda, but it's his choice."

"Can't you do something?"

Therein was the problem, he wanted to tell her. As much as he loved them both, getting between them was a bad idea. "Mike's his own man. I can't—as much as I would love to help—I can't."

"Mike listens to you, David."

"I hate to say this, Bren, but I think it's too late for intervention by anyone."

"Goodnight, David!"

He whispered the same to the person no longer on the phone.

Surprisingly, Toni didn't harbor any harsh feelings toward Mike. If he didn't love her anymore, she told David and Brenda, it wasn't his fault. Shit happens. What she didn't reveal to either was that the suddenness of the change in their relationship had left her feeling cold. Just a few months ago, they were lovers, bathing in the heat of their love as if they were lying under a blazing sun on some beautifully romantic beach. Then the impossible happened. While still in laying out under a steaming hot sun in her sexiest bikini, the weather had suddenly changed, and it had started to snow. "It never snows in paradise," she shouted up at the heavens.

Before she knew it, everything that was green and beautiful was now covered in white. The slowly descending flakes had become a blowing blizzard. How, why? Something had gone wrong in the cosmos. She was so surprised by their break-up, it felt as though it had really snowed on their imaginary tropical paradise.

In the days that followed, the loss of their intimacy was such an upheaval to her psyche she had to slowly wean herself from him by sprinkling his cologne on her pillow at night so she could get some sleep. The only way she found to cope with the hurt was to convince herself that he just stopped loving her and that it wasn't another woman. She still had her pride. If he didn't want her anymore, then they were doing the right thing in calling a halt to it before anyone got hurt, she decided, feigning the courage she wished she possessed. The real reasons for the tears running down her face as she tried accepting that lame excuse was ignored.

CHAPTER 10

The shape of the zinc coated steel strip looked flat, David thought as he watched it moving up into the exit accumulator. He was a little surprised at that, considering the poor shape of the incoming raw sheet steel. "Don is making good shape with the levelers." His voice was drowned out by the in-plant noises.

With that inspection out of the way, David walked over to check the temper mill rolls for marks. There was nothing he found on the rolls that would mar the required super smooth strip surface. After inspecting the rolls, he turned to leave when he spotted Mike walking in his direction. In the moment or two he had before Mike reached him, David wondered when he should ask him about his break up with Toni. *No*, as he had told himself over and over the last few weeks, *it's none of your business. If he wants to talk about it, he'll make the first move.*

"Hey, Dave," Mike said as he neared his friend and boss. "Lauren said you wanted to see me. Was he joking around, as usual, and pulling my leg?"

"No, I asked him if he had seen you." David never looked directly at Mike as they were talking. Mike had a way of reading his moods and David didn't want him to know he was concerned. "Joe, that geek over in material control, called me and said he is expecting up to thirty incoming trucks from the steel mills by tonight. And, as a blind man can see, we don't have room for all those coils on our raw coil section of the floor."

"Yeah, material control, now that's a misnomer," Mike said sarcastically. "Look, David, they knew yesterday that we were out of room on the floor. I told that jag-off myself."

"I know that," David answered, while taking note of the anger building in his buddy's voice. "Their excuse is they order correctly but can't control the other mills when they want to ship us raw steel. All they can do is give them a window, something they aim for and sometimes they miss. That may be true, I don't know, but it doesn't help us any. There are still thirty trucks with over fifty coils headed our way, and we've got to decide where to put these coils when they get here."

Mike walked away from his friend and looked out over at the crowded coil field. Most of the coils were double-stacked to conserve space. Safety wasn't a major concern with doubling up the coils, he knew, because the bottom rows of coils were all in steel racks to prevent them from slipping. Some genius from the office, he recalled with a smirk, had once asked him if they could triple stack them. The fowl look Mike gave him answered his stupid question. *Funny*, he thought then while watching the shirt-and-tie walk angrily back toward his air conditioned office, *how people freely suggest dumb things that only put others in danger.*

"We will have to close one of the receiving doors and store the coils in that truck bay," Mike suggested when he heard David walking up behind him. "That will take care of about half of them. The rest, I guess we will have to put in the walkways or in whatever corner we can find."

David struggled to listen to Mike as he pointed out the spaces they could put the overflow of incoming raw steel coils. It wasn't that he was he ignoring what Mike was saying. David knew Mike could handle the challenge that was why he assigned it to him. It was that, every time he looked at him, he couldn't help thinking about Toni DiNardo. They were together so often, he had once thought them inseparable and joined at the hip.

"Dave! Hello, McFly, is there anyone in there?"

"Huh, yes?" David answered as the picture of the dark-haired beauty faded. "Sorry, Mike, what were you saying?"

"I said we should be all right. I forgot we were running a lot of small coils today and they take up a lot of space in the raw coil field. By the time the trucks start rolling in, we should have some empty bays."

"Good, Mike. Let the others know what the game plan is for handling the incoming coils. I'm going over to the material control department and explain what we're going to try and do with the over-crowded field."

Both felt the indifference as they walked away. The unasked questions were a wall they couldn't climb over or go around. For the last few weeks, they had chosen to ignore the wall. David recognized the grief his buddy was carrying. It wasn't a large chip on his shoulder like some people might carry to gain sympathy. You would have to be close with him to see it, that's how well Mike disguised his hurt. David saw it clearer than perhaps anyone, with the exception of maybe Toni. Then again, she wasn't around to see how their break-up had affected him. It was there in the harsh tones Mike used when he was talking to almost everyone. Not enough to raise the ire of the person he was conversing with, but enough for David to sense he wasn't quite himself. It was also evident in the way he walked, or in reality, didn't walk. Gone was that silly gait, that swagger of his that bugged David to no end, but often was a beguiling lure that amused women when he approached them. That was then. Now, he seemed to be carrying the weight of the world on his broad shoulders. What was most noticeable and distressing to David, was Mike's loss of his sense of humor.

One of the maintenance guys had cracked everyone up when he slipped on some nails and fell on his butt, tossing his paper cup full of coffee up in the air. The amazing cup tumbled around in the air without losing a drop then landed on top of his head, spilling the contents down his face. David waited until he knew the guy was all right before he lost it. Mike was the only person who didn't see any humor in that. David was more surprised by that than the amazing spinning cup of coffee.

Mike wasn't alone in having once felt the amazing transformation from experiencing unbridled love for someone, to the empty, barren, feeling inside from the loss of that love. It was also amazing how many people longed for the chance to risk everything just for the opportunity to know that kind of love. David was one of those who had never found that deep a relationship. That was probably why he couldn't find the nerve to ask Mike what really happened between him and Toni.

Their open devotion to each other was a carbon copy of the daydream David had concocted for himself. Somewhere, in the group of girls he dated, he dreamed he would meet that certain woman, and they would immediately hit it off. She would be beautiful, of course, passionate, with a spontaneous ability to integrate her emotions with his. What Toni and Mike had created for themselves was the same portrait he had painted for his future. Unexpectedly, something had happened to Mike and Toni to destroy their love. That shocking discovery, David unconsciously feared, threatened his own vision. He saw Mike and Toni's failure as the failure of every man who envisioned there was a real chance to experience that special kind of tenderness and affection. The real reason he didn't discuss Toni any further with Mike, David reluctantly admitted to himself, was because he really didn't want to know the ugly truth.

CHAPTER 11

They danced together, as if no one else was in the room, their sultry moves obviously choreographed to entice him. But, instead, he felt embarrassed for them. Their intentions were so clearly apparent, David half expected them to start swapping spit any minute.

The doorbell had rung just as he finished dressing. The long, hot, shower was just what he needed after playing four physically demanding games of basketball down at the rec center. When he opened the door, and Mike walked past him, leading two unmistakably inebriated women, David could have screamed.

"Hey, buddy, this is Rachel and...and Donna," Mike said to the man staring at him after the threesome walked in.

"Her name is Dara, not Donna, Mikey," Rachel corrected him. "And who is this handsome man?"

"This is David, girls, my best bud. He also likes to party and can do it all night, he can."

David looked at a grinning Mike, knowing he was trying to draw him into his plans for the night.

"I bet he can," the skinny blonde said and stuck her finger in her mouth in what she must have thought was sending an obvious signal.

Dara...something...David couldn't understand her slurred speech when she walked up and introduced herself—and Rachael Thomas had audaciously sauntered into his apartment and made themselves right at home. They turned the stereo, playing softly in the background, up loud and were dancing before David had a chance to say ten words.

Mike motioned for him to sit down on the couch as he directed the evening's entertainment. While David watched the girls dancing, an already intoxicated Mike excused himself and went into the kitchen, looking for the cold beer he knew David kept on ice.

Dancing Dara was a dyed-platinum blonde about five feet four inches tall and weighing less than one hundred pounds. She had that common bar girl look about her with dark circles around her eyes that belied her true age. She was twenty-five but looked ten years older. Her wire thin figure was a result of her genes, not because she hung out in bars, her audacious life style blameless.

Actually, she isn't that bad looking, David decided when he stopped grinding his teeth and decided to relax and go with…whatever. She had light-colored eyes that he thought were either blue or light green. She didn't stop dancing long enough for him to be certain. She did have a pleasant smile that occasionally gave an air of innocence to her overly made up face. Her little-girl-dyed silver blonde hair was as thin as she was and just hung down to her shoulders. She wore a tight red tube top that outlined the shape of her small, braless breasts. With her painted-on tight sky-blue jeans, her outfit looked very seductive on a woman with a young girl's small figure.

David looked at the other woman as she spun around in front of him. Raunchy Rachael, he later learned, was the woman who Mike first approached. He talked Rachel's friend Dara into coming along to party to meet his best friend, David.

Rachael was a stocky cocoa-skinned woman with a very cute, round face, and long sexy eyelashes. She looked the part of the woman that people invariable said, "She would be so much better looking if she lost some weight." It was true. Yet, from the fluid way she danced across his living room, it became obvious to him she carried her weight very adroitly. Her loose fitting skirt waved about her body, revealing most of her shapely thick legs. David was sure they were the alluring bait that caught most men's attention at the bar, but he knew what made Mike salivate were the two large mounds wrapped precariously in her low cut tight yellow sweater.

Take thirty pounds off her frame, David decided, while he watched her spinning around his living room, and she would be, in his eyes, a perfect size for a woman. His interpretation of perfect wasn't the textbook skinny figure most women wanted for themselves. *Take the extra pounds from the brown bombshell*, he thought while watching them dance, *and put them on the blonde pencil, and they would be perfect bookends.*

"I like him," Rachael whispered to Dara about the quiet black man sitting on the couch watching them dance.

"He is damn good looking," Dara added.

"The way he's staring at me, I think the feeling is mutual."

"Good, because I think I like the other one. Hey, girl, maybe we'll have some fun tonight, huh?" Dara said, giggling in her dance partner's ear. Both women snickered as they looked over at the flabbergasted man on the couch and winked.

That was David's cue to leave. "Where did you find these two?" he asked Mike, pushing him back into the kitchen after excusing himself from the Soul Train Dancers.

"What's wrong with them?" Mike snickered. "They have all the necessary parts." He jerked his arm out of David strong grasp and put the four bottles of beer down on the table. "Hey, buddy, you've got to chill out. They're old enough to know what they want. Do you have a problem with having fun now, David? You haven't in the past, if I remember."

"What's wrong with them? Mike, open your eyes," David said, louder than he meant to. "What did you pay them, twenty bucks a piece?"

"No, ha, ha, ha, they would be over paid," Mike laughed.

David just stared at him. This was the second time this week and sixth or seventh time this month that Mike had come over unannounced with some of the women he had met at the many bars he frequented.

He was right, however, and David felt a little hypocritical in objecting to them because he had joined in on the festivities on more than a few occasions. Mike hung out in the better establishments then, and so was the class of women he met. They were nice girls, just looking for Mr. Right and there was nothing wrong with that. As Mike's drinking increased, the class of the establishment he frequented decreased, and that mattered less and, unfortunately, so did his taste in women.

David felt a little guilty judging him. Obviously, there was nothing wrong with Mike dating. It was what Mike was trying to erase over the last six months that cheapened the experience.

Some of the girls they met were sweet, sincere, and only looking for someone to share their lives with, like most people. But Mike had no such intentions. That, "I'll call you" he left them with was a perfunctory promise. He couldn't be honest with any of them, David knew, until he stopped lying to himself. *None of the women you are with*, he thought as he looked his best friend in the eye, *will be able to help you forget about that dark-haired beauty.*

"Don't ruin a fun evening, Davey." Mike picked up the bottles of beer, made a quizzical face at David, then pushed open the swinging door with his back and walked into the living room. David leaned back against the sink, drained by the effort to arrest Mike's new lifestyle. The still swinging kitchen door held his attention as it swung back and forth, oddly changing the pitch of the music blasting in the living room with each swing. He tried to think of another way to reach out to his friend but was side tracked by the sounds of merriment drifting into the kitchen.

No matter what he did with Mike, they had always managed to have a good time, he warmly recalled. Even if an evening ended in disaster and their dates stormed out, they had fun saying goodbye to them. The two girls guzzling down his beer in the living room were probably okay David thought. It was just that the shadow of Toni DiNardo hung over everything Mike did.

Their laughter beckoned to David to join them in the living room. Past evenings of both fun and pleasure teased him with pictures of what he could be missing, offering more reasons why the *"I should march in there and throw everyone out"* thought had lost its sting.

David moved toward the door then stopped. He wasn't quite in the mood to join the party yet. He didn't want to embarrass Mike by acting rude to the women, but he was beginning to grow tired of Mike's adolescent attempts at having fun. Well, it wasn't the fun he really objected to, it was more the fact that he knew Mike was still in love with Toni, and all this was just his poor way of dealing with the pain. *If what Toni said was correct*, David thought, taking a deep breath and blowing it out slowly, *it was Mike who suddenly broke it off with her. If that's case, why is he so miserable?*

He knew Mike still loved her very much. Women fell out of love quickly, not men. Men were like the dog that permitted its master to beat it over and over before he turned and bit him. David saw it in Mike's eyes the few times when he mentioned her name. It was written across his face whenever they talked about beautiful women, and he grew quiet. David knew he was still haunted by her memory.

When David had asked Toni why she thought they broke up, she said she didn't know why, only that Mike suddenly started avoiding her. When she confronted him, he coldly said that it just wasn't working out for him. Seeing the sorrow on her lovely face when she talked about him was something David had a hard time forgiving Mike for. David was still dropping by to see Toni on occasion and considered her a close friend and debated daily if he should tell that to Mike.

One memory he always treasured was one day when he stopped by their place with a birthday gift for Brenda. He had called Brenda the night before and knew she would be at work. Toni, he found out when he followed her into the kitchen, was baking a special chocolate cake for Brenda's birthday.

"Hi, Davey," Toni had said to the person ringing their doorbell.

'Hi, Toni," David answered the woman with flour on her hands, clothes, and face.

"Sorry, I look a mess," Toni said and closed the door as he stepped into the house. "I'm baking a cake and cookies for Brenda's birthday. You know she isn't home."

"Yes, I did. I wanted to be sure to drop off her birthday present when she wasn't home to surprise her."

"How sweet, where is it?" Toni asked as she led David to the kitchen.

"You're looking at it."

She stopped and turned around. "Oh, hell, is she being punished again for being bad?"

"Ha, ha, you are just jealous, Betty Crocker. It's the same present you have desperately wanted since that day at the park. Own up to it, you poor girl."

"Poor girl" gave him the finger and walked into her kitchen. "I would ask you if you would like to taste some of my cookies, but we both know the answer to that," she countered.

David ignored the snicker on her face and the truth of her words when she winked at him.

"No thank you, Pillsbury Dough Girl, the last ten volunteers are still trying to get that taste out of their mouths. So there."

Toni had to laugh herself at that come back. So, went the evening as David sat down with a cup of great coffee in her tantalizingly-smelling kitchen and talked to her while she cooked.

Something she said about her hair reminded him of the day at Kennywood Park when they first met. When David told her about the wig-less girl on the roller coaster, she started laughing so hard that when she turned around tears were streaming down her face. That image was seared in his mind as he touched his kitchen door and ran his fingers softly over the dark stained wood as if it was her skin. He had never seen a woman look as good as she did laughing at his story. He couldn't remember what it was about her that so impressed him that day because she always looked good. Maybe it was something in him, he wondered.

"No smartass answer from you, but try one of my cookies," Toni said, after taking the tray of hot chocolate-chip treats from the oven.

David zipped his lips closed but mumbled something. She rolled her eyes at him and rescinded her offer by moving the tray out of his reach.

"Sorry, sorry, but that was too tempting an offer the lovely lady most eloquently described."

"Okay, the lovely lady comment gets you a second chance. You are rude, but at least you aren't blind."

"Mmmm, they are good," he said, after taking a small bite of the very hot cookie.

"Really? They are Brenda's favorites. I'm going to put some on a plate, and you can take them into the living room while I put my cake in the oven. Take your coffee with you."

David did as ordered and, five minutes later, Toni joined him.

"My Granny said to never have some big foot man in the kitchen when baking because their walking around makes the cakes fall. I don't know why," Toni said to the confused look on David handsome face, "I think it's that the vibrations allow the steam to escape...or whatever. Now, tell me about yourself, other than dreaming about my roommate, what's up?"

They talked about themselves and some of the things that they saw on TV, about their jobs, and other trivial things without mentioning anything about Mike. He was the skeleton in the closet. But each time they were alone together, it would eventually come up. They couldn't talk about him around Brenda because she would become angry and ruin the moment. They understood her frustration with what Mike had done, but neither of them wanted to point fingers.

"How's Mike doing?"

It was always at that point he would look into her soft blue eyes and, for a moment, they would stare at each other until one looked away.

"Mike is getting by. Like I told you before, Toni, he won't talk to me about his feelings for you or what happened. He is still hurting over you, I can tell."

"I know you think that, Davey, but—"

"Look, I know him best, and I can't figure out what's going on in his head. I can't."

"I just want him to be happy, Davey, that's all."

"I know sweetheart, I know." David leaned over and kissed her cheek. "I wish there was something I could have done to—"

"None of us saw this happening, I know I didn't, or I would have done something different. I just don't know what."

David saw the pain in her expression and wanted to change the subject but couldn't. "How are you doing, Toni?" *Should have changed directions*, he noticed immediately.

"I—I still hurt, but it's getting better, it really is, Davey. But it will be a while before I can let go again and trust a man. Not you, baby," she said to the look in his eyes, reaching over and rubbing his leg.

He knew what was coming next. They had skipped over it all evening.

"What about you and the birthday girl?" she asked.

She didn't disappoint him. "The same, Toni. You know we care deeply for each other, but we are just letting thing happen naturally."

"Davey, don't wait too long. I know both of you are dating others, but I would hate to see you—I'm sorry, there I go again, wishing you two were together and I couldn't even hold on to my man."

"What a group we are, huh? Speaking of the devil, I should be going before the redhead tyrant gets home."

"You don't have to run," she said, placing her hand on his leg again as if holding him there. "She will be pissed to know you didn't wait around to see her."

"I just wanted to drop off her birthday gift," David lied. "I would hate to look in those green eyes and tell her I have to work tomorrow and will miss her party."

"You're kidding!"

"I'm sorry, but I have to work."

"That's a better reason to stick around, I'm sure she would like to thank you in person."

That comment silenced the room, as it often did when anything was hinted that might push the two of them together. Both Brenda and David knew that it was Toni's desire that the two of them find happiness in each other's arms. It was something they both wanted but were unsure if the other was the answer. They both realized the dark-haired beauty sitting across from him had no doubts they were.

Toni knew she had made him uncomfortable and regretted speaking her mind. "What did you get her? Hopefully, not the gift you said when you walked in. I would hate to watch my best friend be that disappointed," she said, changing the subject.

When he stuck his tongue out at her again, she realized she was successful.

"Those earrings you mentioned she liked," David answered and produced a small, beautifully gift wrapped box.

"Oh, Davey, she will love them. Are you sure you can't call off or something tomorrow? I invited some of our girlfriends. Who knows? In a room full of drunk women, even you might get lucky," she said with a snicker.

"I wish, but we are very short handed at work, and I'm the boss."

Toni knew how important it was for David to always do the right thing at work. She understood that was just who he was. Even the thought of a thankful Brenda lavishing him with kisses couldn't defer his sense of duty as crew boss.

Long after she had finished putting the finishing touches on Brenda's cake, Toni sat on the couch thinking about her Davey. She had found her love and lost him. Davey was looking for that love and couldn't see it was right in front of him. "You can lead a horse to water but—" she whispered as she got up, finished the last sip of her coffee, and headed for the kitchen to clean up before Brenda got home from work.

While the notes from his favorite song were playing on the car radio, David recalled how Toni would reprimand him for staying away so long between visits. He would feign ignorance while struggling to name reasons for his absences. Nowhere on that imaginary list of excuses did he mention the time he needed to be away from Toni to get her out of his mind. Was it because he was in love with her? he often questioned. He had tried to honestly examine his feeling for her in the past, but it was a question without an easy answer. The whirlpool of emotions he felt after Toni's break-up with Mike made it all but impossible to weed out the truth.

On one side, was the question what could that gorgeous woman have done to piss Mike off enough to break up with her and then drive him to desperately seek others to sooth the hurt? And why would Toni want to let go of a person who she was still pining for, and then date no one else? Hell, he understood she could have had almost anyone she wanted. David resisted the urge to include himself on that list.

He loved them both very deeply. It was those strong feelings that made him hesitate at his kitchen door. On this side of that door, he possessed his own free will. It was his apartment, but the three souls partying on the other side of the door didn't recognize his rights.

On the other side, he knew he would eventually yield to whatever the evening's direction and/or director took them. It was Mike's party, and David didn't want to dampen the fun. The last time he tried that, they didn't speak for days, and it didn't stop Mike from drowning his life away in the bar scene. Renewing their friendship gave David the chance to be there should Mike crash land, David finally decided and had apologized to him.

He pushed the door open and was abruptly met by Rachael. He stopped, and she didn't.

The message her body sent by pushing into him wasn't missed, just ignored.

"There you are!" she shouted above the din of the stereo. "I was coming to get you, honey." She reached out, took his hand, and guided him out to the middle of the floor. She put his arm around her and slow danced.

"You have a nice place here, not like most single guys. You are single, aren't you?"

"Yes."

"What?" she asked, leaning in closer.

"Yes, I'm single."

"Great, but even if you weren't, it's okay to dance with a married man, right?"

Contrary to any of his prejudgments, she felt wonderful in his arms. Her eyes were bright and full of life. Her perfume was strong but not offensively so. He sensed she was probably a different person sober and felt a little guilt at prejudging her. That was something he had to deal with often when others thought less of him.

As they danced, David looked over at Mike sitting on the couch being eaten alive by the skinny blonde sitting across his lap kissing every exposed inch of skin on Mike's face and neck. David thought he saw a bit of contempt in the eyes of the man struggling to hold off the she-cat in heat.

As David danced with the strange woman, he felt a little pleasure in the dilemma Mike had gotten himself into. When the song came to an end, David took Rachael back into the kitchen, allowing the lovers some privacy. He knew the solitude of the living room would unleash the she-cat all over Mike. At least that was the plan. He intended to take his time in the kitchen by asking his "date" everything about her. With that in mind, and a snicker on his face, he opened the kitchen door for...*what's-her-name*?

CHAPTER 12

Brenda sat in her car outside David's apartment, angrily trying to decide what to do next. She had rushed over to tell him she had a great idea about how to get Mike and Toni together again. When she pulled up and started to get out of the car, she noticed that Mike's car was parked next to David's. She slammed her door closed. He was the last person she wanted to see right now after what he was doing to Toni. She wanted them together for Toni's sake, not because of her affection for Mike, she said to her confused anger.

From the shadows she saw moving past David's living room window, there was more than just Mike and David up there. She had previously reprimanded David for letting Mike bring over his low-life women after hearing stories of Mike's latest amorous rendezvous at his apartment.

"Now what?" she mumbled to herself as she struggled to control her temper. "Who knows how long they'll be up there?"

Brenda stared up at the window as if it would give her some psychic insight into how long she might have to wait in her car. They appeared to be dancing or something, she figured from their movements. She took a deep breath and looked down the road as she tried to figure out her next move.

Toni was still in love with Mike, Brenda thought as she gritted her teeth and then looked up at the apartment window again. Each day she was more certain of that. What she needed to know was if Mike still wanted a relationship with Toni. David had hinted that he believed that to be the case, but she wanted more than a hint before risking her friendship by trying to get them together again.

Brenda decided she might as well listen to some music while she made up her mind to leave or to stay. Turning on the radio, she searched the pre-set channels for a song to listen to while she waited. As was the case when you really wanted something, no music was playing. Each of the stations was either talking about news, sports, or playing an advertisement.

Peeved, Brenda turned off the radio and looked up at the windows to David's apartment. She noticed that the light in the window was now dimmer. It had to be coming from another source illuminating the shears and curtains drawn across his windows. The same shears she had helped him pick out and hang up. *They look good*, she thought as her mind drifted. A small smile forced its way out as she recalled when David asked for her help in remodeling his new apartment that was only minutes from his job. He had taken her advice on most of the items they bought and even the things she insisted he throw away that day—with the exception of that ugly brown floor lamp.

Helping David clean and furnish his apartment was still a treasured memory. She had so much fun arguing with him over what was too feminine and what was masculine for his apartment. She never let him know, but she admired the way he stuck to his opinions on what he wanted in his place. Even her hints that, if she got her way he "might" get his, failed to deter some of his terrible choices, that ugly brown lamp in his living room being a constant reminder.

"You know I'm right about this ugly lamp." Brenda stood in front of the floor lamp with her hands on her hips, frowning, but her complaining wasn't having the desired effect on the man who stopped cleaning and looked at her.

"No, I don't," David said. "I think that lamp has character. Yes," he explained, "it adds character to my apartment. It's not perfect, unlike a certain someone blocking my view, but has character, like me."

"Oh, you!" That complement stole her argument. She walked past him toward his bedroom. "Hey," she turned around and added, "Now that we're done, I need to change out of these dirty clothes. Do you mind if perfect uses your shower?"

"What? Did you say you wanted to shower with me?"

"You wish," Brenda answered, rolling her eyes and sauntering toward his bedroom. She didn't have to turn around to know he was watching her. If he wasn't so stubborn about that stupid lamp, she might have considered a co-ed shower, she angrily claimed as she closed the door to the bedroom. It wouldn't have been the first time, she recalled.

During a long shower, she lost her frustration with the stubborn man in the other room. They had a great time shopping for things for his apartment. And after they finished putting away all his purchases, hung the shears over his windows, and cleaned up, she felt sweaty. Wrapping a towel around her, she walked into his bedroom.

"Okay, Brenda," she chastised herself, "quit pouting because you didn't get your way. If he likes that stupid lamp, so what?"

After towel drying her hair, she realized her brush was in her purse, and it was on his couch. She thought it would serve him right if she walked out in only a towel to retrieve it. Instead, she put it up in a ponytail. She was about to put on her clothes when she remembered an idea that crossed her mind in the shower. Looking in his dresser, she found some sleepwear and walked out the room wearing his pajama top. It was too big on her and hung down to mid-thigh. But rolling up the sleeves helped. And the leg show did get the expected results. She caught him stealing glances as she pranced around his apartment. The strong-willed man didn't disappoint her. The effect she had on him was obvious, but she remembered he maintained his cool all that evening.

David looked up from the couch and was surprised when Brenda walked in wearing his PJ top. Obviously, it was too big and fit her like a short dress. But seeing her in his clothes warmed him. The doorbell rang just as he was about to say how nice she—

"That's the pizza I ordered," he said.

"I'll get it."

"Not in that outfit, you won't," David injected and rushed past her to the door. "The poor delivery kid will get blue balls."

Brenda grinned at his jealous response.

It was while sitting on the couch, finishing up an amazingly delicious pizza he ordered and cold beer, that she again realized why he was so special to her. Everything about her outfit that night hinted she might be willing to give herself to him. Brenda shook her head acknowledging she probably would have let him had he had come on to her, but he didn't try. David had correctly read the no in her eyes. What little she was wearing, and the teasing, was because she wanted to play with him, not because she was aroused. Brenda wasn't trying to get him in bed, that would be easy. She was just being playful. David was the only man she knew who could look past the obvious, look past her leg show, and tell the difference. Thus, she could playfully push her teasing further with him without any apprehension.

"Thank you for helping me, Brenda," David said, sitting back on the couch relaxing after they ate. "You thought of some very nice things I needed to make my place look better. I love those pictures on the walls that you picked out and the couch pillows. They add class to everything."

"If you mean that, then get rid of—"

He suddenly sat up and cut her off. "The lamp stays."

"But it's so—"

"That's why."

"What?"

"I know it's ugly." David smiled at her confusion. "I only kept it up because I knew it would bug you. Hell, it bugs me. But when you made a big deal about it, I had to keep it."

Brenda's mouth dropped in shock.

David thought she would find that a reason for more of the same teasing they had done all day, but she didn't. There was a little hurt he read in her eyes. He spoke to that hurt. "Brenda, that lamp means a lot to me now. I was going to throw it away like you asked when it took on a different meaning. That ugly lamp— that wonderful lamp—will be a reminder every day, when I look at it, about the sweet lady who took the time to help this color-blind decorator…ah, decorate." David shook his head at her and playfully frowned when the eyes of the emotional woman seated beside him started to water.

She was so touched by that she almost—almost—decided to do him right there on the couch. But what his sweet words did was deeply touch her soul and not inflame her body. Brenda remembered how much she enjoyed being around him. She could always be herself around David, either a flirt or a friend, and not worry he would misread her actions. That was another reason she debated waiting longer in front of his apartment—to see if Mike and his women left—or driving home.

Brenda looked up at the window again and remembered they were sitting there staring at each other that evening, his light brown eyes talking to her soul. Maybe it was the relaxed atmosphere, or what little she was wearing, but she felt a familiar stirring. She was just about to change her mind and—when dummy picked that moment to jump up and start cleaning up empty pizza plates and beer cans. Had he waited another minute, Brenda recalled, she would have been all his that night.

That memory put a smile on her face as she stared out her car window. They had so much fun buying things for his apartment, but he was stubborn about a few things in the stores and she made up her mind, as the hot water rinsed the soap from her body in his shower, to just wear his PJ top and panties, and use her assets to get the upper hand—all woman have over men. But his sincere response to that stupid lamp touched her in a place she didn't expect. But that was her David.

She didn't remember falling asleep on the couch as he took his shower, but she did waking up in his arms as he carried her to his bedroom. A quick decision was made to pretend she was still groggy while in his arms. The reason was obvious, she wanted to see if he would finally take advantage of the situation. He carefully placed her in bed where he had previously rolled back the sheet and blanket and then covered her. Her confidence in him was again confirmed, but it left her ego a little bruised. *What does it take to shake this guy*? she wondered, as he covered her with the blanket, kissed her gently on the forehead, and walked out his bedroom.

The next morning, he was up, dressed, and making breakfast for them, she discovered, when she woke up and peeked in the kitchen. She returned to his room and got dressed.

"Hey, I see you're up," David said when the slightly tussled but still-striking-looking young woman walked into his kitchen.

"Yes, you have a wonder bed. I slept hard all night. Did you— you must have. You didn't have to give me your bed and sleep on the couch." Brenda smiled innocently as she waited to see what he would say.

"I'm glad you slept well. Come grab a seat, breakfast is ready."

"Mmmmm, thank you," she said and tabled what else she

wanted to say. "Everything smells wonderful and I'm starving."

It was the same deep value she placed on that friendship that swayed her from driving away when she looked up at his apartment.

The special feelings of that day still moved her, she realized, more than having great sex. She took a deep breath and slowly blew it out. Coming to grips with what she felt for David would have to wait, she decided. Toni needed them now.

For a brief moment, after Brenda looked up at the window, she thought Mike and his friends were finally leaving and she might yet get the chance to talk to David alone about her plans for Toni. *He's finally putting his foot down*, she cheerfully decided, believing the darkened room to mean he was throwing them out. Then another light came on.

"Damn it," she cursed. Brenda slammed her car into gear, pulled out into the street, and accelerated away from David's apartment. "That's the last time, I let him touch me," she swore. The direction of the light had suddenly become clear to her. It had to be from his bedroom. What ignited her anger was when that light suddenly died out.

"Why are you so mad at him?" she asked herself as she turned left onto Penn Avenue, "You're not dating. It's—it's just so disappointing," she answered herself, "because I thought, I really thought he was better than that." Brenda dabbed the water out of her eyes when she came to a red light. They had been intimate on several occasions since that night they first met at the amusement park. It was always a spontaneous reaction and never something planned, at least that's what she tried telling herself. She ignored the one time she set out to seduce him, wearing the little football outfit she talked Toni also into wearing to David's football party.

After that first time, they made love, she knew he was a very dangerous threat to her freedom. That passionate man had left a lasting impression on her. As she once told Toni, he was so kind and genuine he was one guy that she could do again anytime, anywhere, and anyway, and not feel guilty or cheap.

The men in her life she usually dated quickly came to understand who was in charge, and not just from the fact that she was a red-headed "ten." Her strong personality usually reduced the hardest male ego to putty. Loving her was something she granted, not that you seduced with your charm, unless she wanted you to think so. And she quickly tired of men whose egos couldn't handle a strong, opinionated woman.

In David, she discovered a man who could relate to her on a different level. The steamy passion she found hidden in his calm smile and controlled demeanor burst forth, surprising and impressing her with his intensity. And he was so physical. She loved the way he held her that night, as if she was weightless, and demonstrated amazing self-control. He had repeatedly taken her almost to that point when physically a woman just has to say to her passionate lover, "enough!" And as if reading her thoughts, he would stop short and ease her back to reality. He was gifted, she learned from weighing her experiences with men, gifted.

Brenda remembered how he acknowledged that the two women looked beautiful that day in their gold miniskirts, black silk blouses, and the black and yellow knee high socks they wore for the Steelers football party the four of them had over David's old apartment. He tried playing off the obvious effect it had on him and failed.

"What wrong, Bren?" Toni asked as they sat on the couch sipping screwdrivers.

"Nothing, Toni."

"Well—"

"I can't believe that guy," an obviously upset young woman alleged.

"I hope it's not Mikey you're pissed with."

Brenda rolled her eyes at her BFF.

"Okay, what did David do?" Toni asked as the boys were out on the back porch grilling food for the party.

"That just it, babe, nothing. I know I look amazing in this little outfit, we both do."

"He said we looked amazing when we walked in. Did you see the look in his eyes? Oh, that's not enough for you?"

"No! He said *we* look amazing."

Toni shook her head at her self-centered friend. "Do you want to leave or something?"

"No, I'm being silly." Brenda took a deep breath. She placed her hand on Toni's knee. "I just hoped he would—"

Toni knew her dressed-a-like friend was in love with David but wouldn't admit it to her or herself.

Brenda had found his composure around her both frustrating and so intoxicating. Later that night, after having a fun day with her friends at David's football party, she succumbed to her ego, and a decision was made.

"Hey guy, I—I think I drank too much. My stomach feels queasy. Could I just sleep if off here on your couch, Davey?"

David looked from the young woman lying on his couch to Toni sitting with Brenda's head on her lap and shrugged his shoulders. They knew she drank a lot, only Toni figured out why. They also noticed she nodded off a few times on the couch while they were sitting around talking. None realized she was pretending.

"Are you sure it's okay if she sleeps on your couch, Davey?" Toni asked after freeing herself from Brenda and spreading the blanket David got for her over the already sleeping girl in the identical Steelers colored outfit.

"Of course, Toni, that's no problem. If she wakes up, I'll either put her in my bed or take her home, whatever she wants."

"We can stay around until she—"

"No, you guys go home. I'm off tomorrow and Brenda said she was, so she can sleep it off. You probably have to get up early for work Monday, and I know Mike does."

Mike nodded in agreement, but David thought he saw something else in the momentary smirk on the face of the lovely, slightly inebriated, woman in the identical sexy outfit. Toni surprised him a little by just staring into his eyes before hugging and kissing him and then following Mike out of the apartment.

David wondered about Toni's hesitancy as he locked his door. *What did she want to say?* he questioned. He then walked over and stood looking down at the sleeping red-head. She's such a special person. Beauty, brains, and if you could get close to her, he had learned, you will find she has a kind and giving spirit. According to Toni, Brenda wasn't looking for another one night stand or another boyfriend to date. She now wanted something more meaningful. Toni had shared that with him, he thought, with her own motives in mind when he asked why Brenda seemed depressed lately. "Don't we all?" he had answered her and regretted it when Toni stared at him like he was missing the point.

"She doesn't want to just date guys any more, Davey, ya know. I think she's just tired of the dating scene," Toni explained as they chatted over coffee one day when Mike and Brenda were working. "She was thinking about quitting and going to work at another hospital, but what good would that do? She would be hit on there. She isn't looking for another guy, or just another lover. She's looking for a person who can reach down to her soul and forever plant their seed in her heart like I hope I have with Mike. Do you understand, Davey?"

He understood David told her. "Hell, Toni, I'm looking for the same thing." But he also understood the woman sitting on her couch with him had decided for them that each was "That" person for the other. They had gotten very close, but, again, something was missing.

The woman now lying on his couch, with her face covered in red hair, he considered a special friend. Watching her, David took a deep breath, slowly blew it out, and started to clean up. The left over pizza was wrapped and placed in the frig. Unfinished drinks were poured out and cans tossed in the recycle garbage, glasses rinsed and placed in the dishwasher, while softly singing to himself. The remaining snacks were either tossed away or the bags resealed with clips and placed in the cupboards. He took a damp paper towel and started wiping off the table and counter tops.

Brenda woke up and, when her head stopped spinning, heard who she figured was David singing in the kitchen. She didn't remember dozing off but, obviously, she must have. There was some truth to the story she told Toni when they were ready to leave. She did feel like she might throw up. David's comfortable couch looked like a better option then. That quick nap did the job, she thought. After standing and stretching, she felt much better. Maybe Davey would take her home now, she was thinking as she picked up the blanket covering her off the floor, or—

The other reason for her "nap" returned, and with it, her plan.

While washing and drying his hands, David decided it was time to check on his sleeping guest. He tossed away the paper towel and headed for the living room.

When he stepped into the room, he was stunned by—

It had only taken her a moment of vacillation before she decided to follow through with her plans.

There in front of him was another reason why he believed there were threads of his soul and spirit that were eternally interwoven with the soul and spirit of the amazing creature he was gazing upon. There in front of him stood a woman most men would have crawled up to and begged her to allow them to love her. There in front of him stood a woman who was more than she appeared, and she appeared amazing. There in front of David stood Brenda. She stood in the center of the room with one finger in her mouth and holding in front of her the small blanket Toni covered her with in her fist. It was all that covered her. He looked at the couch where her clothes were neatly folded then back at her.

David knew his mouth was hanging open, and it took two tries before he remembered how to close it. His eyes then traced the angelic figurine from her beautiful face, with her long red hair down over her shoulders, down her body. The sports blanket failed to cover enough to satisfy modesty, leaving both her shapely breast almost completely exposed as only her fist between them holding the blanket provided coverage. Her body, like a corona, outlined the lucky black and gold striped blanket that hung down from her fist, providing coverage down to her thighs.

The look in his eyes was what she had wanted to see, what she had dreamed about, and the reason for her brash display. His reaction erased all her doubts—almost.

"Amazing," was all he could think to say, but nothing came out. She looked breathtaking, standing there as the blanket in her hand both revealed and hid just enough to steal his breath. He had purposely avoided those enhancing green eyes when he took in the vision in front of him because what he wanted, craved, the moment he walked in and saw her, was so obvious he felt embarrassed and tried hiding it from her. When he finally surrendered to the urge, she surprised him when her eyes revealed her need was the same. David walked up to Brenda, never taking his eyes from them now.

"Bren," was all he was able to say because, when he took a step forward, she dropped the blanket at her feet, silencing him. He looked in those green pools, wondering if she knew how grateful he was for this magic moment. He took the moment she gave him to feast on the beauty standing there.

The woman's body, as he already knew and the slow inspection his eyes took confirmed, was flawless. He walked over and picked her up in his arms. He followed their direction and carried her to his bed.

In the past, they made love with power and confidence. Both were physically gifted and built for the long haul. They had practiced different positions and explored areas most have shunned. Both were experienced and more than understood how to give of themselves until the object of their affection was completely satisfied. Racing toward a common goal, both sensed the other was more than capable of giving them, numerous times, everything their soul and body desired and, in the past, often leaving the bed in wild disarray with pillows missing and sheets tangled as evidence of the physical struggle that had just occurred.

This time, as he gently placed her on his bed, their eyes asked for something new, a gentle reaching of the same goals. This time mouths and hands, that, in the past, roughly raced over their bodies, searching out every pleasure, cautiously touched as if crossing uncertain territory. David spent time between her legs letting her know—yes, he wanted her—but she was all that mattered. After convincing her of that three or four times, she reciprocated. Stopping just before he couldn't. Then long, slow, and deep, echoed in their minds as they rode together giving them time to smell the roses.

This time it wasn't just to appease their craving, but their caring spirits. At the finish, it didn't leave them soaked in each other's sweat and gasping for breath as in past forays. She didn't bite down on his shoulder or dig her nails into his back, as she often did to stifle another scream as he slammed into her. Neither did he roughly grasp her taunt ass cheeks in his powerful hands and toss her about as his face took on another grotesque mask when the power of the moment raced from his toes and out his mouth like exorcising a demon. They reached it together but without the climactic violence. This time, afterward, she softly cried and he, trying to resist the emotion bubbling up in him, silently joined her.

Somehow, they sensed it would be the last time they made

love to each other. There were no post-copulation promises made to restrain themselves the next time as there always were after they recovered from the bliss and realized nothing had changed between them. No pulling up the sheets to cover themselves after the insanity was over and their modesty returned. In fact, no words were spoken as they cuddled up, minus any covering, and fell asleep in each other's arms.

That subject remained the elephant in the room after the morning sun welcomed them into a new day. Now they shared the same reality—that it would be the last time they would cross that line, unless...

Maybe they each considered that but felt forbidden to ask if the special tenderness and emotions they shared this time was their souls finally releasing the threads that bound them together, freeing them to go out and find their real soulmate.

That night at home, Brenda acknowledged her copulation in the past with David produced toe curling effects, but it was always just physical. She loved the way he would possess her body as if he had the right to do whatever he wanted to her. Yet he always waited until she was fulfilled before seeking his own pleasure. Others had taken her there, maybe not as quickly, or as completely, or as deeply, but she wasn't alien to pleasure. Other men had made her scream before, but none had made her cry. What happened during and after that last night together was alien to her. Long after the physical effects wore off, the memory of the tenderness they found continued. The woman he awakened made a decision she wouldn't or couldn't settle for less, any more, from anyone.

After that memorable evening together with David, Brenda started turning other guys down for reasons she knew were bogus, who were just trying to get a date with her. A few were great guys she had led on until they finally thought she was willing to go out with them. The real reason she turned down their friendly advances was that David had touched something new in her that no one else ever had.

What scared her was how easy it would be to surrender to those powerful feelings she felt for him and become his other half. That realization prompted a renewed effort to get back into the dating scene. She had often vowed to Toni and Katie, when they were together usually making their famous screwdrivers and talking about men, not to ever become someone's other half.

They had talked it out after that first night they were intimate together, as Brenda lay in David's arms, to declare a shaky truce until they were sure about what they felt for each other. Each acknowledged they weren't ready to make a commitment in their lives and yet conceded the powerful effect the other held over them as a threat to that life style. They had agreed to let their friendship grow unrestrained but put the kibosh on their physical relationship. They only broke their truce on a few occasions.

But the powerful emotional ties that bound them to each other they both tried to ignore by labeling it as just needing to scratch an occasional sexual itch, thus ignoring the truth. It was that emotion she had held in check that caused her to cry over "just a close friend" while driving home on the Parkway West.

CHAPTER 13

Dancing Rachael ended up being fun to talk with, David realized, much to his surprise, as she humorously told him the story of her life. She was able to add some things that would normally be risqué by giving it a funny twist. Something about explaining it that way made her stories more interesting, David thought.

When they first sat down in the kitchen, Racheal made him smile when she made something unmistakably clear.

"Look, David, I find you cute and sexy, but it isn't going to happen tonight."

"What isn't going...oh, okay."

"Yes, okay. Look, it ain't 'cause I don't want to. You're a nice guy, but it's that time a month, ya know. So there is no way you are going to get in my pants—tonight."

David paused, looked at Racheal, and feigned disappointment, letting the not tonight comment float away. What he was going to explain to her, before she volunteered her reason, was that it wasn't in his plans for tonight either. That was before she graphically explained her monthly reason.

They both laughed at what Racheal called nature's 'bad' timing. She laughed, with a drop of remorse mingled in because the more he opened up to her, the more she liked him. His laughter was infectious, and he was damn good looking to boot. He had a nice body and white teeth. She had a thing for guys with white teeth.

The more they chatted, the more David found Dancing Racheal fun to be with. He knew she would have been very difficult to deny tonight, if they had started to get amorous, with her bedroom eyes, gentle mannerisms, and her sweet dimples—an alluring bait.

David opened his car door and held it as Racheal got in and thanked him. He closed her door and, as he walked around the front of the car, looked up the street at the traffic stopped at the light a block away. He wasn't sure, but it looked like Brenda's car that drove past as they came out. Probably not, he decided. David looked up at his apartment and noticed it was still dark. They had evaded detection when they snuck out. As he got in and started up the car, he was thinking of how surprising it was the way the evening had ended. He chuckled a little when he pictured the look that would be on Mike's face when he discovered they had left him alone in his apartment with that she-cat.

"Shall we see what the two love birds are doing," David had suggested after they finished two beers in the kitchen. But when he held the door open, they walked into an empty living room.

"Let me guess," Rachael said, nudging David, "your bedroom is being occupied by two semi-naked and sweating individuals."

"Wrong on both counts," David whispered. "Mike wouldn't have the nerve to be in my bed, sweating or anything else. This is a two-bedroom apartment, and he knows the other bedroom is his whenever he wants. And two," he said, winking at her, "they are probably completely naked and sweating."

Rachael put her hand to her mouth and smothered a laugh.

For a moment, just a moment, the way Racheal looked at him, David thought about kissing her. But another devilish thought consumed him. He put his finger to his lips and motioned for her to be quiet and to follow him. He tiptoed down the dark hallway toward the bedrooms. As he expected, his bedroom door was wide open, and everything looked as he had left it. The next room was the bathroom, and it also was unoccupied. As they approached the last door in the hallway, the breathless sounds of passion trickled into the hallway. That was a needed buffer from the occasional creaking sounds the floor made as they approached the last bedroom door. David slowly leaned forward and looked in the crack of the partially opened door. After a minute he then backed away and motioned for Rachael to quietly take his place.

He wasn't surprised that the door was ajar. He knew Mike hated to sleep in a closed, dark room. It had something to do with being punished as a small child by his parents when he did something wrong, Mike had confided to him. Those childhood fears followed him into adulthood. Whenever David told him to confront them, he just claimed he liked the night-lite on so he could see his women. David never bothered to ask him why his bedroom night-lite was on and his door cracked open when he slept alone?

David pulled a reluctant Rachael away from the door.

"They're doing it with the lights on, how kinky," she whispered. The gleam in her eye wasn't from embarrassment, David noticed, she was enjoying being a peeping tom-acina.

"Yes, I know. He likes it that way," he whispered in the ear of the snickering woman.

"I've never seen anyone actually doing it before," she said under her breath. "Well, in the back seat of a car, but not in a bed with the lights on." When he gave her an inquisitive stare, she shook her head at him. "Don't get me wrong," a smirk forming on her face, "I'm not a pervert or anything, but it is a kind of rush to see them going at each other."

They leaned against the wall for a minute and listened.

"Damn!" Rachael said, fighting the urge to ask could she look again.

"Shhhh," he said in her ear. "What's wrong?"

"Mother Nature sure has lousy timing," she answered with a resolute look on her face as she squeezed his hand. She thought about offering him and alterative but decided she didn't know him well enough.

It only took David a moment to realize the intensity of the sounds that were now escaping the confines of the room had provoked her outburst.

"That's the truth," he lied. David had to tug on the reluctant woman before leading her down the dark hall and away from the exhibitionist. Looking up at the ceiling, he whispered a very sincere, "Thank you."

დიდ

Brenda stood outside their door trying to get herself together before entering and having Toni give her the third degree about her flushed face and probably red eyes.

Three deep breaths later, she opened the door.

"Toni, I'm home." Nothing. No music playing. She must be out. Brenda hung up her jacket and walked into the kitchen. A quick look at the bulletin board hanging in the kitchen explained everything. That was where they left messages for each other.

Brenda, off the next two days, spending it at home with Dad. Love you.

Good, Brenda thought, she needed to get out more.

As mad as Brenda was at David for his indiscretions, her concern for Toni's happiness drowned out those bitter thoughts, and she reviewed her plans to reunite Mike and Toni. "The only important thing is doing what's best for her," she said to the silence as she walked up the steps to her bedroom to shower and change. Brenda stopped and stared at the phone on the end table near her bed. David was a big part of her plan, but she was still angry with him. She walked over and sat on her bed. Gritting her teeth, she dialed his number. What am I going to say to him, she wondered as his phone rang? She knew what she wanted to say.

"This is the residence of David Jackson, I'm not home now. Please leave a message."

"David," Brenda spoke into the same answering machine she talked him into buying, "this is Brenda. Toni is visiting her dad and I'm alone tonight, would you mind coming over? I have something very important I would like to discuss with you about her. Call me back if you can't make it over." She hung up and had to close her eyes until she calmed down. She held back the tears until she was in the shower.

Something about a hot shower and getting clean does lift the spirit, Brenda confessed as she finished blow drying her hair. She debated putting it up in a ponytail, but questioned if it was completely dry so she just brushed it out and let it fall down over her shoulders. There was a visitor coming over maybe, that she knew loved it that way but that wasn't why, she lied to those accusing voices.

The next debate should have been what to wear if her company does come over. Wearing just her robe, Brenda walked over and sat on her bed. She looked around her quiet room as if hoping for some kind of inspiration. Brenda was accustomed to men

swooning over her since puberty. She knew she was a great looking woman. She wasn't living in a cave without mirrors. She had
accepted the gifts men offered for a chance to win her heart. They
came in every type, age, race, and financial standing. But it took
one that only wanted to be close friends with her that broke
through her façade and saw the little girl hiding behind the sensual woman, that none of the other men in her life had discovered.
Getting in her shapely pants being the only picture they saw.

Sex with David had been the best, and from his reaction,
damn great for him. She loved the way he sought out every inch
of her and physically possessed her without her worrying about
him finishing too quickly. He was a long-distance runner, Brenda
recalled as she lay back on the bed and allowed her robe to fall
open. The last time they were together gave weight to that prem-
ise. She closed her eyes, and as that picture colored her thoughts,
allowed her fingers to… She quickly jumped up after her hand
slid over her stomach and touched the hair between her legs. "Oh
yes, what to wear?"

"What to wear," Brenda questioned again as she tossed her
robe onto the bed and walked over to her closet. "Comfort or seduction," she said as she continued talking to herself. Getting
David in bed was easy, she admitted, he was a man who found
her very desirable, but that wasn't the problem. She knew any
woman standing in front of a healthy man in next to nothing
would garner the same response. What to wear to cause him to
surrender his heart to her, that's what she was looking for in her
closet. None of her designer clothes made that promise.

What she felt for him tonight was clothed in hurt and that
pained her deeply. The amazing relationship she now demanded
of life was probably driving in her direction as she stood there
naked trying to decide. Brenda was given a vision of what could
be, and she was persuaded that if they could just let go, there
wasn't any place their love couldn't take them.

Toni and Mike had gotten close but stumbled. It wasn't too
late for them to get up and try again, and that was why she invited
David over. If only…

She chose her yellow silk PJs. They were comfortable and
sexy she thought. The shirt fit her comfortably and was loose
enough to wear without a bra. The bottoms were shorts that

loosely hugged her bottom, and she knew David had a thing for her long legs. She rubbed perfume in a few places, picked up her robe and hung it up, then walked downstairs.

A little over an hour later, Brenda was watching TV when she heard someone driving up to the house. A quick peek confirmed it was David parking outside. She tried to remain calm. That lasted until she opened her door after he rang.

"David! What the hell is wrong with you?"

"What?"

"When are you going to learn? You can't just put your dick anywhere and not pay the price sooner or later by catching a venereal disease or worse. What's wrong with you?"

The heated and frank conversation caught him completely by surprise. He stepped into her house expecting the usual warm greeting he had come to enjoy and found an irate vixen. Her green eyes were aflame with indignation and every word tinged with anger, accusations, and a finger in his face. David was speechless as she backed him up against her door...trapped. He thought she was near tears and knew he would do anything she asked to prevent that, but he was at a loss to figure that out.

"I came by your place earlier this evening to talk to you about getting Toni and that idiot back together and saw his car parked there. When I looked up at your window, I saw the shadows of women. You said you were done with his bar whores."

"And I meant that?"

"Then why did your lights go out?"

"Lights going out, I don't know anything about lights going out. But I know nothing happed with me. I promise you, Brenda, nothing happened."

"Don't touch me," Brenda said and pushed away his hands when he tried to hold her.

It took a lot of talking to convince her nothing did happen. What was more confusing to him was why he had to defend himself in the first place. It's true they had been lovers on those random nights when they found themselves mutually horny. Nothing they had planned by any means, just the luck, great luck of the draw. Neither had he ever suggested taking their relationship beyond being close friends and occasional lovers. Yet, there was Brenda lambasting him for sleeping with one of Mike's drunken whores and screaming about all the possible STD's he could catch from them and how she's afraid now to touch him.

Finally, relieved that he was telling her the truth, her disposition changed. Brenda was again the soft talking, usually always cheerful, happy-go-lucky woman he had come to know and love. The quick change in her mood had further bewildered him. It was the first time he could ever recall seeing such strong opinions and emotions from live-for-the-moment Brenda.

When he sat down on her couch, Brenda realized she was still emotionally charged. She was no longer angry, but she felt the growing need to release some of her pent-up energy. Like every woman, she knew how easily she could remedy that problem with the unsuspecting, but more than willing, handsome remedy-reliever sitting across from her.

"David, would you like a cold beer? I know I sure could use one." She asked breaking her train of thought that would only lead to the bedroom upstairs. There was only so much relief gained from squeezing the couch pillow in her lap.

"Yes, I would honey, thank you."

"Come with me and we can chat in the kitchen, or maybe down in the family room would be better."

Have the rules changed? he wondered, as he followed the leggy lass as she pranced off barefoot. He came over to discuss something she claimed was very important. Could that have something to do with their sex life? Staring at her in that bedroom outfit, as they descended the stairs, he shook his head hopping so. They had talked before about how to reunite Mike and Toni, and after hearing her message on his answering machine when he returned home from dropping off Rachael and noticed Mike and his date were gone, he thought maybe she had found a way. David debated just calling Brenda when he arrived home and heard her message, but with Mike gone, he decided that to see her tonight might be fun.

But Brenda's angry reaction when she opened her door had caught him off-guard and put a different spin on everything. He should be asking her why she was so upset, he thought as he headed for the couch in the family room. David put his questions on hold as she sat down beside him and a hint of her perfume drifted over caressing his thoughts.

He had to stubbornly admit that another reason why he remained silent was she looked too damn good to argue with.

"I'm thinking all we need is to get them together…"

David noticed her haunting green eyes sparkled with joy now that he had "come to his senses" as she put it. Her flawless skin now was flushed with excitement over her plan as she talked. The gold pajama top she was wearing, and that occasionally outlined the shape of her breasts, totally distracted him when her nipples would harden. She was wearing matching loose shorts that alone could spark a man's imagination. He wasn't sure why she was ready for bed so early in the evening. Is there something she's hinting at, or was she just being comfortable? David took a deep breath. He speculated on it but didn't pursue that ego-generated wish any farther.

"You never know, Davey, what might happen when they see each other."

What Brenda doesn't realize, David thought, distracted by the woman explaining her ideas, *is her vibrant personality is all the spark a man would need to fall in love with her, in or out of those pajamas*. The frown that greeted him when he arrived had given way to a cheerful smile and body movements that were at times, suggestive. He had seen that gleam in her eyes before. At least, he hoped it was the same glimmer.

"I'm not crazy about Mike, but if she loves him then I should be all for it, right?"

He nodded in the places he was supposed to and hoped Brenda hadn't noticed he was more watching than listening. Not that he wasn't interested. Getting Toni and Mike back together was also on the top of his list. It was just the beautiful woman across from him at times took his breath away. Any man that would hesitate to try and win her heart, he had to admit, was an idiot. Right idiot?

Brenda waited until David finished taking a swig of the cold beer before she started explaining the rest of her plan. "I was thinking some place like the mall. We pretend to just bump into each other and see what happens."

Brenda was very pleased by the excitement she saw in his eyes. *David wants it to*, she mistakenly gleaned from the aroused look on his face, *Mike and Toni back together again*.

"Okay, let's give it a try 'B,' but something not too obvious. We have to be very cautious and really make it seem like it was an accidental meeting. I know Mike, he would smell a rat and run away. Remember our first meeting in the park."

"I know, Davey, but from talking with Toni, I'm convinced she still loves Mike," Brenda explained. "I don't know why but…"

"The why isn't important," David said cutting her off before she could say anything negative about Mike. "The fact we both agree it would be good for Toni is all that matters."

"You know we are risking our friendships?"

"Yes. This could all blow up in our faces."

"I know, David, and I'm very worried about that. But I think they were meant to be together."

"I'm not sure about that, but they both are still in love with each other. I still can't figure out why that went sour."

"I blame…"

"Don't go there, Bren, we don't know what happened between them. Let's stay out of it and let them find their own way. That's how I approach life."

She looked longingly at him before looking down and nodding in agreement. She knew what would be good for her, she thought hiding her face from him. This was new to Brenda. It was usually the guys that were dealing with the desire for her. Brenda could feel herself sliding into that emotional trap of needing him again. It was in the hot flash she was feeling on her skin and the cold longing in her heart.

"Okay," David looked in those soft eyes and said. "I will find a way to get him to go wherever we decide," David explained as he stood up and paced around the room. Every inch of the woman sitting across from him becoming a big distraction, and those damn pajamas shorts riding up her legs didn't help. "I've got to get him to stop drinking first," David looked at her and clarified. "Give me a little time, Brenda. He needs to have a clear head. I think he is finally ready to move on.

"Sure, that's no problem."

"So, let's say on the first of each month, we review where we stand with them. When the stars align, we'll kind of bump into each other at one of the shopping malls or a park or someplace."

"Getting Toni to go shopping will be the easiest. I just hope we can make it work, Davey, timing is everything."

"That we can do," David said and returned to his spot on the couch this time a little closer to her. "If there is something there it will come out. If not...well we have to let them move on with their lives, agreed?"

Brenda reluctantly nodded.

In the comfortable silence of the family room they traded looks. Each wondering if the other realized that the person across from them was quickly becoming the only thing on their mind and not so much the welfare of their closest friends.

Better get going, David was thinking as Brenda looked at him with those soft eyes of hers. "It's a date then," he said and stood up.

"Yes," Brenda answered standing with him and innocently adjusting her clothes.

"Good." David watched and held his breath before he took a step toward her and they hugged. Not intimately close like they normally would, but with space between. He kissed her on the top of her head and then started walking toward the steps.

"Davey," was all she could force herself to say. Every step separating them sent a chill.

He stopped walking but didn't turn around. "Yeah," was all he could bring himself to answer as he lowered his head.

"I...nothing, I just hope it works," she lied. His reluctance to turn around signaling to her his struggle was the same as hers. Even from behind, his powerful body was imposing. Tell him *'I love you,'* her heart said to her mouth. *'No don't,'* her pride answered vetoing those explosive words. *Only on your terms, remember, only on your terms or it won't work. Do you want his body or his heart?*

"Me too," David answered, holding on to a tenuous tread of restraint. Knowing one more look into those emerald eyes would rip that thread from his grasp, he started walking toward the stairs. The urge to flee before he made a fool of himself was strong, but not as strong as his need to show her respect. He stopped, turned, and indicated he was waiting for her to lead the way up the stairs.

Brenda was battling to keep the truth between her lips and

was slow to read his gesture. When she finally did, she hurried over and slipped passed him. She turned, smiled, and made the way her hips moved walking up her stairs a clear message.

Watching her ascend, David almost regretted acting chivalrously, almost. Inhaling the fresh scent of the woman lit his match and the lithe figure climbing the steps, she was the fuse. All that was needed to ignite his stick of dynamite was to touch the fuse.

"Good night, Bren," David said as he leaned forward and kissed her cheek.

"Good night, Davey." Brenda closed and locked her door after he left. That was followed by gently pounding her head against that door. *So close*, the pounding in her chest indicated to her, *girl, that was so close*.

Brenda punched her pillow a couple of times in bed that night and then turned over onto her back. She laid spread eagle on top of her bed. Her goal of getting to sleep early for the long double shift she had to pull tomorrow was blindsided by David's visit.

Brenda turned over and buried her face in her pillow as visions of her last visitor started touching places she struggled to resist when he was sitting beside her. "He is so damn handsome, so damn sexy," she told her pillow.

They had spent times alone together just chatting about life without mentally raping each other—times when laughter and fun was their goal, and times when they opened up to each other about the secret things we all keep hidden without judgment. But like the "Sand in the Hour Glass," when each word between them started to fill their intimacy glass, they flipped it over enabling them to start afresh.

They had made tearful vows to each other and Brenda didn't want to be the first to break them again. She knew she could get him to. He was just a man, and what a man, she thought snickering. One or two loose buttons would have done the job. Davey was so adroit at reading her intentions. That was one of the things that touched a nerve when he was around her. He was so quick to pick up on things she never had to be vulgar, not that she was above that. But it's nice to know a man that was somewhat attuned to her in and out of bed.

Brenda knew they both lived on the edge of passion. A touch here, a smile there, and they could find themselves naked and

sweaty in a heartbeat. Both struggled, unknowingly unsuccessful-
ly, to hide that fact from the other. Only their mutual respect for
the other person cooled the coals and allowed them to be close,
but in some control.

He was gone, and yet still here, Brenda acknowledged as she
took a few deep breaths and then tried thinking about work tomorrow. That worked for only a few minutes. The silky, cool
touch of her PJs on her skin did little to dissuade the mood. Brenda squeezed her legs together in a final desperate act. David Gary
Jackson was again the lead actor in the sensual movie playing on
her pillow. Brenda knew how to stop it but, try as she might, she
couldn't stir up the strength to pull the plug.

"Oh, Davey, what I would give to have you love me as much
as I love you," she said in the darkened room. "I wish I was blind
and stupid, but I'm not. I know you love me, but I can sense that
something in you that you won't let go. I can't be satisfied with
most of you, with most of any man anymore. With me, my sweet
lover, it's now all or nothing. The day I see that in your eyes, you
are in for the most fantastic ride of your life. If not you, then
whoever the lucky guy is who finally reads me like a book."

Brenda climbed under the covers and stared up at the ceiling
until she drifted off into a troubled sleep.

David was in a like position, thinking about the same thing.
To him, he was between the proverbial rock and a hard place.
What he shared with Brenda and Toni he felt was special. He
deeply loved them both, that wasn't the problem. Why couldn't
he make up his mind about what he really wanted from either of
them? That was the problem.

"I love you, Brenda. I love everything about you from the
funny way your nose wrinkles when you laugh to how you take
my breath away in...anything. Why can't I fall in love with you?
Why can't I fall in love with any woman? Why can't I..."

CHAPTER 14

The diminishing sound of an approaching car signaled it was slowing down to park, so Mike got up off the couch and looked out his bedroom window again. It wasn't him. The latest arrival was a blue Buick Regal belonging to, if he remembered correctly, that muscular rookie cop living in the apartment building next to his. Watching him workout in the grass beneath his patio convinced Mike he wouldn't want to be the one to piss off that cop. His neck was as big as his thigh, Mike guessed.

The previous car he heard pull up was that of the pretty girl in the apartment next door to him. Mike took a deep breath and looked up the road. No cars were in sight. That's okay, he thought not sure if he wanted to go anyway.

It was going to be a very sunny day from what little he could remember of last night's news. The early afternoon sun gave promise of everything the weather reporter on channel four had predicted. A warm breeze blew past him as he looked out the window for David's car. The smell of newly cut grass, and a sweet downwind whiff of old Mr. Taylor's peach orchard trees on the hill across the street, mixed with the soft summer air to trigger Mike's urge to get out in the sunlight. This was one of those days you dream about he thought, with plenty of sunshine tinged with a cool breeze to keep you dry.

Another urge made its presence felt as he thought about where they were going. Maybe this isn't a good idea, Mike pondered after stepping back from the window. When David gets here he will have to explain to him how he felt about going back to that place. No, can't do that either, got to face it sooner or later he scolded himself. That's what the booze was doing to him he recalled, making him run from his problems. "The new Mike doesn't run, he faces whatever—"

The blast of a car horn signaled an end to his effort to strengthen his resolve. Mike gathered up his keys, locked the door, and walked down the steps from his second floor apartment. David was sitting in his canary yellow Mustang GT singing along with an old Temptation's song on the radio when he walked up to his car.

"Hi, David," Mike said, checking out the car for a blind date David might have sprung on him. Seeing no one else in the car was both satisfying and a little disappointing. *Good*, he tried convincing himself, *we can just hang out at the park.*

Mike had avoided going out to Kennywood Park all of last summer. He reluctantly acknowledged it was because of his break-up with Toni more than anything. Every time David had suggested they run out to the park and check it out, Mike had declined using a variety of lame excuses. He was embarrassed he had to stoop to lying to his closest friend, especially since David didn't buy any of his excuses anyway.

"I thought you were going to ask that girl, what's her name, oh yeah, Cathy, to come along and maybe bring a friend?"

"I did, Mike," David said as he turned around to back out of the parking space, "but she said she had to work today."

"On a Saturday, I thought most banks were closed on Saturday."

David looked over at his friend wondering if Mike really cared that he had struck out with Cathy. "She works downtown in the main office. They work on the weekends sometimes she told me. You would have liked her girlfriend. I met her once. She's a very cute blonde girl with an ample amount of your favorite female quality."

Mike nodded and said nothing else. He felt a little relief in not having to converse with a person he just met anyway. On the other hand, he sadly realized, that would have guaranteed having someone to walk around the park and ride with.

"I'm going to take the Parkway route to avoid the traffic on Carson Street."

Mike just nodded.

Is this a good idea returning to the park, David found himself questioning as Mike seemed distant? He didn't want to put any pressure on him, not now anyway, not since Mike finally got his head together and stopped drinking. I'll just have to play it by ear, David decided. If Mike has a problem once we get there, we'll leave and go see a movie or something.

They were singing along with David's favorite song when he drove right past their exit. They took the next exit, Wilkinsburg, and turned left on to Swissvale Avenue. When they reached the Rankin Bridge the nearness of the park awakened sleeping anxieties that Mike harbored about the place. He wasn't even sure why it bothered him to go there. It engendered nothing but pleasant memories. Those memories, however, were centered on Toni.

There was nothing in their relationship that should have caused Mike to feel anxious about returning to the park. Even his break-up with Toni was accomplished without nasty words or belittling. If it was possible to have a painlessly worded separation of two people who still loved each other, Mike believed, then theirs qualified. Two people who loved each other going their separate ways? That made a lot of sense. That thought lingered a while on his mind.

The old mill town of Braddock passed below the bridge as they crossed. A classic steel town built up as the mills in that town flourished. However, as those steel mills closed and moved to the Midwest, the tax base declined, and the population departed. Once there were numerous businesses flourishing on Braddock Avenue as well as many illicit ones. There were bars for the huge steel mill work force on every block. Some blocks had three or more. Night life in Braddock was notorious in the area for its wild bars and strip clubs. Once the mills moved out, it didn't take long for the legitimate businesses to close. With a declining income base, the town couldn't maintain the remaining buildings. What was once a thriving, but outlaw, town now bore the vicious scars of poverty.

The physical plight of the town distracted Mike for a moment until he looked up and spotted the highest peak of the Steel Phantom, Kennywood Park's best roller coaster ride, perched in the distance above the tree line. It looked like a great wooden serpent lying in wait for them. The feeling of dread returned.

David read Mike's pensive mood. "It's been a while since we were here last, huh?"

"Yes, it has," Mike answered. "I don't know why it bothers me so much, but I'm leery about being here."

"Well, after what happened between you and Toni I can understand why. For a long time, I didn't think you would ever get over her, but I think you may have. Sometimes things just don't work out. No one knows why. They just don't work out."

Mike didn't answer him. He had spent most of the night thinking about nothing else but Toni DiNardo. The sound of her laughter was a phantom that drifted in and out of his thoughts, tormenting him with her sweet memory. Mike thought long into the night about how deeply he still loved her and the remorse he felt over having to break it off. Never in his life, Mike acknowledged between the tears that ran down his face last night, had he ever felt so strongly about a woman.

It was a huge mistake cutting her out of his life, he reasoned as they approached Kennywood Park. He knew that now and thought maybe he should have given Toni the choice. Maybe she would have stayed with him when she found out the truth.

Mike envisioned a dozen episodes where he had told Toni. In all but one, she was forgiving but heartbroken over Mike's dilemma. It only took one bad episode, however, to chill him to the bone. A hysterical Toni screamed insults and striking him repeatedly with her fist. The depth of her anger shocked him. It took Mike a moment to shake himself free from that imaginary picture. She has reason to be angry with him, he grudgingly admitted, but he only did what he thought was right for the both of them.

Guilt had become Mike's constant companion. It had accumulated enough evidence to accuse Mike, in the *Court-of-Conscience*, of numerous love crimes. Revealing the truth was never the goal of guilt, accusations were. On that hypothesis…guilt attacked him.

"Some of his crimes were committed out of ignorance," the voices of guilt grudgingly conceded to the Court. "Others were foolish acts done without thinking. Then there were the times he knew what he was doing," guilt berated Mike's risking everything to obtain momentary pleasures."

"Yes," Mike admitted, "that was true."

"Then there are the women in your life," guilt said, remembering each one of them by name, or face, or distinguishable body parts. "You can't condone your actions? Their caring for you didn't come from a bottle. It was real."

Mike sighed so deeply David looked over and asked if he was all right. Nothing pained Mike more than his unbelievably careless conduct toward some of the women he had met. He should have known better he conceded. Guilty as charged, he pleaded to the court.

Mike looked out the window at the decaying industrial buildings dotting the river. He tried imaging what was produced there before the buildings became rusted monuments to the past, but he was quickly sidetracked again by his guilt. It was the alcohol, he entreated the painful memories. He never acted that way unless he was drinking. That small truth did little to sway the power of his guilty conscience.

Mike looked over at David and only then realized he was talking to him.

"I want to see that movie about the space soldier and their..."

He listened to David long enough to understand it had something to with a movie he wanted to see.

The man driving was the one who helped him come to grips with the fact he was only hurting himself, Mike thought as he looked at David. *God sent him into my life when I needed a friend the most.*

"I might ask that new girl in the office to go with me..."

Short flashbacks of his drinking binges and the surrogate women he had staggered after were sharp and very painful reminders. But thanks to David's constant nagging, Mike thought smiling over at him, he had stopped drinking long enough to see the sorry shape he was in. David was wrong about one thing, Mike thought as they turned into the amusement park parking lot. He hadn't gotten over Toni. He just came to grips with the decision he made, but he would never get over her.

"This is a new beginning."

Mike said nothing, but he agreed with him. Looking around at all the people flowing down the parking lots toward the expected fun of the amusement park, Mike decided it was time to make new memories.

David locked his car and was surprised to see Mike already walking toward the park. He watched him for a moment wondering if he was anxious to meet new people or just trying to erase the past. Today will be interesting to say the least, he figured as he ran to catch up with his buddy.

The drive home was as care free as the trip there was stomach turning.

"Now that was fun."

"You got that right, Davey. But you do realize, no, I quest that goes without saying."

"What goes without saying, Mike? Wait a minute, tell me my good friend, you're not talking about the beauty that you bored so much she ran away. Tell me you don't hold any pipe dreams that she wanted you over me."

"Davey, my boy, you are my best friend, so I don't want to rub your nose it, but she wanted me."

"I agree she wanted you. She wanted you to get lost so she could get her daily supply of sweet chocolate. Mike, I realize you've been out of the flow of beautiful women for a while, but the finger she was giving you didn't mean you were number one."

"But I am, cocoa puffs. She was trying to get through that dense head of yours that I was the one she wanted, the one she really wanted oh Stevie Wonder."

"Are you sure Pewee Herman, I thought she was guessing the size of something else with her little finger."

"Oh, you didn't go there," Mike said laughing. "As the many women who prefer filet to T-bone will tell you, it's not the size of the ship but the motion of the ocean."

The insults poured from them all the way home.

Nothing meaningful had occurred in the park. But they quickly realized the ghosts of the past were absent as they toured. None of the young women they met offered anything more than good conversation and eye candy. It was the one young lady that they met in the arcade that was the source of their conversation. She couldn't decide which of them should spend all their money on her for the pleasure of watching her use them.

She dropped them both when they ignored her and started making fun of each other.

It took a couple of minutes before they realized she was even gone.

The real value of their day at the park was they had fun, simple, clean fun. The kind of fun that required no thinking or planning. The kind of fun that you can enjoy because there are no strings attached and no need for deep commitments. Neither of them was seeking valued memories that last a lifetime, just having a good time. Like other intelligent adults, they wasted dollars trying to win weirdly shaped and colored stuffed animals that cost, and were worth, pennies. The greasy food they consumed was delicious and the drinks cold. There were a few ladies that caught their attention, but not enough to change their outlook that they were there to have fun.

Mike left the lovely young woman they teasingly battled over, and the fears of his past and future, somewhere in the crowd that wove its way through idyllic Kennywood Park.

CHAPTER 15

David studied Mike, as he finally maneuvered his car into the parking space, and shook his head but didn't say anything when Mike earlier drove up and down the rows looking for that special space. He knew from past experience it wouldn't do him any good to question his actions. There was a parking space somewhere close to the mall and Mike Buffer was going to find it. Even if finding it meant riding up and down the rows of parked cars for another twenty minutes.

"Where to first?" David asked as they finally walked into Monroeville Mall.

"Can you believe that woman tried to pull into my spot? There is no way I was giving that space up."

"Yeah, Mike. You know what?" David asked, trying to redirect the conversation. "Let's stop in that computer store for a minute. I want to check out the latest software."

"That woman was crazy," Mike continued mumbling as he followed David into the crowded computer store.

They headed for the section with flight simulators. Both had become addicted to fighting each other on computers. All they had to do was link up, and soon they were up in the air opposing each other in jet fighters. With their computers hooked up by cable, they could oppose each other in a variety of formats. They could even communicate to each other while they were trying to shoot the other out of the sky.

"They have it," Mike said as he pointed to box labeled X-25 Future Fighter.

"Yes! Let's get it. You bought the last set, these two are on me."

"You got it, dude." They spent the next hour reading the covers of most of the latest arrivals in the "New Software" section of the store. There weren't any top war games they didn't already possess. Their collection included the most modern of jet fighters to the old, rickety, World War I bi-planes. Mike, who preferred fighting on land, purchased all the tank and submarine warfare software. David was the quasi fighter pilot. The purchase of X-25 would complete his inventory of every computer fighter game produced worth having. There were some, he would be quick to admit, that he didn't like and had wished he had never purchased. But inwardly he was proud of his collection.

The food court was situated directly under the computer store and, with the right shift in the wind, sends tendrils of enticing aromatic suggestions floating up the escalators into the upper mall.

"Mmmm. Smell that?"

Mike had to admit it was inviting. The aroma of the food finally enticed them out of the computer store. "Come on, we can buy the games on our way out the mall." Mike had already turned and headed for the escalators when David grabbed his arm.

"Hold up. I want to get my lottery tickets before the line gets too long. Let's go this way then we can get the tickets and walk down to the food court." The sour look on Mike's face voiced his disappointment. The smell of the food was enticing enough to argue over, but Mike refrained. Sometimes the ticket line can be very long. There wasn't a line when they turned the corner, but with their poor luck, five people arrived moments before they did. Four of the five were older citizens. David realized all too well he could be there a while. Mike shook his head an opted for a bench he spotted not far from the lottery booth. David was resigned to standing between two old women with a fist full of number slips.

Like most of the older malls, Monroeville Mall had two floors with an open center and walkways that circled the mall in an oblong racetrack pattern. The lottery booth David was standing in front of was situated on one of the three entrance hallways that led to the center of the mall. It was the busiest entrance and one reason why David only saw them in the crowd for a few seconds. He was standing behind a gray haired woman that was purchasing over fifty dollars' worth of lottery tickets when he grew frustrated and looked to his right and saw Brenda and Toni walk past the entrance hallway. Only the ten-minute wait he had already endured prevented him from getting out of line and following them.

David turned in the other direction to see if Mike had seen them. Mike was gone! "Aaaw, shit!" It was after he turned around in a circle twice that he spotted him looking in the window of a camera shop.

"Give me five dollars' worth of Quick Picks on tonight's lottery."

"Pick five on tonight's lottery," the bored young woman behind the counter repeated. She looked at him and broke into a wide grin as she handed him the ticket. She was cute, but too young, he explained to Mike after he teased him that she was overly friendly with him whenever they stopped here to buy tickets. David smiled back and took the ticket out of her hand. '*She always puts the other customer's tickets down on the counter,*' he recalled Mike informing him. '*She personally hands you yours.*'

David hurried over to where Mike was standing. "Got them, let's eat."

"Now you're talking." They stepped out into the crowded main aisle on the top floor of the mall. Fifty feet across from them was another walkway on the other side of the mall. David cautiously looked around for the girls as they headed for the nearest steps or escalator down. There was no sign of them. They could be in any of the stores he realized. Was it really them he questioned? He only had a momentary glimpse. No, it was them, he decided. The profile of that red haired beauty was ingrained in his memory.

It was a strange urge that willed him to walk to the banister and look down at the people on the lower level, but there was no sign of them down there. As they rode the escalator down, he got a great view of the bottom level of the mall. There were plenty of ladies, just not the ones he was looking for. Resigned to hurrying because of Mike's grumbling about his slow pace, David gave up the search and concentrated on choosing from the many different foods the food court had to offer.

Mall food courts were a collection of fast food restaurants sprinkled in with various ethnic food purveyors. One can't help turning in circles as the doctored photographs of their wares reach out to tempt you. Hamburgers so thick and juicy you can't imagine how you're supposed to eat one of those monsters.

Shakes, moist with swollen dewdrops running down the side of the cup, beckon to the dry, parched, throat of the mall shopper.

Mike and David were just about to walk into the food court when they spotted Brenda and Toni as they were riding up an escalator.

David had hoped to spot them before Mike, but the man standing next to him with his mouth open gave evidence it was too late for that.

"Was that..."

"Yes, it was," David answered him before he could finish. "I thought I saw them earlier, but I wasn't sure. Why don't we follow them?"

"Why don't we...not?" Mike chimed in. He started to verbalize his reasons why but the needy recipient of those important words of wisdom had already turned his back to him and slithered through the crowd toward the escalators.

Not a good idea, David, Mike thought as he followed him from a distance. He could have caught up with him but decided against it. He felt safer with David between him and them. Then if David tried something stupid there would be room for him to duck out of the way.

This was fun, David thought as he reached the top of the escalator. He did the mall twist but couldn't spot the women. A quick glance back down the escalator located Mike reluctantly moving toward him. The forlorn look on his face caused David to snicker. It was obvious he wasn't enjoying the chase.

"Okay, Mike," David said as Mike stepped off the escalator, "I don't see them. They must have entered one of the stores. Most of the women's clothing shops are on our left. Let's head that way and see if we can find them."

Only a nod from Mike seconded David's suggestion. Grinning at the reluctant change in his buddy's mood, David led the way toward the women's apparel shops.

The first three stores they passed were a bust, the girls weren't there. They would stand outside of a store and peek in keeping as close a tab on the occupants as they could without suggesting other possibilities. But a couple of observant security guards thought the worst and followed the errant pair in their noble pursuit.

"What are you guys doing?" They finally closed the distance between them and inquired.

"We're looking for our girlfriends," David answered the guard. "They don't know we're here and we just want to see what they buy."

The guards looked at each other and then at David. He had a shit eating grin on his face that rang true. "Okay, guys, just don't cause any misunderstandings."

"No problem." With that said, David led a now very reluctant Mike back on the quest.

Minutes later, they spotted the girls walking into Penny's department store on the other side of the mall.

"There they are," David announced loud enough to cause people to turn and look at them.

Mike said nothing. He had spotted them walking earlier while David was looking in a store window but remained silent. Mike was having a bad feeling about this, as he followed David into the store after them.

They cornered the girls, or were actually cornered themselves, near the store's fitting rooms. While Brenda and Toni were looking at clothes, David led Mike between clothes racks and startled a few customers until they were within listening distance but hidden behind a display.

Mike started to get into the challenge of the game and surprised David when he moved past him and edged closer to where the women were standing. A stunned David watched as Mike duck-walked across the floor beneath the clothing racks until he got within a few feet of them and hid behind a table stacked with jeans. Being that close to Toni was exciting Mike realized. So exciting he decided to stand up and face her.

"You would look great in that blouse with your red hair Brenda, not me."

"Are you kidding girl. Guys couldn't resist you in this."

Guys? On second thought, Mike decided, he would stay down where he was. Dry mouthed, and realizing the stupidity of his actions, he started looking around for an escape route.

"Come on, Toni, why don't you try them on and see? With your dark hair and tan, these are a perfect color for you. I'm too fair."

David waited until they walked into the fitting room before he rushed up to where Mike was hiding. "I don't believe you."

"What?"

"You know what. At first, you were so scared, I thought you were going to pass out. Now you get within smelling distance of them. If they had turned around, they would have seen you. Or is that what you were hoping for?"

Mike thought about it for a minute. "Honestly, I don't know. For a second, I felt like we were still together, and this was some kind of game. Then the truth slapped me back to reality. I was going to stand up and introduce myself to her. Can you believe that? Then they started talking about some guy of Toni's. If I would have stood up, she would have ripped me a new you-know-what."

"I don't think so, Mike. Toni isn't dating anyone. According to…ah Brenda, she's still as much in love with you as you are with her, and maybe more so. And we both know you are still head-over-heels in love with the girl."

Mike looked from the fitting room entrance into the eyes of his friend. There was no need to answer him or to ask him what he meant by that. The pounding of his heart was witness enough about how he felt. Then the guilt returned and stabbed him in his chest.

Mike turned and walked between the racks of "Sale" blouses toward the store's main entrance. David almost called out to him. Instead, he watched him as he stepped around two ladies talking and walked out the store.

David was contemplating Mike's lost opportunity when he noticed two women staring at him. It took him a minute to understand the root of their interest. He was standing in the male forbidden zone, the women's underwear department. You pervert, their questioning eyes seemed to imply.

David sheepishly grinned at the women and inadvertently walked toward the fitting rooms. His situation deteriorated when he heard Brenda's voice. A tall rack of women's coats saved him from bumping into her as she walked out of the fitting room. David peered between the coats and watched her return some blouses to a rack and picked out some others. She was wearing a black beret on her head, a short sleeve thin white sweater, and a thread worn jean mini-skirt with white knee high stockings in almost knee high black boots. She looked amazing he thought, as he studied the very attractive woman.

David stopped staring when he had a devilish thought. He detoured around the clothes racks until he was directly behind her. "Hey, good looking," he said, hiding behind a clothes rack, "what's your sign? It's a wonder you didn't break something when you fell from Heaven." It took all his strength to hold back from laughing.

Brenda was at first startled by the voice behind her. The pick-up-lines was so nerdy she knew whoever said them couldn't be serious, and then there was that voice. "David! Where are you?" Caught off-guard, she whispered the last words as she turned around. Brenda almost laughed out loud when he stepped out from behind a coat rack.

"Hi, Red. How did you know it was me?"

"With that pathetic come-on I asked myself, with as good as I look today in this outfit and boots," she said with her hands on her hips, "who would be so desperate as to use that old line to get next to these great looking legs? There was only one man I knew that desperate." She then stuck her tongue out at him and made a funny face.

What could he say to that? He just shook his head at her because the green eyed lady really was all that and a bag of chips.

"David, what are you doing in here anyway? I thought we were going to meet later in the food court. I know, I know. You're here taking advantage of the sale on women's lace underpants? You can buy them, you can wear them, but they will do you no good unless I'm in them."

He tried not to smile as she blew him a kiss. "Close, oh carrot top. I figured if you were shopping here, they would surely have granny panties in twice my size. The ones, ha-ha, with the months on them so, so you will know when to change them…this time."

Brenda tried ignoring his dig at her. Well, for a moment she did, and then she punched him. "Toni's back there waiting on these clothes. Are you in a hurry?"

"No, actually. I came in here with Mike." The frown on her face told him he should change the subject. He didn't. "We spotted you guys walking in the mall and followed you in here. At the last minute, he—"

She turned around to see what had stopped David in mid-word.

"Hi, Brenda."

The conflict she battled resurfaced. Brenda wanted to both curse him out and adjure him to give the relationship with Toni another chance. She had thought of many different plans to reunite them, but none seem very feasible without his help. "Hi, Mike." The silence that followed just punctuated her inner debate.

Mike was quick to pick up on it. "Are there any other women in the ladies fitting room?"

"No. We were the only ones. After standing around forever waiting on a fitting room attendant—" Brenda's frustration with that was evident on her face. "—we gave up and just picked out our own room."

"Good," Mike said as he headed for the fitting rooms.

"Hey, where are you going?" Brenda asked.

Mike didn't answer her. When he reached the entrance, he stopped for a moment, turned around and walked back to Brenda. "I'll deliver these for you," he told her as he took the blouses out of her hand and then walked into the ladies fitting room aisle on the left. A shocked Brenda turned toward David and received a shoulder shrug.

The men and women fitting rooms were two hallways that branched off in opposite directions from a single entrance. They were constructed the same way each with four small booths.

What's taking Brenda so long? Toni wondered. The booth was exceptionally cool, and she wasn't wearing her blouse. The squeaking door caused her to spin around. The person standing in front of her caused her to frown. "What took you so long?"

"I couldn't find a blue flowered one in your size," Brenda answered holding up a yellow blouse of the same design Toni said she liked.

Toni took the blouse from her and tried it on. "What do you think?"

"Not bad. What about a solid color? You know, like that silky coral one you tried on." Brenda watched Toni as she posed in front of the mirror. "Take that one off, and I'll get a couple of the solid ones."

Toni said nothing as she watched Brenda in the mirror gather up the other blouses and walk out the booth. Slowly she unbuttoned the blouse and decided she was getting tired of shopping and was looking forward to eating...something. Brenda's excitement was the spark that persuaded her to try on another blouse. *After this*, she vowed, *we're outta here*.

"I think this one would look great on you."

Toni closed her eyes for a moment to get herself together, lest her closest friend see her growing frustration and that hurt her feelings. She started faking a smile before turning around. "I hope so because I'm..."

Toni felt herself growing dizzy. Everything was wrong with what she was seeing. Standing there in front of her was, she had only recently admitted to herself, the only man she would ever love. As her head started spinning, she reasoned this must be a vision created by the strength of her sorrow. This was what happens when you allow your imagination to run berserk, she scolded herself.

Then the vision spoke. "Hi, Toni. Are you okay?" The frightened look in her eyes was more than he had counted on. Surprise, yes, and then anger, but fear, no. Mike tossed the olive colored blouse Brenda had shoved into his chest on the floor and walked slowly toward her.

Reality sometimes was a large pill and very difficult to swallow. All of her senses said that the Mike walking toward her was real, but her pain had tempered her to never again trust in those senses. Wasn't it their poor judgment that had delivered her into his arms without regard for the possibility that her fragile heart could be broken?

As she wrestled with her doubts, the image moved closer. Soft brown eyes looked down into hers. Their wet sparkle reached beyond the hurt and touched damaged feelings, gently healing them. Toni felt the pain of that healing process in her chest.

"Mike," she uttered softly.

Mike had felt the tug on his heart the moment she turned around. Her beauty impressed him more now than she did that first time he saw her. She was standing there in white jeans, an unbuttoned blouse, and her taupe bra was almost invisible next to her tanned skin. She made no effort to close her blouse but tilted her head to the side as she was wont to do when perplexed. He saw the look on her face and cringed at the thought of what could be soon spewing out of her lips.

For an instant, she looked as if nothing bad had transpired between them. Then reality arrived. When Toni took a step back, his knees almost buckled. He had obviously caught her off-guard. Brenda's intro, and her push-in-his-back, had served to completely catch Toni unawares, and he wasn't prepared for the look of fear he thought he saw in her eyes.

When he instinctively moved toward her to try and allay her anxiety, she inadvertently stepped back to clear her head of the confusion she was feeling. Then Toni watched as he moved closer and felt the soothing touch of his warm hands on the cold skin of her arms. Her response was spontaneous. She moved into his arms as if knowing the warmth that awaited her there.

Mike, overcome by her response, squeezed her tightly to his chest. Her gentle acceptance broke him down, and his emotions burst out. He cried softly on her shoulder. His muffled sobs provoked a soothing back rub from the woman crushed in his strong arms.

Brenda suddenly felt as if she was peeping in their bedroom window. She waited until Toni looked at her before she let the door slowly close. When she turned and looked down the hallway, she saw David standing guard. Her voyeurism had a purpose. She felt responsible for whatever happened between them after she intercepted a retreating Mike Buffer. A stern countenance and a finger in Mike's face changed his mind about chickening out. When Mike questioned the wisdom of her suggestion, she all but shoved him into the booth. Hearing Mike sobbing and the look that Toni gave her removed the heavy weight she felt for interfering.

Drained, Brenda had started walking down the hallway with her head down when she bumped into someone. She stepped back and was ready to apologize when she noticed it was David. The nervous watchman had decided to walk down the hall and meet her. She looked up at him with a blank expression on her face. Slowly a gleam appeared in her eyes, when she read his, and was followed by her pixie-like grin.

David looked around and noticed that no one was near the fitting rooms when he decided to enter and see what was going on with his friends. He passed the first booth when he saw Brenda walking toward him with her head down. Reading her body language, he was prepared for the worse until when she saw him and smiled. That was followed by a look he was unprepared for...but remembered. That told David all he needed to know. He took her by the hand, looked around again, and entered the nearest booth. David locked the door and slowly pulled her into his arms. Now Brenda was the one surprised.

The idea was fresh, but it took David a minute to overcome his concern that they would get into trouble for their impulsive actions entering the ladies fitting room side. When the vivacious redhead gave him that look. He didn't care if they did get caught.

Brenda let him kiss her. Cautiously at first, then passionately she returned his warm embrace as her arms slipped around his neck. It felt right to both of them.

Mike's tears washing down Toni's neck and shoulder did more to wash away her pain than all the remorseful words he could have offered. No dozen beautiful long-stemmed red roses or a gift of sparkling diamonds ear rings could have torn down so quickly the walls months of pain and regret had built. It took a Mike as contrite as she had ever seen to warm her cold heart enough to forestall her bitter accusations. It surprised her how quickly tearful nights of accumulated clear evidence of her undeserved heartache she let float away in the winds of forgiveness.

Toni pushed Mike back at arm's length. He slowly raised his head and looked at her. His face was puffy, and his eyes were red. Toni held no lofty expectations, no preconceived notions on how she should feel. As she looked at Mike, all she felt was his sorrow and a desire to ease it. Her own pain was gone. His heartfelt repentance all she needed to heal her soul.

"Michael, I love you." The words flowed easily from her heart. They weren't tinged with the bitter taste of revenge. "I have always loved you, and I know now, I always will." There was so much she wanted to tell him, but she stopped when she felt his body spasms. She began to realize that every kind word she spoke beat him with remorse, like lashes from the taskmaster's whip. The Mike that stood in front of her was an open, remorseful spirit with no means of protecting itself. She would have to wait until he forgave himself before they could face their feelings.

Toni took her pink blouse off the hook and put it on. Tucking it into her white jeans, she suggested they get out of here. Mike smiled softly and nodded. Toni took him by the hand and walked out the booth. She stopped for a minute when she heard some muffled sounds coming from the middle booth. She turned and looked at Mike. He had this wide, little boy grin on his face. When he raised his eyebrows, the truth came so quickly it surprised her. Toni put her head briefly on his chest and laughed. The urge to knock on the door and startle the occupants held sway for a moment and then departed. Toni led Mike out of the fitting rooms. As they re-entered the store, the noise of the department store music drowned out her best friend's sighs.

They walked out the Mall caught up in their own ozone. Toni only worried about Brenda for a moment until Mike reassured her David had spare keys to his car and would drive her home. "That is," he whispered in her ear, "unless the mall police decide to do so."

They laughed about that as they walked, hand-in-hand, out the mall.

As Toni drove, Mike struggled with what he was going to tell her. *The truth, you couldn't stand the truth!* he thought, remembering the much-published line from an over-rated movie. *It's decision time mister*, he thought, *you're going to have to explain it to her*.

"Shit!" Toni said. The panic in her voice ripped Mike from the daze he was in. The severe side motion of the car tossed him hard against his door. He was just able to get his arm up against the window in time to reduce the blow. He knew they were in trouble.

"Dumb ass!" he heard her screaming at the U-Haul truck now in their lane and close enough to count the dents on the bumper. "The stupid driver didn't check his mirror before changing lanes."

Swallowing the lump that rose up in his throat, he turned toward her. Her eyes were ablaze with a mixture of righteous anger and genuine relief. They had missed being hit by the errant truck by an even smaller margin than he realized.

"So I noticed," Mike whispered to the enraged woman behind the wheel.

They arrived at his apartment without further incidents. Toni had forgotten the near miss with the truck and was dreading an even more dangerous head-on collision. She was apprehensive talking about the past but knew they would have to sooner or later. The deep wound Mike had cut in her heart had healed, but there would forever be the scar. It had to be explained, or it would continually be a sad reminder of its creation and creator.

Toni's growling stomach gave both of them the excuse they craved to delay the confrontation.

"What was that?"

"I'm sorry," the embarrassed female said, blushing a little, "I haven't eaten all day, and I'm starving."

"Well, I could throw together a salad, and…and I have some steaks thawed out that David and I were going to cook after we got back." When she looked at him but said nothing, he tried plan number two. "Or we can go out and eat somewhere you would like."

"A salad and steak—sounds like an offer I can't refuse."

It wasn't what she said that built a bridge over the rough water, but more the look on her face.

"Let's go."

Making dinner granted them time to luxuriate in their reunion. To play and cavort aimlessly as if their relationship wasn't saddled with the ugly hurt and pain of the last year or so. While she whipped together a great toss salad, Mike pulled out the steaks he was thawing out to throw on the grille and pan fried them, presto, dinner. It was seasoned with loving stares and silly looks, as they mooned over each other.

The dishes were done, and the man who was now drying them made a quick decision that should never have been made so abruptly. The first time he thought about a similar decision he panicked and broke it off with Toni. He had done so spontaneously, unaware of the depth of the pain his abrupt actions would cause. He had looked down that terrible road of life, saw where it ended, and became frightened. Mike's decision that fateful night should have been to U-turn after entering that highway ramp, ignore those beeping their horns at the idiot going the wrong way, and drive away as fast as he could.

Now, after weighing his impulsive behavior and recanting, he made another decision. Again, he consulted no one, but this time he had thought it through. Long before he stumbled on his love at Monroeville Mall, he had come to a decision. Now he really felt good about it because fate—David and Brenda—had timely thrown them together the day he had come to grips with that choice.

Mike towel dried the last of the dishes Toni washed and who was now busy wiping off the table. When he finished drying the silverware, he leaned back against the sink and watched her. *This is my Rubicon,* he thought of the decision he was going to make, *my point of no return.* He was flush with love for the fair maiden toiling in his kitchen. The road ahead was clear to him. He held no vain, narcissistic images of salvation from the inevitable. "Once the die is cast," he whispered.

He daydreamed about walking over and roughly squeezing the right back pocket of the wench in the white denim jeans. The shapely owner of those jeans would abruptly turn around and swing at him with the dishtowel she was using. He'd duck, and the blue and yellow dishtowel would pass harmlessly overhead. Deftly he would grab the wrist with the deadly weapon in it and disarmed the culprit before she did any serious damage. Weaponless, she would quickly succumb to her more powerful adversary. Begging for mercy, she'd allow him to gather her up in his arms. She would gain no pleasure from this brutal act. The kiss she planted on his lips would be just to demonstrate how much she abhorred him. He would misunderstand her kiss—as she would expect him to—and the loathsome oaf would drag her into his living room and cruelly toss the wench down on his couch.

Mike stopped daydreaming when he noticed Toni was finished wiping the table, so he took the dish towel from her hand, led her by that hand into the living room, sat her down on the couch, and knelt down in front of her.

"I've got to explain to you why I acted like such an ass-hole, Toni."

"Wait, Michael. Not too long ago I wouldn't have given a

damn about your reasons. Then I would have told you and your reasons to go and fuc—ah get lost. But do you know what happened to me?" she said, pausing and looking down at his hands as they held hers. "I realized that you must have had a reason for acting like you did. Granted, I couldn't figure out what in the hell that was, but I thought you believed you had one. I know you, Michael, looking back, I knew there had to be a good reason."

Mike looked at her in guilty disbelief, swearing to never let those forgiving blue eyes out of his life again—never.

"Sweetheart, I thought I was doing the right thing when I broke up with you. I tried to do it slowly because I thought it would hurt you less if you thought I was just falling out of love with you." The intensity of her stare almost silenced the confessor. "I was trying to find a way to spare you the bad news I learned about myself. So, I lied to you. The truth is—" There were voices in his head saying *don't chance it, lie again!* "I found out—I'm sterile."

Toni leaned back in shock and disbelief. Her world became fuzzy again. She searched his face for some sign he was lying. His eyes were bright and looking directly into hers. If he was lying then he was also lying to himself, she judged, from the sincerity in his eyes.

Mike watched as the reality of his bitter words gripped her. Very little about her expression changed. She didn't make a face, frown, or let her mouth drop open. He wished she would have reacted stronger, her blank stare of possible indifference hurt far worse.

Toni felt the breath leave her chest. Problem was, it didn't return very quickly. Did he say sterile? *Oh, my God! Don't fall apart Toni, get a grip. He's expecting you to show some disappointment but don't fall apart. Oh, my God.*

"Yes, sterile," he said to the growing surprise now bursting forth on her face. "I haven't told anyone about this, not even David, and I don't want you to either."

Toni was still speechless.

Mike was so caught up in what he was going to tell her he failed to notice. "It was after your last visit to my parent's house that I found out I'm sterile. I was joking with my dad about him becoming a grandfather someday when he gave me this odd look.

I know how much he likes children, and I thought he might enjoy talking about it, but he shrugged me off. Then a week later my mom tried to hint around about not having children being more acceptable today than when she was young. It took a while, but the light finally came on in my head.

"It was the next weekend I was over the house. I think you had to work. Anyway, I finally had to ask them about it, and that's when my world came crashing down." Mike took a moment to catch his breath. Telling her about this was painful. She was the most caring and attractive woman he had ever met, and he knew this was a huge disappointment to her. Being her man had made him ecstatic and gave him unbelievable confidence and self-assurance. He delighted in listening to her dreams of having a house full of children, believing he was going to be the lucky recipient of all those attempts at wonderful procreation.

"I waited until I caught my mom alone and then tricked her into telling me. I asked her why she was keeping a secret from me. She grew so pale I thought she was going to faint. Immediately I was sorry I asked. She promised me if she could sit down she would tell me everything. Toni, I thought she was going to say I'm adopted or something like that. But you know what, now that I look back, I think I could have dealt better with that news.

"It happened when I was fifteen, my mother reluctantly explained to me. I was very sick with the flu and somehow I also contracted the mumps. I remember those scary days in the hospital even now. I was so sick, my mother thought I was going to die she later told me. I was in there for three weeks before they let me go home. I was still so weak my dad carried me into the house. It took days of my mother's home cooking to get me back to normal.

"Toni, she said the doctor told them that because I was very weak from battling the flu my body was open to infection. That was when I also contracted the mumps. It attacked my testicles, and they became swollen and infected or something. The antibiotics they were giving me worked, but very slowly. She said she didn't quite understand all of the medical terms, but one thing she and my father did understand was the doctor said I was now sterile. My testicles were damaged and had stopped functioning. It was an 'internal vasectomy,' I think they said he called it, that made me completely sterile. It shut down my body's ability to produce sperm."

Toni saw the hurt in his eyes and squeezed his hands. Sadly, she remembered how often they had discussed having at least five children. There was no need to try pretending to him that she wasn't disappointed.

"Honey, I understand how that must have affected you," she warmly admitted, "but didn't you know how much I loved you? I would have dealt with it. Having your children would have been the second greatest thing in my life."

"Toni, I knew you would be terribly disappointed in me but would tell me it was all right. You've got to understand. It wasn't just about how you would feel. You have your dreams, and I have mine. I knew it would haunt us all our lives. People constantly asking when we were going to get pregnant and relatives snickering behind our backs. You're an only child. I know your dad wants grandchildren. And…and you…you are so bright and caring, you would be the best mother." Mike watched as her eyes watered up. "No, Toni, I didn't want to put you through that. I felt it was my fault and you shouldn't have to suffer all your life because of me."

"But look on the bright side, Mike," Toni said after leaning forward and kissing him on the forehead, "I don't need to take those darn birth control pills anymore."

Mike gave her a puzzled so-what look.

"Hey, don't knock it, pal. Those darn pills used to make me sick. I hated taking those things. The last year or so my body has never felt better."

Mike faked a smile. Her admission of voluntary celibacy almost passed right over his head.

It worked, she thought about her attempt at some humor, as a small grin broke through his stone face.

He just stared at her. The story about the pills she obviously concocted to make him feel better. It didn't work. What did work was the fact that she was still in love him. For that, he forced himself to smile.

Mike forgot the apologetic words he had practiced saying as they had driven home from the Monroeville Mall. After drawing a blank, he said whatever came to mind. "Please forgive me, Toni, for letting my disability affect our relationship. There's nothing in the world more important to me, now or then, than you."

Toni's eyes spoke for her. Their forgiveness gave him the strength to approach a potentially mood destroying subject.

"Toni, there is something else I want to explain. Please forgive me baby if you can for trying to erase my love for you by dating other women. And Toni, I wouldn't blame you if you could not."

"Mikey—" Toni closed her eyes for a moment before explaining, "—the past is over. I'm not jealous about anyone you were with. You weren't unfaithful to me because, at the time, there wasn't a me in your life. I would have done the same—if I could. And yes, if you need to hear me say it, my love, I forgive you. What's the alternative?" Her blue eyes pleading with him not to answer that. "I don't want to live without you," she said. "It's as simple as that. The past, as I look at it, only goes back as far as the fitting room in the mall today. Now you need to forgive yourself."

Mike put his head down on her lap and, after a moment, Toni softly stroked his hair. The emotional strain of telling her his horrible secret, and her inspiring response, threatened to break through the strong facade he had struggled to show her. She was worth dying for he decided.

Toni leaned over and kissed his cheek. "There is one thing all this has taught me," she added, "and that is I love you with all that is within me. I love you if we can or can't conceive. I will love you even if you don't love me. See, Michael, I finally realized that it has nothing to do with you. I will always love you and that is that. We may not always be together, but I will love you none-the-less. If we don't work out, I may find someone else, but I'll always love you. Regardless of what tomorrow brings, I'll never stop." She placed her hands on her face and softly cried in them. Mike felt his own emotions bursting out and hid his face in her lap.

After a few minutes, they gathered themselves and held each other on the couch. For the next hour, they let all their pent up emotions out. They shared the private hells they had endured the last year. Toni tried explaining how she battled the cold fingers of depression that tried to convince her to take her life and for a while, she considered that an option. Only her faith in God helped her. Mike felt guilt rip through his insides as he fought the picture of her beautiful face laying somewhere cold, stiff, and dead because of him.

He told her of his spiral down the road of alcohol addiction and the beginning of a dependency on getting drunk almost every night. He explained that the booze and women he was with, as David finally was able to get him to see, was just his futile attempt to try and erase her memory.

The common salvation they each found was in the strength and friendship of two friends that refused to pity or turn their backs on them. Two people whose love for them was without conditions. That just affirmed what they already knew, they were real friends.

Sated, they turned out the lights and went to bed. In the quiet darkness, their passions grew beneath the cool sheets. Mike stepped out willingly onto that highway, with the woman he has born to love in his arms, and led them both up the ramp and accelerated into the passion of the moment. The lusty pleasure from the soft nurturing woman under him, as they made love again, was momentarily interrupted as a memory he kept secret flashed across his mind...

CHAPTER 16

David was making one of his routine furnace checks at work when he reached the entry end of the over two hundred foot long structure. Thoughts of a report he had to finish writing caused him to stop and plan out the last two hours of his shift. By chance, he looked up and spotted some large tears on the edge of the steel strip coming down out of the entry accumulator and about to enter the furnace. He ran over and grabbed the phone by number two bridle rolls. "Frank, this is David. You've got a section of torn edges that just entered the furnace and is headed your way. Open up your air knives."

Pot operator Frank Sanders was standing in front of the hot zinc-filled pot using a scoop to remove accumulated dross from the top of the liquid metal hot zinc bath when he heard someone shout over the intercom something about tears in the strip. He dropped the scooping tool and hurried into the pot control room.

"This is the pot, who called?"

"Frank—" The temper of David's voice echoed his concern. "—there are tears on the drive side of the strip that have entered the furnace. Open up the air knives."

David hung up and rushed down the furnace walkway toward the pot area.

Frank started spreading apart the air-fed zinc blow-off knives the moment he heard that tears were in the furnace. His quick action was rewarded as that section of the strip with torn edges came out of the zinc bath just missing catching on the spreading air-knives and tearing the strip in half. David reached the pot as the trailing damaged edge was reaching up into the cooling towers. It was his call on whether or not to shut down the line and cut off the bad edge. He looked in the pot control room at Frank his pot operator for advice. Frank shrugged his shoulders. David accepted that non-answer and hurried over to the strip cooling area by the water quench tank. That was where the damaged section of the strip would come down out of the air blowing cooling tower, if it survived that far, giving him the next opportunity to judge the condition of the damaged strip.

His training of A-crew paid off when he saw three of the material handlers arrive and hurry over to plug in the strip cutting shears. David climbed up on the water holding tank just as the damaged section of the strip appeared overhead coming down toward him. He signaled to Frank to slow the line down. In a procedure practiced often during the trying early years of learning the operation, David took the shears and cut diagonally into the edge of a clean section of the slow moving strip a few feet before the tears started. He cut across the strip about five inches then turned the shears upward cutting against the direction the slow moving strip of steel sheet was traveling. One of the material handlers grabbed the sheared off section of the strip he was cutting off and pulled it out of the way.

David braced his feet on top of the water quench tank and tenuously held on to the strip shears. The force of the downward moving strip threatened to yank the shears out of his hands. His arms started to ache as he struggled again the motion of the steel strip. David looked up and was able to see the strip as it cleared the turnover roll and started down the exit side of the cooling tower right toward him. He quickly estimated there was at least twenty-five feet remaining of damaged strip coming down.

The pain in his arms increased, but he held on to the shears. He looked up again and, seeing the last of the tears coming down, aimed the shears closer to the damaged edge of the strip. As the tears grew smaller, so would the piece he was shearing off. As the last of the torn edge was sheared off, David aimed the shears toward the edge and cut off the last section. Frank took the nod from David as he signaled that everything looked all right. Frank waited until David was out of harm's way before he started taking up the line speed.

"Good job, guys," David told his crew when he climbed down.

Bob, Mike, and Donna, the first material handlers to reach the pot area when they heard about the tears, just looked on in relief.

As a group, they had learned the many ways of cutting out problems that would have shut them down for hours only a few months ago. Shearing off strip tears was just one of the bandages, and a potentially dangerous way of applying that bandage.

A soft feminine voice giggling behind him caught David's attention. He turned to face his only female crew member. Under the yellow safety hard hat was the diminutive, but very cute, smiling face of an imp.

"What are you up to, Donna?" David asked, knowing that somehow he was the butt of her amusement.

"Nothing, boss, I was laughing at something Mike Buffer said."

Now he was worried. Who knew what Mike was doing behind his back. David looked from Donna to Mike suspiciously. Her eyes danced under the brim of the plastic hard hat. His buddy had said something smart-assed about him that she found funny. David was sure of that.

Donna Winger was one of the most capable employees working at Zinc Coater. Every man who worked with her had learned to respect her ability. There was little doubt that she was next in line to be picked for the next operator position that opened. You never have to tell her what to do twice, David often boasted to his superiors.

It had caught all the men she worked with off-guard when she came to one of the company dinners in a low-cut, sexy dress. Her blonde hair was styled up in a bun accentuating her petite face. She was blessed with a very curvaceous figure that caused more than a few eyes to roll.

Donna was such a valued part of the crew that no one took into account her femininity in their bulky company uniforms—that was, until after that dinner.

She never asked or permitted anyone to help her because she was a woman. In fact, David thought, recalling his own rebuke at her hands, she became very cross with anyone suggesting she might not be able to handle a job because she was a woman.

Mike stepped forward when he saw Donna about to burst out laughing. "I just commented that the only time a team leader does anything is when things are going wrong," he relayed to David with that shit-eating grin of his.

"Yeah, I bet, buddy. I'm sure it had nothing to do with the tear in my pants I got from climbing up on the quench tank."

"What tear?" Mike asked, tongue-in-cheek.

Donna's face turned a deeper shade of red as she tried not to laugh in the face of her favorite boss.

"I guess I better go and change them, huh?"

"That might be a good idea," Mike volunteered, "before something jumps out."

Donna's attempt to smother a squeal failed. She then turned and quickly walked away.

David looked at Mike and gave him a thanks-a-lot look. Mike just shrugged his shoulders in innocence at the man shaking his head and now walking toward the locker room.

David was untying his shoes when he heard the locker room door open. He looked up and saw Mike hurry toward the urinals. The room was silent as he watched Mike's race to unzip. The deep breath he heard from the bathroom signaled he was success-ful—barely.

"Hey, Dave," Mike shouted from the urinals.

David was slipping on a new pair of pants when Mike called him. It occurred to him that Mike had called him Dave instead of David again. He had started doing that a lot lately. As David thought back, he realized it started after Mike and Toni had got-ten back together. "Yeah, Mike."

"Toni asked me to try again, so here goes. There will be a glass of wine on her table with your name on it, and she expects you to be drinking out of it on New Year's Eve. If you're not there, these are her exact words, '*She won't talk to you any-more—forever.*'"

"Sure, she will. Tell her there's no way she could keep her big mouth shut for ten seconds, much less forever. She just wants to get me drunk so she can have her way with me. Tell her I said that."

"What? Do I look that stupid? She would rip my tongue out."

"Look, buddy," David said from the locker room, "I would think the two of you would want to start your New Year alone together, right?" No answer. David figured Mike's silence was because he was finished tinkling and was trying to shake off that last stubborn drop. Every man knew it required a good degree of concentration, patience, and true fortitude, to get that final drop. Procrastination would cause it to magically reappear in your shorts after you had put away your johnson and pulled up your pants.

Mike turned the water on, picked up a bar of locker room generic soap, and washed his hands. As he washed, he thought about David's answer. He had expressed his apprehension to Toni that David wouldn't want to be *"a crowd."* With Brenda gone to her grandparent's home in Scranton to be with her family for the holidays, he knew that was how David saw his being with them.

Mike took a little longer to wash than he normally would have, stalling for time to think of another way of talking David into changing his mind. He really missed spending time with him. Mike's reuniting with Toni had occupied most of his free time so who could blame Davey if he felt left out. The only time they had together was usually at work or at few times over at Brenda and Toni's place. After the third washing, he gave up and decided to change the subject.

"How is Legs's new job coming along?" David asked, beating Mike to the punch.

Mike smiled as he dried his hands with the cheap, rough, paper towels they always supply in washrooms. David's referral to Toni as "Legs" reminded him of how close the two of them had become during the time he was quote, *"Lost in Space."* Many a romantic evening lately was lost as the two of them verbally sparred, to the neglect of him and at times, poor Brenda. No man loved Toni more than he did, Mike figured as he threw the used paper towels in the wastebasket, but David was a close second.

"She loves her new job, man. That's all she talks about when I see her. I think she likes being in charge for a change. I told her she would regret it eventually. As you know, dealing with people can be a pain in the ass sometimes."

"Present company included," David whispered.

"I heard that. She's on cloud nine, and I don't want to say anything to bring her down. Being a manager at Horne's is very important to her self-esteem."

When Mike walked from the washroom into the adjoining locker room, David was sitting on his bench putting on his steel-toed shoes. Mike sat down on a bench across from him. He felt a warm sense of camaraderie with the brown man putting his big feet into those even bigger shoes. Their friendship was one of the few things he truly believed in. Three things, he often would swear, are eternal in the universe. "There is a *God*, I'll always love Legs, and I'll always have at least one true *friend*."

David untied his right shoe and started again. It didn't feel as tight as his left shoe and gave him an off-balance feeling. He knew Mike was watching him and that he was going to ask him about coming over for New Years again as he pulled the strings on his shoe tight.

David was very happy for Mike and Toni. They were two of the most important people in his life. He knew, however, with Brenda gone home for the holidays, he would only be in the way. They would do their best to entertain him while ignoring the significance of their ushering in the year together.

Then there was Trisha Tipton, the very foxy lady he had recently met. Circumstances had prevented him from being able to introduce her to Mike. He had planned to take him on a covert trip to Denny's last Monday where he was planning to get his unbiased opinion, but Mike had left work early that day to pick up Toni.

David stood up and pushed his shirt into his new pants. His thoughts drifted to the newest woman in his life. He had met Trisha after breaking one of his cardinal rules. Never pick up a hitchhiker. The most important component of that rule was definitely not a female hitchhiker. The potential for false accusations was obvious.

David had spotted her walking alone on busy Route 30, about a hundred yards after passing a pulled over red Buick Regal with steam pouring out from under the hood.

"Whoa, what's going on here? Someone's car is overheated, I'm guessing," he said, answering his own question when he noticed the vehicle pulled off to the side of the road. As he passed the vehicle, he noticed it was empty and spotted the potential owner walking up the road ahead of him. "No hitchhikers, remember, and seeing that's a female, no way."

After spotting no traffic behind him, David slowed as he neared the stranded motorist. Seeing her close up, wearing tight fitting white slacks and a coral colored sweater, he decided to rethink his iron clad vow. He was able to justify breaking the rules because he assumed that was her car and, technically, she wasn't a hitchhiker but a stranded motorist. Truthfully, he wasn't convinced about stopping until he got a good look at the unfortunate "stranded motorist." She had her back to him as he slowed down. "Well, she has a great looking rear—from the rear—or one could say her behind looks great from behind." Wiping the grin off his face from those corny remarks, he lowered his windows as he approached.

When she happened to turn to gauge the approaching traffic, David decided he had to assist the poor great-looking woman. "The fact you are a knockout lady," he lied as he slowed down and pulled over in front of her, "has little to do with my helping my fellow man." He was correct in his assumption—she was the frustrated owner of the red Regal.

The stranded motorist stopped when a car approached, slowed, then pulled over off the road in front of her. She weighed the need to get to her destination with the apprehension she felt when she noticed there was no traffic as she approached the driver side of the vehicle of someone obviously offering…something.

"Hi. I was wondering if you need some assistance or a lift to a garage?"

As she suspected the stranger asked if she needed a lift. But when she saw the good-looking man behind the wheel, her first thought was no way. Great looking guys', experience had taught her, motives were always suspect.

David was, at first, taken aback when she looked at him as if he had some ulterior motive when he asked. Thankfully, no traffic was behind him for a few miles, he noticed, worrying the woman standing in the road might be endangering herself. "I figured that was your car back there with steam coming out. Can I be of any assistance? Maybe drop you off somewhere, maybe at a repair shop?"

She looked at him and then took a few steps up the road before stopping and considering the kind offer. She still had a long walk ahead of her and wasn't sure what to do about her car. She looked up the road where she was headed and back toward where her crippled vehicle was parked.

David thought she was considering it when she stood there looking up the road. He silently hoped the nice-looking young woman would say yes. *Please say yes*, he thought as he used her hesitation to give her the once over. *Oh, please, good-looking lady*, he prayed after a thorough inspection of her attributes, *please say yes*.

"Okay, yes. Thank you," she answered, smiled, walked around the front of his car, and climbed in the passenger's side.

David was a stickler about keeping his car clean but, when she opened his car door, he quickly looked around for anything he might have missed. He felt a little weird when she climbed in and put as much space as possible between them by leaning against the door and staring at him. He looked at her and smiled. Watching the traffic, he waited for two cars to pass before pulling out.

"I have an idea if you don't mind," David volunteered after sneaking a look at his passenger. "See, I'm off today and was just heading up the K-Mart to pick up a few things. If you don't mind, I think I know what's wrong with your car, and I don't think it would take much to fix the problem."

The lady started to relax and now looked across at him with a poignant, thankful gaze. One that men had foolishly begged, robbed, and sold their souls to see on the faces of the opposite sex.

"You don't have to do that, you know," the lady said, knowing what troubled her most, as she walked that dangerous road to work, was how to get her car repaired.

Her voice touched him like soft fur on bare skin. "I don't mind," David answered as he slowed for a red light. "I'm off today and have the time to kill. I don't think it's anything major. If it is, I'll let you know, Okay?"

She only hesitated for a moment. "That would be so great if it's not a problem for you. I was wondering what to do. I'm new here and don't really know anyone good with cars."

"Good. Now, do I need to drop you off somewhere first?"

"Yes, I work about a mile farther up the road. I was in a hurry, and wouldn't you know it that's when my car breaks down. I've had it for three years and never a problem until today when I was running late for work. That why I decided to leave it until after work and started walking. Right there," she said pointing at a Denny's Restaurant. "I'm a waitress at this Denny's."

David turned into the Denny's parking lot and stopped near the entrance.

"This will be good," she said as she quickly opened the door. "Thank you very much."

"You're very welcome." David was about to ask her for her name when she hurried out the car and toward the restaurant. He watched the shapely lass as she quickly strolled toward the building. Each step she took planted her image deep in his consciousness. All he could say looking at her was, "Damn!"

She possessed long, hazel-brown hair that reached down past her shoulders in ringlets. Broad shoulders and a torso that curved to form a tiny waist then flared outward in a distinctive line, carving out hips that made him groan as he watched her. All he could think to say as she walked away was "Jay Lo." It was said that perfection was also in the eye of the beholder. He labeled the winsome lass as nearly perfect. He was totally impressed with the attractive lady hurrying toward the Denny's.

David didn't consider that the woman he was scrutinizing knew she was the object of his attention and used that opportunity to plant that impression in the fertile mind of a guy she thought very sweet for offering to help. He had no way of knowing that her hips carried a little more swing than normal as her legs worked in perfect union. Upon reaching the building, she suddenly turned around and ran back to his car.

"I forgot to give you my car keys, didn't I? How silly of me."

David just smiled and nodded. He had intended to ask for them but got distracted.

She returned the smile, made an "I'm crazy" sign by circling her finger against her head, giggled, and then ran off, laughing, minus the perfection of her first exit. She was late and this time forgot he was watching. The second exit did more to dazzle him than the first. He had thought her out of his league, as she sauntered toward the restaurant the first time like a runway model. Other than his closest friends, he quickly judged her a woman a notch or two above the class of women he usually met. Nothing would come of this meeting. He had already conceded that, other than hearing her saying "thank you." The fact that would be enough was evidence of the effect the charming young woman initially had on him.

When she ran back to the car, David saw her in a different light. He was able to see beyond her looks and realize she was just a female like every other female. As she reached the door of the restaurant, she tripped but managed to catch herself on the handle of the door. Embarrassed, she turned and looked at him with this big grin on her face, waved, and then disappeared into the building. That small blunder removed her from the pedestal he had placed her on and now gave him the confidence that something just might come of this, after all.

Checking under the hood of her car, he found out it was, as he had expected, only a blown radiator hose. *It must be my day*, he thought when he discovered it was the top hose and easily replaceable. Sometimes the bottom hose could be a bitch to reach and remove. Within an hour, he had purchased a hose, new clamps, and antifreeze at the K-Mart store he was headed to anyway, installed it, and tested the cooling system for leaks. He checked all her fluids and then added some oil and windshield washer from his supply in his trunk. Now what do I do with her car? he questioned. He wondered where the nearest carwash was and then realized it was relatively clean inside and out. The sensible thing to do now was to give her the keys, and she could get a ride to pick up her car after work. That was the rational thing to do. David didn't feel rational. He wanted all the credit from that grateful lady. The reason? Maybe, just maybe, she was unattached.

An idea popped into his head. He turned on his car's emergency blinkers, locked it, got into hers, and drove off.

He proudly pulled into the Denny's parking lot and parked in full view of everyone inside. Other than a few customers, no one came out to greet him. Undaunted, he drove around the building once and then parked in front again. This time the side door of the restaurant opened and a woman came out. She was dressed in an excellent fitting Denny's uniform—if there was such a thing. *Never had orange and brown combined with a mid-thigh skirt to look so good*, he thought. He got out the car and handed her the keys.

"You didn't have to drive my car here. I would have gotten

someone to drive me down to get it," the grateful owner of the Regal said, her bright eyes dancing.

"It was my pleasure," he enjoyed saying. The look on her face was reward enough...almost. For that brief moment, he was someone this foxy chick appreciated.

"Where's your car? You didn't leave your car?" she asked while looking around. "But what if someone—" She put her hands on her hips, pouted, and shook her head at him. "Wait here a minute," she said and hurried back into the building before he could answer.

Like I would go anywhere, he thought as he watched her. David took that pause to check his zipper, shirt buttons, and face in her car mirror. A few minutes later, he looked up in time to see her walking toward him. *My, that girl looks good*, he thought as she approached.

"My boss said it was okay for me to take you to your car for helping me, like he had a choice," she said, rolling her eyes at the thought. "Come on, my darling black knight, I owe you."

"Look, you're at work. It's no big deal walking back to my car. I could use the exercise."

She just laughed, got in on the driver's side, started her car, and waited.

He remembered how great he felt sitting across from her as she drove. When she asked about what he did to fix her car he used that as an opportunity to observe her more closely than he had been able to when he was driving. She had long brown hair with lighter highlights blended in that hung in ringlets. It was beautifully styled and added a flair to an already pretty picture. Her face, however, could stand alone. She had dancing light brown eyes that seemed to imply her thoughts before her mouth could say them. They were bigger than normal but added character to her face. They were not quite bedroom eyes, as they were often referred to, just more oval than most. Her nose and mouth were small and proportioned. Her lips were full, revealing some of her heritage.

David found it hard to listen to what she was saying, fighting the urge to take more than a cursory look at the rest of her anatomy less she catch him in the act.

"I was rushing to work today," he remembered her saying,

"when I heard something pop and then all that smoke—"

"It was steam," he interrupted.

"Okay, steam came out from under the hood. I knew it was important to pull over and stop before I damaged my car. What bugged me was I was only a few minutes away from work. So I grabbed my purse and started walking. I wasn't going to thumb a ride, even though I would be late, but I need this job. You wouldn't believe the nice tips I get."

Yes, yes I would, David thought, looking at her.

"Here we are," she said. Carefully the lady made a U-turn, pulling up behind his parked car. She searched in her breast pocket and took out some rolled up money.

"Noooooo, I can't take your money."

"Trisha Bey Tipton always pays her own way," she insisted with just a hint of attitude. "I don't like owing people."

"I understand that. I'm the same way. But this was my good deed for the day. If I accept money, it's not a good deed."

He added a big smile to the end of that baloney. There was something he wanted from her. *Take a chance*, David thought as the engaging woman insisted that he take the money.

"It's fifty dollars. If that's not enough, I'll get more."

"That's twice as much as necessary, but I can't take it. Thanks, but no thanks. It's not your money I want."

Their eyes met. His were wide with apprehension, her eyes started to close as she awaited the proposition. "There is something you can do for me, I—" David hesitated when she started to frown and jerked her money back. "Wait—wait, I was just going to ask would you allow me to take you out to dinner this Saturday night?"

Her engaging smile slowly returned to her face as his words found root, and her eyes answered him, yes. *So, you like to play*, she thought, okay, my handsome prince, I'm game.

"My name is Trisha Bey Tipton," a soft voice whispered between rose-colored lips, "I'm single, and I was born on July twenty-eight. And when you finally tell me your name, I'd be delighted to accompany you to dinner on Saturday."

Stupid, David realized, *you didn't introduce yourself.* "I'm sorry, I was—never mind, I forgot my manners. My name is David Gary Jackson, single, born eleven-eleven."

They sat for a minute, smiling across at each other, as each mentally tried to figure out the others age. She didn't give hers, so he decided to play her game.

"Oops, I've got to be going," she told him after looking at her watch. "I told my low-life boss I would be right back."

"Why do you call him a low life?" David asked, prompted by the scowl that appeared on her face, and an opportunity to delay her departure a few moments longer.

Trisha grabbed an order tablet out of her hip pocket and started writing. "Because he's always looking for a chance to fire me. He doesn't like people who won't suck up to him, especially people of color."

"I hope this doesn't get you fired."

"Don't worry," she said, handing him the sheet of paper, "I draw in too many returning customers. I get great tips, and he gets the business. I have a lot of customers that ask for me when they are seated. That's my phone number. Call me tonight after midnight. I get home around eleven and that gives me time to shower."

David got out the car, reading the number over and over again, committing it to memory.

"One more thing," she shouted to him. She then motioned for him to come back to her car when he looked at her but didn't move. With the noise of passing cars, she wasn't sure he heard her. When he leaned in on the passenger side window, she said, "Thanks for not hitting on me," blew him a kiss, and slowly drove off. *That should keep him interested*, she thought as she watched him staring at her car as he shrunk in her rear view mirror.

They had gone out on four dates and always had a great time together, David favorably recalled as he sat looking at his locker. When he turned and looked over at Mike, his decision to bring up the subject of the new woman in his life was tempered when Mike had his back to him reaching in his opened locker. Trisha was open, friendly, funny, and a very opinionated young woman, David admitted, yet she never tried to dominate their conversations. They talked often on the phone, and she would always ask him to please call tomorrow if he was free.

Those conversations helped them draw close very quickly.

David learned Trisha loved watching sports, movies, and experimenting making meals from her cook book. She was at ease on the dance floor at a club in a dazzling little black dress as she was snuggling on the couch in cotton sweats.

What he liked best…well, another thing about her he liked was that she made time only for him when they were out together. No making eyes at other guys, no chatting away on the phone when they were together, so he was careful to give her the same courtesy.

After dressing up and going out on those four wonderful dates, she surprised him with a suggestion the next time he was free.

"Hello, Trish."

"Oh, hi, Davey, what's up?"

"Just dropping a line to see how my girl's doing."

"She's just great. Off this weekend for a change, hint, hint."

"That's why I'm calling. I was scheduled to work this weekend, but the schedule is light so they canceled running, so now I'm free. You want to go out and shake your moneymaker at dinner and a club dancing?" When she paused answering, David got nervous.

"You know what? Can we just chill here tomorrow evening with some hot popcorn and rent a movie? I thought you were working evenings this weekend, so I promised my girlfriend Jenny I would spend Saturday at the mall looking at wedding dresses with her. I know she will walk my legs off."

"Oh, I hope not, I simply love your legs."

Right on cue, Trisha thought of her new almost steady boyfriend. She had noticed during their first few dates he was a leg man. Every time she crossed them, it got his attention, which meant, of course, she was going to cross them often, which she did. "Why thank you sir."

"I could bring over pizza with that movie."

"As much as I love pizza, no. I'm sure Jenny and I will eat enough at the mall. You can for yourself if you want."

"No, I'll just eat before I come over."

"Okay, babe, see you around eight."

⁜

They were sitting on her couch, eating popcorn, and watching a movie that turned out to be boring when they started chatting about growing up, family, and some of the people they dated.

"I have two sisters and a big brother," Trisha explained. "I guess we all got along well for siblings. I'm the youngest so I'm sure they would tell you I was a spoiled brat."

"Your sister called me and said you still are."

"Yeah, right. Did you tell her off?"

"No, I agreed with—"

Trisha raised her head from off his shoulder and gave him the eye.

"I...ah...had she really called I would have told her I agreed with you and she was out of her mind."

"Yeah, I bet you would."

"Well, I'm an only child and I know I was spoiled," David volunteered and they both laughed. "Growing up was normal I guess," David added when she lay back in his arms. "I played a lot of sports and dated the same girl, Jeanette Goins, through most of high school. My parents couldn't afford college, so I started working right after school. I lucked up and was hired at a new company and was able to get promotions while working there and became a team leader at the second new plant they started."

"Were you in love with her in high school?"

David looked at Trisha and realized what was on her mind. "I thought so, but her parents were very well educated and wanted the best for her. At least that's how she quoted them. I took it to mean I wasn't good enough for her in their eyes and, when she didn't speak up for us, I broke it off with her. 'If you're not going to fight for what we have,' I told her, 'then it's obvious to me you don't love me enough.' She tried to convince me she did, but it was never the same. She went off to college, and I never heard another word from her. Don't get me wrong, she was a good person, just not a fighter. Looking back, maybe she did love me but not enough to put us before her parents."

Trisha took the girl's trying to convince him as meaning one thing, and she almost asked him about that. "I agree," she finally said, took the bowl of popcorn from her lap, and placed it on the coffee table. "I was dating a guy named Marvin in high school. I thought what we had would last, and everyone thought I was sleeping with him, but I wasn't. It's funny. I was kind of in the same situation as you were. I had the chance to go to some prestigious art schools but turned them down, wanting to stay in town to be with him. I guess he's the reason I'm here. I discovered he was sleeping with my best friend, can you believe that? At first, I didn't believe it when other people saw them together and told me. I didn't want to lose him so, to prove them wrong, I gave in and we became intimate. But now I only regret wasting my time and my virginity on him and neglecting my art career.

"To top it off," she continued, "when I came to Pittsburgh to enroll in one of the art schools here my friends had recommended, I registered too late to start the fall semester by a few days—a few days, David. Undaunted, I wasn't about to go back home so I decided to work and save my money. I got the job at Denny's my first day looking. It wasn't where I wanted to work, but they offered me the job on the spot so I took it. I wanted to make as much money as I could before the next semester started in late January. After the great tips, I'm glad I took the job there and this is where I met you."

David looked in those eyes and kissed her.

"Speaking about that, there's a problem.

"What?" he asked. "One kiss and you are breaking up with me?"

"I should," she teased. "No. David, listen. I'm going to be very busy, I guess, when my art school classes start in January with school during the day and working nights."

"Are you making excuses not to see me already, you spoiled brat." All that got him was a punch in the side.

"No, baby, just the opposite," she said then leaned over and kissed him. "I brought it up because I don't want you to think I would be ignoring you. I'm enjoying my time with you."

David saw that enhancing look Trisha gave him that made his mouth go dry. Her eyes seemed to hint at things and places they had yet to discover as an intimate couple. Then he thought her worrying about something long before it might become a problem could mean she was looking ahead and wanting to keep him in her life.

That's a good thing, he decided as he smiled at her. "Well, we will just have to make the best of whatever little time we have together."

When the handsome man sitting beside her made that suggestion, it prompted the lady to climb into his lap and smother him with a flurry of butter-flavored kisses.

Trisha is a very interesting woman, David thought. Although she was built like a brick house, she never was overt with her obviously blessed physical trappings. Other than very alluring evening wear, when she dressed up to go someplace special with him—much to his aversion, she liked to wear loose and oversized clothes at home that hid or softened her tantalizing attributes. She must have sweats in every color and material, he figured.

They had kissed often and held each other, but that was as far as it had gotten. When Trisha wanted to be kissed, he quickly learned, she would look at his lips and then his eyes. When he moved to kiss her, she would quickly close her eyes. David found that sweet and amusing. Trisha was a gentle kisser, unlike Brenda—who was aggressive and her tongue was a wild thing. He called it Roto-Router, because it would clean your pipes. Trisha seemed to like the softness of an embrace, lips touching gently and tongues softly caressing. A kiss was a kiss, as far as David was concerned.

And unlike the physically demanding Brenda, whose taunt muscles he could feel when he held her, Trisha gently melted into his arms as if she was weightless. It was like hugging…a pillow.

Why am I comparing Trisha to—Never mind," David whispered louder than intended in the quiet locker room.

"What did you say, David?" Mike turned to ask when he heard David's voice.

"Huh, oh nothing, Mike, just thinking out loud."

Things were moving along smoothly between them, David recalled, until he asked Trisha, after one of their more passionate dates, to meet Mike and Toni. Her face changed so abruptly it was scary. He had seen the faces of hatred and prejudice before, but usually on white faces that resented him for whatever reasons their sick minds told them was acceptable. This was the first time he had run into it in such a demonstrative manner in a person of color. He was floored.

"I won't go near them," she shouted at him, and then she put her finger in his face. "It's bad enough I have to work for them, I damn sure don't have to party with them."

David let it drop when she handed him her coat, seeing her eyes threatening to tell him something he didn't want to hear. Obviously, something painful had happened to her, something hurtful that scarred her. Whatever it was, it must have cut deeply. *Had I seen this display of hate when we first met*, he thought when reflecting on that day, *her car would still be sitting on the side of the road with "smoke" pouring out from under the hood.*

Her reaction had caught him off-guard. The Trisha he thought he knew possessed genuine kindness in those soft eyes that smiled back at him everywhere they went. It was that fact that slowed his annoyed response and saved their relationship.

"Look, beautiful, we have to get one thing straight," David had said as he helped her put on her coat and then turned her around and looked in those angry eyes. "Mike and Toni are two of the most kindhearted and loving people I know." Then he put their relationship to the test. "I love being with you, girl, but not at the cost of losing my dearest friends. You decide."

She rolled her eyes at him and put her hands on her hips.

He didn't flinch but wondered if this was the spoiled brat her siblings saw. Those sandy colored eyes staring back at him were beautiful, but dangerous.

Trisha felt hurt that he had picked them over her. Her response had reached the tip of her tongue, and she strained to keep her mouth closed. Just before she was about to say something stupid, she remembered how wonderful she felt when she woke up this morning singing about the new man in her life. After closing her eyes and slowly shaking her head, she reluctantly said "Whatever."

They had little to say to each other as they walked out of her house on their way to the cinema to see Will Smith's latest movie. As they got into the car, each thought, as the evening progressed, that they would be able to convince him/her that they were wrong. This time, they both were wrong.

"There's something I've been waiting to tell you, Mike," David said as he walked over and sat down next to him on the locker room bench. "I've got a date with this girl I just recently met. Her name is Trisha. She went home for Christmas but is coming back so we can spend the New Years together." David read the surprised look on Mike's face as his left eyebrow went up, as it was wont to do when he was surprised. "I was waiting for the perfect time to introduce her to you."

Mike said nothing.

David took note of that and pressed on. "Look, I'll see you guys after the holidays. Tell Legs I'm sorry for missing another chance to put her, and all women, in their place behind their man," David teased.

"Yeah, sure, I'll tell her that and get my lights knocked out. You can tell her that when you see her."

"Coward."

"Yes, but a live horny coward."

"Tell Toni I promise we'll get together with Brenda after she returns." David cringed and was sorry he said that as soon as it left his mouth. He was certain of that when Mike didn't comment further on his faux pas.

Mike knew Brenda was still a sore spot with David, something that still troubled him, and that after many tries, he had obviously failed to resolve his feelings for her. Anyone knowing her would have understood his dilemma. She was a mindblower. No way was Mike going to touch that subject with him. Mike was following his advice to Toni to let them find their own way. If it was meant for them to be together, he had just told her again last night, love would find a way. If not, he implored her, let them just be caring, close friends.

CHAPTER 17

Brenda pulled her feet up under her as she sat on the sofa. The room—and the house, for that matter—was crowded with family and friends celebrating the Holidays. There was the tantalizing smell of various foods cooking, a hint of eggnog in the air, and the familiar scent of pine from the huge Christmas tree in the living room. Every window and room contained holiday decorations. It was a warm house full of warm people.

It had been a wonderful, joyous last ten days. They were minutes away from the New Year, and the majority of her family was already sauced. Trays of drinks and food passed by her, but Brenda politely declined. She was sober for a change during the Holidays. As she sat in the chair, her thoughts were with Toni, Mike, and, of course, David. She envisioned the quiet atmosphere of their house with her friends toasting and laughing in the New Year together and was sure David was with someone tonight.

Among all the gaiety and cheer in this crowded home, she felt very alone.

"It's my fault," she whispered as the room filled with partying people gathering in the living room around the big screen TV. The sound was turned down as music played, but everyone's goal was just seeing the wild goings on in Time Square New York. It was her fault she was lonely because during the week before Christmas she was doing some last minute shopping with her two cousins, Emily and Janice, when she stumbled into Jack Towers at the local mall in Harrisburg.

Jack was a cute boy all the girls liked, and she had dated for a few months during her senior year in high school back in Pittsburgh. Everyone thought they were a perfect match because he was a handsome guy and a very successful quarterback on their school football team and carried all the trappings that go along with that highly visible position, and she was the prettiest and most popular girl at Washington High School. They got along great at first and had some fun times, but, for some reason, he thought he deserved to date her. It only took those few months for Brenda to finally realize his ego was bigger than his stat sheet. They had a fun time together until Jack started calling audibles in their relationship. He got demanding, and she decided to sack the quarterback her senior year.

"Brenda McShane?" he said when he saw her.

"Hi, Jack."

Out for some last minute Christmas shopping with her cousins, Brenda had spotted Jack looking in the window of a men's store. Her attempt to just say hi, ignore him, and walk past was thwarted by her cousins, Janice and Emily.

"Who is this hunk?" Emily asked, when she spotted the guy calling Brenda, and then grabbed a retreating Brenda by the arm and dragged her toward him.

"Yeah," Janice seconded.

"Hello, Brenda."

"Hi, Jack," Brenda said to the smiling man with eyes only for her. "Emily, Janice, this is Jack Towers. We were friends in high school back in Pittsburgh."

"We were more than—Hi, Emily and Janice. What are you doing here in Harrisburg? Wait a minute. Stupid me. You're here for the holidays at your grandparents, right?"

"Yes, we are, and we have to be going."

"No, we don't," Emily claimed as she stepped closer to Jack.

"Yeah," a grinning Janice added.

"Well, you have a great holiday, okay?" Jack said to an obviously reluctant to chat Brenda, ignored the others, and walked away from the threesome.

"Brenda, why the cold shoulder?" Emily asked when they caught up with Brenda.

"I'll tell you guys about that later."

"He's cute."

"Yeah."

On the ride home, as her cousins regaled over the gifts they bought, memories of Jack Towers silenced Brenda.

"Brenda, there's someone here to see you," she heard someone shout up the stairs, a couple of days before Christmas.

"Maybe it's your David," her cousin Janice suggested when they heard the announcement. They were upstairs trying on clothes in one of the bedrooms and talking about the men in their lives.

"If it is, bring him up here so we can tell him the truth about our cousin," Emily teased.

"Yeah," her cohort Janice agreed.

Brenda shook her head no way, but the thought of that wonderful guy at the door made her hurry out the room, stop, come back, and check her hair in the mirror, ignoring the teasing from her cousins for that, and then run down the stairs with her cousins' laughter in her ears. She ran through the large house to the open front door. Standing there with a gift in his hands—wasn't David.

"Hi, Brenda."

"Jack, what are you doing here?"

"After bumping into you and your cousins at the mall, I had to bring the prettiest girl in high school a Christmas present."

"That was a long time ago, Jack."

"Trust me, Brenda, you are better looking now than ever. Here."

"What is this?"

He smiled. "Well, you will have to wait until tomorrow at Christmas, now won't you, Grinch?"

Almost everyone had arrived at her grandparent's house a few days ago, and they were having a great time celebrating the holidays. It was a custom for the McShanes to spend the week before Christmas up until New Years' Day here with family for those who could get that much time off. But those who couldn't came whenever they could. It was that warm feeling, generated by her last few days here around some wonderful people, that altered her usual opinion of the man standing at the front door.

"Who is it, baby?" Brenda heard her mother ask from the kitchen.

"It's Jack, mother, you remember Jack Towers from Washington High back in Pittsburgh." When her mother didn't answer Brenda shook her head, remembering that she never liked Jack.

"Can we go for a walk or something?" he asked.

Again, this was a Brenda who was warmed by her family. "Sure," she said while looking into blue eyes that always impressed her. "Let me get my coat. Mom, I'm going for a walk with Jack. I'll be back in a few. If I'm not, Dad, it's okay to shoot Jack." Brenda knew wherever her dad was in the house, he was smiling if he heard that and—her mother was not.

Jack helped Brenda put on her coat, and they started walking down the driveway and turned left up the road. The sun was shining, but it was still brisk out, she noticed as they walked, but not unpleasantly so for a stroll. The road her grandparents lived on was sparsely populated, so traffic wasn't a problem as they walked down the middle of the road, taking turns looking at each other but not speaking.

"I saw that look in your eyes when we bumped into each other at the mall, Brenda," Jack finally said. "I know I screwed up when we were dating back then. It's just after seeing you again, I wanted to let you know I'm sorry about that."

"That's sweet of you, Jack. But what have you been up to since those crazy school days?"

"Well, you remember, after I tore my MCL that season, my football career was over. So, I started working with my dad and went to school at night for auto mechanics."

Brenda did remember how upset the school was when their star quarterback went down. He was a being a dick to her, and she didn't care back then. But now?

"My family moved back here after I graduated to help my grandparents with the farm. Gramps was getting on in years and needed our help."

"Yeah, Jack, I remember you telling me your family was thinking about moving during our last days at school. Remember, we were laughing because we discovered my grandparents also lived near Harrisburg."

"Yeah, in the same area and they even knew each other."

"That was crazy."

He got quiet as they walked. Brenda knew it was because he once claimed that was another reason for them to be together.

"What about you?" he asked.

"Me?"

"Yeah you. You were close with…what's her name…in school. That sassy girl with the dark hair."

"Toni."

"Yeah, Toni's was her name, and there was…"

"Katie."

"Katie, yeah, her older brother was starting quarterback when I joined the team. He played college ball somewhere down south I was told."

"Katie went to school on the west coast and is working out there with her sister. Toni and I are still very close and actually share the same house. My parents insisted I go to school so I became a nurse. No night nurse or head nurse jokes," she warned him with a scowl when he stopped and looked at her.

"No, no, being a nurse is great, but I always thought you wanted to be in the spotlight or on stage."

"See, again you never figured out what I wanted."

"And, believe me, that is something I will always regret."

She turned and started walking back toward the house. Not because of what he said. She thought his admission sweet, but she was getting cold. He quickly caught up with her.

"Can I ask a personal question?"

She just looked at him and smiled.

"Okay, okay. I was just wondering if there someone special in your life now?"

There were a lot of things she wanted to tell him but thought better of it. "No," she decided to say, "but there are guys trying."

"Hell, I'm sure of that." He laughed. "Have you looked at yourself in the mirror? If I was back in Pittsburgh, I would be trying."

"That's sweet. What about you?"

"Same here. My sister, Wendy, do you remember her? Well, anyway," he continued when Brenda shook her head, "she is always setting me up with her girlfriends. But, no, there isn't anyone special in my life…yet."

"Remember?" Brenda asked, trying to change the subject. It wasn't because of his curiosity about her love life, but because it made her think of someone she was trying to forget while here. "We talked about how hard it was for you losing your dream of playing college football?"

"I do, Brenda, all the time. But you know what? Seeing you again rekindled another lost dream."

He stopped walking when she did. When she grabbed his jacket and kissed him on the cheek, he thought about grabbing her in his arms and kissing her hard on the mouth, but being unable to read her intentions was what lost him Brenda in the first place. Instead, he watched as she turned and started walking down the road. From that moment, Jack knew, as the woman with the long red hair blowing in the winter wind walked away, he would forever be in love with Brenda Joy McShane.

When they reached her door, Jack did ask Brenda out, and they went on a few friendly dates the week after Christmas. Brenda thanked him for the expensive gold cross and necklace he gave her for Christmas, but she made it plain she was here for her family during that time. Still, in between, whatever free time she had she was open. A much wiser Jack Towers accepted that. For all but one "date," she took her cousins along with her. If he objected, and what man wouldn't want to be alone with her, he hid that from everyone. Janice and Emily were also good-looking young women so he didn't openly protest.

On the evening before New Years, they went out to dinner and a movie alone.

"Thank you for a beautiful evening, Jack," Brenda said when he pulled up in front of her grandparents' house.

"You're welcome, and seeing you again has been wonderful. And may I say again you look beautiful tonight?"

"And again, a girl never tires of hearing that sir."

"When are you guys leaving?" Jack asked when the attractive woman staring at him stole his thoughts.

"My family is leaving New Year's day. I believe everyone is leaving that day."

Brenda sensed he wanted to say more but remained silent. Some of the harsh words she threw at him when they broke up seemed right then, but they seemed wrong now.

"Don't say it," she said as he opened his mouth to speak. "This year is ending, let's let the past float away and with it all remorse and mistakes."

"A clean slate?"

"Yes, a clean slate." With that, she leaned over and kissed

him, patted his cheek, and started to get out of his car. "Wait," Brenda said when he started to get out and walk her to the door. "Let's part here as friends."

"Okay." He watched disappointedly as she walked up to the house. The woman wasn't only beautiful, but elegant and classy. She turned, when reaching the door, and blew him a kiss. Jack Towers knew at that moment he was going to leave the dairy farm and move back to Pittsburgh. When, he wasn't sure. *Yeah*, he thought as he drove off after she was gone, *all things being equal, 'You can only win if you try and try as hard as you can,'* quoting his old football coach.

Brenda was sitting up in bed with her cousins, Janice and Emily, talking about her date. Two of their teenage female cousins were lying on a mattress on the floor watching TV. That was their room and the assigned sleeping quarters for the five during their stay.

"You know he has fallen for you again," Janice said, low enough not to be heard by their younger relatives.

Brenda looked over at the teenagers on the floor and whispered, "I think he always has had a thing for me, Janice. I was going to tell him that hurting his knee was the best thing that happened to him with his big ego, but I thought that might be too cruel, true…but cruel."

"Why is that?"

"He was such a jerk when he was BMOC. He figured I was just another of his trophies. Talking to him now, had he been the same person then, we would probably be together now. When his head is out of his ass, he's a great person."

"And a very handsome cuss."

"That he is, and my first," she leaned over and whispered that last part in their ear.

"Really."

"Yeah. I was also caught up in the school frenzy over Jack the star quarterback. I thought he loved me. He only wanted to date me so he could boast to his friends he got into my pants, I later found out."

"Wow!" Janice said louder than she intended. "What a jerk," she then whispered—too late.

"Wow, what?" Linda, one of the two teens lying on the floor, sat up. She was quickly joined by Shay, the other teen.

"It sounds like boy talk," Shay added, a smirk breaking out on her freckled face.

When their older cousins failed to comply with their inquiry on the subject, the two teens climbed up on the bed and the five of them shared view points on boys, sex, and dating.

CHAPTER 18

The meal was both memorable and delicious, and the company even more so. Trisha's kitchen, illuminated only by scented candlelight, was transformed into a French café and carried with it an air of mystery that tantalized and excited David. The enticing image of the lovely woman seated across the table in the flickering candlelight was, in itself, very captivating. It was clearly apparent that she had put a great deal of effort into a delicious dinner, the warm and sensual atmosphere of her apartment, and, most of all, herself.

The light from the four candles seemed alive as it danced across the walls. Their flickering ballet put him in a very romantic mood. Combine that with the sultry bass voice of Barry White, singing/talking from the living room, and the evening offered dreams of a desert far sweeter than the pound cake sitting on the sink counter top. The mood, the food, the woman, and the wine were skillfully combining to fire up his expectations for tonight.

"This was sooo good, Trish, but I can't eat another bite."

She had prepared a delicious salad as starters and then topped that with a tender rendition of surf & turf. "Are you sure there isn't something else I can give you?"

They both paused, and wanton eyes looked across the table at teasing, sultry ones in the silence that followed. Then she turned to her left and pointed, the snicker on her face partially hidden in the candle light. "Don't forget the pound cake. The bakery where I bought it in the 'Rocks,' I'm told, makes the best."

She hid it well, but he wasn't buying that she was referring to the cake. "Maybe later, after we work off some of this delicious food…ah, dancing in the New Year." *Back at you*, David thought. "Besides, it's getting close to twelve."

"Okay, take two of the candles into the living room while I

put things away. It won't take but a few minutes. Don't start without me."

"No way, that's a promise."

Following orders, David moved two of the four candles from the table where they were eating into the living room with Barry. Her apartment didn't have a dining room. It had a large living room, a nice-sized kitchen, and a surprisingly large bedroom and bath. He had only seen the bedroom when given a tour. The large kitchen served a dual purpose with an eat-in area.

Under normal lighting, the living room was painted in a very light pink with rich tan carpeting. Trisha's couch was also tan, but a little darker than the carpet. Her tables and accessories were all dark mahogany. He had thought of asking her why she mixed the two extremes but decided it wasn't worth possibly offending her.

Another strange thing he noticed, at least he thought of it as strange, was that she had no pictures of anyone in her house. There were no family members or old friends decorating her tables or walls. David thought that odd, but again not odd enough to risk offending her.

"Ten minutes to twelve," David announced as he carefully placed the candles down on top of the coffee table like she had suggested.

When he turned around, Trisha was standing in the doorway to the living room with her arms extended out to him. She was even more breathtaking standing in the dancing light of the candles. Her hair was up in a bun with tendrils of hair curled at the sides of her face. It made her seem taller to David. She was wearing long string silver ear rings that only added to her classic beauty.

The stunning dress she was wearing clung to every curve of a body with plenty of them, like it was poured on. The shiny silver gray material highlighted all her assets. It was floor length with a long split down the front of her left leg. It had string straps that tied behind her neck, and the back was bare down to the flair of her hips. The front of her dress, David noticed when they were eating. from her waist up was loose-fitting material with a deep, revealing cut allowing enough of the curve of her ample breasts to keep his attention. She looked awesome! From where he stood, he couldn't find any flaws, and it wasn't from lack of skillful searching. After seeing how beautiful she looked, he felt guilty not showing her off to a host of New Year's Eve partiers. She was far too elegant looking tonight for just his eyes, but she had turned down his offer to paint the town, settling for quiet intimacy.

From the moment, he walked into her candle-lit apartment, he couldn't take his eyes off her. She never mentioned anything to him about working out but, as toned as she was, it either came from working out, or she was one of those fortunate few born with great genes and didn't have to work hard to stay in shape. From what David could gather, her lovely genes were the only thing under that silky gown.

☙☙☙

"Turn on the television," Toni suggested.

"No way. Let's turn on the radio or the stereo and let the music take just the two of us into the New Year," Mike suggested as he danced alone in front of her. "Screw the rest of the world."

Damn, she thought, *does that guy know the right things to say.* "But it's tradition, honey," she pleaded in her best helpless-female voice. "I've got to watch the ball at Times Square come down. It wouldn't feel like New Years if I didn't see that."

Mike shook his head at his lovely superstitious mate and turned on the television. As a compromise, she turned down the volume and then turned on the stereo. The first station she found was playing "oldies." From the nod of his head, that was good enough for him. Mike took Toni in his arms and slowly danced around the room. She was wearing a white silk jump suit that felt like cold skin in his hands. When touched, it offered no resistance to the feel of the woman wearing it. He liked that a lot.

This was going to be her year, their year, Toni silently vowed as she slow danced with the man of her dreams. Mike's arms felt sooo comforting as he held her. They wouldn't be able to welcome in the New Year like she wanted, but even that was a blessing. At least it meant she wasn't pregnant.

It was the gut-wrenching fear she had endured during the week delay in her body's usually very actuate monthly cycle that had threatened to steal her holiday spirit. As she lay alone in bed this morning, wondering how she was going to explain to Mike that he was a fertile-turtle, her period came. She cried. A part of her, she began to realize as she buried her face in her pillow, wanted to have his miracle baby. A voice in her head, one that she was starting to nurture, suggested this pregnancy was a blessing given to them because of their great love for each other. Another voice she heard suggested Mike had lied about being sterile all along. She swept that negativity out of her mind.

Somewhere, in the crying spell that gripped her, it turned from sorrow over not being able to have a baby to now one of relief. The week of uncertainty gave her a chance to take an objective look at her life. It would be the last time they would have unprotected sex, she vowed, and she would go back on the pill. There were other sexually transmitted diseases out there, she remembered, trembling at the thought of his being with other women. If she and Mike had a future together, she decided, she wanted to enter it unencumbered.

ↄ৲৻৲ↄ

Brenda reached for the glass of champagne Grandma Sarah insisted she take and returned Grandma's loving smile as if to say, *I'm all right.* Everyone had noticed today that Brenda wasn't quite her usual spry self and decided to give her some space—that was, everyone but Grandma. They were all standing in a semi-circle around the television, counting down as the Times Square ball started its descent.

Grandma Sarah and Grandpa John McShane had opened their home to their four children, their spouses, and grandchildren for the Christmas and New Years holidays. With the ten grandchildren they brought with them, added to a few close friends, the house was overflowing with McShanes and friends.

Christmas Eve had turned out to be one of the most remarkable days in Brenda's life. Although she deeply missed her friends back in Pittsburgh, she was genuinely glad to be around her family. Her grandparents had rented enough beds to make everyone comfortable in the five bedroom house. There was food, booze, and deserts to feed three times as many, twice over. But it was the joyous spirit that filled the big McShane home that amazed her. She felt like she was a little girl again, and Brenda had to admit that felt good. The holidays fostered old feelings of new birth, new beginnings, and happiness. Brenda's mom and dad saw it in her and felt better that they had all but insisted she come along. She thanked them again Christmas morning as they opened the presents everyone received.

The McShanes had the same sibling rivalries that blemished most families. This holiday was different, in that they never once surfaced. Not a mean-spirited word was spoken between adults or the children. Brenda was able to spend some fun time with two of her cousins, Janice and Emily, which were around her age, and that made the time go fast. They never got along well before because Brenda was always the prettiest cousin and got most of the attention growing up. This time, none of them held that against her, and that opened doors that revealed they had a lot in common. Janice and Emily weren't as tall as their leggy cousin, but they could fit into her clothes, and they had a great time switching outfits. They loved the same music and movies Brenda did and also loved to dance. Brenda began to realize how wonderful it was to have so many of her loved ones in one place.

That realization, as she sat and observed the happy faces about to toast in the New Year, helped her finally shake the funk she had fallen in tonight and to forget about a certain man back home. She stood up and put her arms around her sweet grandma.

"Happy New Years, Grandma," she whispered into the small woman's ear.

"Thank you, baby. Happy New Years to you too," the old woman answered.

As she hugged the white haired matriarch, she closed her eyes and sent a thought home to Pittsburgh. *Happy New Years, David, happy—*

Her grandma interrupted her message when she started dancing with her. Brenda opened her eyes to the wrinkled, loving smile of the woman her mom had said she was the spitting image of in Grandma's youth. They danced to the howls and clapping of everyone in the room.

e/ne/

"A toast to our having a very happy New Year," Toni suggested as she raised her glass of wine.

Mike joined her and touched glasses. "I second that emotion." He then touched the face of the woman standing in front of him with the back of his hand. "To my beautiful lady, may this year bring you nothing but happiness. You deserve it."

"To my incredibly handsome man," Toni said as Mike teasingly looked around the room for the person she was talking about, "and to my best friend in her absence, happy New Year. To another who shall remain nameless because of his stubborn absence but thinks, correctly I might add, that I have great looking gams, happy New Year."

Mike smiled at her.

She took his glass and set it down with hers. Mike watched her, a bit curious about her intentions. Didn't she say—

When she grabbed his hand, he understood that all she wanted was to dance with him again. He held her as the year and their future started anew.

꿈꿈

David and Trisha slowly danced to the soulful voice of Luther Vandross singing on her stereo and watched the clock as the second hand moved past the six on its way up to the New Year. David had to admit he was enjoying celebrating the holiday with just her.

He missed his friends but the wonderfully scented woman in his arms more than made up for their absence.

Four days ago, they were sitting on his couch sipping eggnog enhanced with vodka. Well, David was, Trisha tried but couldn't stomach the taste of eggnog she had purchased for him. Having just returned from a visiting her parents over Christmas, Trisha claimed she had a nice time.

"So, are you glad to be home?"

Trisha looked up the man holding her.

"Is that smile a yes or a maybe?"

"Of course, silly."

"So, you had a good time with your family?"

"A great time. Some of my relatives from out of town were

there this Christmas, and our house was full. Other than my uncle getting too drunk, we had a ball."

"There's something you're not telling me."

Trisha squeezed his leg before answering. "There was my parents' constant asking me to come home and go to school locally."

"What did you tell them?"

"I was being held hostage here by this handsome man."

"Great! Now your dad is going to come to town and shoot me. Thanks."

"You're welcome, baby."

David decided now was as good a time as any to decide what New Year's Eve party she might want to go to and celebrate.

"T, I have four invitations to some rocking parties for New Year's night," David revealed to the woman sitting across his lap resting her head on his shoulder. "Now that you're home, you can decide which one you would like."

Trisha saw the excitement in his eyes and had second thoughts about what she wanted to tell him. They always had fun when they went out, and she was sure they would again, but it wasn't what she wanted--this time. Flying home she had come up with a different suggestion and was hoping he would understand. "Baby, I'm sure they are great parties, but I had something else I wanted to do that night."

David remained stoic.

"I always get invited to someone's wild party on New Years and end up starting the year drunk or hung over," Trisha said, shaking her head and laughing. Then she stopped, and a more serious expression colored her face. "I was thinking when flying home from Atlanta—" She paused to read the questioning look on his face. "—I need to change my luck with relationships. This time," she continued, poking him in the chest, "I want to be with just you. I'll think of some place intimate to go, is that all right?"

David felt an ego boost as he read her words to mean she wanted their relationship to succeed. "I would love to spend that night with just you. Where do you want to go?"

"I'm not sure, Davey, you just get dressed real nice and come over, and I'll make up my mind where, okay?"

A kiss was his answer, many kisses later was her reply.

Now, as the second hand waved past the eleven, he took Trisha's face in his hands and kissed her. The New Year began with their eyes closed and their mouths opened—as it should.

David was enjoying the evening with the woman in his arms more than he ever thought he would. The food she cooked was great, they were having fun talking, and now this beautiful woman was in his arms dancing as Luther sang, "This house is not a home." The strong attraction David felt for her only multiplied the confusion he had over someone else.

He wasn't buying that you-can-fall-in-love-with-two-women-at-the-same-time crap. It was more of make up your mind which one you want to draw closer. Tonight, he found it impossible to be that rational. There was nothing illogical about what he was feeling for the soft woman in his arms, yet he didn't want to be unfaithful to whatever he felt for another.

The New Year, and David's need to make a decision, was rushing at him before he was ready. He was confident of one thing—he was determined to be honest with both of them and, above all, with himself about his feelings.

You've fallen for him, Trisha resolved as she put her head against his chest as they moved in step across her floor. *Damn, why do you keep doing this to yourself?*

But he's different than the guys I usually date, she argued with herself. She knew he really liked her, but he was being so cool about it, and that was a turn on for her, she playfully admitted.

This evening was her attempt to break through this handsome man's wall of masculinity. There were a few places she had in mind for them to spend a beautiful evening, mooning over each other in relative privacy as the clock struck twelve. This morning, however, she awoke with another idea. When she opened the door and saw her handsome man standing there in a beautiful black suit, she knew her first choice was the best choice. The grin on his face, when she shared with him what she had in mind, more than confirmed it.

Other than that dreamy, cute look on his face when she first opened the door, she recalled delighting in the memory of his stunned expression. Her dress had failed to make him grovel. *It could be he sees more than a great-looking woman with a hot body in this dress,* she humorously thought as they danced. He must like her for her, and not what this dress suggested she could do for him, she concluded from his hesitancy. That was how she added up the facts as *she* saw them.

This guy she was going to fight for, she had vowed when standing in front of the mirror while getting dressed. Her girl-friend Linda had claimed that her problem with men was her re-luctance to let them know just how much she liked them. Trisha's thoughts were jumbled by the feel of his rough hand as it moved seductively across the smooth skin of her back. Trisha moved her hips into his, as she forgot about past missteps or mistakes, closed her eyes, and melted into his arms. *If he ever really falls in love with me*, she decided as they moved in rhythm with the music, *I will never give him the chance to think about another woman. He will be the center of my universe.*

She smiled when hearing the words to a Gladys Knight song her older sister Cheryl loved to sing that started playing on the stereo, "If I were your woman." She also recalled a youthful promise boldly made to her sister that she would never do all that to keep any man. Now she admitted she finally understood what Gladys and her sister Cheryl were trying to say. She would do whatever for the man she loved, and if he couldn't handle that...well, that was life.

Moved by that thought, Trisha put both arms around his waist and rubbed the hard muscles in his back. The one thing she de-cided was, after tonight, she wasn't going to lose him by holding back, no way. She would do whatever, whenever, however, once she could trust in his love.

That vow was a total reversal for David's adroit dance partner. Although she'd dated freely since high school, there was only one man to whom she gave herself—as her luck would have it, the one least deserving of her affection. It took two years of heart-ache before she finally saw through him. Advice from family and friends only strengthened her stubborn resolve to prove them wrong.

When she dropped by his apartment unannounced and caught him in his bed with another woman, her world crashed down around her. In her immaturity, all men were now guilty, and all men should pay.

Everyone she dated afterward found a kiss to be a worthy gift after months of courting, if they were lucky. Maybe tonight, maybe with this man.

David was different in so many ways, she advocated. For one, he always took the time to try and read her changing moods. Something that even her family grew frustrated with. He carefully handled her sometimes fragile feelings and showed empathy about her fears. He was always honest about how he felt and wasn't afraid to let her know he had a different opinion. He seemed proud to be with her when they were out, and she never caught him showing interest in other women who often blatantly tried hitting on him in some of the clubs they frequented.

Trisha had taken him to a friend's sorority party, and it wasn't long before the little whores were flashing him, but he ignored their obvious flirtations. One was so brazen, Trisha punched her in the mouth, and when her boyfriend acted like he wanted to retaliate, David stepped between them and, without saying a word, the look on his face made it plain that wasn't going to happen.

Trisha knew David wanted her. It was obvious in his eyes and actions. But he only went as far as she let him and without whining or begging if she gently stopped a wandering hand. She loved that about him. And also, she thought, he would always try again.

She also liked that he never bragged about the other women he dated or asked her about the guys she did. She found his self-confidence arousing. She had teased and tempted him—it was what women did—and he remained both interested and cool. That allowed her to begin to trust in a man again. And for Trisha, that was a huge mountain to climb at this time in her life. Because of the pain and betrayal of her last close relationship, she needed someone patient like David to ease her into loving again. More and more, after each time together with her David, she gained the confidence to finally shed that heavy chip on her shoulder. After dates when she was joyous and happy, or the occasional time when she knew she was being a bitch, how he treated her never wavered. He would quickly put her in her place when he felt he had to, and she loved that he did that calmly without putting her down in any way.

They had come very, very close to consummating their intimacy on a few occasions, but she knew she wasn't ready yet. It was the day after she returned from visiting her family for Thanksgiving that they had come the closest. Maybe it had something to do with her needing to get *very* close to him after putting up with her family nagging her. She had heard the same questions. Why didn't she move back home and go to school, and when was she going to settle down?

She was sitting on David's lap, liked she loved to do when they were sitting on the couch, and were kissing when the vision of having him in her was all she could imagine. Like plugging in the toaster, she became very hot, and her kisses became deep and probing. The recipient of those kisses returned her ardor, and his hands wandered over her soft body. It took removing both their hands from their private places, climbing off his lap, embarrassingly excusing herself, and walking into the bath room to re-snap her bra and for a cold face washing to try and calm down.

Only a few minutes after returning to his strong arms, did she realize the cold water didn't work. They were again fondling each other, but somehow she found the strength to come to her senses and put the brakes on.

His disappointment at her sudden change in direction was obvious, but he handled it like a man…like her man. Disappointment painted his face, but there was always a weak smile that said he understood her reluctance and, most important to her, the why. Damn, she loved that man, she thought later in her bed that night after a very long shower. But she admitted that, had he pushed a little she would have surrendered to him.

With his eyes closed as they danced, David imagined they were alone somewhere on a beautiful island and the evening would offer them all the passion they could handle as he felt the firm outline of her body against his. The scent of her ushered him into daydreaming again about what it would be like to make love to her. Was that a new daydream? No, he'd envisioned that union many times. The feel of her against him tonight just gave more color to that dream.

"Happy New Year, David," she whispered in his ear.

"Happy New Year, gorgeous," David answered and stopped dancing to look her in the eye. Holding her at arm's length, he gently spun her around, taking in every impressive inch of his willing, and now blushing, beautiful dance partner. "I want to thank you for this wonderful evening you prepared. You look totally awesome in that dress and feel even better in my arms." He spun her around again and cursed. "Damn, you look good all over, girl."

Laughing, she shook her head at his theatrics.

"I'm a lucky man." He took her hands, raised them to his lips, and kissed them. "I thank God every day for your radiator hose bursting."

"You say the sweetest things, Mr. Goodwrench. It took me three tries to cut that darn hose," she teased, "when I saw you approaching. And then I had to strut my stuff just to get your attention to help a lady in distress."

It was David's turn to smile. He kissed her hands again but, this time, when his eyes locked onto hers, she sensed his mood had grown serious.

"The attractive woman I saw walking along the highway that day had no trouble getting my attention. But what I didn't realize then was how special the woman I saw that day was, and how completely she would capture my heart."

She made that impish face that always moved him when she became embarrassed and couldn't think of something to say. Her head tilted to one side as she waited for what came next.

"Trish, I never thought I would care so deeply for that lady strutting her stuff as I have. But I have discovered she is even more beautiful inside than she obviously is outside."

The way the lady whose hands he was holding looked up at him, the message those toffee-colored eyes were saying, weakened his knees and his resolve. When that beautiful woman stepped back out of his hands, David used that moment to feast on the amazing female standing in front of him.

Trisha was weighing making that next step with David when a Roberta Flack song came on the stereo. She stared into his eyes as the words, "Like the trembling heart of a captive bird," spoke to what she was feeling. The next verse became her acclimation. What Trisha did next took only a moment of thought, but was an action she uniformly underlined. All her doubts were erased, and her questions answered, looking into his eyes. She did have to swallow and catch her breath first, but in a movement that caught him by surprise, she reached behind her hips and pulled down the zipper to her gown. Then after a moment of hesitation, as if needing to look into his eyes for affirmation one last time, she reached up and untied the straps around her neck to the beautiful silver evening gown that had captured his imagination all night. After another momentary hesitation, she took a deep breath and let go of the strings. The beautiful gown slipped effortlessly down over bare skin and lay bunched at her tiny feet.

When his eyes failed to follow the dress but remained locked on hers, she knew that offering him her heart, soul, and now her body, was the right move.

A startled David stared into the suddenly intense eyes of the beautiful statue in front of him, as she allowed her gown to fall, but he didn't miss a moment of the unveiling. For her, it was an act completed in seconds, but for the man appreciating every special moment with her, time slowed, permitting him to feast on her every shapely inch. As he gazed upon her, the shimmering silver material slipped, as if in slow motion, silently off her brown shoulders. He gasped as the shiny material, moving teasingly slow down over her breasts, slowed to a stop as if snagged by the tip of both firm nipples, only to then be wonderfully freed as the aroused woman took a deep breath. Then it continued its journey revealing two stunning breasts. Her cleavage was impressive in whatever clothes she wore. Never obscenely or distracting from the rest of her body, but just enough to advertise she was blessed—everywhere. Now they were unshackled, and he realized the lady was adorned with breasts that needed no support.

Now moving faster, the gown slipped downward, revealing a tiny flat waist and diamond navel pin before slowing again as it hugged shapely hips that he constantly found himself captivated with. As the beautiful gown slowly exposed more of her, he inhaled. It slipped over the curve of her hips and down her thighs before it came to rest on the floor around her feet.

David bit his bottom lip as he beheld the statuesque nude woman standing in candlelight. He stepped toward her and caressed her face in his hands. Looking in those soulful eyes, he understood the gift she was offering and how much it meant to her. He kissed her gently on the lips. There was a fire ragging in him to take and possess this beautiful woman who had tormented his dreams for months, but he knew that whatever he did at this moment would forever direct their love life. He understood there would be other times to enjoy every inch of the woman in only high heels who was offering him her everything. Instead, he reached down and picked her up in his arms. Standing there for a moment, he again kissed her softly on the lips and said, "I love you, Trish."

When he picked her up and spoke those special words to her heart, she put her arms around his neck, tightly hugged him, and kicked off her heels. Now she felt completely vulnerable and found that liberating. "I love you too, David." With her eyes closed, she felt him start walking toward her bedroom.

Knowing how often they had come close to what was about to happen, Trisha wasn't afraid of the strong man carrying her like a child. When he placed her on the bed and started undressing, she got a clear look at what she had only once fondled and knew this would be more than that. She was giving up control of her body to this powerful man who wasn't only handsome as hell, but he was also…ah…gifted.

David resisted the urge to finally relieve himself of the strong need to have her. Oh, how he had dreamed of those shapely brown legs wrapped tightly around him as he gave her pleasure. But instead, he lay beside her and took a moment to look at all she was offering before gazing again in those waiting eyes. He slowly lowered his head and kissed her hard on the mouth as his hand slid along her body caressing one firm breast with his fingers. He felt her breathing become deeper as he again stopped and looked into those eyes. If there was any hesitancy, he wanted to give her time, while he still could. When Trisha pulled his head down to her waiting mouth, he had his answer.

Seeing her desire matched his, he started kissing down her body, stopping at each breast. Hearing her moan as he took her swollen nipple in his mouth, he knew not only was she growing impatient, but so was he. His moist tongue then continued its journey down her body until it slipped between her taut legs. There he quickly drove her to frantically grab for a pillow to smother her face just before she screamed—four different times.

Trisha's head tossed from side to side as she fought her own growing craving to entwine with the man exasperatedly exploring her body. She had now experienced multiple times the breath robbing experience she always desired and had failed to reach with anyone else. As wonderful as that felt there was another sensation she craved, she had to feel him inside her. At the end of her patience, she reached down and pulled him on top of her. That was all she needed to do. He took over as she closed her eyes and wrapped her legs and arms around him.

What she expected and thought would happen next, in a way, did not. There was no frantic and pounding race to reach the mountain top, as in the past three times she had tried to climb that high peak with Marvin—and three times fell far short, and very quickly.

What she learned that night was, with her David, when you climbed that mountain, you need not run wildly and out of control up its steep cliffs if you intended to reach the top. Instead, when he asked her to relax and dance with him, she throttled the panic she felt and followed his moves. She danced with him thrust for thrust, with each taking her a step closer until her body locked, and she actually lifted him off the bed before falling back, lost in the pleasure. Remarkably, what she failed to reach on those three failed attempts she reached three glorious times, in one attempt in his strong arms, before he did.

They would welcome in the New Year again that night in each other's arms, after she told him how wonderful she felt and how much she loved him, and once more as the sunshine filtered into her bedroom on the first morning of the New Year.

CHAPTER 19

E xcuse me, miss, where is your juniors department?"
Toni stopped folding blouses, turned around to face a
short, round, older woman carrying a bulging store shopping bag in each hand with an enormous black purse hung over
her shoulder. The tired lines in her middle-aged face spoke volumes of the kind of day it had turned into for this exhausted bargain hunter.

Toni smiled sympathetically and pointed in the direction the
woman had just come. "Somehow you walked past it," she pa-
tiently explained to her. "See that mannequin in the far corner of
the store, the one dressed in the denim clothes?"

"Yes," the woman answered, while still trying to find it
among the myriad of colors that were blending together at that
range. She didn't want the pushy young woman directing her to
know her vision was another thing that was failing. "Yes, I see it.
Thank you. I don't know how I missed that."

"No problem, it's in a bad location that's hard to find anyway," Toni said in her most courteous voice. "You'd be surprised
how many people walk right past that department."

The woman gave Toni an odd look, as if to say *I'm not other
people*. She then shuffled down the aisle toward the barely visible
image of the denim-dressed mannequin standing like a hazy
lighthouse in a cold sea fog. Toni smiled back at her. It was one
of those days when the sardonic, nagging little idiosyncrasies of
her customers couldn't break through her veneer of tranquility.
Everything was right with the world today, and those things that
weren't, she didn't want to think about.

"Hey, wipe that dumb grin off your face."

An exasperating grimace replaced the blank look one got
when the mind decided to leave the present and go drifting off in

search of past memories. She turned to face her rude attacker.

"Really, Toni," the rude attacker moaned, "can't you get him out of your mind for a minute. You're making me ill."

The grin she wore was chiseled into her face. A blush of pink suddenly blossomed around it, and Toni couldn't comment.

"You're going to make me puke, you know that, don't you?"

"Well, if you were working instead of abusing me, you wouldn't have to worry about holding down that junk you had for lunch," a still-smiling Toni replied.

Barbie Shuster—Yes, her mother named her Barbie—watched her boss try the tough approach to disguise the man-made high she was on.

"Barb—" Toni couldn't handle calling her Barbie, at least not with a straight face. "—like I was telling you over lunch, I had a great time, and I'm still warmed by the glow."

"You mean after-glow, don't you?"

"Okay, smart-ass, back to your counter. You better make more than five grand today, or you're going to work in sporting goods tomorrow," Toni said in jest.

"Miss DiNardo, I believe your fangs are showing. All right, all right I'm leaving. But I want you to keep your promise about sporting goods. As blind as you are over Mikey, I'm sure you've never noticed that tasty hunk of a man they hired there last week."

"Gawd," Toni muttered when she figured out whom Barb was talking about. "Look, I love my man, but it should be illegal for any man to look that good. Whoooooo," she whistled.

"Mmmm, I know what you mean, girl, but what a waste," Barbie said, stopping to look at a pair of designer jeans on a clothing rack.

"Waste?"

"Oh, yeah, he's too good looking to be straight."

Toni watched her always-opinionated co-worker as she picked up a pair of jeans, held them against her body, and posed. Barbie was one of the first people to warm up to Toni when she was hired as an assistant manager. Her quick tongue and wit was more than a match for whatever Toni threw at her. What endeared Barb to Toni, was her willingness to teach Toni the small points of her particular department.

With Barb's help, Toni had impressed her floor manager with some of the ideas Barb had suggested. When she deflected all the praise and a nice bonus to Barb for her suggestions, a friendship was formed.

At lunch, Toni had shared a secret with her. "David—" Whom she explained was the other man in her life. "—had asked me something," she laughingly described. "He put it as discreetly as seeing a hung, seven-foot-tall Black man running naked through an Irish nunnery. Were men and women's ring sizes similar and could I guess his size. He said he was interested in buying a ring and wondered what size he was. Would you believe that, girl? Oh, oh, and then he said, 'Since Brenda and I wear a lot of rings, what was both our sizes?'"

"Seriously?"

"Barb, it was all I could not to laugh in his sweet face," she explained. "But he was so sincere, so pleased with his detective work I had to play along. He looked so vulnerable and cute"

"Hey, girl, exactly—"Chew. "—who—" Chew. "—are you—" Chew. "—in love with?" Barb asked between bites of her peanut butter and mayonnaise sandwich.

Toni kept her eyes fixed on Barb's green eyes less the dab of mayonnaise, sitting in the corner of her mouth, force her to stop and point it out to her. "Listen, Shuster, David and I are very close friends. He has always been there for me and holds a special place in my heart, and always will."

Barbie bit down on the last of her sandwich. Toni read the *are you sure that's all he is* look on her face and choose, rightfully so, to ignore that.

"What do you think your *'good friend'* was up to?" Barb teased.

Toni took a deep breath and waited until she was over that snide comment. "Obviously, he was trying to trick me into giving him my ring size for Mike," she replied.

Barbie wiped her mouth, thankfully catching the errant tuff of mayonnaise on her face—much to the delight of an interested bystander—and weighed carefully her response. "That's what I would think he was up to also," she lied. She knew that was the right answer when the light returned to her friend's face.

"Me too, me too," Toni said, giggling. "I really think Mikey Mouse is turning into a tiger."

Mikey Mouse, Barb though, *yuck! People in love are sickening.* "I think you're probably right, Toni. If he was to ask you, what would you say to him?"

"I'd say yes before he got the words out of his mouth," she boasted.

Barbie felt a wave of jealously sweep over her and resisted the sour feeling it put in her stomach. She was glad for Toni, genuinely glad, she told the *voice of envy* whispering in her ear. "Toni, I haven't had enough success with men to offer any advice. All I can say is go slowly. It hurts less if you're mistaken."

Toni just grinned at her and nodded in the affirmative. She then asked Barb to move the remainder of the winter coats that they had reduced this morning to the sales area.

"No problem, boss lady," Barbie replied.

That cleared the heaviness they both sensed in the air. Toni fought the eerie sensation that she felt in the pit of her stomach that maybe Barbie was jealous of what she had with Mike. She hoped not, they had a friendship she really cherished. *Maybe I do think about him too much.* That prompted other memories that she resisted only for a few moments as she continued her inspection of her department.

The start of the New Year was everything Toni and Mike had hoped it would be. Old wounds had completely healed, and they seemed closer than ever.

They weren't living together, but they were together almost every day.

"If anything has changed," she confided to Katie when she called from Los Angeles, "our passion is more intense. He's like the Ever -Ready Bunny. It's wonderful, Katie. It's as if Mike feels driven to prove himself each time we make love," she happily confessed to her other closest girlfriend. Katie's come-back caused both of them to laugh until they burst into tears.

"Yeah," her naughty BFF said, "I know you hope he never gets over the guilt, you slutty girl."

"Hell no, every time he looks as if he forgot what he did, I drop hints, and he drops his pants."

"You are so bad, Toni," Katie said after they laughed until

one was choking. "You have spent too much time around Bren and me."

"The only negative," Toni said when answering Katie's other inquiry about Brenda, "is I now feel my other BFF, and the other hunk in my life, David, are drifting apart. They are still very close," she revealed, "and I can sense the sexual tension between them when they are together, but each is dating someone else now."

"Who is Brenda dating?"

"That's the funny part, Katie, it's someone she once dated in high school. Do you remember Jack Towers?"

"Jack Towers, Jack Towers, isn't he that football player back in school that tore up his knee? The quarterback, right?"

"That's the one. They only dated a short time if I recall."

"Yeah, I think I remember him. He was very nice looking if I have the right guy."

"Yeah, he was a looker, and it started to get hot and heavy between them until he started getting demanding, Brenda claimed."

"Wow, you know what, Toni? I believe he was good friends with my stupid boyfriend back in school. He was also on the team."

"Friends with Darwyn? Well, that explains his ego."

"Sure does, and it's a shame too because Darwyn was good in the sack."

Toni giggled. "Katie, stop it."

"It's true, girlfriend, the boy was an amazing kisser, if you know what I mean. I hated dropping him, but no boy in school told *us* where to go."

"Or how to get there," Toni said, laughing.

"I remember now, yeah, he was trying to tell Brenda who she could talk to and things, and our girl cussed him out. He was apologetic if I recall, Toni."

"Oh, he was the rest of our senior year, but you didn't want to cross that fiery redhead in high school. What did we always say to the guys hitting on us?"

"Do it right—because you won't get a second chance to make a first impression."

"You got it," Toni said, laughing.

"So, did she see him again at a party you guys went to or what?"

"No, Katie, Brenda said she bumped into him when she went home to Harrisburg for the holidays last Christmas, and he took one look at our pretty redhead and moved back to Pittsburgh two months later and, not long afterward, traced her to the hospital she worked and asked her out. She was so impressed that he went through all that to see her she couldn't say no."

"How romantic."

"They are supposedly just friends, Katie, at least that's what she told me. She said he's nice and she likes being around him, but he doesn't turn her on any more. But he was her first, so you never know how that will turn out."

"Her first, I didn't know that, Toni."

"Yeah, they were hot and heavy but only for a few months. But we have yet to meet the girl David is seeing. I think he's worried about bringing her around Brenda."

"Why?"

"Like I told you, Kate, there's something between those two that they can't seem to get over. You should see the way they look at each other when they think no one is watching. I know they love each other, that's not the problem."

"I still don't understand. The Brenda I knew, when she wanted a guy, just turned on the charm, flirted with those darn green eyes and long legs, and the guys came begging."

"I know, right? But not with David. But, Katie, if you met him you would understand. He's a handsome sucker but so down to earth and real. Next to Mike, he's the other man in my life. They both seem happy with this new arrangement," Toni went on to say, "so I've finally resigned myself, like my Mike is always telling me, to staying out of it and let fate decide…their fate."

The woman on the other end knew Toni, wasn't convinced about doing that but didn't say anything.

Later that evening, and home alone, as Mike, David, and Brenda were all working evening turns, Toni realized that she was so into Mike lately that she knew little about the other people in the lives of her closest friends. In the past, not a week had gone by that the four of them didn't usually get together to eat, go out to a movie or something, or just hang out at each other's homes.

But just the four and not five or six. That would have to change, she decided while watching TV, that would have to change. With Brenda's birthday being three weeks away, Toni remembered, that sounded like a get-to-know-their-friends reason for a party.

The next day at work, Toni was sorting through some of the newly arrived blouses in the storage room. She was off the clock but determined to find the one she had spotted earlier for a display she wanted to create. She was sure she saw that blouse in the warehouse somewhere. It was twenty minutes past her quitting time, but she ignored that fact because she was never out of Horne's Department Store on time anyway. There was a satisfaction, a certain feeling of accomplishment she had to have before she could walk out the door each day. A yellow blouse, size two, with French cuffs and collar was the fly in her soup. It was here somewhere, she swore, and she was going to find it.

Toni was just about to admit defeat when Donald Mizer, the store manager, walked into the women garments section of the storage room.

"Miss DiNardo, I'm glad I caught you before you left. Would you have time to come up to my office when you're finished here? There's something I would like to discuss with you."

"Sure thing, Mr. Mizer. I was just about to quit. Give me a few minutes to put this merchandise away, and I'll be right up." Toni couldn't find the blouse she was looking for anyway. She was taken aback, however, when he just turned and walked away. *Boy that's odd*, she realized as he disappeared around a corner, his attitude was usually the opposite of his name. Toni couldn't shake the feeling that something was wrong.

Mr. Mizer was never a very talkative man, Toni thought after he left the storage room, but he usually had more to say than that. Some of the women gossiped that he was a little intimidated by the opposite sex. She wasn't sure if that was true or not. As far as she was concerned, he was the stereotypical boss. Warm, when he had to be, but all business. He was tall, lanky, and walked as if his joints hurt. Maybe they did, she thought.

Toni caught a momentary glimpse of herself in the strip of mirror on the sides of the elevator as it raced to the ninth floor. She had felt a sigh of relief when it stopped on the fifth floor and emptied itself of the two maintenance men who stood nervously by the door. When they rushed out of the elevator, she found their quick exit humorous. "I don't bite," she whispered at their backs. *That's not true Toni*, she thought, snickering as the door closed. She had bitten Mikey a few times.

Toni took the few seconds of privacy she had to take a more thorough view of her reflection in the mirrored walls of the elevator. The dark blue cotton suit she had picked out held up well, she decided while turning little pirouettes in the mirror. She still had her flat tummy and just enough of a shapely ass to keep guys interested in looking when she walked past. Her skirt was probably an inch shorter than company policy but gave her both a business air and left a little devilish doubt as to her true intent. She liked that. She believed that keeping people guessing was much better than having them know what you were about. "'Easier to ask forgiveness than to get permission,'" she muttered, quoting that much-used phrase.

The braking elevator put an end to the fashion show. Toni put on her game face, waited impatiently for the creaking doors to open, and then stepped confidently out of the elevator. She had been up on the ninth floor on only one other occasion and that was with Donna Glass, the women's floor manager.

The ninth floor contained the offices of the president, treasurer, store manager, and the majority of the office secretaries. Donald Mizer's office was at the end of the corridor to the left. As Toni walked past the desks of the various secretaries, she couldn't help noticing that many of the women had stopped what they were doing and watched her as she approached or walked by. One quick turnaround confirmed that they seemed to know something about why she was there when she noticed all the women suddenly looked away. The question of why they were all still here this late didn't cross Toni's mind.

Toni gathered herself and took a deep breath. The door in front of her had a fake gold placard that read, *Donald Mizer, Store Manager*. Toni hesitated. *Go ahead*, she scolded herself, *what could possibly be wrong?* She turned the doorknob and stepped into his office.

"Hi, you must be, Miss DiNardo?" An affable older woman looked up from her desk and stated.

It was a small room that contained her desk and various cabinets aligned along the walls. Off to her right was an impressive dark wood door that she gathered led to Mizer's personal office.

"Ah...yes, I am."

"Mr. Mizer is expecting you. Just walk in."

The secretary pointed to the large door. Toni said thank you and walked nervously across the room toward Mr. Mizer's office. She debated knocking first like they did in the movies but thought better of it. She was reassured that wasn't necessary when she turned to look at Miss Pleasant Smile again, who signaled, with a wave of her hand that it was okay to just walk in.

Donald Mizer wasn't at his desk when she opened the door. It was a massive antique mahogany desk that was stacked with papers and books. Its bulk seemed too large for the room, but it did offer an impression of authority. Toni held on to the doorknob for a moment longer and was about to close the door and leave when—

"Come in, Miss DiNardo."

Toni pushed the door open wider and saw that the room was much larger than she first thought. As she stepped in she saw a table set up in the far-right corner of the room. Mr. Mizer and three other people were seated there. She was taken aback by this odd setting.

"Come in and close the door please."

Toni hesitated for a moment, looked back at his secretary, and became dry mouthed when she noticed her now stern countenance. Then she did as Mizer directed. She took a deep breath and walked toward the table.

"This is Mrs. Langston," Mr. Mizer said, pointing to the woman on his left. "She's from our personnel department."

She appeared to be a no-nonsense-looking older woman who, Toni guessed, was in her fifties and was wearing a gray pin striped suit. When she nodded at her, she got no reply. Toni didn't know her but did recall seeing the woman in the store a few times. She always wore too much makeup, Toni now recalled, her hair hung limp and lifeless, as it did now, and the clothes she wore to work each day differentiated only in the color, not in style or imagination. But what she remembered most about her was she never answered when Toni said good morning to her. She seemed to have incessant bouts of PMS, Barb once remarked. Toni fought back a snicker, remembering Barb's barb. Now wasn't the time, she sensed, to act silly.

Toni walked over to shake her hand.

"That won't be necessary, Miss DiNardo," Mr. Mizer said as he pointed at a chair set up in front of the table where they were sitting. "Just take a seat there, and we can get started. The two gentlemen on my right are from the law department. Mr. Reeves has been with us for over twenty years and knows Horne's as well as anyone. Mr. Anderson is new to Horne's, but brings a lot of expertise to the job."

Toni didn't let on to Mr. Mizer, but this wasn't her initial introduction to either of the two men. The Anderson guy tried hitting on her the day she was hired. Only after being rebuffed repeatedly did he get the *hint.* He was a short, round man, about five foot two and also in his fifties with strange looking eyes behind his unflatteringly thick eye glasses. He had an untrustworthy look to him, she had decided, and no matter how nice he tried to be, she never felt comfortable around him.

Toni nodded a hello to Mr. Anderson. The look she saw in his eyes and the smirk on his face screamed *revenge.*

Mr. Reeves was a different story. He had a wide grin on his face. Again, she felt uncomfortable after she acknowledged him because he never made a pass at her or indicated any intentions of doing so. *Why the grin?* Toni had, on occasion, noticed he was staring at her from a distance. At first, she was leery of his odd attention, but after a while, she grew to believe he was harmless. Reeves always dressed in the best suits and acted like he was born with money. At least that was how she associated his aloofness.

She guessed he was about forty or forty-five years old with a luxurious head of wavy black hair and chiseled features. Toni recalled hearing some of the older women snickering about how handsome they thought he was. Today, she sensed she had misjudged grinning man.

Toni gave each of them a courteous nod as they were introduced to her. They returned it but lacked any real sincerity. Toni knew then that she was fired. What she couldn't fathom was why? She was always early and left work late and had yet to miss a day.

Indignation flared up in her as she waited for the unwarranted ax to fall.

"Miss DiNardo, I'm sure you're wondering why I asked you up here and why Mr. Anderson, Mr. Reeves, and Mrs. Langston are present," Donald Mizer said as he tried to make small talk.

The nervous woman seated across from him wasn't amused. He sensed she knew why she was here and was just waiting for confirmation. After all, how many new managers got called up to his office after hours?

Toni squirmed in her chair as her anger started to get the best of her. Struggling to hold it in, she crossed her legs again and tugged down on the hem of her skirt. That didn't help. Her mouth was very dry, and her deodorant decided now was the time to quit working.

Distracted by her fidgeting, and the ill-perceived skin show, Donald Mizer lost his train of thought. He, like most of the men here, considered her one of the most attractive woman in the store. If it wasn't for—no, he shook his head and admitted this was something they had to do. He was about to speak when he sensed somehow that the power he had welded over this employee seemed useless now. This attractive woman wasn't the least bit threatened by him or any of the people in this room. Mizer had insisted they be here to help in confronting her with the results of the test she had taken. Their presence here was to buttress the ugly, but necessary, deed he had to do.

Mrs. Langston correctly read her boss's hesitancy in part as his being flustered by the leg show going on in front of them. The little tart's brazen display wouldn't save her, she vowed. "Miss DiNardo, what Mr. Mizer is trying to tell you is that we have a problem with your job application form. On it, you stated that you did not have any, ah...any venereal diseases."

Toni didn't grasp what Mrs. Langston said right away. She heard her, but she wasn't listening. Her mind was off on a journey somewhere trying to figure what she had done wrong in her department to warrant this unusual meeting. She had received three letters of commendation for her department's sales and appearance—

What did she say? Toni wondered as the older woman was talking? *What—what venereal disease?* Toni was back!

CHAPTER 20

The furniture mover tried one last attempt at making the room's furniture look balanced. The couch and love seat were pushed into the far corner, giving the living room more space like Toni requested. However, it also made it difficult to see the new TV he picked up as a surprise for them from the love seat. Exhausted, Mike didn't care anymore. After sweeping up the now exposed dust, dirt, and assorted lint balls he discovered under the couch, he questioned the necessity for further changes. Without Toni or Brenda home, he wasn't sure where they wanted everything. *Hell*, he thought, grinning, *they always change their minds anyway, they're women.*

After slouching down on the sofa and getting a whiff of body odor, he realized he needed a shower. Glancing over at the wall clock, he jumped up. "Darn-it," he bemoaned, "it's after five." Mike rushed upstairs to Toni's bedroom throwing off clothes in every direction knowing she got off after five o'clock and was only twenty minutes away. He knew he had time because of her commitment to her job. She wouldn't leave until everything was just, just so. Mike picked up his sweaty clothes and stuffed them in the already full bathroom hamper and then got the water temperature of the shower as close to his norm as time would allow and climbed in.

❧❧❧

The drive home, if it did nothing else, gave Toni time to reflect on what her boss had said. She was dumbfounded and stunned. She drove in a trance and was surprised when she found herself parked in front of her home. She honestly couldn't recall how she got here. A part of her dreaded seeing Mike's car parked in front of her place when she drove up. He was here like he promised he would be when she got off from work. They had made plans to go out to eat tonight.

Toni sat for a long time, just staring out her car window, painfully reliving the unbelievable afternoon's events. *You have to tell Mike*, the voice of her conscience whispered amid the confusion. *Yes*, she reluctantly agreed, she had to warn…ah…tell Mike what—what she'd done to him.

"Uuuuh," Toni moaned in anguish as the thought of what could be growing in Mike's body slapped her so hard that she cried out in pain. The realization she could have sentenced the man of her dreams to death was unbearably painful. "Oh, Mike, oh, Mike," Toni groaned as the guilt cruelly flayed her open wounds, "—have I sentenced you to die?"

"Breathe slowly," she warned herself as a wave of dizziness swept over her. Heeding her warning, she closed her eyes and took a couple of cleansing breaths.

The image of Mr. Mizer pointing his finger at her and accusing her of lying about her condition caused Toni's eyes to pop open as she recoiled in her seat. His searing words were spoken with such accusations it had taken the fight out of her, and the man seemed to revel in the pain he had caused. The four of them sat smugly across from her, waiting for the venomous news to break her. It started when she put her hands up to her face and audibly gasped. The four wolves moved to the edge of their seats, voraciously awaiting the mournful wail of their hopeless victim. It was if the arid scent of the wounded woman's desperation fired their lust. Seeing that she was obviously injured by their savage attack, they waited for the arrogant employee to crumble so they could pounce on her and rip her broken spirit to shreds. It never happened.

Toni's pride took over. She wouldn't let the heartbreaking news crush her spirit, at least not in front of them. She stood up, straightened her skirt, turned, and headed for the door.

Her bottom lip now trembled as she replayed Mizer's words over and over in her head. *It can't be true*, she decided, finally turning off her car engine. She had to tell Mike, she resolved after battling with her conscience, that was all there was to that.

How could this happen? she asked herself. What did she do so wrong? Why now?

She felt a wave of emotion surging up in her chest. The one person who could make some sense of the chaos that had befallen her was just beyond that door, she realized as she stared at her house. Grabbing her keys and purse, Toni ran toward her house.

Mike had heard what he thought was her car pulling up and was delighted when he reached the window and looked out to see that it was Toni. He ran his comb through his hair one more time, quickly sprayed a burst of cologne on his face, picked up his towel, and stuffed it in the hamper. Then he hurried down the steps to greet her. He reached downstairs just as the door burst open and a hysterical Toni ran into his arms bawling so hard he couldn't make out a word. Mike held her close as she continued to mutter something between gasping for breath.

"Honey, what's wrong?" he asked, as his panic started to paint vivid pictures in his mind. "Did someone hurt you?" That panic quickly evolved into anger.

"Mikeeeee, you...doctor..."

"The doctor, what doctor?" Mike grabbed her by her shoulders as if he was going to shake the truth from her. "You need a doctor?"

"No, no," she muttered. "It was the lawyer that said—that said—I'm fired from my job."

"Toni, what are you talking—never mind. Come over here and sit down." Mike took her by the arm and all but carried her over to the couch. When he sat down beside her, she started crying even harder and collapsed in his arms.

At first, Mike was angry. He knew this had to involve more than just losing a stupid job. The woman he loved more than life was sobbing so hard he realized death must have claimed someone very dear to her. Then, as his anger vented, he tenderly rubbed her shoulders, wondering who it was she lost. He had never seen her so distraught. Even during the dark days of their relationship he had never seen her allow their break up to drag her to this level of despair. She confided to him that, during her weaker moments when they were apart, she had often harbored suicidal thoughts. Never seriously, she proudly proclaimed, but she had listened to that stupid answer for the pain she felt.

Toni felt the crushing weight of her lost future lift off her enough to arrest the tears streaming uncontrollably down her face. Three deep breaths gave her back some control. Slowly, she sat up and looked disconsolately at Mike. His face was red with anger or frustration, she wasn't sure which. *Does he already know?* she wondered. *Did someone already call and tell him?* Toni felt her throat tightening up as her worse fears seemed to be happening.

"What happened, sweetheart? Who hurt you?" Mike calmly asked, restraining his impatience.

A new wave of hot tears rushed out of her sore red eyes and down her cheeks when she saw his concern for her. She tried to stop them, but there was very little fight left in her. Only this time, she didn't cry out. The concern on the face of the caring man in front of her was a stalwart shield against the pain. She knew his anger was fed by the belief that someone had done her harm when he was the unknowing recipient of the evil.

Toni wrestled with a wave of regret as Mike reached out his hand and softly touched her cheek. She would rather have died than tell him that he might have been exposed.

"Mike, I was fired today," Toni whispered.

"I know that. But I don't think that's what you're crying about. There's something else, isn't there?" He watched her closely. If she was going to try a keep the truth from him, he was hoping to see some sign of it on her face. She had eyes that that you could trust. Honest eyes that would have driven a poker player to the poorhouse.

Toni swallowed before speaking again. She grimaced a little when it hurt. His eyes were so full of concern for her that she struggled with the words that she had to tell him. "I love you, Mike. No matter what happens, I want you to know that."

That beginning stole what little strength he had remaining. A mind-numbing feeling of dread climbed up trembling legs, weakness gripped his stomach, and he heard the wind whistling in his ears. "Toni, please, what are you trying to tell me?" he struggled to ask. "I know you love me, you don't have to tell me that." He felt more frightened than he did when she was crying hysterically in his arms.

She was trying to prepare him for something bad, he was sure of that.

"Mike, I have—HIV." Toni closed her eyes when Mike sat back in shock, and she silently prayed he would understand it wasn't her fault.

"Toni, did—you— say—HIV?"

Toni kept her eyes closed. The way his voice cracked when he said that scared her. It gave weight to all the horrible premonitions she envisioned would happen when he found out. She squeezed her eyes tighter and nodded. The darkness had become her friend. She felt his hands gently rubbing hers. Slowly she opened her eyes and looked nervously into his. There was nothing, nothing but love in those wet brown eyes.

He leaned forward and whispered in her ear, "I love you, Toni, and I always will." He then kissed her on her cheek. "If you do have it, we will work it out somehow. Don't worry, I'm not going anywhere."

She reached out and hugged him as tight as she could.

Toni knew, when his hot tears painted the side of her face, that she had given her body to others, but this was the only man she would ever give her heart, soul, and spirit.

"Why is the door wide open?"

Still stunned, they both turned toward the questioning voice and were greeted by a figure wearing hospital greens outlined in sunshine.

"Hi, guys."

Brenda was inconsolable when Toni told her about the results from the physical she took for work coming back testing positive for HIV. Brenda had walked in full of exuberance on Mike and Toni comforting each other. From the sadness on their faces, she knew right away that something terrible had happened. At first, she thought someone had died in her family when Toni ran into her arms and burst into tears.

"David?" she mouthed at Mike.

Only after he shook his head and pointed at Toni did her heart beat again. Whatever it was that happened had apparently happened to Toni. She wasn't happy about that, but relieved that Toni was alive. Then Brenda felt a little guilty. It was that guilt that helped set her off when Mike told her the truth. It was a concerned Toni and Mike that now ministered to a weeping Brenda.

"Mrs. Langston," Toni struggled to explain to them, "had accused me of lying about my health when I applied for the managerial position. Mizer said my blood test had revealed a venereal disease. At first, that shocked me, but I told them I didn't know that and would get medical help and take care of it if that's true. They looked at each other for a moment as if I said something weird. Then the lawyer, Mr. Anderson—no, it was that older guy Reeves—stood up and said, 'Damn it, girl, you have AIDS.' He said that those samples I gave for the physical when I was hired were misplaced. They decided to hire me anyway. When they finally found them and had them tested and re-tested, both returned the same results. My mouth dropped to the floor when I heard that," she told them. "Then Anderson corrected Reeves by saying I didn't test positive for AIDS, but HIV. The two of them then started arguing about the difference between AIDS and HIV until that grinning bitch Langston shut them up and said, either way, I was being terminated.

"I was dumbfounded," Toni said as she let go of Mike's hand, stood up, and walked around the room. "I was so, so shaken that I couldn't even defend myself or ask them if they were sure they had the right person or something. I just sat there in my chair and took it. Then that witch told me they had to ask how many men and women I had slept with at work. I was so angry at what she was asserting, I was going to jump up and kick her ass—but I couldn't move. The horrible news that they dumped on me had put out my fire. I just got up and walked out. At the door, I regained a little of my pride, turned around and faced them. I then said, 'Isn't it a strange coincidence that the only person that I've slept with at work is also in this room?' Having sowed that seed, I walked out the room leaving them to their suspicions."

"Toni, Mike, you've both got to be tested," Brenda later explained to them as she dabbed her sore eyes with a tissue. "They could have made a mistake. And even if they didn't, Mike needs to know if he's infected."

"Brenda is right, Mike. Maybe there's a chance you're clean, honey. I might not have infected you." Toni raised her hands to her face, closed her eyes, and swallowed, choking down the pain that word caused. "Anyway," she continued, "we've got to have you checked."

Mike said nothing.

His silence hurt her more than his justifiable anger ever could. He had a faraway look in his eyes. *He's worried I've poisoned him*, she thought as she turned and looked out the window. *If by some chance I did, please forgive me, my darling.* She closed her eyes and prayed. With the silent prayer over, Toni opened her eyes and groaned. The bright sunny day was now gray and wet with a driving rainstorm. *That's an omen*, she determined, *a very bad omen.*

CHAPTER 21

"Jon, if you would try throwing the ball once or twice, I think we can beat these guys," Mike told his panting teammate. They were playing a five-man, two-hand tag football game and taking a water break.

"You guys were covered, Mike," Jon said, wheezing. "That's why I've been running with the ball." He then took his bottle of lukewarm water and poured some of it over his head.

"Jon, you've lost yards with your running. Quarterbacks are supposed to throw the ball, remember?"

Jon threw some of the water he was guzzling on his teammate. That was the third game of tag football in a row for Mike. It was a usual occurrence on weekends during football season on the grounds behind his apartment buildings weather permitting. Usually, David was here and their quarterback, but he was working an extra day.

The exercise was Mike's way of keeping his mind off the test results he, they, were waiting for. Brenda had driven him and Toni to the hospital where she worked and had several blood samples taken. Brenda explained that the samples would be shipped out to different clinics for evaluation. Her theory was that it would offer less of a chance for a mistaken diagnosis. Also, Brenda knew an administrator that could put a rush on the results. She set it up to channel all the test results through a doctor friend of hers at the hospital—Doctor Albert Ryan—and it would be up to him to read all the results and break the news to them.

The last few days had been hell on Toni. In the weeks since they found out she might be HIV positive, there had been little passion between her and Mike. He had found that both troubling and a relief. He had nightmares about how some nasty, squiggly germs had worked their way from Toni's body into his when they made love. Last night, it was hard to even hold her while they were sitting on the couch watching TV without thinking about that nightmare. He was sure, from her reluctance to kiss or touch him intimately, that she too was feeling the effect of her fears.

"Hey, are you guys going to lose another game to us or just sit there?" Sam, one of the players on the winning team walked over and asked them.

Mike was about to snap off an insult at Sam when Jon nudged him in the side. Mike looked inquisitively at him and then turned in the direction Jon was pointing. There, standing on his balcony overlooking the grass yard where they were playing, was Toni. Mike searched her face for a sign that she was here because the results had finally come in, but she just stood there, unemotionally, staring down at him.

"I got to go, guys," he said, never taking his eyes off the person on his balcony. Jon called Mike a part of the female anatomy as he walked away, but he never heard him. His eyes were glued on the lady, standing apathetically with her arms crossed, watching him approach. Toni was wearing a white flowered summer dress that the breeze whipped around her tanned body. It was a scene that would have captured most men's imagination, but not this time. As he drew closer, her piercing stare and the fact that she didn't utter a word made Mike nervous. The words "Hi, baby" made their way to his lips but were never spoken because, as he approached his building, the expression on her face took on an even more menacing air.

As he ran up the two flights of back stairs to his apartment, it was only the depth of her bad news, in his opinion, that was in question. He walked in the back door and stopped in his tracks when an enraged Toni rushed in from the balcony.

"You—You bastard!" Toni shouted as she hurried over to him. "To think, all along I was feeling so sorry for you and—and it was your fault all the time. You used me, you bastard!"

"Toni, what are you talking about?" Mike pleaded as she quickly closed the distance between them.

"Don't play stupid. You know—"

"Wait a minute, will you?" Mike said, cutting her off. "I don't know what you're talking about. Did Doctor Ryan get the results back, is that why you're acting so...so irrational?"

"Irrational." Toni slapped him hard across the face. "Yeah, Doctor Ryan called, but he only talked to me when he couldn't get in touch with you. Seems he was more interested in telling you first!" she shouted.

She watched in renewed anger as Mike rubbed his cheek with the phony hurt look of the innocent on his face. She wanted to slap that look off his face but thought better of it.

The message she carried would be revenge enough, she vindictively decided.

Mike started to mouth a question, but Toni beat him to the punch.

"I asked Doctor Ryan why he couldn't tell me, since we were in this together. At first, he said it was a private matter and he couldn't share privileged patient information with anyone. After I cussed him out and told him we were both affected with his news, he changed his mind and told me."

"Told you what, that I also have the HIV virus?" Mike asked with amazing calm.

The unemotional tone of his voice impressed her. The fear of those three initials had caused her to cry so much over the last few days that she had to go to the drug store and purchase eye drops to stop the burning. Here Mike stood as if he had said ABC and not *HIV*. *Well, let's see if he can shake these other letters off so easily.* "You don't have HIV, Mike, but don't rejoice too much. The doctor said you've tested—positive—for—for—" Toni said, spitefully dragging it out, "—AIDS!"

Mike staggered backward until his back hit the wall. His mouth dropped open, and he stared wide-eyed at her. The shock subsided, but his knees grew weaker. The wall was a kind, strong friend that offered much needed support. He clearly understood that her words had pronounced his death. AIDS, how was that possible? He struggled to understand first how he could have it, and even more shocking, how it could have progressed so fast.

"It seems you're further gone than I am. Isn't that a kick? I wanted to come over and tell you that in person."

Mike battled with Toni's announcement and the cruel, painful way she was wielding that terrible information. In his confusion and shock he couldn't find the words to stay her attack on him.

"I thought I had found the one man!" she screamed at him,

"the one man that I could trust enough to give my love too unconditionally. I've done things with you I swore I never would with any man, but I did for you. Don't you know I would have done anything for you, Mike? I would have sold myself on the street corner if I thought that's what you wanted from me. You bastard, you've used me far worse than a pimp would have. You coldly sentenced me to death, and for what, sex? Was screwing me worth my life? Answer me you—you—" Toni slapped Mike again. She was trying more to knock him out the stupor he was in than trying to hurt him. "Why, Mike? Tell me why, dammit. How could you hurt me that much?"

"Toni, I don't understand. How could I have AIDS?"

Toni lost it. She thought he was thinking only of himself and not what he had done to her. She gritted her teeth as her body trembled with anger. The sadness that had broken her spirit was replaced by a surge of animosity. It swelled up in her chest and exploded. She threw punch after punch, that Mike weakly tried blocking as his focus was more into mentally deflecting those painful letters. Blow after blow landed, bloodying his nose and lip. Finally, he was able to see through the self-pity that had dulled his mind, and he grabbed her wrists. He was just about to explain to her how all this must have happened, when she kicked him as hard as she could in the groin.

Mike dropped to the floor in a heap and groaning, curled up in a fetal position. Toni stood unrepentant over him as he moaned in agony.

"I hope you burn in hell for what you've done to me, Michael Buffer," she shouted down at him. "I was willing to give you my future, but you stole it from me." Toni watched indifferently as he writhed in pain on the floor. "I didn't even care that you couldn't give me kids," she continued. "Don't you understand that having you to love meant more to me than giving birth? There one good thing about your betrayal, I don't have to worry about giving birth to something you helped create. Or did you also lie about being sterile?" That cruel possibility almost prompted another well-placed kick from her. Toni opened his front door to leave and looked back at him. "The only satisfaction I have now is that *you* will die before me."

Mike lay on the hard floor for a long time after Toni slammed his door and stormed out his apartment. The speed in which his world came tumbling down sapped his will to fight. All he could think about was the enormity of his loss that had walked out his door. He repeatedly replayed the scene that had just transpired, as he lay curled up on the floor. The storm had blown in so fast, he was caught completely off-guard.

He had AIDS. The letters were so frightening, he labored to repeat them. *That means I'm going to die in less than five years or maybe half that.* Even worse, he no longer had Toni, which meant he was already dead. This time he fought his way through the funk that he was in, through the pain caused by her kick, and made the terse calculation that Toni was gone—again.

It took more effort and pain than he first judged to get up, but he was standing. Each step he took gave him a sharp reminder of the anger of his last visitor. He made it to the couch and dropped down. He sat there with legs drawn up under him staring out the patio glass doors. The day had turned into a fog that he couldn't quite see his way through. Stunned, Mike lay down and silently stared at the walls. Every time he tried to think about what Toni said, his chest tightened up. He was on the verge of coming apart and knew it.

A thousand scenarios crossed his mind as he lay there for over an hour. Who could have given it to them? Was it passed on to some other unsuspecting soul he was with? Was it one of her lovers or one of his who first spread the bug? Different faces crossed his mind's eye. Some were innocent and just shared their precious gift with him, others carried the face of the guilty, but how could one know? He looked innocent—was innocent—he corrected himself. There were only a few times he was so drunk he couldn't manage the task of putting on a condom. As the pain lessened, he knew the answer. How did he forget about—

He had to try and reach Toni, Mike finally decided. They could straighten this out if he could talk to her. Sitting up, he reached over and picked up the phone. Summoning up his courage, he hit the number one on his speed dial. The first ring startled him as he awaited the rage of the answerer. By the second ring, he was determined to explain to her what had possibly happened. Rings five and six stole that determination. By ten, eleven, and twelve rings, he was convinced of the futility of his effort. He placed the phone down and wondered where Toni could be.

He leaned back and closed his eyes. *What a mess this has be-come*, he thought as he rubbed his forehead with his fingers. For any other argument they might have had, Mike would have let Toni blow off steam a while before calling. This was different. For one, Toni blamed him for infecting her with the HIV virus, and that could be her death sentence. Second, he knew she was blinded by fear and not hate, and that she loved him as deeply as he loved her. Third, she was a creature of spontaneity and would do the first thing that seemed reasonable to her. That was what scared him because that was the state of mind of the suicidal, he rationalized.

He called again, and no answer. Then he realized he didn't get her answering machine after the forth ring. She was there, just not answering her calls. Reluctantly, he put the phone down.

"Dear Lord," he prayed as he looked up at the ceiling. "I've done something very stupid with the precious life you gave me. I was so in love with her, I didn't weigh the consequences of my actions. Please forgive me for wasting my life. I'm not angry with her for blaming me. Toni's frightened, and rightfully so…I guess. But what am I supposed to do now?" He was again silent as he stared at the white ceiling of his living room. He was waiting—like we did sometimes when the dam had burst around us and the way out wasn't very clear—for a voice to speak to him from somewhere beyond. The answer, if it came, wasn't shouted from the heavens but spoken softly in his heart. When our pain was severe, which his was at that moment, we often fail to hear the *whisper* in the wind.

℘≈℘≈℘

"I'm going, Brenda," Toni said.

Brenda didn't move from the bed she was sitting on but watched as her best friend angrily tossed some clothes in her suit-case. "Toni, are you sure this is what you want to do?"

"Yes, I'm sure," Toni abruptly answered her dearest friend while closing the last of her two suitcases. "I've got to get out of this damn town. There's nothing here but heartache." She was sorry the moment the words left her mouth and she looked into a pair of dispirited eyes. "Not you, Bren, my God, I wasn't talking about you."

"Duh, I know that." A hint of the hurt still broke through Brenda's façade as she walked over and looked out the window.

Toni dropped her suitcase, ran over, and embraced her best friend. The ringing of the phone interrupted their hugging. Brenda felt Toni's arms around her tense up, the suspected caller breaking the sanctity of their embrace. Toni backed away from Brenda and stared at the phone until it quit ringing. She had disconnected the answering machine downstairs, expecting him to call. When it stopped ringing, her intensity had returned.

"Toni, don't go. You can't solve anything by running away."

"I know that's true, but I'm hurting too much. There are too many things here that remind me of him. When we broke up the last time, I was to the point of killing myself over losing him. I thought it was something I had done wrong or hadn't done right, like loved him enough. This time, he just used me to get—I feel worse now, but I know I did everything I could to make it work. So, don't worry, Red, I have no desire to commit *hara-kiri.*"

"But, Toni, there's no proof Mike gave you HIV."

"Brenda, stop defending that ass-hole. The doctor said Mike probably contracted it before I did that's why he has advanced HIV or AIDS. Mike even admitted to sleeping around. Who knows? Maybe one of his bar whores gave it to him. Maybe he already had it and gave it to them, I don't know. Chances are he already had it before we met, and those poor girls might also be infected."

Brenda shook her head. "Toni, I'm a nurse, and I don't pretend to know as much as Doc Ryan about AIDS, but I do know it affects people differently. It can hide in one person for up to ten years and yet burst out in another in two. There's no way of knowing when he got infected. Doc Ryan knows that as well as I do. I can't believe he told you Mike was to blame."

"All right then, explain this to me. Why didn't Mike try to defend himself when I accused him, huh, why didn't he? I'll tell you why, he got busted. He knew he was infecting me all along. I was just another receptacle, another conquest. Bren, Mike deliberately used me, knowing all along, that son-of-a-bitch, that he was putting me at risk. No, he was the cause of my acquiring HIV. If he didn't know he had it, Bren, I could forgive him for that. Hell, remember I thought I unwittingly gave it to him. But, Brenda, I would never knowingly put my worst enemy at risk for AIDS. The only saving grace is that not all people with HIV have acquired AIDS. There's a slim chance that I might live a long life."

Brenda saw an opening and jumped for it. "There's a great chance, that's why I want you to stay. We can fight it together."

"I understand—"

The phone rang again, breaking the thin thread of logic Brenda had established with her angry friend. Toni grabbed her two suitcases. As the phone rang, she walked out of her bedroom. Brenda thought for a moment about answering it and then decided against that, wondering what would she tell Mike, if it was him.

She heard Toni closing drawers and rushed downstairs to see what she was looking for.

"Brenda, did you see my diary?" Toni asked her when she entered the living room.

"You always keep it on your nightstand," Brenda reminded her.

"Yeah, I know. But I brought it down here before talking to the doctor. I wanted to record what he had to say if he called. I had no idea what direction his conversation would take."

"I bet," Brenda answered.

"Look, Bren, you don't have to take me to the airport. I don't want to bring you into this. I can call a cab."

"No way, Toni. No one else is going to say goodbye to my best friend but me. You look for your diary, and I'll get my keys."

Toni remembered she was in the kitchen when the doctor called so she walked off in that direction.

Brenda used that momentary respite to speed-dial David's phone number. "Come on, come on David. Please be home." When she heard his answering machine kick in, she swore.

"I found it," Toni shouted from the kitchen.

Brenda put the phone down just as Toni stepped into the living room. She wasn't sure if Toni saw her when she entered. If she did, she gave no indication. "Ahh, have you talked to your dad about leaving?"

"Yeah right, like he would understand. I'll call him from Florida."

"Florida, you're going all the way to Florida."

Toni didn't answer her. One slip of the tongue was enough. She had called and learned there were a few remaining but expensive seats on a USAir flight. Grabbing her suitcases and diary, she headed for the door. She was out before Brenda could say anything else. Brenda stared at the opened door for a moment until she heard the door of a car slam shut. She threw her keys up in the air, catching them without looking, and headed for the door, knowing she had until they reached the airport to change Toni's mind. If only she could have reached David at home.

ᘒᘉᘒᘈ

David had trouble getting into the baseball game he was watching on TV. It was too early in the season to establish a love, or hate, for any particular team. The Pirates weren't on TV today so he was reduced to flipping between the channels until he found a game between the Tigers and the White Sox. It had taken two innings of boring baseball before David bothered to look over at his answering machine. For some reason, no one had left him any messages lately, so when he came home today from grocery shopping, he didn't bother to check. Lately, he was either home when someone called, or they didn't want to talk to his machine. He had heard there were people who refused to talk to a machine when they called, thinking it was too impersonal. Trisha usually only called late at night after work or during the day she was at school.

Distracted by the boring game he looked over at his phone and was surprised to see the red light on the answering machine flashing in a series of three blips indicating there were three messages. "Three calls?" He slid over on the couch and pushed the play button.

"Hi, honey, are you coming over tonight? I'm off today. If not, let me know because I just remembered my girlfriends at school are meeting for a few drinks at Karen's house around six this evening. I would like to go but if you want, I'll gladly stay home with you if you're off. Really, I mean it. If you don't call me back in time, that's where I'll be. Bye, sweetheart." Beep.

David decided to call Trisha back immediately. As bored as he was, spending the evening with his "Sparkling Brown Sugar" seemed like a great idea.

Her picture was erased from his mind by the next message.

"Hello, David, Mike here. Look, could you stop by later. It's very important I talk to you. If you're busy, it can wait. Bye." Beep.

The defeated tone of Mike's voice cut through the building excitement of spending the evening with Trisha.

"David, this is…To…lev…tttt…nn."

David frowned, as the third message was barely audible. What in the world was that? he questioned. With his older model answering machine, he had to replay all of the messages to get to the last one. He hated that feature and was going to buy a newer model but recanted when he remembered how little he paid for this model and who had picked this model out for him. Besides, it had been very reliable and always worked. While the first two messages replayed, he turned off the TV and put his head next to the speaker of the answering machine and listened carefully as the third message began.

"David." He could clearly hear now. "This is Brenda. You've got to help me. Toni is leaving town. Can you—" Beep.

David jumped up as if he had sat on a live wire. *My God*, he wondered, *what's going on? First, Mike calls sounding like hell, and then Brenda whispers for me to—*

David bolted out of his front door, all the while feeling his pockets for his keys. Twenty minutes of weaving between cars and racing through yellow lights had cut ten minutes off the usual time it took to reach Toni and Brenda's apartment. During the drive, David replayed the messages over and over in his head. The obvious conclusion he came up with increased the speed of his car as he tried to arrive before she left.

He pulled up in front of the duplex immediately noticing the empty space where Brenda always parked. She would walk the couple of blocks to work and often left her car for Toni to drive to her job downtown if she or the buses were running late. Hope's faint heartbeat gave David enough strength to get out and check the house for an answer he already knew. The unlocked door surprised him when he tried it, *Strike one*. When he walked into the house, he didn't hear music playing, *Strike two*. "Is anyone home?" No answer, *Strike three, you're out!*

After walking upstairs and noticing Toni's open and empty dresser drawers, David knew he was too late. Solemnly he walked downstairs and looked around in each room. Funny, he thought, how the spirit of a place becomes as empty as the space when people move out. He felt the difference as he walked from room to room. He was here before when they weren't home, but one could still sense their presence, their spirit, and sometimes— their fragrance. Knowing now that Toni was gone, he could also feel the loss of her aura.

David tried calling Mike and got no answer. Was he also trying to head off Toni? David wondered. Hopping they had their keys, David walked out of their house, looked around at the world passing by unbothered by what had happened here, and locked the front door. Brenda had said Toni was leaving, but not why or where? He sat down on the top step of their doorway and tried to figure out what he should do next. "Brenda asked for my help, and I tried," he acknowledged, and after a few minutes, he stood up to leave. His guess was the girls had a fight, and he never thought that would ever happen. Once they calmed down, he decided as he reflected on how very close they were, it would all work out. But now he was going home to see if he could rescue his evening.

He took a few steps when he spotted something black in the bushes in front of their house. He stuck his hand in and retrieved a book. When he turned it over, he realized it was a diary. He was going to leave it on the doorstep but wasn't sure if that was a good idea. With the door now locked, he couldn't put it in the house. David looked for their mailbox and located it. They had a mail slot in the door. There was no way that thick book was going to fit through there he realized.

He decided to try and identify whom it belonged to. Written on the first page were the words:

> *To Toni,*
> *from her best friend,*
> *Brenda.*

eᴐeᴐ

They argued all the way to the airport. Brenda tried every angle she could but couldn't dent Toni's resolve. She was leaving. This was a part of Toni that Brenda had never seen before. They had become so close there never was a reason for either of them to show the other anything but their better side. That damn Mike Buffer, an angry Brenda acknowledged as she drove, had pushed her across that line, exposing a side of Toni that she was totally unprepared to deal with.

Their differences of opinion continued to paint the drive to the airport. Brenda felt the futility of her argument but felt compelled to try. When they drove up to the USAir terminal, she had given it her best shot. Brenda was now resigned to the fact Toni was leaving.

"I'll say my goodbyes here," Brenda told a quiet, sullen Toni as they sat in the car beside the USAir baggage curb check-in. Looking out the windows, they both took note that the entrance to the airport was unusually empty of cars and people unloading their luggage. "I couldn't stand to watch you board your plane, Toni. I think you're making a big mistake in leaving like this, but I understand you honestly believe it's the right thing to do. Please take care of yourself and call me as soon as you get there. Wait a minute, where in Florida are you going?"

Toni smiled at her, reached over, and squeezed her hand. She got out of the car without answering. Toni grabbed her suitcases out of the back seat and sat them on the curb. She then walked around to the driver's side door. "Look, Bren, you're the one person I will miss the most, and I think you're right. It is best we say goodbye now. Please don't tell anyone, but I'm going to Daytona Beach," she decided to tell her best friend. "My dad and I spent our vacation there once, and I always wanted to go back. They have great beaches." Toni wanted to tell her more about that vacation, but she knew she would only be delaying the inevitable. She reached in and kissed Brenda on the cheek. "Goodbye, babe. I'll call you as soon as I can and tell you where I'm staying. Don't worry, it may be a while before I make that call. I think I'll want to clear my head first so don't worry about me. And, if you don't know where I'm staying, you can't tell anyone that might bug you about that." The more Toni thought about it, the way she was feeling now, it would probably be a long time before she could call.

Brenda also knew that when she saw the look on her face. She was right about one thing, the men in Toni's life would be frantic to find her. If they thought she knew where Toni was they would descend upon her like flies on shit. Hell, they probably would anyway.

Brenda watched as Toni walked determinedly into the airport. Her shoulders were straight as she carried her pride for all to see. The length of her long strides proclaimed she wasn't running away, she was leaving. It was a very poignant and touching moment for Brenda. She sagged down in her seat and brought her hands up to her face. Her fingertips comforted her trembling lips as her best friend walked away. Brenda also felt a little pride as Toni took this step on her own. Look at her, she thought. Toni had a certain air about her that seems to stand her apart from everyone else in the airport. She was like a bright star in a clear night sky. You could see the other stars, if you look hard enough. But then there's that one that catches your attention as if it was calling you or touched you on your shoulder making you look up.

Brenda's trance was broken when she noticed Toni suddenly stop. Just before hope was buried six feet under, Brenda embraced it again. She bit down on her bottom lip afraid to own the hope she had changed her mind. Toni turned and looked back at her friend. Then she put down one of her suitcases and waved. Brenda just stared back. She wanted to smile at Toni and return the gesture as a show of love, but she couldn't move.

Toni stood there for a moment as if waiting for a reply. Then she blew Brenda a kiss, waved again, and freeing Brenda from any compensatory obligations, turned, and walked away.

The gentle gesture was a moving statement to the weeping woman sitting in her car. Brenda waved back, but after Toni had turned around and walked away. "Hang in there, girl," she whispered to the retreating image.

Brenda sat for a while replaying the day's events, wondering if David or Mike could have talked her into staying if they had been here and was even more surprised when an airport cop hadn't come by and asked her to move her car.

Brenda drove off blaming herself for not preventing Toni from leaving. Overcome with sadness, she pulled over to the shoulder of the airport road and reviewed her conversation with Toni. She knew the guys would grill her about what happened and where she went. Brenda was about to drive off when she noticed the planes were taking off on the runway beside the road she was on. According to Toni's schedule, she was running late when they arrived, and her plane should be taking off in another twenty minutes. Brenda was determined to watch for her plane until they chased her away. Symbolically she wanted to say goodbye to her closest friend.

A signature silver plane, bearing the USAir logo and a blue tail fin, roared down the runway and screamed as it rose up over her car. An assurance passed over her, as the plane banked left, that Toni was sitting there looking out her window at her car as the plane flew overhead. Brenda waved out the car window up at her. "Goodbye, girlfriend."

享み☆

David walked in his apartment, placed his keys on the hook by the door, and then walked over and flopped down on his couch. He was tired. Well frustrated and drained was more like it. Battling a nagging suspicion something bad had happened between Toni and Mike or with Brenda, and not knowing what, was tormenting him. In the last few years, they were his family. David was raised by his grandmother after he was taken from his drug addicted mother at twelve. He never knew his father. His grammy always said that was a good thing. When she died five years ago, a part of him died with her. Meeting and befriending three white soul mates was never envisioned by the black man sitting on the couch, but it had happened, and they were the dearest people in his life.

"I can't call Trish, not tonight," David said, talking to himself. "I would be lousy company. I've got to know what is going on with my friends."

Mike's phone continued to ring without being answered as had Brenda's a call before. *Where are they?* David started to have second thoughts about what to do? He had two hours before Trisha was going to leave for that shower. Should he go over Trisha's house anyway? he pondered, or try and find Mike? David sighed deeply then gingerly got up and walked into his bedroom. He was out of his clothes and showering in less than a minute. The vision of that spirited vixen in his arms won out over the confusion that was Mike, Brenda, and Toni.

David was drying himself in front of the TV when the phone rang. He wiped his hair one more time and sat down on the couch. With his towel wrapped around him he picked the phone.

"Hello."

"David, it's me, Brenda."

"Hey, Brenda, what the heck is going on with you and Toni? What was that message on my machine about?" David asked in rapid succession.

"Toni, left town, David," Brenda all but whispered.

"What? Toni left town?" David shouted into the phone.

"She's gone. I just got home from taking her to the airport. I tried to stop her, but she wouldn't listen to me. That's why I tried to call you. I was hoping you would get the message and help me, but it's too late."

David felt a chill. His apartment was warm, and he was still sweating from the hot shower, yet he found himself wrapping the towel on his lap around his shoulders.

"David, did you hear me?"

"Yes, Brenda, I'm sorry. It's weird. I've had this funny feeling all day that something was very wrong."

"Something is very wrong, David." Brenda told him the whole story. Between her pauses, he knew she was either crying or fighting to hold back the tears. He wanted to reach out and comfort her and thought about rushing over and doing just that. She was broken hearted over Toni being ill and leaving, David realized. Yet, he felt removed from it all, having yet to recognize the battle raging within his spirit. The nothing he was feeling was the realization that this time it was really over between Toni and Mike. The nothing was the huge emptiness he felt over hearing for the first time his best friend had HIV. The nothing David felt also resulted from their apparent decision to keep that terrible secret from him.

Brenda couldn't find the strength to tell him Mike had AIDS.

"Where did she go?" he asked in an unmistakably defeated tone.

Brenda read the sadness in his voice but tried to be upbeat about everything. "She's off to Florida," Brenda told him. She felt an odd need to withhold the exact location. "Maybe the change in climate will do her some good. Toni's angry, David, very hurt and angry. She blames Mike for giving her the virus. I tried to explain to her that there is no way of knowing that. But she's sure he gave it to her."

"Brenda, I know Mike. He would die before doing something like that to anyone, much less the one woman he idolizes. Toni means the world to him. Well, she was his world."

Brenda's hesitation almost made him regret his next words.

"If he did give it to her, it was because he didn't know what he had."

Brenda hesitated again before answering. "That's the viciousness of this disease, David," Brenda's explained, her voice raising another octave. "You can have it for years and never know. It's the curse of our generation. It can pass from ten different people before anyone shows any sign of the infection. By then those ten people could have passed it on to a hundred others and so on and so on. Toni is so angry she can't see that."

"Did you try explaining that to her? Never mind, dumb question."

"Of course I tried!" Brenda shouted before absorbing his apology.

"I'm sorry," David said, after sensing the anger in her voice, "of course you did!"

"No, I'm the one who should apologize. I'm sorry for shouting at you."

"What did she say when you told her those facts?" David asked, trying to ease the tension.

"If you would have seen the fire in her eyes, Davey. She wasn't about to listen to me or anyone." Brenda groaned. "But she had a good argument."

For a moment, he questioned if he should continue this line of thought. He should have—not. "What argument?" The silence on the other end convinced him he should have let it drop.

"What I was trying to warn you about when he involved you

in his whoring. That could be when he got infected. You might be—"

"No, no, Bren, I always wore protection—always."

"Nothing is one hundred percent, David, you know that."

"Then we are all carriers because the elitist social status of a person doesn't guarantee safety either. And you know that." *Calm down*, he chastised himself. *It's too late to argue who is right.* "Brenda, good people and bad people carry the virus. None of those girls could be infected."

"And they all could have been, that's the problem our generation faces."

"Wait a minute."

"What?"

"After Mike finally came to his senses and stopped drinking, he said he was through with that life, and with the bars and the bar girls. I told him great and talked him into getting tested for a possible STD. He was reluctant, at first, because we had just completed our required yearly physical at work and nothing was reported in the results we received. I explained there was no way of knowing all of what they were checking with that physical from company doctors.

"But we did get this very cute female physician that poked us everywhere. Some places only a finger with nail polish could go." David waited for a silly comeback, but she remained silent. "Mike really was reluctant to be rechecked when the results of that physical came back and we both did great. My cholesterol was a little above average and his iron was a little low. Other than that, we passed with flying colors, Brenda. But I insisted we both take a STD screening.

"Brenda, I went with him and was also tested. That was before they got back together this last time. It took longer than I realized but the test finally came back clean for both of us. They didn't find any HIV virus or any other STD. And I know he hasn't been with anyone other than Toni since."

"Why didn't Mike tell her that?"

"I don't know. I don't know, Brenda."

"But, Davey, you know that only means he probably didn't when tested, but it doesn't mean he couldn't have it show up later. Sometimes the virus remains hidden. The only way to know if you have it is when it starts to attack the body's white cells. There is no test to find it while remaining hidden. The frightening part is either Mike or Toni could have had it and escaped detection. See, that's something you could have explained to Toni or I could have if I knew about the results of that test. But that might not have stopped her anyway."

David felt compassion for Brenda sensing she was feeling guilty about not being able to help her closest friend in the world. "Well, Red, I know you tried to do all that you could to change her mind, other than kidnapping her, nothing would have worked I suppose. No one was closer to Toni than you."

They both were then silent. David's reference in the past tense stirred individual morbid pictures. This time they each sensed their dark haired friend would be gone a long time.

"Brenda, have you talked to Mike?"

"No!"

David was surprised by the sharpness of her answer. She said she didn't blame Mike for giving Toni HIV, but she must blame him for causing her to leave.

"I've got to call him, Brenda. He's probably crushed by all this." The dial tone he heard in his ear answered one of the questions on his mind. He took a deep breath and hung up.

"Hello."

Thank God he was finally home, David thought after calling him for the third time. He took a deep breath. "Mike, it's David."

"Hi, Dave."

"Where have you been? I tried calling your house. Brenda told me about what happened with Toni. Are you all right?"

Mike didn't answer right away. David waited, giving him the time he needed.

"I guess so. Sorry I didn't tell you about the test. Toni didn't want you to worry about us. I guess I should have told you, anyway."

David wanted to say something smart-assed in payback but thought better. "You guessed right," he finally said. "Don't worry about it. She's always trying to play my big sister." He hesitated as he pondered how to ask the next question. "Is it true, Mike? Did you test positive?"

"Yes. I just came back from seeing the doctor to verify Toni's claim. The doctor was one-hundred percent sure of the results. Both Toni and I tested positive. David, she thinks I knew about testing positive before we became intimate again, can you believe that? You know me. I would never do anything that cruel to anyone. I thought Toni knew me better than that. You would think getting news like this would be the most frightening thing you can imagine. It isn't. Having someone you love doubt you, that's the most frightening."

David wasn't sure if Mike was only talking about Toni's reaction. "Look, Mike, I think the news frightened her more than you realize. Somewhere…ah, deep inside her was a fear we never knew about, a crack in her foundation. A small crack that it took an earthquake to split open. And when her house crumbled and fell in. It was something she, and I guess we, never imagined could happen, so she became frightened and ran off to Florida. In the same situation, we might have reacted the same way."

"Wait! Did you say Toni went to Florida?"

David didn't take in account Mike couldn't know that.

"David," Mike said his voice barely above a whisper, "Where's Toni?"

After a deep breath, "She's probably landing somewhere in Florida as we speak."

"Where?"

"I don't know where. Brenda just said Florida."

"I'm really hurting inside over this, David. I never thought Toni would ever doubt my love for her. I want to get angry at her, but I can't."

How do you reach out and hug someone on the phone? David wondered. "I'll be right over."

"No, wait. I know you mean well, but I want to be alone for a while. Don't worry. I'm not going to do anything stupid. I've just got to get myself together. You know what I mean?"

David could empathize with him because he did. "Okay, but, Mike, promise you'll call me if you need anything, or before you really do something…stupid."

The dial tone was his answer.

CHAPTER 22

Spring arrived without a word from Toni. Her father, Anthony DiNardo, was frantic at first and blamed everyone for her running off. Later, after Mr. DiNardo calmed down, he admitted it was something he would have expected Toni to do when she had to face tough problems. Brenda tried to explain that Toni just wanted to get a fresh start, but it was obvious Mr. DiNardo wasn't buying that.

"That's just who she is. My daughter doesn't like to face things. Toni should have straightened that boy out and not let him chase her away from her family."

Brenda was out of excuses and just let him rant. She also didn't expect Toni to cut everyone out of her life.

For Mike, he quit working at Zinc Coaters before anyone found out about his having AIDS. He had a large amount of money in his bank account, he explained to a surprised David, from the will of his late grandfather and really didn't need to work.

"I never wanted to use the money he left to me because I never liked him very much. He and my dad hated each other, but I was his only grandchild, so they had to deal with each other. With AIDS, my time is short anyway," he rationalized and shrugged, "why spend my last days working?"

"If I had money," David countered, "I wouldn't be working period!"

Brenda, as expected, took Toni's departure the hardest. Each day, she rushed home from work expecting a letter or a message on her new and better answering machine she purchased just for that reason. As the weeks evolved into months, Brenda became resigned to life without Toni. David dropped by on occasion, but he was dating Trisha and couldn't offer her the intimacy she needed. The holidays without word from Toni were the worse.

Thankfully, Brenda followed tradition and spent time with her family during the holidays.

There was a deep sadness etched in Brenda's beautiful face that kept everyone else at a distance. She started working as much as she could to avoid their house and the silent memories in each room, on each piece of furniture, and from each keepsake.

David was battling his own demons. Everyone who has ever been near a person with HIV understands what those demons are. He had to come to grips with that fear before he could honestly look Mike in the face. It was important to him that none of his anxiety revealed itself. Mike must never wonder, David decided when he thought about the chances of his catching the disease, if he was afraid to be close to him. There was some fear, the horror of HIV prompted that rationalization, but David knew he would risk everything to allay Mike's concern that he might be leery about being around him.

In the ensuing months, David tried to constantly keep Mike's spirits up. He had read somewhere that most patients that resist the debilitating emotional effects of HIV live longer than those who live as one without hope. Mike did surprise David with how well he accepted the loss of his future. It was as if he always knew an early death was waiting down the road for him.

David remembered something his cousin Bobby had confided to him when he was in his teens. Bobby had always claimed that he would never live to see thirty. He wasn't upset about that. It was just something Bobby understood to be a fact of life. Two years removed from his thirtieth birthday, Bobby died of cancer. Mike seemed to have a similar, relaxed acceptance of his fate.

The afternoon sun surprisingly warmed the day beyond the need for a jacket. One appreciative worshipper sat on his balcony enjoying the fresh air. David thought about getting up and going over and seeing if Mike wanted to go somewhere today but decided against it. In the mood David was in, he would be lousy company for Mike after a bad week at work after numerous strip breaks and power outages. Couple that with one of the few times David had an argument with Trisha. She got upset with him because he seemed preoccupied lately, when he was there, and had too many excuses why he couldn't see her. He was distracted, waiting on the test he had decided to take again, but didn't want to tell Trisha it was because he was worrying about the virus he might have given her.

This week, with their work schedules, they had seen each other only once. That evening, while driving to one of their favorite restaurants for dinner, she shared something.

"Honey, everything is set."

"What is, Trish?"

"Remember," she said ignoring the questioning scowl on his face as he drove, "I mentioned trying to get off and fly to Atlanta for the annual Tipton family reunion? Well, I got the time off from work. Isn't that great?"

"That is, babe."

"My ignorant boss kept me guessing if I could get the time off until yesterday. A week before I'm to leave. That meant the plane ticket prices were higher. I bet he did that on purpose, the jag-off."

David noticed she had the same frown she always got when mentioning her boss. *And calling him a "Jag-off," the girl has spent too much time in Pittsburgh*, he thought as she talked. He had planned to get some of the biker-looking guys together after work, walk into Denny's with about a half dozen of them, and scare the hell out of her boss. Maybe when she got back.

Her going home for two weeks was a godsend, David now realized, after being a little cold to the idea when she first told him. They hadn't been intimate in the last few weeks, as David stalled while he waited for his test results, but the woman walking out of her apartment when he pulled up looked dazzling in a body-hugging tan dress. "Damn," was all he could say when he saw her. "Damn." With her figure, she looked stunning. He got out of his car and opened her door.

Trisha saw the look on his face. There was a more important reason for wearing this short, tight dress than seeing his tongue handing out, but, as a side benefit, that was cool, she thought as she demurely got into his car while tugging on the rising hem of her dress.

"You look amazing, Trisha," he said as he climbed in and took a moment to watch as she struggled to cover what she could.

"I just threw this on in the last minute. I was tired of wearing jeans."

Yeah, right, David thought. *Something is up, and I don't mean just me from looking at that little dress.* "Then I should go home and change out of my jeans."

"Not on my account. You look great, baby."

Needless to say, she was the object of everyone's attention when they strolled into the steak house. Admittedly, David was proud to have her on his arm.

"Baby, I have something to ask you," Trisha said after they had made small talk over a surprisingly delicious cup of restaurant coffee after dinner.

David was sipping on his drink when she put down her cup. Looking into those bright eyes, he knew the reason for her looking like a million bucks on a simple dinner date was about to present itself.

"Every year...well, every year since I was a kid, I told you the Tipton's have a family reunion. We have it in different places or cities for a week to ten days. This year it's in my hometown of Atlanta next week. Funny," she said with this big smile on her face, "two years before I met you it was here in Pittsburgh before my cousins moved away. Most of my family lives in the south, but just about everyone comes. It's a tradition. And if you don't want my aunts bugging you all year, you better have a good reason not to show. And those old bitties know how to bug you."

"Sounds like fun, Trish," David garnered from her joyful countenance.

"It's a lot of fun. We do a lot of fun things as a group. We have big dinners. Some of the younger people throw parties. There are tours, there's a huge picnic scheduled at the park, all the food you can possibly eat and alcohol to drink. And it's a hoot just getting together each day with my crazy family. I have a lot of very nice-looking cousins that would love to show off for you, the hussies," she said with a chuckle and then looked down at her plate.

Her hesitating to come right out and ask, surprised David. Usually, she said whatever was on her mind, regardless of whom it embarrassed, he thought while fighting to keep a straight face. *You have changed, haven't you, pretty lady?*

"I would love it if you came with me." There, she said it, Trisha thought and coyly looked up at him for his answer.

There, my overly dressed sexy woman said it, David thought, now to somehow get out of this…gracefully. He had to find out about that test before being around all those people.

He didn't come right out and say no, she realized as she watched him considering her offer.

"Normally—"

That's a no, Trisha quickly grasped, the disappointment creasing her face in a frown.

"—I would love to go with you anywhere, babe," David said ignoring the disappointment on her face, "but next week is very short notice. Ten days you said?"

"Actually, it's for two weeks this time because there is so much to do and see in Atlanta for those who have never been there. But we only have to stay a week at the most."

"Well…I'll put in for it, but it doesn't look good. This month is full for vacations."

"Try real hard. I promise you will have a great time."

"I'm not worried about that, girl," David said while trying to ignore the hints and the sassy looks she was giving him. "Whenever I'm with you, it's a great time."

He would have normally thought she meant meeting her family and seeing the Atlanta area, that was until she cocked her head to one side. That always meant something extra. And with them, "extra" meant all of 38-24-38 he could handle. Lately, 38-24-38 was seven for seven in getting her way when that pretty little head leaned to one side. He was more than happy with the amazing benefits granted from losing seven straight times to whatever she wanted, but, this time, it was important.

Two days later, he took the cowardly but smart path and told Trisha the bad news over the phone. One good thing. Brenda had promised the results would be in, proving again they both were free of the antibodies that fought HIV and AIDS before Trisha returned, maybe even before she left.

"Think positive, Davey," Brenda had told him. "It's better to be sure, right? I have positive vibes we are clean, but after what happened to Toni and stupid, we both want to be sure."

David sighed over the "stupid" insinuation, but didn't comment. Her words helped alleviate some of the weight on his shoulders from maybe having to give an undeserving young woman worse news than that her boyfriend wasn't going with her to Atlanta.

Taking Trisha to the airport to catch her flight wasn't easy. But David gave Trisha credit. He had expected her to pout and make both of them miserable, but she didn't.

"Honey, when I get back, will you help me paint?"

"What?"

They were at the Greater Pittsburgh airport, having arrived early, and were sitting in one of the many eateries sipping a delicious cup of coffee as they killed time before her flight, when Trisha surprised him with that request.

"I decided I want to paint all the rooms in my house. I want a fresh start."

"Sure, baby, anything you want. I love how you pay your painters."

Not lately, Trisha thought, but having learned it was not always a good idea to speak her mind around a man that she knew loved her, she kept that to herself. "That's great," she said with a big smile. He bought it.

He hugged and kissed her on the cheek and then watched her walk into the security line. A wave and she headed for her gate.

It was three days later when Brenda received their second test results that would affirm the earlier results.

"Hello."

"We are clean, David! Thank God, we are clean!"

The joy of those words made him sit down and take a deep breath. "That's great, red. So, let me get this right. I don't have any of your cooties."

"No, and believe me you never will again, smart ass."

"I'm sorry, I—"

"Yes, you are, but isn't that great news?"

"I feel like I have my life back again. What are you doing tonight?" When she hesitated answering, David feared his attempt to make light of their near miss might have hurt her feelings. He needn't have worried.

"I'm going to have sex with my boyfriend who, unlike you, can last for more than a hot minute."

Her teasing lifted that fear off him. "Yeah, but you have to admit, it was an amazing hot minute."

"The best ever, Davey, the best minute ever."

After they placed the phones down, two like minds allowed themselves to resurrect some "Best ever" memories for probably the last time. After granting those treasured recollections their due, they moved on with their lives.

CHAPTER 23

"Trisha, have you seen your sister?" her mother called from upstairs.

"No, Momma," Trisha shouted from the couch she flopped down on as soon as they walked in the house. The fun and sun had sapped her strength. She smelled like chlorine from the public pool, as did the other females sitting on the couch, but she was too tired at the moment to care. They were all wearing shorts and shirts over their swimsuits, and now she was trying to push herself to get up and take a shower before the house became full of the other visiting family members from out of town like it had each night this week.

Her parent's friendly home was the place to be, at least that is what most of the younger relatives thought. They always had the biggest big back yard in the neighborhood where they, and the local kids, would hang out, dance, roughhouse, play different sports like badminton or shoot some basketball.

"I think Cheryl said she was going to pick up her boyfriend, Momma!" Trisha shouted so her mother could hear. "Who knows where they are now?" Then she whispered, "Or what those two are doing."

"That's the truth," her cousin Beverly seconded, also sitting on the couch beside her.

Occupying the other seat on the couch was her cousin, Donna, eighteen. Billie, twenty, was sitting in the recliner. Donna and Billie were sisters who lived in Mobile, Alabama. Beverly, also twenty-one like Trisha, lived here in Atlanta and grew up with Trisha and her older sister, Cheryl, twenty-four. Only six years separated the oldest from the youngest, so the five single young women were often in competition for the best-looking guys their age when they got together. Cheryl usually won that race and the gold medal. She wasn't the looker her younger sister was, but was expert at hinting with a look, or with body language, what boys might find if they picked "Door number One." As more than one lucky guy discovered, they weren't empty promises.

Trisha had the most desirable physical qualities of the group, but her reluctance to use them gained her the silver medal. Beverly, Donna, and Billie, when they were around, were left to fight for the bronze. Donna was the wildest of the five and unashamed of that title. And that usually got her the bronze metal, but none of the cousins were above having a good time.

"Trish, I thought you said you were bringing your new boyfriend down with you."

Trisha sat up and looked at Beverly. They had already discussed that when they were driving to the picnic. Why bring that up? Oh, okay.

On cue, the two sisters joined in the ribbing.

"You aren't ashamed of him because he's ugly, are you, cousin?" Donna asked teasing her.

Trisha stuck her tongue out at her.

"Or are you afraid one of us would take him away from you? That wouldn't be the first time."

That prompted laughter from the other three young women.

The seeds of their taunting might have been planted earlier at the outdoor family reunion picnic where they were able to reserve the best shelter at the park for their reunion. Having a Tipton on the Parks and Recreation Board didn't hurt any. It was what was located next to that shelter that made it a highly sought after spot that sometimes was rented years in advance. Situated very close to the shelter was a very large public swimming pool, two ball fields, a basketball court across the street, a large playground nearby for small kids, a new bike trail, and even some horseshoe pits.

Of the almost one hundred Tipton family members, friends, and dates attending the picnic, about half that number had planned to enjoy that refreshing public pool on a stiflingly hot day nearly one hundred degrees and very humid. Of that group, nearly twenty were young women under thirty years old. Half that many were there without a boyfriend, husband, or a date. The young ladies sitting in Trisha's parents' home constituted some of that small party.

Trisha's sister Cheryl announced she had a new boyfriend, surprising no one. She usually grew bored with her dates quickly. They learned he couldn't be there today for the picnic because he had to work, but he promised to come by the house later she told everyone.

One would think with a group that size, in a public pool filled with plenty of others seeking relief from the hot day, one person wouldn't stand out. One would think that and would have been wrong—today.

In the past, Trisha often earned silver medals when competing for guys with her sister and cousins, simply because she possessed the best equipment. This day, that "equipment" was clothed in a tiny white bikini, the same one that a certain guy back in Pittsburgh loved, covered by an opened white shirt and white shorts. There were others walking toward the pool wearing similar swim wear, but none were as toned and eye catching as the young woman in white over white. The same curvaceous figure that made a stranger stop, pick her up, drive her to work, return and fix her car for free, and then drive hers to her job leaving his more expensive model, was walking toward the pool and, like a magnet, pulling every male and most female eyes in her direction. Her white swimwear seemed to glow against her copper skin as if illuminated.

The other young ladies, including the three now sitting in the living room, had a chance until she slipped off the shirt and stepped out of her shorts. Game over! Even Cheryl realized offering "Doors" now wouldn't distort the image her sister's near-perfect figure seared in the minds of male and female alike. Like a fat man hearing the dinner bell, available males decided as a group to swim any where she was sitting. Growing bored with the constant come-ons, Trisha announced she was leaving.

"Hey, guys I'm going back to the picnic," Trisha told her cousins and the five or six guys sitting around them. She picked up her clothes and put them on.

"Why are you leaving, Trish?"

She looked at her cousin, Beverly, and then the sharks surrounding them. "I have a man." With that said, she walked back to the family picnic grove. Like a pied-piper, she induced a line of young men to leave the pool and follow her at a distance, stopping only when they saw the size of the gathering she melted into.

"I'm sorry, honey. Did you say where Cheryl was?"

Trisha looked up as her mother walked down the steps into the living room. "She said something about picking up her new boyfriend I think, Momma."

"Yes, she did, I forgot about that. Is Dad still out back?"

"I think so, Momma. He said he was going to fire up the grill again, in case someone came over tonight hungry."

"After all, that food today, heck, my refrigerator is still full of leftovers."

"I would like a freshly grilled steak myself," Trisha said, after standing up and kissing her mother on the cheek.

Momma Tipton had forgotten how much her youngest could eat and not gain a pound. "Where are you going?" she asked as Trisha walked past her and started up the stairs.

"Too get out of this bikini and take a quick bath."

That was another thing her youngest would often do a few times a day she remembered. "Before you do, clean up that room before company arrives."

"Yes, Momma."

Most of the mess in her room was her cousins' doing, but that was all right. They had a great time together this week, sleeping over. She placed their dirty clothes out of sight on the floor in the corner behind the dresser and then remade the bed. Only a few of their makeup and hair products remained, and she wasn't sure where to put them. She opened her underwear drawer and made room by pushing them to one side. That would do for now.

Now, that bath. Part of her wanted to take a quick shower, but that would mean having to go down stairs before she wanted to and face her teasing cousins. It was weird they started teasing her about David, she thought as she walked into the bathroom, because they had a good time last night, laughing and sharing naughty secrets about their men.

Maybe she shouldn't have boasted about how great he was in bed, Trisha wondered as she locked the bathroom door, but it was the truth. Like she readily confessed when they doubted her claims, yes, her experience with men was limited, but her man could go all night if she let him. After the girls accused her of exaggerating, she kept some of the other things he was gifted with to herself.

Thinking about him, she reached in and turned on the shower and then stopped undressing when she realized what she had done. "Oh, well." It wasn't her plan to get her hair wet, but the more she thought about getting the smell of chlorine from the public pool water out of her hair maybe a shower was a good idea, she reasoned. But that would mean having to blow dry her hair, she deduced, as she stepped out of her bikini. "Oh, well."

Twenty minutes later, Cheryl walked into the house arm-in-arm with the new boyfriend.

"Where's everyone?" she asked when she noticed the missing part of the all-girl-band.

"Trisha is upstairs taking a bath," Billie volunteered while staring at the great-looking man beside Cheryl. "Your mom is in the kitchen, and your dad out back on the grill. Is this him?"

"Oh, I'm sorry, yes, this is him." Cheryl introduced "Him" to them. "That's Billie in the recliner."

"Hi."

"Hello, Billie."

"The female staring at you like you're chocolate cake is Donna. Donna and Billie are sisters."

"Hi, Donna."

"Hi.

"The other young woman on the couch is Beverly."

"Hello," Beverly said as she stood and took a step toward him.

"We are all cousins." Cheryl stepped between them and informed her date. "Come on, guys, I want to introduce him to my parents."

"Hell, yes, wouldn't miss seeing your dad meeting one of his precious daughter's lovers," Beverly added as the other two young women jumped up with renewed interest.

The new boyfriend noticed that all the Tipton cousins were lookers. He came over to see one and now there were four nice-looking women surrounding him.

Cheryl stared at the three giggling females now standing next to him, and for a guy who at first seemed totally uncomfortable after hearing that dad and lover comment, he now seemed right at home. Cheryl felt more comfortable now as she led the gregarious group into the kitchen.

Trisha didn't hear the commotion downstairs as she sat in front of her vanity, blow drying her hair. Afterward, she put on a little makeup and rummaged in her closet for something to wear. She decided on white silk lounging pants and a matching blouse, clean yet comfortable. Standing in front of her mirror, she thought she looked great, and she felt even better. The only negative was that her dark underwear was visible. It was evening wear and usually too shear unless wearing certain sometimes uncomfortable undergarments or nothing at all.

She didn't mind the outline of her underwear showing, that was common now days, but not the color. It was a look she cherished at home when it caught the attention of David, the smile on her face giving evidence of that naughty memory. The question, change outfit or underwear? After she hammed it up in a few different poses, the outfit won out. As she changed, she momentarily tried on the outfit bereft of panties and bra. Like looking through a thick fog, her assets moved about…freely, but remain tantalizingly just short of being revealing. "Mmmmm, another look to thrust on poor Davey," she decided as she took out some white underwear from her drawer.

"Trisha!" Cheryl shouted up the stairs as they passed on their way to the kitchen, "get pretty and come on down. I want you to meet my new boyfriend. Once again, I get the best-looking guy."

Her three cohorts giggled in agreement.

Hearing Cheryl boasting about her boyfriend almost put a dagger in the David-induced high Trisha was feeling and relishing in. The picture of him getting caught sneaking a look at her assets in this outfit, while bare underneath, was still a strong image and a smile her sister's teasing couldn't erase.

"Coming." This wasn't a contest, she planned on telling her cocky sister, because she had already won. Her David was both handsome as hell and—Could a female be cocky? she wondered. "Come on, girl," she whispered as she sprayed on perfume, "get your mind out of the gutter."

Trisha heard the commotion going on in the kitchen as she walked down the stairs. She shook her head, guessing that their mischievous cousins were giving Cheryl's man a hard time. For some reason, she also found that description amusing in a naughty way.

All week, her parents' house began to fill up each night as out of town family members stopped by to shoot the breeze after spending most of the day together...somewhere...and sometimes stayed until late in the morning—if they left at all. Some, like her three cousins, just stayed the night. It was fun being around them, tiring but fun. It was one reason why she wasn't worried about dressing to impress. What she decided to wear was more for comfort. This was family. They had seen her at her best and worse.

Trisha stopped at the bottom of the stairs, and, hearing laughter coming from the kitchen, she took a deep breath and prepared to be courteous to the young man caught up in the whirlpool that was her gregarious family. When she stepped around the corner and walked toward the kitchen, she noticed everyone gathered around Cheryl's boyfriend who had his back to her. When each looked past him at her, something about the smirk on their faces made her curious.

"There she is," Cheryl said after spotting her little sister walking into the kitchen filled with people, "Trish, I want you to meet—"

Trisha looked from her grinning sister to the nameless man turning around. Words of greeting reached her mouth and froze there as did her body. He didn't say anything, at first, and that was a blessing. Cursing in her parents' house was frowned upon so she swallowed those words. The young woman staring in shock needed that air anyway to breathe—before she fainted.

"Trish," her mischievous sister claimed, "this is my new boyfriend. What did you say your name was again?

"David."

"Oh, yes, his name is David. We just met about an hour ago when I picked him up at the airport. We are in love, aren't—"

Trisha wasn't listening anymore. Seeing the man of her dreams standing in her parents' kitchen was more than she could—

Seven people watched as tears leaked down her face. Each of them had shed many tears in their lifetime. It was only strange to them when a girl that rarely did—did.

David sniffled, trying to hold back his emotions. It didn't surprise him when he heard others doing the same behind him. She looked amazing in her white outfit. It was obvious from the glow on her face, it was good for him to be here. Enough. He walked up and hugged her. What her tears did, David couldn't have accomplished with those in the room who deeply loved the family member now hidden in his arms, sobbing, if he had a year to impress them. Anyone who could touch their headstrong daughter, impulsive sister, and strong-willed cousin that deeply was now family. The ladies in the room had already accepted the handsome man. It was the other male in the room that her emotional reaction to seeing David here impressed the most.

Over the years, John Tipton had shared his daughter's secret with no one, as he promised her that terrible night. But he never told her of the many nights he sat in the bushes at the park with a bat in his hands hoping to see them attack another helpless victim. Hell, he was just praying to see them. Or the times he followed her when she was going someplace alone, or the many nights he cried about her stolen innocence…

∽∾∽∾

She was leaving the movie theater late. Trisha knew her curfew was less than an hour away, but if she hurried, she would make it home in time. She decided to run after she got off the bus four blocks from home believing that the earlier she got home, the better. Hopefully, her father wasn't calling around, looking for her. Her mother would have, but she and her sister were visiting her mother's parents down in Jacksonville. Trisha had a busy weekend of homework to do, or she would have gone with them.

Trisha was counting on her dad being too engrossed in the football game on tonight to notice how late she was. He was a diehard Atlanta Falcon fan. As she neared Hensley Park, she stopped running. She was now only a few blocks from home and didn't want to walk in the door all sweaty and have it appear she was running to make curfew.

Hensley Park was very familiar territory for her. It's a very scenic park surround on two sides by woods and large maple trees. On the east side of the park was the ball field. The south end was mostly grass and was used for picnic outings. Growing up near the park, Trisha knew every path. Her family would often walk their dog, JoJo, there almost daily before he died of old age. She grew up playing many games of softball and hide-an-go-seek in that park located close to home.

But familiarity often bred inattentiveness. Unconcerned, she walked on the dark side of the street next to the woods adjacent to the park. The constantly broken street light on that side of the street was an almost monthly victim of teenage boys and their rocks or BB guns. Anywhere else she would have instinctively crossed the street where the lighting was better, but this was their park, and she was almost home. The dark shadows offered no warning, set off no alarms with the teenage girl thinking about how gross the movie was she had snuck out to see.

Trisha only felt a sharp pain in her neck for an instant, and then darkness. Some might have said that was both a blessing and a curse, shielding the unconscious young girl from feeling her body being drug farther into the woods surrounding Hensley Park. The darkness of the park, and of her mind, hid what was being done to her body once she was tossed on the ground. Only the last few minutes of her third attacker registered as she slowly regained consciousness.

She heard voices but was too groggy and couldn't ascertain who was talking.

"Come on, hurry it up, Tommy. Someone might hear you."

"Shut up, Cory," Jake said.

As the cobwebs started to clear, Trisha began to realize what was happening and groaned from the painful assault.

"Listen to the bitch, those people love it. I—I told you guys," the man assaulting her said to the two watching.

As she gained more clarity, Trisha quickly discerned her situation and punched her attacker in the face, knocking him off her.

"You bitch!" he shouted at her as he sat up trying to stem the flow of blood from his bleeding nose.

Trisha screamed, as she tried to get up and never saw the blow in the dark that silenced her screaming and knocked her out as she fell into some nearby bushes.

"I'm going to kill the bitch," her third attacker boasted as he stood looking down at her unmoving form.

"I think Jake might have done just that with his blackjack,"

Cory told his partners in crime. "Let's get the hell out of here. Someone might have heard her."

Trisha woke to silence. She was dazed and just lay there, looking up at a star dotted black sky. There was an air of peace in the quiet she heard. Nothing about the last hour or so immediately registered in her thoughts. Then fear arrived and with it cold reality, shame, then tears, and finally pain. After a bout of crying, her anger took hold, and she ignored the pain and sat up looking for her attackers.

She was normally a gentle soul, but with a fire she kept in her chest. It was that fire that caused a young girl, lying in the weeds with her clothes torn, not to plead or beg but to punch her attacker in the face.

On shaky legs, Trisha stood up wary of another blind blow from out of the darkness. She only relaxed her fist after carefully looking around. They appeared to have run away.

"Trish baby, where the hell are you?" John Tipton whispered as he looked out his front door and down their street. This was his third attempt at spotting her maybe walking home. She had mentioned going over a girlfriend's house, but he didn't remember who and it was already past her curfew. Thankfully his wife and older daughter were both visiting his wife's parents. She would have the police and FBI out looking for Trish. Maybe should he call the police, John questioned. Not yet, but soon, if she didn't show up soon, he anxiously decided.

When she asked could she go over her girlfriend's house something about that request didn't sit well with him, he remembered thinking then, but he was so engrossed planning for the Falcon's football game that was coming on TV he didn't get the usual information on who, what, where, and a phone number like his wife would. She was that careful with both their daughters growing up. He had thought that overly protective sometimes, but never voiced that opinion.

He was just about to go and randomly call around, hoping someone knew where she was, when he thought he saw someone walking in his direction in the middle of the street about a couple of blocks away. He stepped out the house and held his breath. He already had a tension headache. The person was walking unsteadily and constantly turning and looking behind them. When that person walked under a street light, he gasped. It was Trish. Just the way she was walking sent shards of remorse ripping through his soul. Something was very wrong with his princess, his baby.

Trisha saw her father standing in the yard looking down the street at her. She knew he would be worried sick about her being late. Thank God, her mother wasn't home, she thought as she took another painful step toward arms that would protect her from bad guys.

When his delinquent daughter got closer, he spotted the disheveled conditions of her clothes, and the truth of what happened to her slapped him hard across the face. But when he saw the bruises on her face, he almost had a heart attack. He put his fist to his chest to stem the pain.

She ran to him when she got close. "Daddy."

He ran to her and scooped her up in his arms. He stood there in the street, holding his baby in his arms like he had many times when carrying her up to bed or home when she sprained her ankle a few years ago at the park playing in a softball game. There were tears then, but he knew they would end, and she would heal. He wasn't sure either would happen this time.

Trisha put her arms around her father's neck and squeezed as tight as she could. She was safe now. The squeezing was meant to hold back the flood, but it didn't work. She cried.

He cried.

CHAPTER 24

After he carried her into the house and placed her on the couch, she vehemently refused his insistence he take her to the hospital. She spared telling him about the terrible headache she had from the blows to her head.

"Honey, you could have an infection or something. You need to have them check you over," he pleaded as he knelt in front of her.

"No, Daddy," Trisha said as she held her torn blouse closed with her fist. "I can't have anyone else knowing what happened to me, I can't."

"Honey, your mother and sister will need to know."

"Then I might as well stand naked in the street, Dad, and shout to the world what happened to me. Neither of them can keep their mouths shut. I can't have kids at school talking about me like that, I can't."

"And, baby, I can't keep something this serious from them. It will break their hearts if something bad comes from this, say you get pregnant, and I—we—didn't tell them."

"If it comes to that, Daddy, I will say I just had sex with a guy I met at a party," she said as she stood up. "It happens all the time these days. Not to me, Daddy," she said to the pain that remark caused him. "I'm going to take about ten baths. Don't worry, your little girl is tough. This is between you and me, okay? Please, Daddy."

John Tipton sat back on the couch, after watching his little girl walk up the stairs as if she had just skinned her knee. She was disheveled, but there was a fire in her eyes. John started rubbing his chin, as he was wont to do when perplexed about something. She was handling this shame like a girl twice her age, he surmised. Had they left all their tears outside in the yard? he questioned. His wife Mildred had often claimed Trisha was more like him with her stubborn streak and pessimistic attitude to life, and Cheryl more like her with her optimistic approach to everything. She may be right.

He debated forcing her to go to the hospital. He knew she would obey him but what of the repercussions? If her fears of embarrassment came to fruition, she would never forgive him he feared, knowing his daughter.

Trisha showered and took a bath so hot it burned her skin when she put her foot in the steaming water. She gritted her teeth and groaned as she slowly lowered the rest of her body into the steamy water. Something about her assault floated into her thoughts as she waited for the burning pain to subside. Yes, when she punched that punk in the face, and he rolled off her, she was going to kick him in the balls when someone hit her in the head from behind. What was it? She was going to say she was lucky they didn't kill her, but nothing that had happened to her in the park was lucky.

After her second shower, she realized she could wipe their touch from her skin but not the memory. She walked into her bedroom and looked at her torn panties on the pile of clothes she had worn and was tossing away. Now she was glad she didn't take them off and dispose of them like she wanted when they irritated her as she walked home. What she didn't discover on them lifted her spirit and evoked a "Thank you" aimed skyward at her Maker.

Her dad was a six-foot-three-inch and 250 pound hunk of a man. Even approaching fifty, he was in great condition. And Trisha knew she was always special to the big man. He loved her sister and mother, but, with him, she was special.

An emotionally drained John Tipton never heard his daughter's bare feet descending the carpeted stairs. She was in all white silk PJs that gave her a very clean appearance as if she was just baptized and the sin she carried into the house was now rinsed away.

That somewhat reflected the prayers he had tearfully offered as his daughter was upstairs. Startled, when he realized she was standing there staring at him, he first noticed her softness had returned. Looking at her walking toward him, he could almost believe his baby hadn't just been through hell. What to say to her now? he questioned.

Trisha sat across his lap. "I love you, Daddy."

He cried.

She held him. "I'm okay."

She wasn't. His baby, whose bubbling personality was the source of the family's joy, turned into a reclusive, rebellious teen after the attack. Only her love and devotion for the man crying and holding her tightly to his chest that day on the couch, kept her from falling completely off an emotional cliff. It took years for her to get over that night. As perplexed as her mother was over the change in her daughter, they were always in her corner.

Her dad had joined the rest of his family in warning her about her latest boyfriend, Nate Jones, being a low life. She had shunned his opinion of Nate but never cussed out her daddy like she did nearly everyone else who dared question their relationship.

Yet, when she found out he was also a cheating dog—again, it was only her daddy she confided in and told him how much that hurt. Seeing her mature into a young, strong woman was very rewarding after that. She dated others, but it was clear who was in charge. They were just tires on her car. Tires she changed whenever they wore out or made noises she didn't like. He wasn't happy about her past choices, but it was obvious to him the man she was now hugging today in his kitchen had become the tires, the engine, the whole damn car, and she—

Trisha lifted her head from David's chest, as she regained some control. Her family, her dad, was watching but she ignored them. "What are you doing here, David?"

"You were so disappointed when I couldn't come with you and meet your wonderful family, I had to do something. I bribed and threatened a couple of guys to work some of my days," he said, answering the next question written on her face. "I could only get four days off, but it is worth it to be here with you."

Trisha caught herself wanting to jump into his arms again when he said that, but Daddy was watching.

"It took me a while to find your family online. I called three Tipton's in this town before your lovely sister answered the phone yesterday."

"Yesterday?"

Cheryl moved behind her dad, when Trisha quickly turned and glared at her. She stuck her tongue out at her scowling little sister. "Don't look at me that way, sis," she added. "Everyone here knew he was coming."

A stunned Trisha looked from laughing cousins to parents who weren't laughing but did nod with smiles on their faces.

"Why do you think we were teasing you, girl?" Beverly said.

"Yeah," one of the other cousins added.

One last person she needed to get an affirmation from. The man she respected the most growing up.

Her dad looked at his daughter with a love she understood and had once desperately needed. He was the only one Trisha ever told about her rape at fifteen by three white boys when walking home late from a movie she wasn't allowed to see. She didn't confide in him because she loved him more than her mother—she didn't—or because he was the only one at home. But because she knew he loved her too much to deny her wish of privacy. There was no way her mother would have honored her request to keep it a secret. There would have been a dozen cops outside their house and news people sitting on her couch as she told them what happened to her baby girl.

It was a secret they kept from everyone all these years and rejoiced once she later took a physical and they learned she wasn't pregnant or had contracted any diseases. Well, there is one terrible disease his precocious, trusting daughter caught. It was the same hate and prejudice that singled her out as a victim as she walked home alone near a park she played in all her life.

After her dad gave her the look, she hugged David again like she would if they were alone. "I'm so glad you came for me," she said to him.

Trisha only questioned what came next for an instant before reaching up and pulling his head down. With the kiss, she wasn't showing off. It was her way of letting her dad know what this guy meant to her. She had dated others but never allowed any show of affection, even holding hands, around her dad.

After the greetings were over, they sat around in the living room telling stories about the trouble the two sisters and their cousins got into growing up. Surprisingly, none of the other rela-

tives came over that night. It was suggested everyone was probably drained from the hot weather at the picnic.

David was having a great time hearing about the sisters and
especially the one leaning against him. But he noticed it was getting late and there were a few yawns in the group. "I should be
going," he announced.

"Already, you just got here," Trisha said.

"It's getting late. Where's the nearest nice hotel?"

"Where's the closest hotel?" Trisha asked the room.

Then Father Tipton offered a suggestion. "Son, you can stay
here."

That caught everyone by surprise. Trisha looked at her father,
half expecting him to say "Sike, I'm joking." He was the only
male allowed to sleep in the same house with his daughters. They
had all heard him make that declaration many times as they grew
up. Even their male cousins knew that rule.

"Thank you, sir," David said, looking from the startled woman next to him to her father. "But I think we drove past a Holiday
Inn." He looked at Cheryl.

"Nonsense, that place has bed bugs."

No one believed that, but they laughed anyway at Cheryl. She
only looked at her father for a moment when she saw the question
on his face.

"We have a sofa bed in the basement," their father added after
debating on asking his oldest daughter a question. "I'm sure Trish
won't mind setting it up as your bed, and there's a bathroom with
a shower down there you can use."

Stunned, Trish looked from her dad to David and then happily
nodded. It was plain to everyone, with the exception maybe of the
matron of the house with the startled look on her face, that it was
a good idea. Mom wasn't too convinced about that with five
young women swooning over him, but if Dad thought it was a
good idea, then so be it.

It was for him because Trish had a look he hadn't seen on his
daughter since before that terrible day. Everything he and his
family had tried to do for her had failed to elicit that look they
had all come to expect from his always vivacious daughter. Back
in his kitchen, in front of everyone, the man she was holding had
breached the years of pain she carried and returned that look to

her. *Hell, for that*, he thought but held the humor of it inside, *he could sleep in my bed.*

"If it won't be a problem, sir," David said, looking from Trisha's mother, obviously contemplating everything disastrous, to her unenthusiastic father.

"Oh, from the looks on my swooning daughters and her cousins, I'm sure it will be a big problem," the father said, shaking his head, as did all the grinning young women in the room. He threw his hands up, walked away from the gaiety, and out on his deck to cover his grill for the night.

David only had four days off, but they were spent with Tipton's all around him but, unfortunately, not much time alone with the one he came here to see. Word quickly spread among the family reunion what he had done just to be with "them." He was never alone until he went to bed in the basement family room late every night. There the sofa bed Trisha set up for him was remarkably comfortable, and he had all the amenities, a bathroom with shower, a laundry room where he could hang his clothes and get dressed, and the largest TV in the house. A kiss goodnight, after she set up the sofa-bed for him, was as intimate as they got. He debated each night if the smirk on her face, as she climbed the stairs and said goodnight, was her teasing him.

Each morning, he had breakfast together with the family and then got dressed for the next reunion tour or activity. That would take up the brunt of the day. Evenings were spent with a house full of people, laughing, drinking, and having a great time. By day two, David felt comfortable around all of Trisha's relatives but a few. One was an older female that he avoided after she twice fondled him when they were alone for a few minutes. Once in the back seat of a car as the two of them sat waiting on the rest of the family to load up for a trip around Atlanta, and another time in the basement when he went to change clothes from swimming. Oh, and another time while in that same pool. It wasn't that she was unattractive, but he only had eyes for Trish and guessed correctly he was just entertainment for her.

But on David's last evening there, Trisha's parents gave her a big surprise when they learned he had to take the redeye home that night so he could be at work first thing in the morning.

"Okay, everyone, let's get going. You know I hate to be late."

"Daddy, we are just going over Uncle Larry's, everyone there is probably still getting dressed," Cheryl said as she walked into the living room. "Aunt Patty is probably still in the shower."

Everyone knew that was probably true. Their aunt was habitually late for everything, even at her house.

"Nevertheless, let's get going everyone."

David was dressed an hour ago and was sitting on the couch, watching TV, as the family got dressed and were ready to go. He was enjoying watching the Tipton women parading past him as if he wasn't sitting there. They were a collection of sassy, but very nice-looking women.

"No, Davey," Cheryl said and walked up to him when he stood up to leave as they all gathered in the living room. "You are staying here with Trisha."

He looked from her to her smiling cousins in the living room. It was obvious from their snickering they all knew something he didn't. When he looked at Trisha's father, who had walked into the room from the kitchen, he smiled at him and then walked out the front door without saying a word.

"It was wonderful meeting you, Davey, please come back." That said, Cheryl kissed him on the cheek and followed her father out the door. She was followed by her cousins, who first duplicated her goodbye kiss. David stood there wondering what was up when Trisha walked down the stairs and into the living room, arm-in-arm with her mother. David looked at her, wondering if she knew what was going on. The two women walked over to him.

"It has been wonderful meeting you, David," Trisha's mom said and softly touched his cheek with her hand.

"It has been my pleasure, ma'am. You have a wonderful family, and everyone has been so kind to me." David looked at Trisha, but she remained quiet.

"Well, I better get out to the car before my husband pitches a fit. You know how he hates to be late, Trish. Again, it has been nice meeting you, David. I hope—" She stopped and looked down at the floor when she sensed maybe she was saying too much. A smile and she was gone.

"What's going on, Trish?"

"Oh, you mean them leaving us here?" she asked as she walked over and closed the front door.

"Well, yes. I thought we were going over to your dad's brother's house for a few hours before I go to the airport for my flight."

"That was the plan." Trisha walked over and hugged him. "But my daddy decided we needed some alone time before you leave." She kissed him quickly on the lips.

"Wait—wait. Your dad suggested that?"

"I know, right? But he knows how much I love you."

"Your dad suggested we should spend tonight alone together. Didn't he see how I was looking at his youngest daughter's ass the last few days?"

She hugged him and smiled that captivating smile of hers. "I know my sister and cousins noticed. They told me so all last night."

☙❧☙

"I can't believe how quiet it is in here now," David said as they sat on the couch after a very delicious dinner of leftovers— leftovers, mind you, of perfectly cooked spare ribs, three different styles of potato and macaroni salads, various cooked veggies, three different recipes of tasty chicken. Each item had been cooked by one of the family members and brought over to the house. Other than the ribs and breakfast, Trisha's parents had to cook nothing during the four days he was there.

"I've had a wonderful time down here with all you family. Like you said, they do like to party."

"I told you my family loves to have fun when we get together."

David just nodded. He had mixed feelings about leaving. Having grown up with just his grandmother and no siblings, being in the midst of such a large, loving family was euphoric. Their accepting him as if he was one of their own added weight to the Trisha side of the scales of justice. A scale already leaning more to her side than—

"I can't tell you how much your being here has meant to me," Trisha said and started rubbing his leg. "My dad letting us alone in his house means he's accepted you, and that's a big deal with him. I'm his baby, and he is very protective. He must like you."

"I like your family."

"My crazy sister is in love with you, mister," she said and lovingly punched him on the leg. "When you asked her to dance yesterday when we were out to the club before the other girls, if she wasn't earlier, she was sold on you then."

"I kind of figured that might work."

"Well, it did, but I think she was already there."

David reached over and lifted her chin, kissing her briefly on the lips.

"David," Trisha spoke more to what she wanted than the gleam in his eyes, "I would like to be intimate with you tonight but not in my parent's house."

"Honey, I admit thinking about being with you every night, with you a couple of floors over my head, but there is no way I would do anything here to disrespect the kindness your family has shown to me."

That didn't surprise the woman with her head on his shoulders. "I'll make it up to you."

Trisha was sitting on the couch alone when her family walked in later that night, minus her cousins. They noticed her looking past them for the three trouble makers.

"We wanted to talk to you alone, sweetie," her mother said to the look on her face. "Your cousins are staying with Aunt Deloris tonight." Her parents walked over and sat down on both sides of her. Cheryl sat across the room and watched.

"Sweetie, your daddy and I just wanted to know where the two of you are headed. David is a very nice guy, and we all like him."

Trisha felt a little trapped, as if there was something negative about to happen. Did they know something she didn't?

"Did he catch his flight?" The question was asked by her father more to sooth the silence in the room than concern about David.

Trisha knew they were waiting for her to say something, but her throat burned with emotion. It wasn't easy for her to talk about her feelings for David. She could talk for days about him but not how she felt. She loved him more than she wanted them to know, more than she wanted anyone to know. It was like a weakness, like an addiction. It was so powerful sometimes she feared what she would do if he fell in love with someone else.

Trisha had to look at her sister for strength before she could talk. "Mommy, Daddy, I love David with all my heart and soul. He is everything I have ever wanted in a man. If he—" was all she could say before the tears came.

Her mother reached out and hugged her.

"I would—marry—him tomorrow," she continued.

Her sister crossed the room and joined their parents. The three of them hugged her, but it was the caring look from her daddy that eased her fears.

CHAPTER 25

Even as the bright sunshine burst between the trees and right into his eyes, causing him to look away, the spring-time was always his favorite season. The smell of the air blowing across his balcony carried a freshness that signaled a new beginning. After hibernating most of the cold Pittsburgh winter, the newness of spring stirred a restlessness in his spirit. Summer was coming, the warm rays of the sun signaled, and David was ready for it.

He spent Thanksgiving at home with Trisha, who cooked an amazing turkey dinner, and Christmas in Atlanta with her and her parents. This time, David did get a beautiful hotel suite, and Trisha surprised him by stating she planned to share it with him.

"Baby," David said as he watched Trish hanging up their clothes. For a moment her shapely figure held his attention, and then he thought, *Are you sure you want to ask her this?* "Maybe you should stay with your parents while we're here," he said with little conviction.

She stopped what she was doing and looked at David sitting on one of the beds. "Are you throwing me out?"

"Hell no! I'm just trying to keep your daddy from killing me."

She laughed. He had a point. "Well, tell me this," she said then walked over to her opened suitcase. "Would it be worth piss-ing off my daddy to see me in this?" With that question, she held up a couple of pieces of very shear pink negligee.

"Damn, girl, to hell with your daddy." David jumped off the bed, but he was too late. The girl holding the tiny pieces of cloth ran laughing into the bathroom and closed the door.

Minus the picture of her wearing next to nothing, he again tried to talk her through the closed bathroom door, but she would have none of that.

"Look, babe, I'll even sleep downstairs again."

"Nope," she said from the bathroom, "I'm not staying there. You spent your money in advance to get this great suite, and we are going to enjoy it." What she modeled, or better yet, what little she modeled, when stepping out the bathroom, did all the convincing needed. Instead of getting dressed to go over her parents,' they got undressed and would be an hour plus another shower later than expected.

And as expected, their sleeping arrangements didn't sit well with her dad, but after the first few days of not saying much, he was his gregarious self again.

Going Christmas shopping with her family was a new experience for David, and he relished every moment. Watching them fight their way through the crowd and battle for items they wanted was eye opening as was observing the other people out there obsessed with bargain hunting.

Trisha looked so happy being around her sister and some of her cousins he didn't feel slighted at all when they went off doing girl things. In that time he got a chance to male-bond with her father. Following Trisha's hint, when he mentioned Falcon football to her father, he no longer scowled at the man sleeping with his daughter and that kicked open the door and her father spent the day talking sports. Later he even made him lunch while the girls were out shopping.

The Tipton family had a tradition he was unfamiliar with. They opened their gifts at midnight on Christmas Eve, and that was different but fun. Everyone was wide awake instead of waking up half asleep in the wee hours of the morning. It didn't hurt that most were inebriated by midnight.

After they returned, he didn't get to spend as much time with Trisha as he hoped. She was right about working nights and school during the day stealing most of their time together. But the girl sure made up for it when they did find the time. There was no pretending what they both wanted when he or she walked in the door. The clothes they were wearing, after their being apart for sometimes as long as a week or more with their conflicting schedules, never made it to the bedroom on the wearers.

Christmas was fun with her family, but after returning home on New Year's Eve, they celebrated the anniversary of their first time making love by copying the act. Trisha wore the same dress, and, as the minute hand reached twelve, it started another slow trip down over a body that still, a year later, took his breath away.

David was looking forward to spending some hot summer days doing things with her in the beautiful outdoors like swimming, bike riding, a picnic or two, and always seeing her in a bikini.

Mike had finally gotten over a bad case of the flu and had mentioned he was also looking forward to the spring.

Thoughts of warmer weather caused David's mind to drift southward toward that long sandy peninsula that jutted out into the Atlantic Ocean and the person marooned there. In a moment of loneliness, Brenda had called him and let the location of the soul she was lamenting over slip out. She was so down, David wasn't sure if she realized that or maybe did it intentionally, hoping he might be able to do something about their missing friend.

Over the last few months, Brenda had come to accept Toni's absence. The few times David came by to see her, she was upbeat about a nice guy she met, and they talked less and less about Toni. Did she miss her? Sure, they all did. But she said being with her family over the holidays let her see that she was loved.

"David, I want what my grandparents have," Brenda shared with him as they sat talking one evening after the holidays. "To meet someone and grow old together. My grandpa was just an ordinary guy, grandma told me, not the one she liked or wanted, but he loved her with all his heart, and that was enough for her. She is right you know. Marrying the richest or handsomest guy or prettiest girl isn't enough. If that's all the relationship has going, it won't last. Here, fifty years later, they still in love each other and draw a house full of family there with that love."

"I believe that, Brenda. That's why there are so many divorces. We all love pies and cake, but if that's all you eat, it will kill you. We were great together, red, but, for some reason, it just didn't click with us. You don't know how many times I prayed it would."

"Really, I didn't know that. But I know you're right." Brenda thought about it before bridging a subject the two of them had avoided. But it was David who brought it up she decided. "We were good together, weren't we?"

"We were great, girl. I never told anyone this, but, when we were out together, the fact that you always made me first won me over even more so than your long—"

"Don't say it, I know."

"Well, they are amazing," David teased.

"Yes, they are." She grinned at him. "But yeah, I always wondered why we couldn't bridge that gap, except—

"—in bed," they said together and laughed.

"Now you are with someone you care for and so am I." Brenda wanted to say he loved but couldn't, and that bothered her.

He looked at her and smiled.

"I always thought I would be happiest being free, ya know," she said when he gave her that look. "Just dating and enjoying life, but now I know that isn't what I want, Davey. Did I tell you my parents are moving back to Harrisburg to help my grandparents run the place, and I'm seriously thinking about joining them?"

That came as a surprise to him but, seeing the peace that had come over the vivacious redhead, it seemed like it was the right move for her. "Brenda, whatever makes you happy. If you go and don't like it, you're young enough to start over again anywhere."

"That's how I feel, Davey."

She seemed happy with her decision, David remembered from that day they chatted. Knowing that Mike and Toni had also found happiness would be the final piece of the puzzle. But just seeing her again would be a start because Toni was a woman who drifted in and out of his dreams over the last five months. But thoughts of Toni had become more intense as the cold weather broke.

As the beauty of the virgin green blanket on the ground erased cold memories of the bitter winter—and Toni's disappearance—David began to sense a change in the air. It was as if he could see the tiny sprouts of spring's handiwork working their way through the softening ground. Hope was the image David saw in those sprouts. Tentacles of optimism reached out to him and stirred his faith.

"Toni," he whispered as memories touched a familiar cord.

Like an abstract thought that appeared out of nowhere, he remembered Toni's diary. He searched through his junk drawer until he found it. Holding it in his hands almost reverently, he walked back out onto the porch. The soft black cover had a feminine touch to it, David thought.

The lively song of a bird off in the woods somewhere momentarily broke his séance. The avis-songs timbre sounded like the voice of their runaway girlfriend. Its similarity helped ease the sting of his guilt. David slowly opened the book. Maybe there's a clue in here about where she is staying, he tried reasoning. His private vow not to violate her personal written thoughts, when he hid the book in the drawer, he felt was now invalidated by his sudden concern for her safety.

David looked up to the Heavens and silently prayed for the intuition to see only the words he needed to find her. He failed to acknowledge the seed of fear that he might read something that would change his feeling for her. Something that would mar the caring and loving picture of her he had painted and that, after all this time apart, was unmarred.

At one point, Toni had been the quintessential perfect woman in his eyes. A strong friendship and mutual respect colored their close relationship. What worried him, as he stared at the book in his hands, was what if she wasn't as impressed with him as he was with her? That was the real reason he had tossed the diary in his junk drawer and forgotten about it.

He sensed she was looking over her shoulder as he thumbed through the pages. His palms were wet. Stopping for a moment, he took a deep breath. Again, he convinced himself of the importance of finding out where she was. It was almost a year, and no one had heard a peep from her. The visions of her already very sick or worse he, like both Brenda and Mike, hadn't allowed that ugly possibility to fester in his thoughts. Surely, Toni would have let them know, and they shared that belief silently.

Mike read one of the pages.

> *Sept. 16,*
>
> *Mike thinks I should quit working at the Foodmart because there's no future there for me. I agree…*
>
> *David is funny. The way he looks at Brenda when he thinks no one is looking, reminds me there's a little bit of boy in that big guy. I know he loves her, diary.*

"A little bit of boy, great—she thinks of me as a little boy," David mumbled. He looked around forgetting no one could see him on his porch. He closed that page and leafed through the diary. The absolution he felt for transgressing her memoirs dissolved in his concern for how she viewed him. Guilt directed him to avoid the pages until the last one. He now felt to read anything in between those pages was an invasion of her privacy. Truthfully, he was now more afraid of what else might be written about him.

> *Jan. 16,*
> *That bastard, how could he do that to me? How?*
> *The doctor wouldn't tell me the truth at first until I screamed at him. Then he told me that I have HIV, but Mike has AIDS.*
> *I asked him how that was possible. He said Mike must have had it years earlier, diary.*
> *Mike had AIDS, and he gave it to me. How could he do that to me, Diary? How could he hate me that much? Wait until I see that bastard. I might cut off his—*

David slammed the book closed on her last unfinished sentence. He was in shock. Could she be right? Could or would Mike do something that despicable. Her painful description of the conversation with her doctor triggered feelings of anger that were new to him. Being angry with Mike violated their friendship. He had to find out the truth. Even Mike, David decided heading for the door, couldn't get away with that shit.

᭰᭰᭰

Mike tossed the two aspirins into his mouth and washed them down with a glass of cold water. He could feel the fever in his body through his clothes. That was one of the frequent effects of AIDS, the nurse told him on his last visit to the hospital. He picked up one of the four books David had dropped off a week ago. He had promised to read up on his affliction but never could crank up the determination to see just how bleak his future was.

Testing for AIDS, the title read. Mike skimmed through the acknowledgments and found the first chapter.

> *The key to testing for HIV is to look for antibodies to the virus. The test doesn't find the HIV virus, just the antibodies that your body produces when it discovers the presence of the HIV virus. It usually takes less than six months or up to a year for your immune system to create antibodies to HIV. It takes time for the HIV concentration to reach high enough levels to trigger the body to produce the antibodies.*
>
> *The immune system attacks and eliminates most of the virus. Some of the HIV viruses, however, change their structure, thus escaping detection. In a new disguise, the HIV virus attacks and destroys most of the same white blood cells that were destroying it. These T-cells are your body's defense against infections. The loss of these T-cells (called T-4lymphocytes) are the first sign of the presence of the HIV virus.*

He let the book fall out of his hand as he leaned back and closed his eyes. The thought of strange, alien, microscopic creatures, climbing through his body and waging war like he was the ravaged city in a grade-B movie gave Mike the willies. He shook himself as if to shake off the coating of despair that constantly built up on him at the thought of his condition and his bleak outlook. He felt in awe of the power of the tentacles of despair that constantly tried crushing his spirit. Even after he shook free from the desire to pity himself, he felt weak from the constant, titanic struggle to remain upbeat. *Can anything offer so little hope as having AIDS?* he wondered.

He remembered when cancer use to scare the hell out of people. But since some treatments had slowed and, in some cases, destroyed cancer, it wasn't as frightening as it used to be. But everyone was scared to death of AIDS.

What was that figure he read? Oh yes, he remembered, *Most people with full-blown AIDS die within two to three years.* Thankfully, Doctor Haney said he wasn't close to having full-blown AIDS yet.

Mike refused to think about the five-year number that Doctor Haney did give him.

Mike heard the hurried footsteps as they approached his apartment door. When the doorknob turned, he knew it could only be—

"Hi, David." Mike turned around and looked toward the door when he didn't receive an answer. "David, what's wrong?" The look on the face of his friend was almost as unnerving as the subject he was pondering over. "David!"

David just stood there unable to speak. The weight of their friendship was a heavy burden on him. "I don't know how to ask you this," he revealed as he walked toward Mike. "All the way over here, I knew what I wanted to say, but when I walked in that door—now I'm not sure."

It had come to a head. Mike had expected it to happen sooner or later. There were things he had wanted to tell his best friend but couldn't. He felt he might lose him if he knew the truth about what he had done. "Look, David, say what's on your mind. If you and I can't talk to each other, what's left of the time I have— left?" That was said with a grin on his face.

David nodded in agreement, ignoring the morbid point Mike was trying to make. His feet felt like lead as he walked over and sat down on the couch across from him. "Look, Mike—" He looked around the apartment stalling for the words to say. "While I was sitting out on my balcony today—ah, enjoying the warm weather—I was thinking about where Toni might have run off to. Then I remembered something I must have pushed out of my mind. I had picked up her diary in the front of her house when I raced over there to try and stop her from leaving. I was going to leave it on her doorstep but decided to give it to Brenda, but, by the time I saw her again, I'd forgotten I had it. Weird, huh?" He felt a twang of guilt over having the diary for the first time since he found it, concerned Mike might think he was purposefully keeping it from him.

"David," Mike said, trying to breach the embarrassing gap his revelation seemed to inspire, "what did you find out?"

David searched his friend's eyes for a glimpse of subterfuge. He found none. The rage he carried over to his dying friend's house melted into shame. He tried to hide that shame before Mike saw it on his face. "I read her last entry. In it she blamed you for giving her HIV. What I can't understand is how she could think that. Either of you could have given it to the other or even caught it from other people, but she was so...so..."

"So adamant about my guilt, right?"

"Yeah, Mike. The way she wrote it," David continued explaining, "as if you knew you had HIV and didn't care that you infected—No, that's stupid, isn't it?"

The pain in Mike's face was so obvious that David could have seen it with his eyes closed. He was immediately sorry for asking him that. "I didn't give it to her, David," Mike said softly.

"I didn't think you did, Mike." David got up and looked out the balcony glass doors. "It was just that she was so certain that you were guilty of something that I wondered for a moment if our friendship had blinded me. I'm sorry, Mike." He turned and faced him. "I think I rushed over here to hear you say that."

Mike got up and walked over to his repentant friend. For a brief moment, he just looked at him. He saw nothing that voided his compassion for the apologetic man standing in front of him. "Well, now you've heard it," Mike finally answered. "Now sit down. It's time I tell you everything." He led him over to the couch and sat down with him. "Don't get angry over what I'm going to tell you. I did it, and it was a very stupid thing to do, but it's too late to change anything." He knew he was leading David on but wanted a measure of revenge for his doubting him. "About six months after Toni and I first got together, we gave blood at the blood bank. There was a blood drive going on at her job that she was in charge of and needed people to sign up, so she asked me to participate. Or course, back then, as now probably, I would have donated an arm if she asked. Well," he continued when David didn't seem to get the joke. "I don't remember where her father was that weekend, probably off fishing. Anyway, there was a special delivery for her. The delivery guy saw me in the yard and walked over. I'm thinking he thought that I was Toni when asked me to sign for it. He was looking for a male—Tony—DiNardo, I guessed. When I realized that, I said okay. He said to sign here, so I signed. David, I sat for a long time trying to convince myself not to open her mail when I saw it was from the Oakland Blood

Bank where she and I gave blood. I was so concerned that it was bad news, I had to know, so I opened the letter and read it."

"Where was Toni?"

"What?"

"Toni, where was she?"

"Oh—she went to the grocery store to buy some things to make dinner. I offered to go with her, but since I was dirty from cutting her grass, she jokingly declined my offer, jumped in her car, and drove off. 'Be back in and hour,' she said. Anyway, my eyes were drawn to a line of bold lettering at the bottom of the page that coldly said, 'You have tested positive for the antibodies that indicate you have acquired the HIV virus.'"

The sudden change in David's expression was predictable. Mike didn't wait for a comment. "David, I cried. Standing there in the middle of her front yard, I cried. I questioned God on how he could let someone as sweet as Toni become infected. That was the worst day of my life, at least I thought it was then. The night before we had the house to ourselves. It was the most wonderful night I can remember. We were so passionate. I don't know how we didn't end up in bed. You know what? Not one of the tears I shed that day, as I read that letter over and over, were for myself. After waiting all my life for the perfect woman to come along, now I find out she has HIV. How cruel is that? I would have gladly given my life to save hers, but it was too late. The woman of my dreams was infected."

David looked at Mike in total disbelief. First, Toni said Mike had it and gave it to her, and now it was Mike trying to say she had it first.

"I know what you're thinking." Mike stood up and looked at David. He knew his story was kind of unbelievable. "Wait here."

David tried to piece together the fantastic yarn Mike had spun. Now Mike was saying Toni had HIV even back then.

"Here."

Mike's appearance in front of David caught him off guard. When he looked up, Mike had a sheet of paper in his hand and a resolute look on his face.

"This is the letter. I've saved it to remind me of Toni after she—" The meaning was transferred via eye contact.

Slowly, David looked from Mike's tortured face to the folded sheet of paper in his hand. He took a deep breath and slowly blew it out before taking the paper and nervously reading. When he finished, he looked up at Mike. He was about to say he was sorry, but knew that wasn't necessary. The pain he must have felt, David thought, to be accused by the woman you love of destroying her life when all along it was her fault.

He handed the letter back to Mike and watched as he walked across the room and slumped down in his recliner staring out the patio doors, his sadness evident by his actions. David stared at Mike for a moment and watched as he folded up the letter and placed it is his pocket. If Toni had it first, he understood that Mike didn't give it to her. But why did he keep that a secret? Surely Toni needed to know.

"I'm a little confused about some things," David said. "Why didn't you say something to Toni about this letter? And—and Toni should have been told right away that she was infected."

"You may not believe this, but I denied the truth of her illness for a long time. She was so vibrant and full of life I thought it had to be a mistake. Hospitals make them all the time, right? It was just after reading that letter," Mike added, ending the silence in the room, "that we started having sex. I know, I know," he said, cutting off an expected reply, "I should have told her before then, but I didn't expect to that night, and when we started to really get intimate, I couldn't stop her or me. I wanted to make love to her so much I decided to risk it. I wore protection after that first night.

"For months everything between us was so great, I refused to even consider it. She was so full of life, like I said, that I figured they had to have made a mistake. I hid the letter from her and myself. You've seen her, she always looked so healthy. I couldn't accept it, David, I couldn't. Then something strange happened. I was sitting with her one day watching TV, and suddenly I thought about the chance that she could pass the virus off to me. From that day on, it ate at me until I couldn't be alone with her for fear we would get intimate. Remember, that's what broke us up—my leaving her alone. David, I fell from making passionate love to her to being afraid to be alone with her. How was I going to tell Toni I was afraid to be around her? It would have killed her. So to keep from breaking her heart, I led her to believe I didn't love her anymore. Stupid, I know. I tried to spare her, on one hand, and ended up slapping her with the other." Mike took a moment to catch his breath. He found that to be the accepted practice when he thought about how he hurt the woman he loved.

David grieved for his friend, but the real reason for his giving Toni the cold shoulder finally made some sense. But that would mean—

Mike leaned back in his chair and closed his eyes. "Even when we got back together," he continued, "I couldn't tell her the truth. So I told her something I've kept secret, I'm sad to say, even from you. I revealed to her that I'm sterile. That was one reason when I was with those women, Davey, I knew I couldn't get them pregnant if something broke." He didn't have to open his eyes to see the surprised look on his friend's face. Again, it was expected. "But you know what, David?" he said when he did open his eyes and look over at him. "As shocking as that news was, she took it in stride. It was only after we broke up that I realized how much I had hurt her by not telling her the truth. I actually thought I would hurt her more by telling her the truth before she showed any signs that test proved correct. I wanted her to enjoy the last few days, and—and I didn't stop to think, until after we broke up, what if she was intimate with someone else. He also would be in danger. I guess I foolishly never thought there could be someone else."

"Yeah, thanks a lot, numb-nuts. I guess I should get checked."

"Funny," Mike answered and shared a finger with his friend. "But according to her anyway, thankfully there wasn't anyone else."

David had a few questions he needed to ask but was afraid of the answers.

"After you helped me get my head together," Mike said, punching him in the arm and distracting him from what he was going to ask, "I realized I wanted her back in my life. Dying no longer scared me. I probably never would have made the first move had that redhead not pushed me into that dressing room. We were very, very happy until Toni found out. David, I was going to wait until she showed some signs of the virus before destroying her dreams of the future. I wanted her to have a period happiness in her life where she could look back on and, hopefully, say I knew what it is like to be loved."

"Mike, how can you be sure one of your bar girls didn't give it to you?"

David worried he might have offended Mike and was a little surprised when Mike smiled.

"I was acting stupid, buddy, but not that stupid. I wasn't so drunk that I forgot to wear protection. Well, only once or twice. I couldn't have lived with myself if I had infected any of those women. I never told you, but on those few days when I was sober, I was tested at that clinic a few times after not wearing protection just to make sure. So up until I got back together with Toni, I was clean. Remember the main reason we decided to get tested together originally had nothing to do with my getting back with Toni, but was after we were with those two wild women we found out later were strippers? Could some of those women I was with have infected me, yes maybe from their doing...well, you know? Do I think they gave it to me? No. The odds are they did not." Mike looked him in the eye and said clearly, "It was Toni that I caught the virus from."

This was getting crazy, David thought as he covered his face with his hands. "Mike," he asked after gathering his thoughts together, "I'm still a little confused. You said you were afraid to touch her. If that is true, and you knew she was infected, why did you continue to have sex with her?"

He couldn't answer David right away. The pain of the question stole Mike's breath away. He looked up and wiped his eyes before the water could leak down his face. "You still don't get it, do you, partner? I purposely let myself get infected by Toni. I tried everything I could to get infected by her. I wanted sex with her so much she questioned my motives. Even after I accidentally cut myself and was bleeding, I continued to make love to her. Well, not cut on purpose, I stupidly caught myself on my zipper. I knew the danger of making unprotected sex to her in that condition. I decided, why not? I wouldn't want to live without her anyway."

The picture that Mike was painting finally became clear to David. When it finally did, his mouth dropped open as if some grotesque thing was trying to crawl out of his throat. It took him a moment to catch his breath. "You did *what*?" he screamed across the room. "You let yourself become infected? I thought it was an accident. I—I thought you just couldn't keep your hands off her. That would be stupid, but knowing Toni, I could possibly understand that but—you did this on purpose?"

Mike didn't answer him. He lowered his head as if to deflect the ire of the man now walking toward him with his fist balled up as if to beat the hell out of him.

"I don't understand!" David shouted, his hands waving back and forth in front of him. "You, you let yourself become infected with HIV, are you crazy? Don't you understand what a heinous killer AIDS is?" He walked around the room in circles, looking for something until he finally had to ask, "Where are those books I got for you? There they are." Spotting them stacked on the floor under the coffee table. "Listen to this, Mike. Where is that page? Here it is. These are the diseases that attack AIDS patients. Cryptococcosis—a fungus that causes infections to the central nervous system. Symptoms are headaches, nausea, fever, and blurred vision. Twenty-five percent of the people who get this fungus die. Here's another, CMV it's called. I can't pronounce the word. But it is a virus common to people with AIDS. The virus can attack the lungs, brain, colon, liver, and eyes, causing blindness. In the colon, it causes chronic diarrhea, wasting, and very painful cramps. CMV infected people die a slow, painful, and wasting death.

"Mike, there's page after page of diseases that viciously violate the weakened body of AIDS sufferers. And you willing let yourself become a victim, why?"

Mike didn't answer or look up.

His acquiescent manner only served to heighten David's frustration. *How could he just let go of life*? he wondered. *Doesn't he realize how precious his health is—or was? What he did was stupid.* "Wasn't it bad enough," he continued, "that Toni had—Oh, oh, no. You did it for her? No, no, you did it for love, right? Well, guess what? I don't buy it. You have no right to take your own life, not even for Toni, not even for me."

Mike stared down at the floor as his friend vented his sorrow for him as anger. David was hurting knowing, as Mike did, that he was sentenced to death.

David knew his words were stinging Mike, but he couldn't stop. Learning his friend had committed suicide on purpose, just as if he had put a gun to his head and fired it, angered him. The fact the bullet would take years to kill him offered no consolation. Mike was going to die. It was suicide, nonetheless. "Dammit, Mike, was she worth it?"

Mike's head shot up, and he glared at David. In his rage, he failed to see the stunned look on his friend's face. "She was worth it then—" he shouted bluntly back at David through clenched teeth. Then he calmed down and whispered, "—and she's worth it now."

David sat down and said nothing for a long while. After reading up on the horrible, painful deaths that awaited most AIDS suffers, he had trouble grasping the depth of the sacrifice Mike had made. It was the light of David's own love for Toni that began to chip away at his anger and add some value to Mike's motives. *For the love of those dark eyes, you might have done the same thing*, he stubbornly began to comprehend. But, more important, two of the few people he had truly loved in his life, were now sentenced to death.

Growing up, David had found he liked being alone more than being out with friends. He also discovered he was very thin skinned with a short fuse. That was a volatile combination, and he quickly learned it was easier just to avoid confrontation than to fight everyone who even looked at him funny. It took him a while, but he taught himself to deal with it and to open up somewhat to people.

Mike was one of a few men David trusted. It was his sense of humor that allowed a reserved David to relax his guard and allow a stranger to get close to him. Now that he had, there was no one he trusted more. Mike knew every high and low in David's life. That trust also carried over to Toni and Brenda. They had all meshed so smoothly that he put all his faith in the strength of their relationship.

"Mike," David said calmly, "Toni thinks you're to blame, and it was kind of both of you at fault. I can understand how you can love her enough to die for her, really, I can. I'm sorry for getting on your case. It's just that AIDS is a horrible taskmaster that demands pain and suffering as penitence. I'm no expert, but you should read the books I brought you. Well, maybe you shouldn't. Now that I think about it, they're very depressing."

"I'll read them, I will," Mike promised. "I need to know the facts. David, what I've told you must remain between you and me. I want your word that not Brenda, my parents, or anyone else will ever hear about this from you."

David tilted his head and made a "Duh" face. Mike looked at him with that impish grin of his. An unspoken "thank you" passed between them.

They changed the subject and talked about the good times with the four of them. David opened up to Mike and told him some of his most private thoughts lately. One that came as no surprise to Mike was that he once had a secret thing for Toni. Mike smiled at his friend and punched him in the arm, acknowledging that he always knew that.

"But I never did or would hit on her."

"Duh, I know that."

The two friends shed what little pretense they had withheld from each other and freely exposed their strengths and weaknesses to the light of day. Time—they both more than understood now—was too precious a thing to waste.

CHAPTER 26

A *pril showers bring May flowers.*
May flowered as pneumonia in Mike's chest. One of the early invaders to attack the weakened immune system was PCP, or Pneumocystis Carini Pneumonia. Thankfully, it was caught in time before it could fill his lungs with fluid. Mike spent a week in West Penn Hospital under the special care of a certain tall, redheaded young nurse. Her gift of bringing cheer into the life of the sick was never more evident than it was in the countenance of her now-favorite patient. It only took her a moment to look into his eyes and forgive Mike for causing Toni to run away. His infamous sense of humor quickly winning over Brenda and befriending the lecherous patient in the other bed infatuated with the attractive nurse and her frequent visits.

Brenda was also a Godsend for the depressed man in room number 315. Mike walked out of that hospital more confident than he had been since Toni's departure into oblivion. David had sensed the change in him but was afraid to bring it up. Mike now had an air of hope about him that added color to the pallid tint of his skin.

When Mike was released, David insisted that he move in with him until he was stronger. Mike had thought about going over to his parents' house to stay for a while but changed his mind. They had only visited him once while he was in the hospital, and then only for a few minutes. The fear on their faces, after he told them he had the AIDS virus, explained their dilemma in words Stevie Wonder would have seen.

❧❧❧

For a moment, it was completely quiet, and Toni thought that odd. None of the caterwauling seagulls were flying overhead, and none of the tourists had driven their vehicles down onto the beach and gunned their engines. No personal boats or jet skis were passing near the shore. Even the ocean breeze seemed to stop for a moment, and for that moment, it was quiet. The next wave silenced the…silence.

The tide rolled in washing the sand off her feet. The water was cool as it struggled to absorb the heat from the sun. Come autumn, the process would reverse itself, she remembered. The warmer water, heated from the hot rays of a summer full of sunshine, would release its heat into the cooling sand. That was one of the many reasons why she loved Florida. The warm spring sun soothed the winter cold from your bones. Then, in the fall, the oceans were like a hot spring as it washed over you, taking the chill from the nippy air.

Today, the beach was her home. Monday and Tuesday were her off days, and like, during the rest of the week, she loved walking along the beach at Daytona. This was where she enjoyed spending most of her free time. The early summer crowd would start arriving soon, Carl, her boss and owner of The Best Beach Chairs Rentals, told her last Friday. Until then, this was their time, he explained, time for the natives to enjoy the quiet beauty of the sunrise and sunset. Soon, he claimed with a sparkle in his squinting eyes, the rich, cold northerners would arrive to fatten his wallet and dirty his beach.

Old Carl was a trip, Toni remembered as she imagined the old man reciting one of his many vivid tales of woe. She thought he was between sixty and seventy. He was too proud to tell, and she too respectful and fond of him to ask. His face was kindly, and his brown eyes still shown bright with life. Thin white hair blew loosely under the faded Cubs baseball cap that he always wore, turned slightly to his left. She felt safe around the old man. His boney, wrinkled hands would act out a drama as if marionetted by someone in the Heavens above. The chatty old man was a natural storyteller, she thought, grinning. Or a very good liar. Toni shook her head and chuckled.

She would sit and listen attentively to him for hours. Between her interruptions, while she rented out his chairs, he told her countless stories of his thirty-two years of experiences on Flori-

da's beaches. From his own frolicking days, as he chased the
wanton women from up north, as he called them, to the last seven
years in retirement renting beach chairs, he seemed to delight in
talking about his life. Try as she might to get some work done, he
would prevail upon her until she stopped working and sat with
him awhile. "Sit down," he repeatedly told her. "The chairs will
sell themselves. But I must admit a pretty girl in a bikini doesn't
hurt business."

That was the same spirited conversation that seduced her into
working for him.

Toni had walked up to the old guy after those first few weeks
of walking along on the beach after spending too many days secluded in her motel room. "How much to rent a chair?"

"So, the very pretty lady that walks past my stand everyday
can talk."

Toni started to regret asking, but the day was too hot for walking, and she just wanted to lie out in the sun and let it warm her
skin. She had spent the last two days indoors, getting over a bad
cold.

"I'll make you a deal," the old guy said. "If you lay out in one
of my chairs near my stand, the chair rental is free."

"I don't need your—"

"No, but I do. If other women see you lying on one of my
chairs, that will encourage them to get out of those air conditioned hotel rooms and do the same. See? When a group of pretty
women are laying out on the beach, that draws guys like flies to
you-know-what."

The last thing Toni wanted was to be hit on by a bunch of
guys, much less this smiling old codger. But something about him
made her relax. His eyes seemed kind, she thought.

"Please. I need the business. Look out there," he said, pointing
up and down the beach. "Where is everyone?"

There was only a dozen or so people walking on the beach
from all the hotels. And, for the last week, she'd been one of
them.

In less than an hour after she lay out in the sun, his words became prophetic. Three women appeared separately, as if by magic, and rented chairs. Then three different couples appeared and
joined them. Each time someone would rent a chair, she would

turn and look back at his tent. Invariably, he would catch her, grin, and give her a thumbs up. She had to laugh.

"Thank you for the chair…"

"Carl."

"Carl."

"No, thank *you* for the business. Now I can afford to take my wife out to dinner thanks to you."

She knew he was kidding, but it made her smile.

"What's your name, little daughter?"

"Toni."

"Well, Toni, you have carte blanche to my chairs any time you are out on my beach."

Your beach, she thought. "Thank you, Carl."

"Wait a second."

She stopped and turned around.

"Forgive me for being presumptuous, but I've seen you here a lot these past weeks. Well, you're hard to miss, and I think you know why," he said to the inquiring look he saw on her face. When a small grin crept out of the corner of her mouth, he continued. "I work this stand alone and could really use some help. I'll pay you ten bucks an hour just to sit and look pretty while renting my chairs. I'll open up, and then you can come to work for me whatever time you want, and then I'll return before dark to close up. You can work one day or seven days, for as many hours as you want. It will give me time to get some other things done at home, what do you say."

Toni was just about to graciously decline when—

"Just think it over, no rush. You can start tomorrow or next month if you want."

That's how it all started. And he was true to his word. She would tell him how many hours each day, and sometimes he would leave but always return ahead of schedule. More often he would only be gone for an hour or so and insist she stay and work with him.

Today she avoided walking near the Hilton Hotel where Carl's chairs were located. Instead, when she stepped out onto the beach, she walked in the other direction toward the pier. Old Carl's voice was the shadow that followed and whispered to her as she walked barefoot on the sand near the water's edge. She had explained her story to him, leaving out the part about her having HIV. Carl's advice had surprised her.

"Look, Toni, I understand why you left. Considering everything, I think you did the right thing. When a man or a woman lets you down, you should leave."

Toni just stared out at the ocean. It was a subject that, after all this time away, still produced emotions she struggled to conceal.

"When I came down here, I was leaving my past to start over," he said. "I bet you most of the people here have done the same thing. Sometimes when the fire gets too hot you have to leave or get burnt. Don't listen to people," he remarked as he sat beside her, sensing she was hurting. "Toni, there's nothing wrong with running away. Sometimes it's the only way to survive."

He was right about that, she thought as she took a deep breath, it was about survival. Had she stayed in Pittsburgh, things would have been crazy. It'd been a year, and the pain still hurt. Toni walked down to the water's edge. She'd never intended to stay away this long, or to avoid contact with those she loved. But every time she tried to call or write, the depression took hold of her and reminded her that she was going to die.

You have HIV, the voices would say, *your life is over.*

It was chatting with Old Carl that finally broke the hold depression had on her. Toni found herself beginning to enjoy his odd brand of humor. She giggled to herself when she pictured him walking around with his chicken-thin legs sticking out of those always obnoxiously colored Bermuda shorts he loved to wear and talking about the people on *His* beach.

She did feel good being around him. He seemed to know when she was depressed and how to touch the right cords to get her out of her funk. During the last few months she worked for him, he never complained about all the days she had to take off because of her repeated battles with the flu virus. It wasn't a coincidence. Toni began to notice that Carl started to bring a thermos of hot soup that his wife insisted he drink. He never did, but always insisted she drink it. "My wife would kill me," he would plead with her, "if I waste her famous soup."

Recalling that lie triggered tentacles of warm memories for Toni. Carl talked a lot, but never too much and always seemed to know when to talk and when she wanted to be left alone. He never said anything crude or disrespectful. Usually, there was always some point to the stories he told her, some valuable suggestion when she seemed lost or bewildered.

Toni stopped and looked back toward the tent that was Carl's The Best Beach Chair Rental's prime spot, as he called it. There was only a hand full of people walking along the beach near Carl's.

It was then that Toni looked around and realized she was alone for about three hundred yards in every direction. She sat down at the water line and ran her fingers through the moist sand. The water touched her toes, prompting her to look up. From the calm waters edge, the dark liquid mass seemed to stretch out forever like a large black table. It was both beautiful and dangerous, she thought.

A distant freighter was the only mar to the perfect seascape and, as it sailed past, she held up her right hand. The ship was about the size of her smallest fingernail. She wondered about the people who were working and living on board the freighter. A myriad of tough, unshaven faces passed before her mind's eye as she imagined the strong, hard men who lived in the floating metal city moving off into the horizon. Where were they from, she questioned, and were they happy with their lives? Did any of them have AIDS?

Thinking about the freighter was just her way of ignoring what was already a given in her heart. The decision was already made. Toni knew daydreaming would only delay having to deal with that decision. She had to say goodbye to old Carl, she told the shrinking ship as it sailed into the horizon.

Toni stood up, wiped some of the sand off her butt, and started walking slowly toward The Best Beach Chair Rental spot on the beach. The salty breeze off the ocean pushed, but she reluctantly dragged her feet across the warming sand. This was a moment she wanted to always remember because only the Big Guy knew if she would ever be in this same spot, having this same great view, and feeling this same way again. She stopped and looked around at the collection of diversely shaped and colored hotels and motels that dotted the Daytona Beach shoreline. It was a beautiful scene and one that invariably drew her to the beach almost every day. It had helped cleansed her spirit when she first arrived. Her panoramic viewing led her to a man in the distance waving at her. She gave Carl a wave, took a deep breath, and started walking toward him.

"Hey there, pretty girl," Carl said as Toni approached his tent. "What, you want to work on your days off?"

"Hi, Carl. No, I just like to walk along the beach. It relaxes me."

"I know. Sometimes, I feel the same way," he said to the striking looking young woman standing over him. "Well, come and sit in the shade of the tent with me for a while. With you standing there, it will draw customers, and I want to be lazy for a few hours."

Maybe he had a point, Toni thought, as they were interrupted twice the moment after she sat down.

"Carl, I want to thank you for being here for me," she told the confused man sipping on a Coke. He had returned from renting some chairs and plopped down in his chair. "Thank you for hiring me to rent your chairs when I needed something to do. But most of all, I want to thank you for being my friend," Toni told the old Cubs fan.

He looked over at the young woman sitting beside him. She was dressed in his favorite yellow bikini. She wore tan shorts and an open white shirt over the swimsuit. The few times she shed her shorts and went swimming, he had envisioned himself forty years younger and trying to talk to that lovely wet mermaid walking out of the ocean.

Toni misread the look on his face when he sat up and placed his drink down in the sand. Oh, oh, she thought, here comes the lecture.

"Look, beautiful," he said as he took her small hand in his, "I gave you the job because you needed something to get you started again. I've seen that crushed look before on young people who are running away from something painful."

Toni watched as a memory caused the old story teller to stop and look down the beach. When he returned and looked at her, his face was flushed with emotion.

"There was this girl I saw once with that same forlorn façade I saw on you when you wandered past me those first weeks. Later, she was found floating in the water out there," he said pointing toward the pier, "not far from here. I—I didn't get involved. I thought I would be intruding. You know, she might think I was just some old guy trying to hit on a young babe, so I didn't offer to help her. This one day, I remember her walking past and stopping at the water's edge. She stared out at the ocean for a long time and then turned and stared at me. She was a cutie, not nearly the looker you are, my dear, but cute. But she had very sad eyes, and maybe that's why I didn't approach her. I sensed she wanted to talk, but before I could get over my indecision and say something, she started walking away. I don't think it was the same day, though." His perpetual grin vanished in a look of regret so deep it touched her. He lowered his head and took a deep breath.

Toni put her hand on his shoulder. "Thank you for everything, Carl," she said when he looked up at her. "I know now that I can't run away from the people that love me."

"And that you love."

"And that I love. The AIDS Center here taught me to live fully the days I have left, not to just exist." *There*, she thought, *now he knows*. "I'm sorry to keep this from you, but I have AIDS. But you were never—"

"I know, girl, I was never in danger. Little one, I knew you had it the day you told me you were running away. It had to be something mighty powerful to make you leave people that you claimed cared so much for you. Usually, people flee pain and cruelty. You were running from yourself. With that tiny waist of yours, I knew it wasn't because you were knocked up. But as pretty as you are," he said, making Toni blush, "that wouldn't have been too surprising."

Carl stood and helped Toni to her feet. "Look, my girl, if it doesn't work out at home, you can always come back and live with us. I've talked to my wife many times about you. She wanted me to bring you home with me, but I told her I knew you wouldn't come. You see my lovely Deana and I never could have children. If you don't find the love you need there, come back, and we'll take care of you."

Toni bit her lip and then hugged the old man. His thin, boney frame offered her little physical comfort, but it was his soft heart that she was reaching out to hold. His simple act of kindness triggered feelings that were sequestered since she arrived under the heavy weight of sorrow. His hands rubbed her lovingly as she sobbed in his arms. He held on to her until his own eyes cleared.

"Thank you, Carl," she answered, sniffling. "I'll remember that. I promise to come back and see you before I—I promise I'll be back."

He smiled at the attractive young woman standing in front of him.

She kissed him on the cheek. "Goodbye, Carl."

He couldn't say anything, so he winked at her. He felt empty as he watched the young woman he had secretly adopted turn and walk away. She had promised to come back one day, but he sensed that it was a blank promise. He was sure she meant it, but life often interceded and dictated a different course you must follow, but he loved her for saying it.

"Toni!" he shouted.

His dark-haired daughter stopped in her tracks, but didn't turn around.

"Please take this."

Toni wanted to say no thanks to whatever he was offering, but she couldn't risk hurting him. Turning around, she was stunned by what he had in his hand. The faded gift shined brighter in the sun than the largest diamond. Carl had taken the baseball cap off his head and held it out to her. In the months she worked for him, and even during the weeks when she just walked past *his* spot, she had always seen him wearing that cap. There was a story behind it that Carl said he didn't want to talk about. A story that was so painful that the old storyteller couldn't find the strength to repeat it.

An emotional Toni walked slowly back to him, tearfully shaking her head. Her heart was breaking. Another man had managed to touch her to the root of her soul. She looked on despondently as he stood there offering her his precious gift. His white hair was blowing around his face like an angry swarm of bees looking for the person that disturbed their resting-place. As she neared him, his rawhide tough, sun wrinkled skin parted in a smile. Those warm eyes were bright with appreciation for her acceptance of his gift.

As she came close, he saw her face was full of sentiment. Carl smiled that devilish grin of his and placed the cap on her head.

He then kissed her cheek. "I want my hat back," he whispered in her ear, struggling with the words he wanted to say.

Toni just looked at him through watery eyes, nodding acceptance of his behest.

The old man beamed as she forced a smile. *She's soooo pretty*, he thought, even wearing his old cap and then told her. "It never looked that good on me."

"You have been a real friend to me," Toni confessed while smiling up at him. "Your vibrant, crazy personality has kept me from thinking about how bad my life has become." She tipped her "new" hat at him and then walked away.

He had given her a job that neither she nor he needed. Her father had put a fortune in her account to keep his relatives from getting their hands on his money. Old Carl sure didn't need any help during the slow season she began to realize after those first quiet weeks. They only rented a few chairs each day.

Toni fought hard not to turn around again. He had done all this to help her find herself she began to realize after a few months on the job.

His constant praise and comments on how pretty she was blunted the picture of the thinning woman she saw in the mirror. She had to do it. Toni turned and waved goodbye to the tiny man standing in front of the red, white, and blue The Best Beach Chair Rental sign.

෴

After a hard day at work, David was just glad to be home. Sitting in his car, he looked up at his apartment, debating whether he should go and get something to eat and bring home, or have the leftovers in the frig. Since he was exhausted, the leftovers won out as he climbed out his car and walked toward his apartment building. Unlocking his mail slot when he entered the building, he pulled out a half dozen letters. He was in his apartment, munching on a cookie, when he sat down and looked through his mail. He tossed the first three envelopes aside. They were the usual junk mail. The forth, however, caught his attention. He held the letter up in total disbelief.

He knew the handwriting was unmistakably hers and the post

office stamp sealed the deal when it read Daytona Beach, Florida. Carefully he opened the envelope.

Dearest David,
I'm coming home soon.

His breaths came in short gasps after he read the first line.

Please don't tell anyone yet, I want to surprise Brenda.
I'll call you in a couple of days when I get there. I'm okay.
I miss you, my brother. Please don't be angry with me, I didn't run away from you!
Love you,
Toni

Short and to the point, that was Toni's style David recalled. She would hate to hear him say it, but she was the image of her father.

David put the letter up to his nose. The scent was definitely Toni's. She still flavored her letters with perfume, he thought, the smile on his face a mile wide. First, Mike came home from the hospital looking better than he had in a long time, and now Toni's letter. This was proving to be a great month, he thought, maybe he should go out and play the lottery.

CHAPTER 27

The warm, soft, and thick cotton towel on her skin was comforting as she dried herself in the steamy bathroom. The bathroom doors had the only locks her father permitted in the house on the advice of his paranoid brother. Her father had succumbed to her weird uncle's need to be able to access and check every room nightly for unseen and unheard burglars. That fat, beady-eyed little bastard Uncle Dominic, Toni angrily remembered, loved to time his room searches with her changing clothes or taking a shower. The need for privacy was one of the reasons she had given her father on why she was moving out and getting a place of her own with Brenda. Now she was back under the same umbrella, and she hated that.

The door length mirror, situated on the far side of the eighteen-foot long bathroom, had steamed up earlier from her long shower. But as she approached it, she noticed the fog had dissipated.

Toni watched the woman in the mirror grow larger as she approached, and she felt the pangs of apprehension as she began to see clearly the body in the mirror. It wasn't that she had some great expectations of seeing the healthy woman she was a few years ago reflected back at her. Her repeated bouts with diarrhea and the flu, over the last few months, had stolen that dream from her. But on her first day back home, she wanted to look healthy for her daddy. He would see it if something were wrong, he usually could. He was always the first to recognize when she was getting sick, even before she could feel it.

"I can see it in your face," he would always claim.

"Well, take a good look, girl, what do you see?" Toni forced herself to focus on the woman in the mirror. Holding her breath, she let the towel drop from around her waist, and it drifted silently to the floor. From three feet away, she could see every inch of the Toni DiNardo reflected in the mirror. She closed her eyes to keep back the emotions that swelled up in her chest. She had avoided doing this for months, inwardly hoping that the Florida sun would return some of the color to her sickly pale skin.

Toni took a deep breath. Sorrow was a constant companion that she had gotten to know well as it forced itself into her life. Now, it stood beside her as both stared into the mirror. After a minute or so, she felt her strength returning. She had always been blessed with a very deep well of optimism. The constant strain of dealing with her illnesses, and its many complications, had almost drained that well dry. Lately, she didn't have her usual upbeat attitude about things.

"Gawd, you look bad," she said to the woman in the mirror. The black hair on the woman looking back at her was still wet and lay limp across her forehead. Toni's eyes trailed down to the dark circles around the woman's eyes.

"Daddy always says," she remembered, "that's a sign of anemia. The body is lacking in something it needs very much."

Toni continued the tour of the woman's body in the mirror. There was very little that resembled the healthy woman of years earlier who had posed proudly for hours in front of the same mirror, regaling in the "hard body" reflected back at her. Today, the reflection looked like someone in a carnival sideshow mirror.

The tightness in her chest was an expected response when she noticed how much things had changed. She took a deep, slow breath but the pressure in her chest only seemed to worsen. The reflection was just another leaf that has fallen from the autumn tree of her life. For a person who liked things very orderly, the fates had played a mean trick on her. She felt the forces of change assaulting her every step and knew that somehow things would ever be the same again.

The scale didn't lie, she acknowledged, turning to look at the sagging skin around her butt. The 125-pound woman of her teens now looked down as the needle struggled to reach the 110 printed on the scale dial. She had lost the weight quickly in the last few months. What was frightening to her, she was eating all the fattening foods that she had avoided to maintain her figure, but nothing helped as her weight continued to melt off. The continued bouts of diarrhea and influenza had taken a toll. She could eat little when she was sick, and the little she ate passed right through her. Worried, she went to the AIDS clinic and was re-tested. The result confirmed what she already knew. She was one of the unlucky ones. Her body had progressed, or rather di-gressed, from HIV to AIDS in a year.

"Look at those breasts," Toni said to the reflection as if it was another person. The slightly sagging bosoms were a far cry from the full, healthy upturned breast of her teens. The many stares she used to garner, when she would get that occasional urge to be rebellious and go bra-less, came to mind. She had thoroughly enjoyed the attention her figure usually created. It was worth all the hard work, dieting, and exercise. Now Toni found them dis-gusting and didn't want to touch them. "No man would find those attractive," she said to the sulking woman in the mirror.

It was the same all over. The toned, healthy body she had worked hard to create had deflated like a leaking balloon, but the narrow waist she had always been proud of remained. Not from the hard work-outs and the strenuous regimen of sit-ups of the past, but from the lack of fat cells in her body. This was more evident in the bones that stuck out at her hips. The figure that once drew enough whistles to finally annoy her was now more likely to induce sympathy she decided. Toni picked up her towel, unlocked the door, and rushed out of the bathroom in tears.

"Why did I come back here?" she cried as she fell on her bed.

The door to her bedroom squeaked once as it slowly closed. Two eyes blinked shut as the scene before him nurtured unfore-seen feelings of shame as he watched the naked, thin girl crying on her bed. Never again would he open her door without knock-ing. His secret lust for her had changed channels. There was something seriously wrong with her that had robbed her of her health, Dominic decided as he retired to his room.

He recalled spotting it the minute he picked her up at the air-port. Her surprised call found him the only one home. Toni's fa-ther and two of his friends were fishing up in Lake Erie, and he was watching the house for him. They weren't scheduled back for another few days. When he pulled up to the TWA curb at Greater Pittsburgh Airport, she was standing there waiting. He had rushed to the airport to pick her up, relishing in the rare opportunity to be alone with his favorite niece. That joy changed the minute she climbed into his car. Her sunken, color-less cheeks were the first shock. He was about to question the sickly looking girl when she sat down in the car and rudely ordered him to get his big ass in gear. That convinced him she really was the same smart-mouthed little Toni.

Dominic made a decision on his way to the airport to be her authoritative adult figure until his brother returned. He now acquiesced. Who was he fooling, he thought, *Control Toni Di-Nardo? Not even her father could do that.*

Toni heard her door snap close as she cried in her pillow. *Hope you enjoyed yourself, you fat pig*, she thought, while making no effort to cover up. She giggled in her crying spell, as the thought of a man enjoying looking at her thin body seemed sadly very funny.

A tired and troubled young woman grabbed the blanket on her bed and rolled over until she was cocooned in the cotton covering. It became the warm, protective arms of the mother she struggled to remember. She missed those loving arms. No, she realized, responding to the budding sensations of her daydream, it wasn't her mother's arms she was reaching out for. It was the powerful, playful, silly arms of the man she thought she would one day marry that triggered the need to be hugged so tight. Toni shook herself, as if the feeling could be gotten rid of that easily. Resigned, she relaxed and let those impulsive emotions grow.

Usually, any thoughts of *him* fired up her rage, but the picture of the gaunt girl in the mirror had made that anger senseless. The old desire to hurt *him* like he had hurt her was losing steam. Her illness had made her very sensitive to pain, given or received. When death's countdown clock started ticking, the many senseless ways we wasted our energies became very clear. Toni was a woman who had always enjoyed revenge on someone who had wronged her. Revenge had become an asinine pursuit to the thin woman on the bed. Today, she needed someone to comfort her and erase the picture of that dying woman in the mirror.

No one came forward to heal her pain.

Her thoughts drifted, as they had continually done lately, to her approaching death. She envisioned it as a tall man dressed in a long black robe standing in the corner of every room she entered. From the cruel gaze on his skinless bony face, he was awaiting her arrival with a certainty that frightened her. Then, inevitably, her thoughts drifted back to the curly, black-haired babies she would never have. The weight of the sorrow she was feeling provoked a spurt of coughing. Starting to feel warm again, Toni hoped this wasn't the beginning of another bout with the flu. Her last battle had taken her weeks to completely recover from.

Troubled, her thoughts drifted to the man she called when she first arrived. It was late, and her father wasn't home, but she decided to call David. Their conversation made her feel glad to be home. He was willing to come over right away, and that warmed her, but it was getting late, so she told him tomorrow would be better. He made her laugh when he faked being put down. Dwelling on that conversation with David helped her relax until sleep claimed the naked woman wrapped in the blanket cocoon.

Bright sunshine lit up her bedroom. It was morning, the little moth sitting up in the blanket cocoon realized. "I've got to get up," she said out loud, trying to find the will to move. She would be seeing David today. A pang of regret caused her to close her eyes as the picture of David's shocked face, at seeing how thin she had become, weakened her resolve, and she started to lie down again. *No*, Toni chastised herself and then unwound from the blanket, *you were the one who called last night and asked him to come over and see you, remember? You want to try and look presentable for him, don't you?*

David was a dear friend, she admitted, as she walked over to her vanity, sat down, and started brushing her hair. That knucklehead could always read her. She would go to great lengths to masquerade her true intentions from him, but he always saw through the charade. No amount of bogus animosity, faked passion, mock frustration, or pretended annoyance could prompt him to yield to her and apologize for his chauvinistic behavior. Their playful games made her feel so good that she was afraid to look any deeper at the feelings she had for David after breaking up with—

They had cemented a special friendship from the beginning, and she wanted nothing to discolor it. Only David's close relationship with that son-of-a-bitch Michael had tempered her desire to see him. Her first few days away were colored by the times she picked up the phone to call David and then changed her mind. In the sad, blackened mood she was in, it was a given that David's voice was what her spirit needed more than anything. But she knew he would be able to talk her into coming home, or at the least tell him where she was, and she didn't want to do that.

Toni hurried over to her dresser and quickly pulled out a pair of panties and a bra when she thought she heard Uncle Peeping Tom walking in the hallway. Already the warmth generated by her soon-to-be arriving guest had renewed her inherent sense of modesty.

She slipped into a pair of jeans and one of her impertinent T-shirts. This one had two starving buzzards sitting on a limb of a dead tree waiting for something to die. Written underneath one of the buzzards said, *Hell with this waiting! I'm going to kill something.*

She had picked that shirt because it was also David's favorite, though she would never admit that was the real reason.

Toni sat down on her bed to put on some socks. While doing so, she caught a glimpse of herself in her dresser mirror and noticed the buzzards printed on her T-shirt. Her lips parted in a grin. Memories, the gift that kept on giving, warmed her troubled spirit. She fell back on the bed as thoughts of David, and better days, came to mind. The good days were like a cup of hot chocolate on a cold night. That's right, she remembered giggling like a little girl, the day she first met Davey was the first time she wore this shirt.

☙❦❧

This was one of the driest months of May that David could recall, and of course, today wouldn't be one of those days. It was a light, but chilly rain that was falling. The kind that you thought wasn't that bad but slowly soaked you to the skin. It was fitting, he thought as he looked up. This dreary gray day matched his mood. It would be different if there were someone waiting for him that could lift his spirits a little. He sighed while crossing the street. But that wasn't the case today. No, whatever joy or happiness that rested upon the shoulders of the woman he was going to see, would soon be shattered by the news he was bringing. It was that news that troubled him. Mike had begged him to never reveal his secret to family or friends. Despite powerful misgivings, David had kept his word. Mike had failed to include Toni in his list so, technically, telling her didn't break David's word.

A gust of wind pummeled him, stinging his skin with the cold rain. His usual warm weather attire of shorts and T-shirt, that had seemed perfect when he walked out of his apartment, now seemed totally inadequate. The last few days had been dry and in the eighties, and this morning started out the same, but quickly succumbed to the sudden cool weather and now this rain. David thought about returning home and sitting out the worsening weather but decided to continue because he was as close to his destination as he was his house. Added to that was a promise he made after receiving a late night phone call.

David had fallen asleep on the couch while watching the news when the phone rang. He looked at the clock on the wall and wondered who could be calling him because Trisha didn't get off for another hour. Taking a deep breath, he picked the phone up after the third ring.

"Hello."

"Hi, David."

It was obviously a female's voice and he was about to guess when the truth snapped him out of his sleepy funk. "Toni?"

"Hi, Davey."

"Toni, where are you?"

His enthusiasm warmed her. "I'm home. I arrived a few minutes ago, Davey."

"That's so great. Are you home to stay, girlfriend?"

Her hesitation wasn't intentional, but she hadn't given it that much thought. "Yes."

"That's just great, baby. I missed you so much."

"Thank you, Davey, I missed you more than you know. When are you coming over to see me?"

"I'm kicking out the three women in my bed as we speak. Okay, ladies, you have to go. Sure each of you are prettier, but she bakes great cookies. Okay Toni, they are leaving, and I want you to know they aren't very happy about that either."

She laughed because she expected him to say something smart-assed like that. "Hey, don't rush them out on my behalf. I can wait those three minutes until you're done."

"Ouch, word got out all the way to Florida, huh?"

Toni heard that but didn't comment and was glad she didn't. She knew Brenda would have kept that secret from everyone— but him.

"Okay, give me a few minutes to take a shower and get some clothes on, and I'll be right there."

"No, Davey, you know what? It's late. How about we get to- gether tomorrow around noon? That way I can get some beauty sleep and look presentable."

"What? That would take you all of five minutes?"

"You are so sweet. You still can't get in my pants, but great try."

"That's okay, but from what the other fifty losers that have tried those granny-panties have said, I'm not missing anything."

They both laughed. It felt so good to spar with each other again. Each had a face frozen with an ear-to-ear smile.

"Okay, sweetheart, tomorrow around noon. Have you talked to Brenda yet?"

"No, you were the first person I called. I thought I would start at the bottom and work my way up."

David just shook his head. Toni was gone for almost a year but nothing seemed to have changed between them. The rules were the same, insult at every opportunity. "Well, smart ass, she's not home, she is working tonight."

"Oh, okay. Well, I can't wait to see you, Davey."

"Tomorrow it is then, lady. Get some rest."

"I will, goodnight, Davey."

That was the push driving him to continue his journey to see her in the face of this suddenly worsening storm. There was someone he cared the world about waiting for him, and even be- ing soaked to the skin wouldn't deter him. Walking wasn't his favorite means of travel, but his car was in the shop for state in- spection, and he was totally confused trying to read the bus schedule. Standing on the corner of Penn and Wood streets for over an hour, he finally realized the buses only traveled outbound on this section of Penn Avenue. Feeling foolish, he decided to find another bus stop. After walking only a few miles, he realized the short cut he chose wasn't on the bus routes, and he might as well walk the rest of the way to Toni's father's house.

The rain started falling in earnest just as he walked out of a side street on to Penn Avenue near Mellon Park. David thought about looking for some kind of cover, but he was already soaked to the skin. He groaned as his cold and wet T-shirt stuck to the skin on his back. He shrugged his shoulders, thinking, *Oh, well, I'm too wet to care anymore.*

Just as he was about to cross the street, a car swerved near him, causing him to jump back on the curb. Before he could react, the car hit a large puddle of water and splashed David from his chest to his shoes. Stunned by the cold water, he could only turn, wild-eyed and enraged, toward the car. The two passengers in the back seat were pointing and laughing at him as the car continued on its way as if nothing had happened.

It was one of those moments when David was very glad he never carried a gun. When the car first appeared, he thought it was his fault because he wasn't looking before he stepped off the curb. So when the wave of water hit him, he accepted it as the price for his foolish decision to continue to walk in this storm and just another straw on the load he was carrying. When he saw them laughing, he knew it was intentional and snapped out. Not an open show of anger, that would please his antagonist too much, but the anger was there just the same. It was there in the eyes that narrowed and squinted as the car raced away. It was there in the way his hands closed into a fist. Yes, he was pissed off.

Yet, despite the baptism, it was the pelting rain in his face that finally detoured him from his destination. The only shelter he could see was located across the street. It was a recessed doorway in the only building in the nearby park. A sudden increase in the sound and volume of the rain falling helped him make up his mind. David headed for the doorway. His new tennis shoes made squishing sounds as he walked. He tried to open the door when he reached it and, as expected, found it locked. He was completely alone in the park.

The sensible people enjoying the courts, playground, and bike trail had long since departed for their homes at the first sign of the approaching ominous dark clouds. Not stupid, David thought, rebuking himself for his poor judgment when it became obvious the weather was turning ugly.

It was only about ten to noon, yet the day was very dark. David leaned back against the door and jerked forward when he felt the cold metal on his back through his wet clothes. Just another irritation on a day that was quickly becoming the pits as the rain was falling so hard now he found it difficult to see the playground or tennis courts only a few yards away. He did spot a white plastic bucket in the grass already overflowing with rainwater. Walking out into the deluge, he dumped the water out of the bucket and brought it back to use as a seat. Somehow it made the situation almost bearable. He did feel warmer now that his back was off the cold door.

Tired, and struggling with the possible consequences of the deed he was going to do, he buried his face in his hands. With a momentary respite, David again weighed his tough decision. The loss of Mike's trust was a very real possibility, one that, until today, he had valued too much to break his word to him. After reading the last page of Toni's diary, the choices weren't as clear as they once appeared. He knew he would have to live with his decision, right or wrong. It was having to live with it that troubled him as he sat on the bucket in the doorway, rubbing his arms in an attempt to erase the chilling effects of the rain. Another chill he felt had little to do with his saturated clothing and more from the reaction Mike would have when he found out his last friend had betrayed him.

A streak of lighting, flashing directly overhead, caught his attention, and the ensuing loud thunderclap startled him. The power of the electric display was impressive as a five-fingered jagged white line reached across the sky. As was wont to happen when nature snapped her fingers, he felt his mountain of problems shrink in significance.

The wall of rain offered David something very helpful—it gave him privacy. There were no distractions to steal his concentration, just the gray, dreary strings of raindrops falling continuously from the sky.

Yes, he realized, his friendship with Mike would probably survive even this. A small smile formed on his face when he thought about all the things that they had faced together. At work, they were called the odd couple and ebony and ivory—among other things—he remembered. Their favorite tag was *ying* and *yang.*

David looked around and reasoned that the rain would continue for a while, so he leaned back on his bucket until the door supported him. The feel of the cold metal was ignored this time as he focused in on the warmth of his friendship with Mike. David always seemed to recall that same incident, the dropped water bottle, as the first time they really noticed each other.

CHAPTER 28

Toni absentmindedly looked out of her bedroom window as the fury of the rain falling in the yard distracted her thoughts. She watched as the drops welded together on the ground, forming large puddles in the driveway. As the rain fell, she began to think of her father and hoped he was having better weather up in Erie. She knew her dad and his friends would find a dry spot somewhere and would be drinking beer, regardless of the weather. Maybe getting a fire going in the cabin and telling tall stories about the ones that got away. Both fish and females. That crazy group knew how to make the best out of a gloomy day. She was very happy her dad could find the time to get away with his friends. There would be plenty of time for her and her dad to spend together when he returned, she reasoned, lying to herself. It was her way of managing the regret that she was battling to control.

She took a deep breath and closed her eyes. The thought of having to talk about her disease with her daddy weighed heavily on her spirit. She knew he wasn't the type that handled sicknesses very well. It was the painful and depressing last two years of her mother slowly dying of cancer that had given her dad his reluctance to discuss her death or anything to do with her being ill. When Toni first realized how much it hurt him to talk about her, she never again asked about her mother's demise. Now Toni was sick and would have to discuss it with her dad. Not only did he deserve to know, she needed to tell him.

Every letter she mailed home to him contained an explanation of her sudden desire to move to Florida. Those letters only made it as far as the nearest trash can by the nearest mailbox. When she finally called him…

"…I know why you ran away, Toni."

Twice she almost hung up on him fearing his famous temperament. She tried explaining it to him in a way he might understand, but failed miserably and finally hung up. Months later when she called again, he correctly sensed that it might be the last call he would get if he pushed her buttons. Toni was very grateful for the space he gave her. It was that space, or avoiding touchy subjects, that bought her time to reason through her dilemma and make the decision to return home.

In the time she was away, Toni learned more about her dad from their phone calls than she had growing up. The questions they couldn't ask each other in person eventually flowed out on the phone. For Toni, the greatest benefit was that she was finally able to get some answers.

For the first three years after her mother's death, Toni remembered how difficult it was to try and talk to her father. Her Aunt Joanna, who came to live with them for five years and help raise his teenage daughter, confided that she had found him crying in his room on a few occasions. Her brother was still mourning the loss of his wife, she informed her niece. Toni missed her too, she tried explaining to her aunt, and needed to share it with her daddy, but he would have none of that. The life and times of Kim DiNardo wasn't open to discussion, he told his prying daughter.

Those arguments would send him running out the door, his face a mask of rage. Toni knew she was the spark, but not the fuel. It hurt, nonetheless, when he stayed away for days dealing with his own demons. He had found out, much to her chagrin, that booze eased some of the hurt. The days spent away from his only child were alcohol induced. He never drank around her, so she drew the obvious conclusions. The virile mind of a teenage girl painted many pictures. None of them revealed that the pain was because of how much he missed his wife as the real reasons for her daddy's behavior. Each picture her hurt feelings painted in her vulnerable imagination was a portrait of a man who no longer loved his only child.

How could he love her, she wondered, and leave her alone like that for days on end? *Think about that*, her demons screamed at her. None of the answers she lovingly gave in his defense seemed to quell their insidious accusations. She knew he had deeply loved her mother, that was without question. It was her lack of a good excuse for his actions that would taint her teen years.

If it was his love for Mom that drove him to run away, then what did he feel for me to cause him to stay away, she often debated with her pain?

As her father drifted deeper into himself, the young teen blossomed alone and vulnerable. Her needs finally gained mastery over her pride and led her into the willing arms of a host of vultures. As she celebrated her sixteenth birthday, lying prone underneath someone in the back seat of his car, her father also lost something that night very dear to him while in another urine smelling cheap bar—his daughter's respect.

In the degrading acts of loveless intercourse, Toni learned how people used other people physically, spiritually, mentally, and worse yet, emotionally. She was able to eventually gain control of her life when she finally forgave her father. In that forgiveness, she saw her own addiction. Slowly she forgave herself for being jealous of her father's inability to cope with her mother's passing. Added to that was a negative in her last EPT test, an answer to a tearful prayer that gave her another chance. She felt that a baby at that juncture in her life would have arrested her future as it had for thousands of other young women.

Funny, Toni thought while doodling in the condensation on the window pane she was looking out, a baby then would have destroyed her plans. Now, she would give anything to hold her son or daughter before she—

No matter how hard she tried to keep death out of her thoughts, everything seemed to center on the short time she had remaining. The old taste of bitterness rose up in her mouth, stinging her throat. She had tried bravely to come to grips with the cards she was dealt. When she first found out she had HIV, she ran to Mike and told him of the danger they both were in. It was then that they found out he had AIDS. The horror of that moment had rippled through her dreams on many occasions, sometimes causing her to lay awake at night, cursing his name.

"How could you?" she had asked him then and continued to nightly in the dark motel room she rented near the ocean in Daytona Beach, Florida, spending the first week locked in her room, replaying her life. She found herself trying to picture the day she was infected, the day when that filthy virus passed from his seed into her. They were intimate often, and he was unprotected as their love grew. She never denied him when he needed her because her needs for him were almost as strong. Mike was the first man she really loved, and he rewarded her love then with tenderness and a caring passion that those rutting elks, who had baptized her into fornication, had selfishly denied her. She welcomed his ardor and learned it was okay to acknowledge her own. Now that passion had come full circle and the beauty of that birth was lost in the ugly dark cloud of death that hung, low and threatening, over her future.

Somewhere, she imagined while hiding out in her dark room, there was a pious preacher in a white, polyester suit, pointing an accusing finger at her, and saying, "The wages of sin is death, young woman. You played with fire and now that fire is alive in you, consuming you. The Holy Bible said, 'It is better to marry than to burnnnnnnnnnnnn!'"

Another memory broke through as she drew a cross on her foggy window glass canvas. Toni recalled the many days and nights wasted hiding in her room and trying to find a simpler God she could understand and a God that could explain why. That gave way to listening to every Bible thumping teacher on TV. She had heard so many sermons that the scriptures they quoted ran together in her mind like wet watercolors. Yet, in her darkest moments, when the cold, harsh pit of suicide began to be a more inviting alternative, it was those random scriptures that came together to lift the burden and permit her to live the days she had left to her in the light of day. When those black clouds of depression cleared, the rays of sunshine illuminated a truth. God wasn't to blame for our poor decisions, we are. It was that spiritual light, that reasoning, that opened up to her the need to be with the special people in her life, as long as she had life, and spend those days with those who loved and cared for her.

Toni remembered when she arrived at the airport full of optimism. But when Uncle Peepers said her father wasn't home but up in Erie fishing, she wanted to strike out at him. As he drove her home, she realized that it was a good idea her father wasn't there because it gave her time to unwind and put on her best face for her dad. It would also give her time to see David and Brenda again.

Tired, she had closed her eyes and let her head rest against the car seat as her uncle drove. Minutes later, her eyes suddenly popped open. It had happened again. Almost every time she relaxed, her mind would drift toward thoughts of *him*. As his face appeared in her mind's eye, she had to fight her way through it. Mike was as much in her thoughts now as he was almost every day they were together.

She unconsciously disguised his name and face when she thought about him. That gave it justification and removed any culpability. In her injured imagination, Mike became a movie star one day or a famous musician on another. That freed her to think about him without dealing with the guilt and to give herself to him in her imagination without restraint. She knew, but would never acknowledge, that it was always him.

Sometimes, in her daydreams and imaginations, he had dark hair or a bright red mane like Brenda's. They would walk hand-in-hand on some romantic beach alone for hours, and then make unbelievably powerful love under a huge white moon that was slowly setting in a picturesque dark blue sea. He was there on her, driving her into the biting sand. Yet, when she rose up to meet him she looked over his shoulders and imagined his face was also in the large harvest moon that stood silently over them, as if judging their performance. When she dug her hands in the moist sand, trying to ground the intensity of the passion that was knotting her stomach as it surged up from their union, he was in the earth beneath them. He was, she sensed, *the* Earth beneath them.

Toni shook herself free from that deceptive trance. "David, I'm going to see David soon," Toni said, trying to silence those powerful memories.

"What did you say, Toni?" her uncle asked, looking in the rear view mirror after her sudden outburst startled him.

"Sorry, nothing really, I must have fallen asleep and was— nothing, Uncle."

He stared at her until he had to look back at the road. Toni looked him in the eye as they exchanged stares in the mirror.

As they drove past familiar buildings and stores along the route home, Toni's thoughts turned to David. He, she imagined, was there in the corner of her dark room every night as she tried to sleep, standing guard over her. *My David is here with me,* she told the voices of fear that tried to frighten her when she was alone. *It is David,* she moaned as she cried herself to sleep each of the first few nights. She desperately needed to believe that.

David would understand, she reasoned in her sorrow. He wouldn't judge her or be repelled by the horror that was growing inside her, not him. He could never hurt her like that ass-hole had done, not her David. It was David she needed to be there with her in that scary and drab room. Only David didn't look like David. He was the same man-with-the-forever-tan, but it wasn't David. She silently knew who her imagined guardian really was.

It had taken months of heart-breaking counseling at the AIDS Care Center to enable her to see the face of the demons that haunted her nightmares. She learned it was okay to be angry with Mike for what he had done to her, and that it was all right to feel betrayed. He had betrayed her trust and given her a death sentence, destroying what future she had by infecting her with HIV.

Tired, and feeling abandoned, she let her mind drift again as the car rocked her. Before she realized it, she was thinking about *him*! She was too weak to resist its strong lure this time. Like a mist, her vivid imagination swirled as if stirred by a large ladle and started to form a face. Toni knew, but pretended to be ignorant about the picture taking shape in her mind. The old hate started to rise as the mural neared completion and became Michael Charles Buffer, her executioner—the man who killed the babies she would never have and the source of the poison in her body. He was as clear in her mind's eye, while her uncle drove her home from the airport, as the day they'd met.

Toni suddenly wiped her art off the wet window and hurried downstairs. She walked into the kitchen looking for something to munch on. *Keep busy,* she reminded herself. *Remember what the crisis counselor said, 'Stay busy, and don't let the past rule your future.'* "That's easy for you to say," she remembered angrily telling them then. Her past had destroyed what little future she may have.

Toni had wanted to strike out at someone during those meetings. The inevitability of her death crushed the well of optimism that usually poured from her. She knew no amount of pep talk could stop the destruction of her immune system. When the loss of her T-cells reached a certain point, it was explained, her body would fight before succumbing to the daily blitzkrieg we faced by a host of viruses and germs. No, she came to understand, optimism was essential to prolong her life, but it couldn't stop the onslaught of the AIDS virus.

Having hit bottom in that dark, lonely motel room, Toni made a decision that gave her back the rest of her life. One, she forgave Mike for poisoning her body. She recognized that if he did—it probably wasn't intentional. And two, she had to face another fact. Like that know-it-all counselor claimed, she wasn't a virgin when she met Mike. Any of the guys she was with before him could have infected her years earlier—and they not know it either.

Toni hated her for that truth. Now, she mentally had to drive down every road she had traveled in search of a clue from guys she wanted to forget. Relive each act as if she might find a clue to who was guilty in the sixty seconds of sex most lasted. The futility of that search eluded her, as if recalling his bad breath or the smell of a guy's under arm odor was a sign that he was the guilty person who infected her.

Only one man she knew had the virus, as much as she wished it to be someone else.

When her anger subsided, she began to consider the distinct possibility that he really didn't know. The Mike she thought she knew—forgiving him finally enabled her to see—would never knowingly give someone AIDS. The Mike she did know was able to wait a long time, even though his frustrations were obvious, until she was emotionally ready to have sex without the slightest complaint. He was her Mt. Everest. For the first time, she realized that the years-long possible HIV incubation period increased the possibility that someone might have infected either of them also without their knowledge. The moment she saw the true reality of the many possibilities, the source of her hate, that had used Mike as the fuel for her reason to flee, lost its hole card.

Having come to grips with the actuality of her situation, Toni then knew her place was here at home. She made a promise to herself, while walking along the beach one beautiful clear day and watching a couple lying out in the sun mooning over each other like they didn't have a care in the world, to live the days she had remaining to the fullest her body would allow. Then, when the time came to go, she would cut the cord that bound her to this world and stand face to face…with God.

Yes, the cord, the blue light cord, she recalled lovingly that day as she walked along the water's edge. The phrase prompted treasured memories of the days when she would sit for hours, listening to David talk about his life. He had so many interesting stories that she never tired of listening to him. After Mike broke it off with her, they found plenty of time to just talk. Sometimes, they would sit and chat over something she baked with wine or a hot cup of coffee.

When she was dating Mike, they were never serious conversations, choosing rather to tease each other relentlessly. Now, they discussed very private things that very close friends do, but not usually male and female close friends unless the male was gay. But that was the special closeness they created. From talking about some things in somewhat graphic details to then laughing about their bungled experiences like losing their virginity to who was their best in bed—Mike and Brenda won hands down—to their dreams for a future.

There were unspoken subjects that they correctly sensed and accepted that should remain private. He was a virile black man, and she was passionate white female. Anyone just seeing how close they had become would naturally assume it was only a matter of time until it evolved into a sexual pairing. By society standards, they would have marked them as two very sexual and desirable animals. Society would have been correct—normally. But what held back their ardor was the missing piece of the threesome. They loved and valued him more than the curious thoughts floating secretly in the back of their minds.

The blue light cord story David told her was her favorite. David swore it was true, and that was enough for her. It happened one evening when she was bored and lonely. On a whim, she decided to make Brenda her favorite chocolate chip cookies and was pleasantly surprised by a knock at their door.

"Hi, Davey," Toni said when she opened the door and was surprised by who was standing there. She walked up to him and gave him a hug. "Nice of you to stop by."

He noticed the bits of flour on her cheek and guessed from the scent of her home she was baking.

"Actually, I came over to see Brenda, is she home?"

"Yeah, right, you know she is working nights this week," Toni said as she put her arm in his and walked him into the kitchen. "You are just hoping, and please don't beg this time—" She stopped and looked up at him. "I hate it when you get on your knees and cry, foolishly I might add, hoping that I might finally be desperate enough to rock your world."

"Am I that transparent?" he said and kissed her on the cheek. "I did come over hoping to see a beautiful woman to do just that with, but you said she isn't home. And you know I have high standards. There is no way I can settle for second best."

"Who are you trying to fool?" the sassy female said as she pushed him away. "As hard up as you are, you would settle for fiftieth best."

"Yeah, that's true," he said as he followed her. "But, unfortunately for you, that number leaves you out in the—"

She turned and stuck her tongue out at him. "Here," she said, offering him one of the cookies she had just baked, "these are the only hot cookies you're going to get tonight."

"Thank you, my dear," he said as he took the cookie from her and examined it. "Let's see...just like the baker, it's flat on both sides with little chips in the front."

Toni wanted to laugh, but she hid it in her frown, rolled her eyes at him, and then picked up a cookie and tossed it at him. Even worse, he caught it out of the air.

So went their evening while she was cooking. After helping her clean up, they sat in the living room, listening to soft music, sipping wine, and chatting about life—from their jobs to the crazy things in the news. Mike the only subject they purposefully avoided.

"Do you believe in life after death, David?"

He was talking a sip of wine and looked at her over his glass. Placing his down on the coffee table gave him time to reflect on an answer.

"I hope so, but I don't believe in reincarnation. I don't think we lived other lives before, but if we did, that's cool. What if in another life you were a man and I was a girl? Wouldn't that be weird?"

"Some people believe in that."

"I know what kind of floozy I would have been."

"You probably were a nun, that's why you're so desperate to—"

"Yeah, right," he said with a big grin. "If there's reincarnation, all bigots should come back as the race or religion they hated. Give them a chance to see all the pain they've caused others."

"Yeah, and all men who beat up their wives come back as battered women."

"See, if we were in charge, we would—"

"Screw it up too."

"True." David laughed. "You asked about life after death. My mom told me something very interesting when I was a kid. She may not have known a lot about the world outside our home but what she knew she was honest about. She told me that one night, as she lay on her bed, trying to get some sleep, she suddenly had this vision or spiritual experience. She said her spirit suddenly left her body and hovered in the air. She looked down and watched herself as she lay on the bed next to my step-father. Then, without knowing why, she started to drift upward. Soon she was outside and above our house soaring upward toward the clouds.

"My mom explained she thought she had died and was going, as she put it, 'To her reward in Heaven.' Higher she soared, past the clouds and into the blackness of space. She looked around and realized she was surrounded by a multitude of dazzling, sparkling stars. Then, suddenly, a star, far brighter than all the others put together, appeared straight ahead. My mom said she knew she was racing toward Heaven's Gate. She said she felt such a feeling of happiness and contentment, and it grew stronger as she moved closer toward that star. The feeling was even better than when she had her children she said. 'Think of your best moment ever,' she told me, 'and multiply that a thousand times' was how she described it.

"In your case, Toni, imagine if I really let you have me, how amazing that would feel."

Toni remembered being so engrossed and riveted by his story that his insult caught her so off guard she didn't have a quick come-back, and the blank look on her face caused him to laugh. But seeing the joy in his dancing eyes, it was worth the put down.

"Then something weird happened to her, Toni," David said after he wiped the tears in his eyes from laughing and continued the story about his mom. "My mom said she suddenly stopped cold in the blackness of space. She tried but couldn't move forward. Confused, she looked around trying to find out what was holding her back. It was then that she saw this long blue cord of light attached to her and extending back toward the earth. She said that was when she became frightened. Then a loving voice spoke to her in the darkness, alleviating her fears. She thought it was the Lord.

"'Fear not my child" she heard him say. "The cord of light is your loving attachment to those you left behind. Your love for your children keeps you from letting go and entering into your rest. Let them go, and the cord will break, ushering you into Paradise.'

"She was torn between her own happiness and that of her children."

Toni felt empathy for the decision his mom was forced to make when David told that story. Fortunately, the decision was made for her, David revealed, when she woke up on her bed. His mom was certain she would have died that night if she had wanted Heaven more than worrying about the welfare of her children if she died. All she would have had to do was let go of this world to sever the unbroken blue light.

The memory of those evenings sitting around chatting about things with Davey warmed Toni as she walked to the front door, opened it, and looked up and down the street. The rain continued to fall in torrents, and there was no sign of David anywhere. She closed the door on the miserable day outside. She was alone. Earlier, she had watched indifferently as her uncle drove off. Now that she was there to watch things, he probably went home, she surmised. Again, she walked to a window, pushed back the curtains, and looked for David.

"Where are you?" she whispered. She wanted to say she needed him, but to acknowledge that was to admit she was lacking something. In her new outlook on things, she was self-sufficient and didn't need anyone. In her heart, however, she ached for the fun-loving times they had together, enjoying the simple things again—a time when the toughest decision she had to make was what to wear.

The ringing of the phone startled Toni. She rushed over and picked it up. Apprehensive, she said, "Hello."

"Toni, Toni, it's me, David."

"David," she shouted into the phone. "Where are you?"

"Look, girlfriend, I'm calling you from a pay phone. I can't come by right now."

Toni's spirits dropped. When she called him last night, he said he would be over at noon, and he was late.

Her silence told David more than he wanted to know. He endured that long moment of silence before speaking again.

"Toni, are you there?"

"Yes, David," she said slowly, "I heard you. I'm sorry. I was looking forward to seeing you again. Why did you change your mind?" she asked.

The skepticism in her voice was obvious.

"What changed my mind?" he asked emphatically into the phone. "I was walking over to your house when this storm hit. I'm standing here in a phone booth, soaking wet, chilled to the bone, and talking to you, girl. I was going to come over anyway, but I didn't want your father to see me looking like a wet bum."

"My father isn't here, David. I know you think he doesn't like you but—"

"He doesn't," he said, cutting her off, "but that's not the problem. I don't want you to see me looking this way either."

"David, I don't care how you look."

"Thanks, I love you too," David said jokingly.

"You know what I meant, smart ass," she said in that sassy voice he had come to expect. "But if you don't want to come over, you don't have to." She knew that would get him.

"Oh, you won't get rid of me that easily, girlfriend. I called to ask if I could go home and change out of these wet clothes and try this again. This time I'll take a cab."

Toni could sense the truth in his voice. He wasn't avoiding her like she feared. It carried the old teasing tone she had come to anticipate from him. From the beginning, they had established a confrontational, loving relationship. He never treated her like she was a breakable Barbie doll or a sex object. His love for her was genuine, and she saw it written in his eyes when he looked at her. She had always loved that about David. She was a person to him, not just a "great-looking chick," which she'd heard all too often as a weak pick-up-line.

What also got her going was that he always seemed to love to challenge her, both mentally and physically—a battle of wits. Unlike Brenda and Mike, the Toni and David were very opinionated. They would argue with each other over anything and everything. Neither would agree on something if they thought there was a chance the other would. Mike came to ignore both of them when they were together. The love they had for each other was far more evident than the constant bickering between them would infer. David was her dear friend.

"No...no, David, you go home and dry off. How about this? I'll come over and see you later after seeing Brenda. I was planning on stopping by the old apartment after seeing you anyway. Now I'll just do that first. Do you know if she's home?"

"Yes, at least she should be. She's started working nights after you left. She said it was easier than being alone in the apartment at night." David didn't realize the weight of his words until after he said them.

Toni swallowed and took a deep breath. She knew there would be some hell to pay for leaving like she did and for not keeping in touch. *Take your punishment like a man—ah, woman,* she chastened. "Okay, Davey, I know it takes you a long time to dry your wide ass, so I'll swing over to your place after I see Brenda."

"That would be perfect, Toni, if you're sure you're not going to change your mind."

"I admit there are a hundred other people ahead of you I would like to see first, but I'm in a charitable mood."

"Yeah, that's what each of those twenty homeless guys said before leaping to their death out your bedroom window." Despite the chill from being soaking wet, her laughter made him feel better. "I'll make us a quick meal when you get here. Hey, girlfriend, I'm very sorry I screwed up, but I have to see you. It's very important," David pleaded.

"I promise. Look, you're one of the few people I came back

here to see, Davey. Don't worry. I'll be by in a few hours at the most. I haven't eaten since yesterday, and I'm so hungry I could eat a horse—watch it, mister, I wouldn't add anything to that if I were you."

"Who me? Neeeeeveeer.

She shook her head at the smart ass as she listened to him laughing on the phone.

"All right then, beautiful," he said. "I'm counting on you. I know we don't like each other, but we have never lied. I'll be home all day so take your time. But knowing you as I do, there will be a knock on my door just as I step out the shower with my hard brown body all soaking wet with white soap bubbles sliding slowly down my chiseled chest, past my six-pack abs, and down to—"

"Oh, stop it, Peewee Herman."

"No, this time, I'm locking my doors."

Toni laughed at that truism because she had caught him in the shower when she dropped by unannounced on a few occasions.

"Well, I was just trying to see why that body caused my best friend to get ill, Mr. Herman. The truth is you probably waited until I knocked on your door and then got undressed and poured a glass of dish water over your head, hoping—and very foolishly, I might add—that you might get lucky."

It was David's turn to laugh. *Might get lucky, huh? Any man who didn't wonder about being with a woman as striking as Toni,* he thought, *is in line for sainthood.*

They exchanged a few more teasing barbs. Toni said goodbye to David and slowly put the phone down. *See?* she thought. *He still knows how to make you laugh.*

Even after her break up with Mike, she knew there was never any real chance of her relationship with David becoming more than a very dear friendship because she was still deeply in love with Mike, and she knew David loved him, too. But there were times when David was also unattached, she recalled as she sat on the couch, thinking about her friend, when she seriously thought about easing her pain in his muscular arms. They would be dancing together or wrestling and, for a moment, she could see how easily it could happen. Sometimes their lips would come close as they clowned around and, for an instant, their eyes locked, and then they would separate and a there would be a moment of silence. Unlike her, Brenda boasted about the sexual encounters she had with men, David being, in her words, "He's a stallion, girl. The other guys were just horses."

There were times he looked so good, and it wasn't just the tempting seed Brenda planted. Sometimes when he smiled or laughed, his eyes would sparkle with promise, the movement of his body, suggesting he was more than capable. But the thought of what that might do to Brenda, and their friendship, afterward, tabled those urges. Not counting what David might think if pushed into that corner. There were times, however, when she sensed he had the same thoughts. The looks he gave her, for an instant, whispered his thoughts. Then that smile would slowly leak out on his face, and the moment would pass.

But sometimes—when the pain was too much, and you just wanted to feel better—maybe.

There was that one day, she now lovingly recalled as she sat on the couch, listening to the rain falling outside, it was a few weeks after Mike had broken it off, that she was hurting and craved the attention of that handsome man. To put it in plain words, she had an itch down below that even she couldn't scratch—and she tried a few times. Just so happened David had called early that evening.

"Hi, lady, it's me, David."

"Hi, Davey, if you are looking for Brenda she isn't here. She's working a double."

"Yeah, I know. That's why I called. Brenda called me from work. She said you were being a little bitch and needed it bad, very bad and begged me to go over your place and let you have your way with me. Calm down, calm down, don't get your hopes up. I told her, hell no!"

"I'm sorry. Did you say, you think it might snow?"

"Yeah, I did. Being alone with you, the room does get cold enough to snow."

"According to Brenda, the cold is the only thing that can make you get—ah, never mind." *Toni, what is wrong with you? Maybe he didn't get it*, she hoped.

He did, but he thought she was teasing him, as usual.

Change the subject, girl, she said to the growing silence.

"Davey, why don't you come over around six, and I'll make us dinner, and we can chat or watch a movie?" It was difficult, but she hid her excitement from him. "That is, if you're free."

"Yes, I am, but please don't beg, Toni."

"Great, and, like with Brenda told me, I'm sure you will only take up a few minutes of my time."

His answer to that made her laugh and her nose run. She hung up on him.

Getting dressed, she sprayed perfume in a few interesting places in anticipation of his visit. The real reason, hidden in her enthusiasm, was maybe stepping over that line with him without acknowledging that. She changed outfits five times, finally settling on shorts and a tank top, the miniskirts judged to be too obvious. David came over casually dressed in this yellow wife-beater and white running pants. He looked simply *hot*! He was so muscular and toned. But it was his perfect white teeth that sealed-the-deal. *Go figure.* She made up her mind the instant he walked past her into her apartment, and his enticing cologne encircled her head.

She was determined to seduce him, but they had so much fun together that evening that the laughter did for her what she thought the sex might.

After chatting with David, for the first time in a long time, she now felt sexy talking to another man. It felt good teasing him. It was one of the weapons she playfully remembered pulling out whenever he was getting the best of her in an argument. She would stand and profile in front of him as if to say *I have the final word because I'm the woman, and I have all the goodies.* All David could do in rebuttal was to cover his face with his hands, shake his head while peering through his fingers at what he could never have.

Toni felt a familiar warmth that held the promise of renewing savored battles. For the first time since she came back, she now felt at home.

"I love you, David," she now whispered toward the man out there somewhere walking home in the rain. "Stupid!" she shouted in the quiet of the empty house. "I should have picked him up," she acknowledged as she stood up and debated what to do about that. "He could get sick walking in that mess."

Toni thought about riding around looking for David, but she didn't know what phone booth he had called from. She would apologize when she saw him, she reasoned, while grabbing the keys to her father's vehicle from the key rack. She had a lot to apologize for.

Toni opened her umbrella, stepped outside, and ran through the rain to her father's black Ford pick-up truck. "Now to surprise Brenda," she said as she started up the truck.

CHAPTER 29

The Buffers sat quietly on their back porch watching the cold rain fall in twisting torrents. The trees waved as the wind raced between the branches. The suddenly erupting fierceness of the storm had interrupted Mike before he could defend himself. His father's angry response, after Mike had set them down and explained his illness, was very distressing. Even more so was his mother's silence.

The pelting rain beating against the enclosed glass patio was like a teacher scolding one of her students for talking in class. They sat quietly, lest the teacher become even more enraged.

Mike leaned back in the lounge chair. He knew the abrupt fierceness of the storm only offered a short respite until his father resumed his tirade. Big John Buffer always spoke his mind. The right of his opinions mattered little. That small glitch never stopped him from giving his biased viewpoints. The trouble his only child was in gave him more than enough reason to speak.

"This patio enclosure was a wonderful addition to the house," Mike said, breaking the silence. "Even on a gloomy day like this, it's beautiful to be outside."

As his words floated into the air, the heavy silence returned. It was like dropping a yellow rose in an outhouse. No matter the beauty and fragrance of the rose, it had no effect on the pungent bouquet already floating there.

Mike sat up and looked over at his mother. She turned away quickly, lest he see the fear and revulsion in her eyes. She wasn't quick enough. Her reaction sent him a very clear message. His worse fears were manifested in two of the people he needed the most. Mike stared at her familiar profile. He loved the comforting softness of her features. Even when she was upset with him, he always knew she loved him. Now, he felt something that was very unnerving. She had looked at him as if he was a complete stranger.

Just the thought of him having AIDS and sitting in their recliner was causing Thelma Buffer's skin to crawl. They would have to throw it away and get another, she decided, fighting hard to resist the urge to get up and fetch her can of spray disinfectant. Yes, she thought to herself, John will have to put on gloves and throw that chair away. There was no way she would ever sit on it again.

She dearly loved her son, but Thelma Mary Buffer was a creature of habit, driven by her sometime irrational fears. Her sterile home was the direct result of her phobias and not from a strong urge to be neat. Now her only child had just told them that he had that filthy Homo disease, AIDS. Thelma struggled with the urge to turn around and ask her son how he got himself infected. His possibly explicit answer glued her tongue still.

How could this have happened? Big John wondered as he stared out at the rain falling in sheets in his yard. When did his son decide he wanted a hairy, smelly man over a beautiful woman? Big John had seen the girls his son dated. He often envied him and his generation for their life style. That last girl, Toni, that Mike brought over the house was so pretty John was often speechless around her. And the body on that woman, it was all John could do not to stare. Why Thelma even asked him, the last time Mike brought Toni over to the house, how come he was so quiet around her and didn't he like her? Why would Michael give up all that to suck-off some man? Big John struggled to keep from throwing up as he pictured aroused male genitalia in his face.

"They say I could live ten years or more—"

"You call that living?" Big John blurted out. "Son, do you know how sick people with AIDS get?" The lines on his face contorted as he spat out the words.

"Dad, I know, really I do."

"No, you don't, dammit! If you had known, you would have picked another life style, another—oh, hell with it. It's your life, just don't ask me to agree with it 'cause I don't. I think it's sick and wrong," his father screamed.

"Dad, Mom, I'm not here to hurt you or to piss you off. I just wanted to tell you that I'm sick, that's all. Guys, I'm not asking you for anything. It took me a long time to build up the courage to come over and talk to you about this. After I told you in the hospital, you looked so shocked I figured that was enough for one day."

"Honey, don't you know you could be passing those germs to us as we sit here?"

Mike was shocked—one, that his mother spoke up when his dad was arguing. That was rare. And even more so, what she said. He stared at her as her words burned in his chest. He wanted to strike out at her, to say something equally hurtful, but she was still his mother, and he loved and respected her. "Mom," he groaned, trying hard not to sound as disappointed as he felt, "what are you talking about? You can't get AIDS from casual contact."

"You don't know that, Mike, no one does," his father abruptly added. "The government would never tell us all the truth. It could cause a panic."

"Dad, it has nothing to do with the government. There are only two ways most people will ever get infected with HIV or AIDS, and that's either with an infected needle or by sexual contact with someone who is infected. You two are both safe. Don't worry, you're safe. I would never put you at risk for anything."

"That just it, boy," Big John tried to explain to his foolish son, "you believe what you're told. You always were gullible. That's probably why you caught AIDS in the first place."

Mike swallowed hard. He didn't expect them to comfort and hold him, but the depth of their coldness was surprising. He looked into their nervous, frightened eyes and sank even deeper into despair. His father was known for his emotionless dark eyes, so Mike wasn't taken aback so much by their hardness. But it was what he saw in his mother's eyes that caught him off guard. They were always so caring they could warm the coldest heart with their soft blue cast. What he saw looking over at him was horror and panic, plain and simple.

She looked at him as if AIDS was a yellow puss oozing out of his nose and mouth and flying around the room, infecting everything.

He had come over to answer any questions they had so they

could draw closer, but he could sense the void between them growing wider. Mother's fears and Dad's pride had won out. It was the one thing he came to understand that each held more sacred than their only child.

Mike had sinned, Thelma determined. Out of his own mouth came the words of his condemnation. It was just as the preacher had said, "Their words shall betray them." Mike had sinned, and the responsibility for that sin fell upon his own shoulders. What he had done, her Bible told her, was an abomination to God.

Thelma battled with her fear on one side and the love she had for her son on the other. He had always been somewhat distant and hid his real feelings in the constant need to make her and others laugh. They had never been very emotional because John thought it would make a sissy out of him. My God, she nervously realized, John would surely blame all this on the few times she had cuddled him as a child.

He did. All kinds of kinky mental pictures tortured Big John as he wondered what had seduced his son to probe into the sick world of the fags. *Probe, that's funny*, he thought. *My son is dying because someone probed someone's butt.* Big John could feel his blood pressure rising again. He wanted to hit something.

He was very sad for his son but was unable to find the words to tell him. These were words that he spoke before but had long ago forgotten them from lack of use. Words that would have explained, far better than he had today, that he understood the fear and sadness his son was enduring. Simple words of comfort and strength that would have given his son the courage to fight this until his last painful breath. Caring words that would have sent Mike rushing into his arms, repenting of the deed that had gotten him infected. Sincere, sensitive words that could have saved his soul before it was too late. Big John searched his memory for those basic terms but failed. They were there, he was sure of it, but he couldn't find them. He could sense them floating just beyond his imagination.

No matter how desperately he wanted to help his son, he couldn't reach through the mind-fog and find them. Tears swelled up in his eyes as he gave up and watched the trees dancing in the gusting wind.

"I've got to be going," Mike finally said. He stood and, when they didn't respond, sighed, and walked into the house. He turned around to say the usual goodbyes, but the room was empty. Usually, he had to fight his way out his parent's home. His dad would berate him for not coming by more often to see his mother, and she would smile and say the he had his own life to live, but he could stay longer when he did visit.

Today, they sat like statues in their seats, ignoring him as he walked into the house.

Mike knew the consequences of walking back out onto the patio and forcing the issue. It was a very thin line of control that held back the hurt and risked the shouting match that would follow. Their insensitivity could crush him at a time when he really needed their support. But he couldn't just walk away. He decided to force the issue, he had to know.

"Look, guys, I know I've hurt you by telling you this," he said, walking back out into the light of the patio. "That wasn't why I came over. I just thought—"

Thelma and John didn't acknowledge him. They sat on the glider, looking forward and slowly rocking back and forth. He knew his mother was afraid to reach out, but he couldn't understand why his father was ignoring him. Their silence gave him license to either leave or continue. Mike found it difficult to keep his emotions in check. Struggling, he tried again. "I'll be okay. David will help me whenever he can, and—"

The sudden movement of his father and the expression on his face when he jumped up from the glider caused Mike to stumble backward.

"Was it that black bastard that gave you *AIDS*?" Big John screamed at the top of his lungs. The powerful man had his hands in a fist when he approached Mike. "Tell me the truth, damn you. I knew no good would come of you and that, that—"

"Hey! Wait just a minute. What are you talking about?" Mike shouted back at his irate father. For the first time it dawned on him that his father thought he was gay, and what was even more startling, he thought David and he were lovers.

"You know exactly what I mean," John yelled at his son. "What in the hell did you think was going to happen when you broke God's law?"

"What damn law are you talking about? I haven't broken any laws. Your prejudice has blinded you to what I'm trying to tell you. Open your eyes, Dad, I'm dying," Mike said, the last word barely audible.

They stood inches apart, eyes searching the other for some understanding of their point of view.

Thelma watched their confrontation as if waiting for Mike to suddenly see the light of the truth and acknowledge his transgressions. "Honey, we love you," they both heard her softly say. "We believe AIDS is God's curse for breaking his law. You may disagree with that, but that's how we feel. Man was created to be with a woman, not a man. God made Adam and Eve, not Adam and Steve."

"Mom," Mike pleaded after hearing her overused axiom. "Please."

Big John swallowed hard. He shook his head as a troubling thought tormented him. The fruit of his loom was a fruit.

It disturbed Mike to see the misery in his father's face, to watch his body slump as the anger poured out of him like a punctured balloon. When he lowered his head, Mike's arms moved out to hold him, to comfort him, to say to him that it was all right, and he understood.

"No, Mike!" his mother shouted with an obvious air of concern in her voice.

Confused, Mike looked down at her seated on the porch swing. She had her hand extended out to him in an obvious attempt to stop him from moving any closer to her husband. The reasons were clear. He had seen her in the throes of fear before. Her phobias were many. He'd watched her scrub the floors, over and over, in an attempt to kill bacteria she was convinced was growing there, and had seen her battle with germs—both real and imagined—until everything in their home was operating-room clean. Mike had seen her terrified before, but nothing like what he saw at that moment.

"Don't, don't touch him."

Mike looked from his frightened mother to the man who had raised him and taught him how to play baseball, how to fish and hunt. In those eyes he found no compromise. He could barely hear his father calling out his name above the pounding of his heart and feet as he ran up the stairs and out the front door.

He would have turned around and rushed back into his father's compassionate arms had Big John called out his name strong and forcefully. It was the weak, vacillating tone of it that convinced Mike that his father wasn't calling him back, but saying in effect, please forgive us for abandoning you.

The drive home through Oakland, the educational and arts section of Pittsburgh, was always an enjoyable diversion for Mike. The exhibition of available young college women never failed to tickle the imagination of all guys riding or driving through that interesting part of town. Today, the same entertainment never caught his attention. He didn't notice anyone as he drove down Fifth Avenue.

Mike sighed, as the pit he had fallen in grew deeper. He had hoped his parents would be able to deal with the dilemma he had gotten himself into and offer some love and support. Who was he fooling? he realized, as someone blasted their horn at the green light he was stopped and staring at. His parents would never understand. But to accuse David of giving him AIDS...well, that surprised the hell out of him.

Mike drove home, replaying his parents' reaction to his illness, over and over in his mind. He wasn't completely shocked by their response, or lack of one. He knew their weaknesses. It was the death of the optimism, planted by a well-meaning friend, that silenced him.

Mike parked beside the car of the lovely brunette in the apartment next door to his. He thought for a minute...yes, Gloria was her name.

As he was about to put his key in the front lock of the building, the door burst open, almost hitting him in the face.

"Oops, sorry," the brunette said.

She spoke in an overtly feminine tone that usually caused most men to lie and say something like this to pretty women, "That's okay, no problem. It's only a broken nose," or "I have another eye, don't worry."

Mike just nodded and walked past her.

His reactions caught the brunette a little off guard. At first, it was his silly grin, whenever they happened to bump into each other like down in the laundry room, that used to annoy her. He was a very nice-looking guy, and she would have welcomed him asking her out, but he didn't seem mature enough to see that. Instead, he just gawked at her when he thought she wasn't looking, like some virginal teenager.

She recalled once catching him sneaking looks down at her as she was sun bathing on the grass below their balconies. Fed up with his peeping, she decided to try provoking him to talk. Armed in her skimpiest bikini, she spread out her blanket on the grass and awaited his inspection. There was so much of her showing she felt embarrassed lying out in the sun, but it worked. Every time she turned around she caught him ducking down on his balcony. For the two hours she was tanning, she figured, he never left the balcony. It had worked. For the next week, he was inflicted with diarrhea of the mouth and never missed a chance to talk to her. So when he walked past her without speaking, his sullen, quiet manner intrigued her enough to stop in the opened doorway and watch him walk up the steps to his adjoining apartment.

In another of fate's games, like the important phone call you made and hung up one ring before the more-than-willing person on the other end raced to pick it up. It didn't matter how many times you let it ring. It was one ring too few. Or resisting the urge to turn around one more time to see if that person you were making eye contact with in passing also turned around to look at you. They did, but you never saw them because you gave up one look too early and refused to embarrass yourself further by looking again. How many times in one's short lifetime did we come up one yard short of our goal? We would never know if the one more ring, waiting one more minute before leaving, giving that untrustworthy person one more chance, or sending that often-rejected manuscript to one more publisher, would be the event that changed our lives forever. Fate laughed at Mike, as the brunette stood at the bottom of the steps, waiting for him to turn around and notice her so he could ask her something…trivial.

She was in the mood to forget his clumsy attempts at getting to know her and was willing to give him another chance, but fate had other plans. The brunette would never know how close she possibly came to getting infected with the AIDS virus. The confused and hurt man, slowly walking up the steps, was in a certain mood of his own. At that moment, he wouldn't have hesitated to ease his pain, loneliness, and frustrations in her soft tanned arms. Only afterward, would he feel even lower when the realization hit that he'd probably condemned that innocent woman to death. Fate saved her and blinded him in one shot.

Later, he would remember what she wore and how good she looked. For now, he just walked up the steps and into his apartment.

CHAPTER 30

Brenda placed the chipped ham sandwich on the counter and hunted for the pickle jar with the last two sliced pickles in it.

"I hope I didn't eat them," she mumbled anxiously, doubting her memory.

The pangs of hunger that tore her away from her favorite soap opera demanded pickles on that sandwich. The doorbell ringing almost halted the search. The pickles were found behind an old bag of hot dog buns in the nick of time. She placed the jar on the counter, closed the refrigerator, and reluctantly headed for the door. She was wearing a pair of old yellow sweat pants, cut off at the knees, and a loose white T-shirt, but that would have to do, she decided as she walked to the door. Whoever it was would have to deal with it because she had just worked a double shift and wasn't ready for company yet. *This will be quick*, she promised the growl she heard from her stomach.

Brenda stopped at the door and hesitated for a moment, hoping it wasn't that pest next door. With her luck, lately, it was probably Mister Wonderful who finally located her and was waiting on the other side of her door, with wine and roses, to whisk her off to some hot, sunny beach. But he wouldn't today, not in this outfit. Well, maybe he would since she was bra-less. She chuckled to herself. When she opened the door, she lost her chuckle.

"Hi, Brenda."

"Toni!" Brenda screamed, totally surprised by the grinning person interrupting her meal.

Brenda started crying and jumping up and down like she was trying to stomp on some yucky bugs. She reached out and hugged Toni before either could say another word. Toni squeezed her tight. The jubilance she saw in her best friend's eyes was the most comforting thing she had experienced in months. Brenda began to sense that when she started to pull away and felt Toni's arms holding her tight. She rubbed her friend's back and leaned her head on her shoulder. If she needed to be hugged longer, Brenda decided, no problem.

"Brenda," Toni finally said, as she held her at arms' length, "it's so good to see you again, girl."

"What—why—never mind, just come in," Brenda said while wiping the moisture from her eyes. "I can't believe it's you. What, you can't call me and tell me you're back in town?"

"It was a spur of the moment thing, my coming back here," Toni said as they walked over and sat down on the couch. Toni kicked her shoes off, as she always did. "Brenda, I came back to see you, David, and my dad."

Brenda looked cautiously at her friend. There was another name she had failed to mention. Toni's sudden need to depart had taken Brenda by surprise because Toni never ran away, never. She was the fighter of the two, the one who stood her ground and took on all comers. Now she had returned. Why? Was it to reconcile with Mike? No, Brenda didn't think that was Toni's purpose.

It only took Brenda a moment to notice that Toni had lost a lot of weight in her face. She had always had that healthy look, the slightly plump cheeks that some people thought were a sign of good health. The cheeks of the girl who sat next to Brenda on the couch were thin and taunt. She had that starving-model appearance.

It was at that moment Brenda knew in her heart that her friend had come back to die. She heard no voices speaking serenely into her mind. No trumpets or horns sounded. She just received a clear understanding of what was happening to her friend. Brenda smiled affectionately at Toni while, at the same time, struggling to keep the grief, that was ripping her apart inside, off her face.

☙❧

David finally arrived home, peeled off his wet clothes, and tossed them in a heap on his bedroom floor. Pulling out some clean underwear, he placed them on the bed and then walked into the bathroom and turned on the water to the shower. *The hot shower will feel good*, he convinced himself, still feeling the chills from the cold rain. He would have to hurry because Toni was always early, and he wanted to cook dinner for them like he used to do before she ran away. Had she changed much in the time she was gone? he wondered, stepping into the hot spray.

They would have the evening to themselves because Mike was feeling better the last couple of days and wanted to spend some time with his parents. Finally, after much debate, he agreed to talk to his parents about his illness. David had battled with Mike for days to do it, even threatening to talk to them himself if he didn't. They had a right, he continued to scold him, to know their only child was dying. He was relieved when he arrived home and saw that Mike's car was gone. "It's about time he took my advice. He'll thank me later," David muttered as the hot water ran down his face.

ℰↄℰↄ

Mike stood looking out his patio door window. Usually, he would be sitting out there with his feet up on the railing watching the usual weekend volleyball games in the court below, but an earlier rain storm had changed that. It had finally stopped, and, after waking up from taking a nap and looking outside again, one would never know it had rained cats-and-dogs. The monsoon had abated, and the sun had reappeared with a vengeance. It was much hotter now than it had been all week. Other than a few small puddles in the parking lot, there was little evidence it had rained hard a few hours ago.

People had come out on the tennis and volleyball courts, doing their imitation of the pros, performing like the weekend warriors they were. Only the fear he might infect someone had caused him to refrain from joining in the pick-up games.

This wasn't working, he decided when he started feeling sorry for himself. He had hoped to get some enjoyment from watching his neighbors play when he realized how beautiful a day it had become, but he didn't. The only feeling he felt was pity because he would never again be healthy enough to compete with the sweating bodies below. He was dying. How long he would live, no one could tell him.

Through the darkness that was his future, he could still see the love he had for Toni. The time he spent getting to knowing her, he decided, was still worth the loss of that future as he leaned back and reflected on his life.

ຄ∕ໆຄ∕ໆ

Brenda tried not to ask, but the many tears she shed over this woman demanded she try. But Toni beat her to the punch.

"I'm sorry, Bren, for not calling, I really am. But I was so depressed I couldn't handle hearing my best friend's voice."

"I cried a lot, Toni, and cursed you a lot."

"That's okay," Toni said to the woman sitting beside her. "I deserved all of that. Am I forgiven?"

"Hell, no! It will take a lot of baking my favorite cookies to get back in favor with me."

"Done," Toni said and rubbed her knee.

"Toni, have you seen Mike yet?" Brenda reluctantly asked after Toni spent time expounding on the reasons why she finally decided to return and face her problems.

"No, and I don't want to see that bastard," she said emphatically.

A surprised Brenda watched the ire rise up in Toni as her face became flushed. Brenda hesitated to answer her friend.

"I'm sorry, honey," Toni said when she saw Brenda's reaction and put her hand on Brenda's knee. "I don't hate him anymore, really. I just don't want to see him," she lied. Toni searched the caring face of her friend for the strength to tell her. "Bren, I'm one of the unlucky ones."

Brenda tried to figure out just what she meant by unlucky. "What are you talking about, Toni?"

"The HIV virus that I was infected with has kicked opened the door. I now have AIDS, Brenda. I'm going to die."

Brenda fell back against the couch and raised her hand over her mouth. She uttered something under her breath that made Toni uneasy. *Please be all right with this*, Toni prayed. Her Florida experience had taught her that everyone took the shocking announcement that someone they knew or loved had AIDS differently, very differently.

Toni fought her sinking emotions, tried to act strong, and didn't want to cry again, but the way her bad news hit Brenda was distressing. She had hoped Brenda would reach out for her when she heard the horrible news. Brenda only sat there with her hand over her mouth.

"Honey, are you sure, do you really have AIDS?" Brenda asked, ignoring what she now knew to be the truth.

"Yes," Toni said after swallowing her tears. "I've had numerous tests in the last few months, and every time it has come back positive." Her head dropped when she said positive, and one stubborn tear ran down her face. Brenda moved over and pulled her dearest friend in the world close to her. They both cried.

Brenda sobbed as she thought how little time that they had remaining to be together, and all the time that they had already squandered. It had taken her weeks to forgive herself for not flying away with Toni as she had implored her over and over, as they drove to the airport, to please come to Florida with her. Brenda, on the other hand, had pleaded with Toni to stay and work it out with Mike. They argued the merits of each other's view-points all the way to the airport without gaining or giving any ground. As Brenda watched Toni's plane fly overhead, she knew she had made a mistake. What she should have done had nothing to do with who was right or wrong, but because Toni needed her. The right thing to do was to go along with her, wherever she was going.

The constant nightmares, depicting Toni suffering horribly and dying all alone in a ditch somewhere, tormented Brenda so much she considered quitting her job and trying to find her. Only David's loud tirade prevented her from leaving. He argued that they had to give her time to sort things out, or she might run away from them forever. As she held her friend in her arms, Brenda knew he had been right.

Toni wept because the word AIDS didn't stop her best friend from touching her. It was only the second time in months that another human being, with full knowledge of her condition, had tried to physically comfort her.

Oh, how she missed this, Toni thought, as Brenda rubbed her shoulders.

"Baby," Brenda said between sobs, "I'm so sorry. I should have never let you leave alone. You needed me, and I wasn't there for you. Please forgive me." She started weeping again.

This time Toni reached out for her. "Don't, Brenda. I really didn't want you to come. I was too ashamed." She put Brenda's head in her lap and gently pulled her hair back from her face.

They were healing. Toni had finally written to her during the holidays but never gave her a phone number to call or a return address. She apologized for that in the letter, claiming Brenda would have either tried talking her into coming home or have come and got her.

Brenda relaxed as Toni's soft hands rubbed against her face and hair. She couldn't help feeling sad for her. She remembered the painful, empty feeling that lasted for months after Toni ran off to Florida and the blame she leveled on Mike for causing her to leave.

Their dreams of opening their own local booking agency also fell by the wayside. The irony was that, without kissing up to anyone, they had finally established themselves with some of the better local bands. Using her father's old ties with agents, they were finally able to get in with some of the bigger touring acts. When Toni left, she took her father's influence with her. Brenda knew the bands and understood the music. Toni had learned the inner working of the business from her dad and had planned out a workable scheme to make money promoting these acts in the local, smaller markets in the greater Pittsburgh area.

Brenda sat up and managed a half smile. Toni bit her bottom lip as she welcomed the show of warmth from her friend.

"I wasn't trying to hurt you, Toni, by talking about—"

"Don't worry about that, Brenda. There isn't be anything you can ask me that I haven't spent nights awake wondering about. I've rehashed every mistake that I've made in my life."

"That shouldn't have taken long, Miss Perfect."

"Miss Perfect's don't have unprotected sex and catch a deadly STD."

"What—"

"You go on and say whatever is on your mind, Bren. If I can't talk to you, I'm in real trouble."

"Thank you for saying that," Brenda said as she placed her hand on Toni's arm. She looked into the troubled eyes of the disheveled, but still lovely, woman. "Toni, there's nothing that can come between us. I know you were running away from Mike, but it felt like you were leaving me. I was really upset with you for a long while. I thought you didn't love me anymore." Her puffy eyes started to fill up again. "But David, he helped me to see how wrong I was. Your coming back proves it. I just wanted you to know I would have been there for you, even if it meant I would catch AIDS." She looked at Toni and saw something in the softness of those eyes that she recognized. "That's another reason why you left, isn't it?"

The silence in the room answered her in a way that Toni, in the anguish she felt for hurting this kind spirit, never could have.

CHAPTER 31

The shower was partially successful. The chill from the cold rain was gone, but, for some reason, David still felt cold. He knew why. He wasn't completely convinced he was doing the right thing by telling Toni the truth about Mike. Instinctively, he looked over at the book lying on his dresser. Her diary's pages could have presented him an in-depth look at the life of Toni DiNardo. There were days when it could have offered him a valuable picture of his missing friend at a time when he couldn't make mental contact with her memory. There, in the loose pages of her writings, was a running biography of the woman that he had come to love very deeply. In her absence, he overcame the voices that tried to seduce him into violating her trust and reading the pages of her private book. They argued, *There might be something in it that would better explain her sudden decision to run away and where she might be hiding. She might be in danger or very ill and unable to let anyone know.*

David rubbed the soft towel through his hair again as he remembered how tough it had been to respect her privacy. They were all worried about her. For weeks, they called each other almost daily, in hopes one of them had received a phone call or letter from their wayward traveler. Brenda did inform him that Toni's father said he had placed enough money in her private account for her to live wherever she desired.

Two days after Christmas, Brenda did receive a letter from Toni, she revealed to David, and in it, she stated she was fine and had no intentions of returning home any time soon. *But she's home now*, he thought, smiling and rubbing the towel behind his back and down his legs. He threw his towel across his bed, sat down, and slipped on a pair of undershorts. There was no way he going to let her run away again, he swore.

cɔeɔ

Toni pulled up into David's driveway. He had purchased this house just after she got back together again with Mike. It was a very nice place, she recalled, and he had maintained it well. Together, they all spent time helping him paint, and Brenda with furnishing the game room downstairs. This was her seventh time here, the last three alone. The house was average size but with plenty of room for one or two people to live comfortably. It sat on a beautifully manicured lawn with small trees lining the property. There was a very large private deck in the back that they used for cookouts with the four of them. She smiled at that fun memory.

Toni was surprised by the strong feelings of excitement that tickled her stomach as she parked. "This is only David," she whispered, trying to downplay her surging exhilaration, "not some movie star."

Her heart wasn't convinced either as it pounded in her chest. She put her hand to her breast and took a deep breath. Turning off her car, she sat there for a minute, looking at her reflection in the mirror. A quick hand through her hair, a shaking of her head, and she was ready.

But just as she was about to step out of the car, her joy was stolen by the sudden notion that Mike might also be in there. No, she thought, David wouldn't be mean enough to pull something like that on her. He must know that would cause her to leave. Toni looked at David's house as if there might be a clue Mike was in there. Her car was the only one there, she realized as she looked around, and David's house only had a one car garage. But the picture of Mike waiting for her behind the front door shook what little confidence that she tried to muster. Did he even know she was back? she wondered.

Toni stared at David's door. Only her longing to see the brown man again prevented her from backing out of his driveway and leaving. *Leave and call him from home,* her fears told her, *and ask him to come over. Then there wouldn't be a risk of seeing Mike. David wouldn't mind, he had started out to do so earlier.* She thought about it for only a moment before dismissing it as foolishness.

Toni took one last look in her visor mirror. She shook her

head, unimpressed with the reflection, climbed out of her car, and walked up to David's door. Suddenly, wearing jeans and an old favorite T-shirt, she seemed underdressed for the occasion. A part of her wanted to dazzle the man on the other side of that door in something short and eye catching. *It's David*, she said to her apprehension. He would be glad to see her wearing nothing. *Well,* she snickered at her slip of the tongue, *that's true, but not quite what I meant.* She shook her head as she walked up to his door. A deep breath was the only pause before she rang his doorbell.

David heard the car pull up into his driveway but remained in his chair, watching TV, as if he didn't know who the driver was. His mouth was so dry he swallowed twice. Each time he had walked past the hallway mirror, he had stopped to check his appearance. The sixth time, he gave up. This was as good as it got, he decided somewhat disappointedly. His hair was a little longer than he liked, but he hadn't expected to be having dinner with a beautiful woman this evening. Well, not with *this* beautiful woman. His beautiful woman was working tonight.

Nervousness had prompted him to drown himself in cologne. It hung over him like a blanket. He had spun around like a top, trying desperately to calm its effect. Finally, he changed his clothes and put on jeans and another shirt. *Oh, well*, he decided, giving in to the stubborn, strong scent of cologne and hoping she didn't gag.

Rrring, rrring.

The walk to the door was accomplished without breathing. Only when he grabbed the doorknob did he finally relax and take a breath before opening the door. He had created a vision of her, closed his eyes, and prayed that the real thing was on the other side.

"Toni," the smiling man shouted as the door swung open.

"Hi, David," the door ringer coyly answered.

He reached out, pulled her into his arms, and hugged her tight. He was so happy to see her, he forgot all about proper etiquette and amenities as he lifted her completely off her feet. Every hug or kiss they had shared over the years was always given with the proper distance and without any sign of intimacy. After all, they were the best of friends and respected the tradition—but not tonight. David held her in his arms and caressed her as if he was her lover.

Toni wrapped her arms around the large man's neck and squeezed him as hard as she could. Her grip had little effect on the powerfully built male, but she wasn't doing it for effect. She wanted him to know just how she felt about him, and that message was received.

Hugging her, for David, was even more exciting than he remembered. How many times in the past had he opened his door and welcomed her into his home? He even recalled a couple of times when he opened that door, saw her, and then playfully slammed it in her face. Not this time. There was little inclination to tease now. The joy of seeing the black-haired beauty was overwhelming.

Toni felt a little strange as David held her. It was a warm and safe feeling, but it wasn't without guilt. That was puzzling to her as she relaxed her grip on him and waited for him to do the same. She didn't owe anyone anything, she thought, as the feeling took root in her mind. She was free to love David or anyone else with the time she had left. Yet a cold chill ran down her spine, threatening to erase the warmth and comfort she found in his arms. The memory of the growing virus that was working hard to evict her soul from her body brought her back to reality.

"Toni, it so good to see you again," David said. letting go and holding her at arms' reach. Ecstatic, he kissed her on the forehead. "Welcome home, girlfriend."

"Thank you, Davey," Toni replied, looking sheepishly up at him. "It's good to be home. I missed you guys so much."

"Come sit down and tell me about the last year," David asked as he closed his front door. "I must say Florida agrees with you because you look great, girlfriend."

"No, I don't. I've lost too much weight. But it's nice to hear you lie." It *was* nice to hear him say that, she thought. "That's why I'm here, big guy," she whispered under her breath as she walked past him. "You always could make me feel better."

When he sat down beside her, the shades were thrown open as he looked closely at her for the first time. David kept the grin on his face, but his eyes carried none of the sparkle they had when he first opened the door. He was seeing her as she was. Her bold blue eyes were as blue as ever, but lacked the fire they were known for. Her cheeks were a little pale and sunken, but the joy of seeing him had disguised their true color with a blush. It wasn't enough, however, to hide the truth. David could see that the strong, healthy glow of the woman he knew, the old Toni, was missing.

But she was here now, he rejoiced, and that was all that mattered, not how good she looked.

He didn't have a chance to say goodbye to her when she ran away. Fate had given him another chance to at least say hello. "That's not a lie, lady, you do look good. Now tell me, what in the world have you been up to while you've been away. I read somewhere that a dozen guys jumped off a cliff and committed suicide today somewhere in Florida, was that because you left?"

"Yeah," she answered, laughing at him, "but, unfortunately, it was at least two dozen."

She told him everything. She talked as he sat there engulfed in the woman telling the story. He could tell the spirit was back in her voice. Toni continued talking as he stood up, took her hand, and led her into the kitchen to prepare dinner.

David stole glances at Toni, as she laughed about someone, while he cut up some additional veggies for their salad. It had something to do with a wonderful old man in a baseball cap.

She was dressed in that crazy T-shirt he always teased her about and jeans. Her hair was styled and a little longer than he remembered, but it looked good on her. David never shared this thought with Mike, but he had never seen his best friend's lady in any jeans that didn't fit as if they were tailor-made for her—until now. They seemed a size too big in places, not the form-fitting painted-on look he was used to from her—heck, Brenda and Trisha too, for that matter. But Toni was still a remarkably good-looking woman.

Words flowed out her mouth between bites of salad and steak. Toni struggled to explain her feelings clearly when she looked into the caring eyes of a man she now realized she had desperately missed. He was so handsome, she thought while watching him eat, and he still thought the world of her. She could tell. She wanted nothing more than to jump into his arms and tell him how horrible it was to be away from him. "I was so angry when I left, Davey."

"I can only imagine."

"It took months before I could get out of the depression I was in, months. Then I met Carl. It's not what you think so quit making that face."

"What face? I was just thinking that, with your looks, girl, there will always be a Carl somewhere."

"Yeah, yeah, anyway, like I was telling you, old Carl gave me a job selling his beach chairs. Well, renting them actually. Sitting and talking with him eventually helped me see I needed to be here near the people I love."

"You won't get any flak from me over that. I agree. Are you finished eating?"

"Yeah, I think so. The steak was delicious, as usual, Davey."

"Thank you. Let's fill up our wine glasses and go sit on the couch."

"What about this mess?"

"I'll clean it up later, don't worry."

Toni smiled and followed him into the living room. Sitting there, fighting through the pain that always flared up in her chest at the thought of the curse that had gripped her future, she finally revealed her bad news...

"Don't worry, Davey," she tried explaining when he just stared at her. "It can't be transferred except through trading of body fluids such as sharing needles or sex." There was a long pause as they looked for something in each other's eyes. Toni read his as fear. "I would never do anything to put you at risk," she said, breaking the silence and answering the nervous gaze she thought she saw there.

Her words didn't have any effect on him, but the defeated expression on her face shook him to his soul. If death planted its seed in a human saddled with AIDS, David thought he saw it. He reached out to her and kissed her cheek, running his hand softly through her hair. He felt the warmth of her skin as they touched. He mistook the heat of the fever that was growing in her as natural warmth.

David leaned back and looked her in the eyes for a moment before speaking. "Toni, you're so beautiful. Put me at risk, please. I don't have any needles, so let's try…what was that other way you mentioned?"

Toni just smiled and shook her head at his silly attempt at humor.

"Seriously, Toni," he said, straight-faced, "I don't care about the risks. I've done a lot of reading on the subject and understand the dangers involved, but I don't care. I'm not going to love you less or limit my closeness to you, if that's what you're thinking. I'm your friend for the long haul, for richer or poorer, in sickness and in health. That's what I would have told you before you ran away. I'll love you in this life and the next."

The lady looked at him as only she could. The message was clear. She then did something completely out of character. She climbed up, sat across his lap, then placed her head on his shoulder.

A surprised David let her. Like holding a child, he wrapped her in his arms and held her. He could only imagine how alone she must have felt in Florida with no one to satisfy her need to be held. He slowly rocked her in his arms, and his heart broke for her when she gently started sobbing.

"It will be okay, Toni. We'll make the best of all the days we have."

She just shook her head and patted him on his chest. "The days we have." Those loving words warmed her as if they were sitting in front of a roaring fireplace. In the quiet of his home, they cemented their love for each other. Without saying a word, it was understood that it was an "unbroken blue light."

She was a little embarrassed by her sudden need to be held like a little girl, but it was her David holding her, and she knew he would understand. Doing that may have put their friendship to the test, but she was proud he read that and allowed her that privilege. A contrite young woman finally broke their embrace, kissed him on the cheek, stood up, and walked down the hall to his bathroom.

David felt so sorry for the pain and loneliness she must have endured. To be so young and beautiful with a death sentence hanging over her head, must be debilitating. If holding her helped her feel better, his arms were hers, he decided in her absence.

Toni checked her makeup. Her eyes were red, but, thankfully, her mascara didn't run. She ran her fingers through her hair, added a little lip gloss, dabbed her eyes, and sprayed a little perfume in the air.

"Thank you, David," she said when she walked back into the room and sat down beside him. She put her hand on his knee and squeezed. "I just needed to be held, I guess."

"Any time you want, girlfriend."

Toni smiled, and again she leaned over and kissed his cheek. She then stood up and picked up her purse. "Thank you for a wonderful evening."

"Wait, Toni, there is something I wanted to tell you."

She nodded and sat back down.

David took a deep breath and looked away. Her bright eyes erupting feelings of guilt. There would never be a good time to say what he had to say. He wondered if she could read the consternation he was feeling at having to bring Mike's name into the conversation. "Toni," he said, grabbing her hand and holding it in his.

She looked trustingly into his eyes. That made what he was going to do even harder.

"Toni, you know Mike also has AIDS."

The strong emotional reaction he expected never materialized. The woman who had raced off into the unknown to get away from that name just looked at David and sighed. "I know. Look, I feel sorry for him, David. I feel sorry for everyone who's afflicted with this damnable disease."

"Do you still blame him?" David asked.

"I would be lying if I said no. But maybe he didn't know what he had when we were together. The counselors at the AIDS Center explained that the majority of people with HIV and sometimes AIDS don't know they have it until tested. They pass it on totally unaware that they are murdering their lovers. Upset with him, yes. I still haven't let that go completely. Blame him anymore?" Toni thought for a moment. "Yes. But not with the anger I had then. Don't get any ideas, Davey. I don't want to see him again. As often as we were intimate, the odds are he was still the person who probably infected me HIV and ruined my life."

"But if he didn't know, then it couldn't have been intentional."

The silence that walked into the room surprised both of them, but they were powerless to break its hold. Toni interpreted the silence as David, believing Mike to be innocent of the crime of infecting her, took his side. And as much as she loved David, she felt a little betrayed about that. Her response? Toni stood and walked toward the door. Only after taking a few steps did she realize the foolishness of her reactions.

"Wait, Toni, please don't leave," David said, his voice subdued. "I want to show you something first."

Toni turned around and looked at him. When she did, he opened the door on the end table beside him. Reaching in, he pulled out a letter. It unnerved her when he stared at it as if it was mystical—that, if handled incorrectly, it could explode. David never took his eyes off the letter as he almost reverently placed it down on the coffee table.

Their eyes met again. Each had questions that tied in with the letter on the table. Neither said anything.

For some reason, Toni didn't want to see what was written in the letter. She looked at it for a long moment and slowly back at David, searching for signs of hope and assurance on his face that it wasn't anything painful or hurtful. He had a solemn look that added to her trepidation.

"I took this from Mike," he finally said. "It's addressed to you, Toni."

"David, please, just give up. Don't ruin this lovely evening. I don't want to talk about him or read some letter of apology or something, 'cause—"

"Read it. Please, Toni, for me."

Now she was getting upset. She looked at those brown eyes, pleading for her to trust them. There was nothing but love written on his face, and only her love for the man on the couch kept her from turning and walking out the door. She was getting angry with him, but she didn't know why.

She fought the negative attitude that threatened to mar their reunion and looked down at the letter as if it was a slimy snake coiled to strike.

David was unprepared for her negative reaction. "Toni, it's from the local blood bank. Remember when you and Mike went down to donate together? You remember, don't you?"

The look on her face said otherwise.

David tried again. "It was right after the two of you became a couple. You were in charge of your company's blood drive. Well, a couple of months later, I think he said, this letter arrived for you at your house special delivery. Mike thought he was doing you a favor when he signed for it. When he saw it was marked personal from the blood bank, he became so concerned he opened and read your letter."

Toni swallowed as the dryness in her mouth became annoying. She wanted to ask David why he was leading her into this pit of ugly memories.

"Toni," David said, pausing to take a deep breath before pointing at the letter, "it proves Mike didn't give you HIV."

Her eyes flared wide open, and she looked at him as if he had murdered her future. If she could have, she would have run out the door and slammed it behind her, but her legs felt too heavy to move. *Can you do that to the man who has so tenderly held you moments before,* her guilt whispered. She desperately wanted to turn and leave, but his words—his words were like a magnet that summoned her closer and closer. What could there possibly be in that letter that could—*No, no, there's no way,* she thought. She didn't move.

"Read it!" David said, a little louder than he meant.

Toni obeyed like a robot. She walked over, picked up the letter, and—

❧❧❧

Concentrating on driving proved very difficult with her mind fast-forwarding from the day she exploded in Mike's face up till the present.

"Move, stupid!" Toni shouted from her car at a slow-moving driver impeding her way.

Her mind a kaleidoscope of emotions and troubled thoughts, she was working on her sixth apology when she ran a red light at Fifth and Shady Avenues.

Screech! Toni swerved left, barely missing the sliding yellow taxi braking to avoid hitting her broadside. She never slowed as she drove around the cab and raced down Fifth Avenue. Her heart beat in her chest like a bass drum as she realized how close she came to being slammed into by the taxi. Looking back at the crowed intersection in her mirror, she envisioned the scene of her accident—her car wrecked and flipped over, smoking, on its side. She slowed down.

Did he really toss away his life for me like David said? she wondered. The respite from her demolition-derby race up Fifth Avenue gave her time to reflect on what David had revealed. Had Mike really known about her being infected with HIV, and if he did, why did he keep it from her? They had made love many times since he would have read that letter, and he never acted like she was ill. David's explanation was too farfetched, Toni determined. No one would purposely catch AIDS, no one. Could she do that for him or anyone? she questioned. The answer she whispered was, "No."

Mike's car was parked in front of his apartment building when she pulled up. *It's a good omen*, she thought. Toni was out of her car and running toward the apartment as soon as she parked. She put her key in his building door and let herself in. While running up the steps to his apartment, she never thought about the many times she had planned to take his keys off her key chain and throw them away. That oversight permitted her to enter the building unhindered.

Toni stopped at Mike's apartment door and gathered herself. On the trip over, she tried but hadn't found the right words to tell him how badly she felt about, about—

That was as far as she got because each time the hurt would swell up and choke off her words. Toni put her key in, took a deep breath, turned the doorknob, and walked into Mike's apartment.

"Mike!"

CHAPTER 32

Mike was sitting outside on the grass, bathed in the hot afternoon sun's warmth. The morning's heavy rain was now an ugly memory. The grassy scent blew over him, and he listened to the trees around him, bursting with new leaves, rustling softly overhead in the breeze. It was an idyllic, serene picture that he savored. He closed his eyes. He had always enjoyed the simple pleasure of sitting in the sunlight. While his friends were concerned with rubbing tanning oil on their skin, he sat beside them, letting his imagination take him on trips into the vast blackness of space. With his eyes closed, he traveled at the speed of thought on mystical journeys around the universe, visiting wild and dangerous planets with even weirder inhabitants.

Today, he was enjoying a voyage to the very edge of our Milky Way Galaxy. Heaven, it was rumored, was a billion light-years beyond that point. *I'm Mike Buffer*, he thought, *captain of the* Star Ship Toni—*ah,* Tomahawk *as it sets sail for the stars.*

A duet from two songbirds chirping in a tree nearby failed to seduce him into opening his eyes. It did, however, stop the take-off of the star ship. The beauty of their song soon captured his complete attention. Again he resisted the urge to open his eyes and locate the chirping duo, but the maiden voyage to the end of the universe was canceled as the beauty of their love ballad captivated him.

A new vision appeared in his imagination. He pictured the two birds talking to each other. The blue male was telling his mostly brown mate how beautiful she was. Mike chuckled to himself as he pushed his imagination a little further. The words the blue bird used to flatter his mate were the source of Mike's amusement.

"You're as lovely, my soft feathered companion, as a long,

thick, juicy worm. You're as tasty as the bugs in that dead branch on the tree of that ugly robin's nest."

She answered him, "You're as mighty as the strong wind that brings the rain, my love."

The idea of birds talking to each other Mike found interesting. What were they singing about? he wondered as their aria broke his train of thought. Was it a message or were they—

Mike was distracted by another sound. He heard someone approaching.

❧❧❧

Toni walked into the apartment after calling out Mike's name. The first thing she noticed was that he wasn't sitting in his favorite chair in the corner of the living room. She quietly closed his door and walked across the living room to the sliding glass doors that led to the balcony. Pushing back the curtains, she stepped out onto the porch, ready to rush into his arms. No one was there.

He must have gone into the bedroom to lie down, she figured. She pushed aside the heavy curtains, letting more light into the room, and walked nervously toward the bedroom. The anticipation of seeing him was quickly evaporating. She sensed he wasn't in there before she turned the corner and looked at the empty bed and the room.

Now, she was worried. David said Mike was driving over to see his parents, she remembered, and then he was going home. His car was outside, but where was he? Toni walked dejectedly back out to the living room. It was still empty. Her prayers weren't answered. The urge to cry swelled up in her, but she resisted. Mike was here somewhere, and she wasn't going to leave until she found him. Her days of running away were over, she told the voices of doubt.

She walked over and sat on the couch. She hadn't been home twenty four hours yet, and her world was been turned upside down. Her attention was slowly drawn to the continuous song of some birds outside. Their happy melody summoned her out to the balcony. Toni searched the trees in the woods near Mike's apartment for the vociferous duo. The expansive grounds behind his apartment were all but empty with the exception of a few people playing basketball. That was odd on such a nice day, she remembered. Usually, in the late afternoons, there were basketball players bumping shoulders with the daily volleyball crowd. Even the tennis courts were empty. It was still humid from the earlier rain. *Maybe that's why*, she thought.

She turned to leave when the bird's song stopped her. Toni looked into the woods, but the large trees hid the songbirds in the awakening green branches. She continued searching for them. It was a welcome distraction from having to think about—

Two, then half a dozen birds took flight from the tree line. After a pause, the songbirds continued their ballad. Toni soon realized they weren't visible from where she was standing. Giving it one more try, she concentrated on looking at a group of smaller trees closer to the last row of apartments to her right, with no luck.

She was getting ready to leave when she thought she spotted someone sitting on the grass across from the last apartment in the complex. It was a man, she realized, with his back to her in an opening between the trees. The opening looked like it was cut out of the woods as a place to put a picnic table because the grass there was neatly cut. Only there weren't any tables that Toni could see at that distance. The guy appeared to be sitting alone on the grass. Toni thought that maybe he was reading a book or something, until he stretched out on his back. She thought it odd, but didn't watch him for long. Other pressing problems occupied her thoughts.

Just then the bird's song seemed to take on a different melody. It sounded odd, as if they were calling her name, Toni thought as she listened anew. Scolding herself for thinking such a stupid thought, she turned to go but found she couldn't leave the balcony.

She stood for a minute with her back to the origin of the fowl music and then turned around as if to rebuke the songbirds for singing her name when she took another look around the grounds behind Mike's apartment. The basketball players, and that person she had first observed sitting in the woods were still there. Only there was something different about the guy on the grass. He was still lying flat on his back in the sunlight but doing so completely dressed. She thought that strange.

"It's him," the songbirds now seemed to be singing. "It's him!"

"Mike?" Toni said under her breath. "Could that possibly be you? What in the world are you doing out—"

രാശാ

Mike listened, as the intrusive sound of footsteps grew louder. Someone was running in his direction. The last few times he had broken the sanctity of his cosmic journey was at the nagging, thumping feet of two overweight women as they jogged. He didn't bother to look up at them after the first time they jogged past. But the next time, he heard them stop as they approached. They must be winded, he though, as the sounds of their footsteps waned.

Mike relaxed and let his mind drift. He was curious to see in what direction it would take him this time. He let his body lay flat against the soft grass and tried to coax his muscles to relax in the warm sunlight. The mental picture of some black, shiny, and hungry bugs climbing up on his clothes had to be resisted before he could reach the serenity necessary to stir his imagination from the depths of common sense. Mike tried hard, but he couldn't seem to single out any particular concept to concentrate on.

What's wrong? he wondered. He checked himself. He felt relaxed. It irked him a little that he kept being drawn back to his launching pad. Being able to lose himself in a fantasy was the aspirin he took for the pangs of reality he faced each day. Now, those tools were also failing him.

Adding to his quandary, he began to realize that the warmth of the sun was missing. In his battle to enter into one of his imaginary trips, he had missed that important fact. That was why he was struggling, he decided. He opened his eyes slowly, lest the sun break from behind a cloud at the same time and blind him. A feeling of satisfaction gripped him as the light of the sun was indeed in his eyes, but not directly. Something was blocking the direct sunlight.

He opened his eyes a little wider, still fighting the bright glare of the sun. He gasped when he realized someone was standing over him. Mike tried to make out who it was, but their head was directly in front of the sun, their face hidden in the bright light, like the corona of an eclipse.

Slowly the glare subsided as his eyes became adjusted to the light. Mike relaxed somewhat when he realized, from the long hair blowing around the person's head, that it was a woman. At least he didn't have to defend himself against a male adversary with the advantage of the sun's glare. He started to speak to the fuzzy image when it dropped to its knees on the ground beside him. He winced as the bright sunlight blinded him. Mike raised his hand to block the light so he could see the person kneeling beside him.

A whisper of a breeze carried the clean, light scent of her over to him, canceling out the crispness of the spring flora growing nearby. For some reason, this interruption didn't garner the usual poor attitude he was apt to display when bothered. The gentle scent of the woman was no bother. It was a pleasure long forgotten. He inhaled it as one escaping a sewer and breathing fresh air.

It only took a moment for his blinded eyes to adjust.

"Hi, Mike," the sun-goddess softly said.

He blamed the glare from the sun as his excuse for doubting what his eyes beheld. The vision didn't waver or show signs of being a case of mistaken identity. The countenance of the person kneeling beside him became clear. Despite the sun's bright rays, he was able to see the contrite, remorseful face of one Toni Di-Nardo.

Her eyes were alive with a different kind of light, a light that revealed much. Mike struggled to speak. The scent of her drifted over him again triggering favored memories. Common sense lost the battle when it whispered, *She's another figment of your imagination.*

"Hi, Ton," Mike said, ignoring common sense.

"Mike," Toni answered, her voice cracking as she spoke, "I came here to apologize to you. I was completely wrong to blame you."

Mike reached out and grabbed her, pulling her down into his arms. She had to be real, he was thinking. She felt real. If this was a mirage, he decided, he was going to make the best of it.

Toni put her arms around his neck as she fell on top of him. "Mikey, oh Mikey," she moaned in his ear. She rocked back and forth in his arms as the joy of being held by him surged through her.

The heat of the sun warmed him again, but now he only noticed the softness of the woman in his arms. Mike entered into another of his fantasies with gusto. It was as though Toni was actually there. This time, it was so real he started to feel the stirring of passion in his body. Then, just as quickly, it was over. Suddenly, her face drifted away with the breeze like smoke from a doused fire when he heard mocking voices. The vision was destroyed by the uninvited comments of some snickering, nosy bystanders. Mike turned his head to the right and noticed those two female joggers looking over at him as he hugged himself. He thought about ignoring them and dwelling only on the pleasure his imagination had conjured up, but he knew it wouldn't work anymore. Their accusing smirks were a constant burr in his ass.

Mike stood and stared back at them. They derisively stood their ground before laughing at him and running off. Occasionally, one would turn around and look back. More embarrassment, he thought, adding to the mountain he had already accumulated. He sighed deeply as pangs of sorrow gripped him. His vivid imagination had become his refuge from the despair of the present. A private place he could go where people were happy, and one person in particular was always happy to see him—again. But each time, reality would reappear, painting a much darker picture. That was the case most of the time when he dreamed about Toni.

He had to get out of here, Mike resolved. Various destinations came to mind, but he turned them down because they all involved other people. He needed to be alone for a while. The little joy he gained sitting outdoors was lost in the mocking laughs of the joggers.

Mike wiped the grass off his clothes and started walking back up the hill. *No one to blame but you-know-who*, he berated himself as he walked around the building toward his car.

One of the maintenance men, picking up loose paper and trash on the grounds, ignored the mumbling man who slowly climbed up the hill past him. Mike left his imagination launching pad behind.

ຕ∕ງຕ∕ງ

Toni burst out the back door and looked around. She noticed two women running in the opposite direction. She swallowed and then ran down the hill to the spot where the man was sitting. When she got to the clearing, he was gone. Toni tried to relax. She looked around and then back toward Mike's apartment to try a get a fix on the correct location of the plot of grass. From what she could figure, she was standing in the same spot the man was. "Mike?" she called out. "Mike, are you in here?"

"I'm over here," she heard him answer.

Thank God, Toni thought, as she ran in the direction of the voice. She turned the corner of a building, right into the arms of—a maintenance man.

Toni screamed.

The maintenance man quickly let her go as she frightened him more than he did her. "What in the hell is wrong with you, lady?" he asked, startled by her reaction. "Why did you call me?"

Toni put her hand to her breast in an effort to persuade her heart not to burst. "I—I thought," she struggled to say. "I'm sorry. I—I thought you were someone else."

"I heard someone call my name," he told her as he calmed down. "I was walking back this way to see who it was when I bumped into you. Were you looking for a maintenance man for something?"

Toni was able to catch her breath after reading the name embroidered on his shirt pocket. "Did you see the guy who was sitting over there?" she said, pointing to the clearing beyond the bushes.

"I was over in that area, picking up trash," he said, pointing to another building behind him.

"No, this guy was sitting over there on the grass by the woods," Toni explained.

"Sorry, lady, I didn't see anyone sitting there when I walked past."

Toni studied him for a minute without commenting. He was about forty, she figured, about the size of the man she thought was Mike. He had dark brown hair that was longer than she liked on a man. He was wearing a blue uniform, and the person she saw was wearing something blue. She didn't think he was wearing all blue, though. She recalled seeing a lot of white, like a white shirt or T-shirt. Could it have been the maintenance man who was sitting in the clearing? She didn't think so but wasn't all that sure. Now that she thought about it, she didn't get a clear shot of him. It was quite a distance away, and the branches of the trees obscured him somewhat.

"Thanks, anyway," Toni said while backing away from him.

Maintenance Man Mike, suddenly cognizant of her apprehensive manner, shook his head in acknowledgement and walked quickly away before she could get him into trouble.

Relieved that he was leaving, Toni turned and headed back toward Mike's apartment. One more glance back assured her he wasn't a threat. Maintenance Man Mike was busy picking up discarded bits of scoria and trash.

Toni weighed her next action carefully. There was the chance that Mike's parents had come by and picked him up. She decided to leave and head home. She had their number written down there somewhere.

The walk up the back steps of his apartment was a quiet, subdued, deliberation on the madness that was her life the last few months. During her reflections, she promised God to spend the rest of her life making it up to Mike if he would let her. She reached his back door just as she seconded her latest affirmation.

His apartment appeared too neat to have been lived in, she realized for the first time when she stepped in the back door. Mike was pretty good at keeping his apartment neat and clean, but there was something sterile about it she thought as she looked around. Then Toni remembered David saying Mike was in the hospital for a while and then stayed with him when he got out. That would explain the antiseptic air the apartment gave off. There were none of the diverse odors people created as they went about their mundane task of daily survival, such as cooking or cleaning.

Toni closed the door behind her and looked around the apartment again for some sign of his presence that she might have missed. "I know what to do," Toni decided as an idea took root. She walked toward the kitchen. "I'll leave a message on Mike's bulletin board." She was pleased when she walked into the kitchen and found it hanging in the usual place on the kitchen wall.

In happier times, they both used it to leave notes to each other when they missed connections. She knew the modus operandi was to take it off the wall, write the message, and then put it on the dining room table where it would be quickly spotted.

Mike. Toni stopped writing after one word. What should she tell him? She started writing, *I stopped by to see you. I wanted to—*

What was that? Toni listened for a minute. She was sure she had heard something. All she heard now was the loud pounding of her own heart. She had checked every room, she affirmed, and the apartment was empty. "Why are you so jumpy, girl? There's no one here but us ghosts." Her attempt at humor failed to ease her reservations as she continued to listen. Then she became frightened when she swore she heard someone breathing behind her. Fear suddenly took on the appearance of a ten-foot-tall, hairy man, who just escaped from some mental institution for the eternally insane for raping and murdering fifty women. Toni held the marker as a weapon and, when she spun around, her mouth dropped, as did the marker.

Mike had heard the door close and waited for David to walk into the bedroom. When he hesitated, Mike thought about calling out to him where he was but knew David would find him eventually. *Ah, hell*, Mike decided while getting up off the bed, *I'll just go out and meet him.* After all, the original reason he walked back into his apartment was to get his car keys and drive over to tell David how great the meeting with his parents went, he thought tongue-in-cheek.

Feeling a little out of sorts, he decided to lie down for a while first. Now, David had saved him a trip. When Mike turned the corner of his living room and saw a woman leaning over his dining room table, he was stunned. The person was obviously unaware of his presence a few feet behind her. At first, he thought maybe his neighbor had walked into his apartment, but that didn't make any sense. Mike took the momentary respite to observe the lady. She was wearing nothing special, only jeans, and a T-shirt. As he wondered what to do without scaring her, she unexpectedly turned around.

"Mike," Toni cried out, dropped her purse, and ran into his arms.

He hesitated for a moment, not believing what was transpiring. The months of idle daydreaming had softened his response.

His entire body felt the touch and weigh of her, but, still, he questioned what he saw. *Is this another dream? Am I going nuts?* The touch and smell of her was the slap he needed to awaken from his stupor.

"Toni?"

"Oh, Mike," she said between gasps, "I came over here to apologize to you. David told me—"

"Don't, Toni, it's not necessary," he explained as he welcomed her hugs, "I'm just glad you're here."

"No, there's something I have to say, I—"

He silenced her with a kiss. It was the first show of passion by either of them in over a year. Terrible shackles of loneliness, the kind most people never experienced, fell from their shoulders. Two warm and loving souls again had a reason to express that ardor. Their lips met with a fervor that rivaled their happier times. Toni rubbed her body into him as if compensating for her disturbing accusations. Mike welcomed it as her genuinely missing him. There were no strings attached, as far as he was concerned, no complex response to some deep emotional trauma. The soft, nuzzling female in his arms wasn't a payment or atonement for past sins.

Mike saw their passionate embrace as the result of their inescapable love for each other. No, he never had a clue they would ever get together again, but when Toni rushed into his arms, the only explanation he garnered from her response was that the fire of that love had miraculously destroyed the walls that separated them.

Mike, oh Mike, Toni thought as his tongue danced around in her mouth. She wanted to cry, but the sheer joy of his embrace stirred feelings she had denied herself too long. Pure and simple, Toni wanted to screw him. Yes, there was something in her, she grudgingly acknowledged, that wanted to try and repay him for the pain she caused. To give him something that would prove her repentance was genuine. It was an unnecessary effort on her part. Mike had given her the absolution her soul craved, but she never stopped to read his response. Her own needs mixed with the guilt she felt to color her actions. There was also a stirring in her that just wanted to feel like a woman again and all that necessitated.

She battled the same guilt that plagued most passionate women—women that society had mislabeled because of their willingness to confront their desires honestly. She wanted a physical release of her pent-up emotions and to relieve the powerful need that was surging through her. The method she chose to allay that need was as old as the need.

Toni thought about her decision, for a moment, and then broke their embrace. In Florida, the additional risks were clearly explained to her. She accepted the gamble, but would Mike? She looked into his eyes for any hint of fear or uncertainty. She had her reservations but couldn't begin to measure his. What if he was repulsed by the act? she wondered. That would hurt so much. When she looked into his eyes, they carried the same loving gaze she remembered. *Well*, she decided, *nothing ventured, nothing gained*. She took his hand and gently tugged at it.

Mike only hesitated for a moment, unsure of her intentions. A blush rose up on his face when those intentions became clear. He allowed her to lead him into the bedroom.

Their bodies came together in a reunion of a love neither could deny—a love so strong that it had rescued them from hell and the cold curse of the grave and gave them hope for the future, however short. Although both were infected with AIDS, the only thing of meaning that passed between them was the realization that, for the rest of their lives, each would never be without the other.

When they caught their breath, Toni tried apologizing again and gave up when Mike attacked her body again and again. She finally understood, before Mike fainted from exhaustion, that he didn't want to discuss it, not now, not ever. From that moment on, they never mentioned it again and forbade anyone else from doing so. Even though, on a couple of naughty occasions, Toni used the threat of bringing it up again to entice Mike into copulation.

The next day, Toni moved in with Mike. From that night on, they were inseparable.

CHAPTER 33

Their decision was as hard to explain to their families and friends as they thought it would be, but, despite their loved ones very vocal objections, they were persuaded. Two months later, when Mike and Toni purchased their recreational vehicle, everyone understood just how persuaded they were.

They had decided to leave Pittsburgh for parts unknown, they explained to everyone. Their vision was to spend the time they had remaining together, seeing the country, eventually ending up in California, where most of the testing for a cure for AIDS was taking place. If there's a cure, they explained to their doubting loved ones, it would be in California first. If not, they would have spent quality time together.

With tempered self-confidence, they withstood the expected wave of protests from concerned and caring loved ones. None shook their resolve more than their heated confrontations with David. They scheduled a picnic at his house to first break the news.

"Hello, guys," David said when he opened his door. "Where's Brenda?"

"She's coming. I don't know if she's waiting for Josh or not, but she said she would be here by two o'clock. Is Trisha here?"

David sighed. "I'm sorry, Toni, but she has classes and then works until midnight afterward. I haven't seen her in almost a week."

"Speaking of the devil," Mike added, hoping to keep Toni from voicing her opinion on that subject, "there she is."

The three of them stood at the door, watching Brenda drive up to David's garage and then get out. She was wearing a short green skirt and lighter green blouse. And, as usual, the leggy redhead looked great, David thought. Just the way she sauntered toward him ignited familiar flames.

"Okay, the queen is here. Close your mouth, David, before you swallow a fly, and get out of my way," Toni ordered as she pushed past the stunned mannequin staring at the attractive lady in green and walked into his house. "Are the potatoes cooking like I ordered?"

David heard her talking behind him and started to say, "Yes, master," but looking at Brenda approaching silenced any snide come back.

"Hi, Davey."

"Hi, gorgeous. No Josh?"

She smiled at him and kissed him on the cheek. "And no Trisha, I'm hoping," she whispered in his ear then strolled into his house. "Hi, Mike, hey, babe."

David turned and watched Brenda hug Mike and Toni. Would he ever be free of her lovely hook? he wondered.

His buddy Mike saw the faraway look on David's face and knew from whence it came. Through thick and thin, he also was smitten by the wiles of the two women now taking over David's kitchen.

"Ready, Mike, the grill is cleaned and ready for you," David said as Mike joined him watching Toni and Brenda talking in his kitchen.

The grill wasn't the only thing ready around here, Mike thought, looking at his smitten friend but keeping that to himself. "No hurry, let's get a beer and chill for a few. The pit boss needs some time to make a few dishes, she informed me while driving over here."

ↄ◌ↄ◌

They were sitting in the living room after a tasty picnic of grilled hamburgers and hot dogs. Toni made her delicious potato salad, and Brenda cooked up some macaroni and cheese and boiled the corn on the cob.

Stuffed from eating, they wandered into the air-conditioned house and were chatting in the living room when Toni and Mike abruptly changed the direction of the conversation.

"One of the reasons we asked for this get together," Toni said, "and by a quirk of fate it ended up being just the four of us—" She paused for effect. "—was to share with our two best friends some great news Mike and I have."

"We have purchased a motorhome and plan to drive around the country," Mike revealed, taking the reins from Toni.

"Hey, that would be a nice vacation." David said, acknowledging the smiles on Mike and Toni's faces. "You guys deserve one."

"No honey, not a vacation. We don't plan on coming back here."

A stunned David looked at Toni and then turned toward Mike. "*What*?"

"Dave, Brenda," Mike said to him and the other person in the room, so stunned she couldn't speak. "We plan an extended trip, seeing everything we always wanted to see and visiting places like New York City, DC, and then travel down to Florida before ending up out in California. We learned that's where most of the AIDS research is being funded."

David shook his head. "I understand what you're saying, I do, but I think you're wrong, Mike. Who knows where or when a cure will be found? I think it would be better to be under one doctor's care. That way, he can monitor any changes more closely."

"Your argument was merit, David, but we want the adventure of seeing the country while we can."

"Then take a vacation, Mike. Toni, that's the logical thing to do." David stood and tried to explain. "Then when you guys come back, you can start treatment."

"Our plans," Mike explained to his upset friends, "we admit, have nothing to do with logic. Logic would dictate that we might as well dig a grave and climb into it. What we are doing is to give our love a chance, and if—when—we die, what a better way of going out."

"If there's a cure—" Toni added, after she stood up and hugged her irate *brother* as David paced the floor, "—love will find it."

It was that love that fueled David's protest. "I don't want you dying alone on some deserted highway," he explained to them. "What if both of you got sick at the same time, very sick? Who would take care of you? Don't you think it might be a better idea to start some kind of treatment program?"

"I agree with, David," an inebriated Brenda added.

She had been quiet most of the day. Her three compadres read the sadness on her face, figured it might have something to do with her missing boyfriend, and didn't press her about why.

"Look, both of you," Toni tried explaining as she took her brother and sat him down on the couch. "We understand where you're coming from, and we don't disagree with you. We came to the simple realization that we want the time we have left to be quality time. How long we have left isn't nearly as important as how we spend that time."

David reiterated his point. "You guys deserve to be cared for," he argued, "as that horrible time in your lives approaches, by people that you love and love you." Then he shook them up with his next statement. "If you are bound and determined to go, I am bound and determined to go with you."

Brenda sat up at that idea. She was in David's recliner across from the three of them on the couch. "I'm going too. After all, I'm the nurse here."

"There's no way, Jose, we would let you either of you," Toni answered before Brenda could say anything else. Toni turned toward David who was starting to stand again and pushed him back on the couch. "What about that girl you are dating…ah, Trisha? Have you considered her feelings? And, and you, Brenda, what about your plans to move to Harrisburg with your parents?" she said as she looked from brown eyes to green. "Your lives are here with them, not with us, you guys."

David tried to get up again, but Toni balled up her tiny fist and put it in his face. Mike only chuckled at their theatrics. They would never hit each other.

They continued arguing their points until Mike put an end to the conversation. "Well, we need to be going," he said to the tension in the room. "You guys have to work in the morning." He knew his buddy wasn't convinced yet and maybe never would be.

"Yes, let's go before I punch his lights out, honey," the dark-haired boxer threatened as she stood up over her stubborn opponent.

David just blew a kiss at her. "Guys, why don't you drop

Brenda off?" their stubborn opponent suggested when he noticed the redhead struggling to get out of the recliner. "She shouldn't be driving in her—"

"Nonsense, I'm fine," Brenda said when she finally extracted herself from the grabby recliner.

David saw her keys on his coffee table by her purse and grabbed them before she could.

"David, give me my keys."

"There's no way in hell you're driving, Bren."

"David, give me my damn keys!"

"No."

It was a stand-off as both stood face to face, waiting on the other to yield. Brenda expected him to because…well, he always did. David wanted to…well, because he always did when looking in her captivating green eyes. And then the final weight that tipped the scales her way was the vivid memory of what this passionate woman could do for a man. Forget the green eyes part, it was more what was beneath those green eyes that caused him to yield—in the past.

David's stubbornness surprised the others in the room.

"Come on, Bren, David is right. Getting a DUI isn't worth the risk, or maybe having an accident."

Brenda rolled her eyes at David, grabbed her purse, staggered for a moment, then walked out his house.

Toni kissed David, made an I-don't-know-what's-wrong-with-her face and then hurried to catch up with the indignant redhead.

"Bye, Mike."

"Bye, David."

"Bren, what's wrong?" Toni asked the quiet woman sitting in the back of Mike's car as they were driving her home. They made eye contact, but Brenda remained mute. Toni took a deep breath and turned around.

Brenda shook her head. "I'm sorry I was in a bad mood today, guys. I—you." They both heard her sighing in the back. "Then I learn my best friend is leaving, and now David wants to leave with you. I feel so—That's why I was drinking so much."

Both people in the front seat knew whatever was bothering her happened before they revealed their plan.

"I'm sorry, Brenda," Toni said, after choosing not to mention that part, "but it's what we want to do with the time we have left. But we haven't given up trying to persuade David that he belongs here."

"You know what, Toni? I don't think it is so much that you guys are leaving that bothered me but something that happened a few days ago."

"What was that?"

"I was—well, we—well, Josh and I were—It was our first time together, ya know. And—and everything was going amazing, then in the middle of everything, you can't guess what I blurted out."

Both Toni and Mike guessed right but remained silent.

"I called out—yeah," Brenda added after hearing her best friend gasp.

"No big deal," Mike added, "I call out all kinds of women's names, Brenda."

Toni punched him.

"I felt so bad. He was so passionate that night, and it felt right ya know, then that happened."

"What did Josh do or—or say?"

"He hesitated for a moment then kept going."

"Smart man," Mike whispered and looked away from Toni.

"I thought that making out with Josh meant I had finally gotten the Ginger Bread Man out of my system, and then there I go injecting his name into my private moments."

"And Josh didn't say anything afterward? And shut up, Mike, I heard your comment the last time."

"Ah—no. He's a sweet guy, Toni. You know what?"

Toni answered on cue, "What?"

"Don't get me wrong, but maybe it would be a good thing to get away from David for a while so I can move on. When—when he held on to my keys and wouldn't give them to me, Toni, when I looked him in the eye, I knew—I knew it wasn't my keys he wanted, ya know what I mean, and neither did I, for that matter. Yeah—maybe—maybe—my leaving would be a good thing."

The car became quiet again as three people encased in the metal, plastic, and glass chariot pondered today and uncertain futures.

೭⁄ꝺ೭⁄ꝺ

In the days that followed, Toni and Mike reluctantly rejected David's caring offer, but after he vowed to either go with them until they got settled in California or spend the rest of his life tracking them down. They relented—temporarily—because they knew he probably would do just that.

David, on another mission to change their minds, pulled over and parked his car about a block from Mike's apartment when he spotted the big white and blue motor home parked across the street. Seeing it signaled just how committed his friends were about leaving. David made a U-turn and drove out of the apartment complex. The thought of arguing with Mike and Toni again proved incentive enough to leave.

He groaned audibly as he drove down Crane Avenue. Their disagreements had been spirited but without any malice. Toni and Mike were leaving, and that was a fact, they explained to him. David had no problem with that, but he was leaving with them.

"Why can't they see that they need me?" he said to that invisible, imaginary listener who sat beside us when we talked to ourselves while driving alone. David blew the rising frustration out his mouth in a deep breath. When he told them he *was* going— and that was that—they finally relented. Then the shit hit the fan. Brenda decided she was also going. Only a long private chat with Toni changed her mind. David was dying to know what Toni had said to dissuade her, but he didn't ask. But it was clear, Toni revealed, Brenda was hurting over Toni not wanting her along again, as Brenda put it.

David didn't ask Toni, but he sensed the new man in Brenda's life, Josh Moser, might have been what Toni used to persuade Brenda to stay. She had surprised them by bringing him to one of their get togethers after they revealed their decision to leave. Josh was a good-looking young doctor at the hospital where Brenda worked and obviously infatuated with the great-looking redhead. She seemed to like him a lot, they all thought.

The amazing thing—Toni and Mike had discussed after their friends had departed their apartment—was the way Brenda still clung to David, even when Josh was there.

"She's letting Josh know David is still second to none with her I think, Mike."

"Well, her date must have assumed that, but I give him credit, he seemed to take it all in stride."

"I know, Mike, but I felt bad for him. There was the guy, she called out in the middle of making love, talking to his date."

"Hey, better he knows what's going on now, Toni. Josh has to decide if being second best with that redhead is better than being first with some other woman in his life."

"Maybe he already has, because he didn't seem to let it bother him."

"David also seemed to take it in stride. He was his usual friendly self with Josh and didn't play up to Brenda's teasing like he usually does."

"Maybe it had to do with who wasn't there, as usual."

"All right, Toni, let's not start in on her again."

"But, Mike, it's true. I know it bothers Davey, but Trisha doesn't like us."

"She was polite when we were together that one time."

"Men—a pretty girl blinds you."

"Present company included."

Toni jumped on Mike and pushed him down on the couch. "It better be."

❧❧❧

David had tried blaming Trisha's absences on her busy schedule. He knew Mike might have accepted that, but not Toni. And for the sake of their friendship, they just let it drop. Another odd thing about this was that Trisha and Brenda had never met.

"I don't think David's lady wants to meet us," Brenda claimed as she ate a sandwich, sitting on the couch with Toni.

"Us or you?"

"What? You think she would be intimidated by little old me?"

Toni laughed. "Maybe it's David who's afraid of that."

"Possibly. But, still, working and going to school can be draining. But you know what? I don't want to be in the same room with them either. That would feel...well, strange, know what I mean?" Brenda told Toni and hinted for her to tell David that was how she wanted it.

So, Toni and Mike met Trisha at David's, but not Brenda. Then Brenda surprised them by bringing Josh to one of their get togethers, but only after learning that Trisha wouldn't be there—again.

David and Brenda might have been playful with each other that day, but, by the end of the night, Brenda was arm-in-arm with a smiling Josh.

Toni wondered if he would still be smiling when he learned Brenda was transferring to a Harrisburg hospital to be with her relatives in three months.

Now that Brenda had decided to move, there was only one person that troubled them. What to do about David wanting to leave with them. They spent evenings debating their options.

"No, Mike," Toni said while they were in bed, "remember I mentioned her to him already. If you bring up his relationship with Trisha again, that might cause a rift between them, and we'll be blamed for that. You know how stubborn Davey is. He has to make up his own mind."

"But what if he doesn't come around? We're scheduled to leave after getting our check up in a few days."

"I'm hoping she can convince him to stay. I think he really likes her, Mikey."

After that discussion, his woman snuggled up against him. Mike decided to table further discussion about his best friend and enjoy the lady in his arms.

CHAPTER 34

"Mike, the last of the antibiotics and medicines that Doctor Brenda recommended we take are stashed aboard the camper."

"Toni, that's a motor home. Campers look more like pick-up trucks," Mike explained.

Toni shrugged her shoulders and walked into the kitchen. Her appetite had returned lately, and she wanted some of that salad they had left over from dinner yesterday. "Okay, mister, the motorhome," she said with her head in the refrigerator.

Two weeks later and their apartment was void of all the keepsakes they valued. They were either given away to love ones or placed in the motorhome. Most of their clothes, and everything else in the apartment, had been given away to friends or promised to whatever charities would come and get them. As if ordained by God himself, their health improved to the point they were itching to hit the road. Mike was over his last bout with the flu and showed no lasting effects. Other than losing five pounds, one would never know he had been ill. His immune system, their doctor had told them, was still strong enough to resist most of the viruses he would encounter. Sunshine, happiness, plenty of rest, and a good diet of fruits and veggies, their doctor suggested, would help support that immune system.

Toni was ecstatic when she discovered she had put on four pounds since returning from Florida. With the return of her appetite, she had hoped to add some more weight. The doctor explained that the measuring tape was their blood count. According to him, it indicated they had acquired AIDS, but AIDS had yet to fully acquire them. When it did, they would see a marked decrease in their body's ability to fight off infections and diseases.

How long that would be no one knew, the doctor explained. It could take six months or six years.

Now was the time to leave, they decided. Like the leaves bursting forth signaling spring's arrival, the good news they heard and the strength they felt were their alarm clocks. Only the painful and undesirable task of saying goodbye to family and friends held their pilgrimage hostage.

☙❧☙

From his seat on her couch, David watched Trisha as she prepared dinner. From there, he could look at the game on TV and turn and watch or talk to her in the kitchen. He had offered to help but was pushed into the living room with a finger in his chest. But every few minutes, she would walk into the living room as if to emphasize a point she was trying to make about her job or the next semester of school. David had told her about Mike and Toni's illness, their plans to leave, and his fervent determination to stop them. She stunned him by saying nothing, but her actions spoke for her. Somehow, in his zeal to help his friends, he had failed to tie in Trisha's increased ardor and the enticing outfits she was wearing when they were together the last few times as anything out of the ordinary.

"Honey, the ham needs to slow cook for about another hour, and it will be perfect," Trisha explained, walking between him and the TV *again.* The shapely lass never failed to snare his attention away from the ball game or whatever he was watching. She wore a variety of nightshirts when lounging at home with him for the evening with matching running shorts underneath. The nightshirts were usually silk and colorful—and, she claimed, airy, soft, and very comfortable. But lately, she skipped the shorts, turning what was comfortable into something totally distracting. The girl did have beautiful stems, he was constantly reminded, as those shapely legs made another inconsequential trip from room to room.

She had surprised him when she mentioned she was a top gymnast in high school, but, before she could commit to a college, she decided it wasn't what she wanted to do with her life. That explained why her thighs muscles would flex like a cat's as she walked. That never failed to catch the wandering eye of one David Jackson because he knew from experience that her coffee-colored skin was as baby smooth to the touch as it looked.

"No problem, Tee," David replied as he looked up from the game. "I'm starving, but I think I can wait that long. Besides," he said, smiling at her, "what choice do I have?"

She stopped glazing the ham and looked at him from the kitchen with that sexy smirk she had developed lately. After placing the ham in the oven and them removing certain items of clothing while out of his view, she walked in the living room and again stood between him and what he was watching. She then slid her hand seductively over her hips, raised her nightshirt a little higher, and then walked into the bedroom. Watching certain enticing body parts now swaying free under that nightshirt made whatever he was watching moot.

Trisha had a charisma about her that made it hard for David to say no to anything she wanted. At times, he felt as though he was being cruel when he stuck to an opinion that she strongly disagreed with. Later tonight, he swore, as he got up from the couch and walked toward the bedroom, would be one of those times. Tonight, he had decided, it was time to tell her he was leaving with Toni and Mike. The real question he wasn't sure of was, when would he be able to return?

What was waiting for him on her bed when he walked in canceled that conversation for later. The naked lady laying there and motioning with her finger where she wanted him to start was all that mattered—for now.

e/୨e/୨

"Did you hear me?" the woman in hospital room 341 asked the nurse standing with her back to her looking out the window.

"What? Oh, yeah. Sorry. I'll bring your painkiller in at six. That's the next time your doctor assigned you medication."

"But I'm hurting now, stupid," the angry woman shouted at Brenda. "I don't care what that asshole doctor said, I want my medication now!"

Brenda heard her but took little note of her protest. She would get the medication on the hour, like prescribed on her chart. This wasn't an ironclad rule with Brenda, but the arrogance of the woman guaranteed that Brenda would observe the rules today.

"Mrs. Haggerty, Doctor Hanno left strict orders to limit your pain medicine to every four hours. You will wait until six before you get any, understand?"

Brenda walked out of that room, thinking only about her friends' scheduled trip into oblivion.

⌒⌒⌒

After invigorating sex, a playful shower together, and an overcooked ham for dinner, David started having second thoughts about leaving her. He wasn't blinded by the brightness of her flame, just deeply warmed by it. They were sitting on her sofa in the thick, soft robes they had worn after their shower and throughout dinner. Trisha had made a pitcher of screwdrivers, and he was sipping his when she slipped her hand under his robe. A very appreciative David slowly began to realize that this was par for the course lately, ever since he told her about Mike's plans. That was why she was so frisky lately, he realized as her probing fingers found what they were searching for and weakened his ability to concentrate. Start talking to her about Mike and Toni and he and Trisha made love before they could begin a meaningful conversation. Then later, when bringing up their journey, she tried working up his passion again.

David didn't feel any anger once he realized the reason for her blatant attempts to distract him. She had to have sensed he might be thinking about leaving with them, so she was offering a strong incentive to stay, and there was nothing wrong with that. Still, he was disappointed that she thought him that easy. But it had worked each of the last three times he came over, David recalled, feeling a little wimpish for his lack of insight and fortitude. But not tonight, he vowed, as his body started to respond to the soft touch of her experienced fingers.

"Trisha, we've got to talk."

"Talk later," she said, climbing up and straddling his lap.

When she did, her robe fell open, exposing her flawless skin and her enticing breast to his exploring eyes. The effect was predictable. The view was captivating enough to silence him as his eyes feasted on the revealing show. The lady was sculptured, toned, and nothing sagged. But when she opened his robe and started kissing down his chest, he involuntarily leaned his head back and closed his eyes.

It was when her tongue tickled down his chest that jolted him out of the malaise he was enjoying just before her wet mouth reached—

No, David thought, *not this time*. He grabbed her and pulled her up into his arms. Trisha was easily one of the most passionate women he had ever made love to. What things she had never done or tried in bed, she quickly mastered them, and he became the recipient of fantastic sex. And what was under her robe promised again to render him sated and happy.

She sat up on his lap and stared at him, puzzled. Why had he stopped her? she questioned.

"Tee." David took a deep breath. "I'm going with Mike and Toni, just until they get settled."

"No, you're not." She leaned forward then nibbled on his lobe a little harder than intended.

"Yes, I am," he answered between painful bites.

She leaned back. "No, you're not!" she shouted in his face.

David held her at arms' length. "Tee, I'm going with them. They need me."

"They need you? What's this on your lap?"

Why was he doing this to her? she wondered. Her worse fears were becoming a frightening reality.

"You don't understand."

"You bet I don't. Davey, I love you with all my heart," Trisha said, swallowing the urge to beg him. She had surrendered more of herself to this one man than all the men she dated. He was almost worth conceding the little of her pride she had remaining and pleading, she decided, almost. "Have I denied you anything?" she said, ignoring the pain that gripped her chest. "What else do I have to do to convince you that I love you?"

"Nothing. You don't have to prove that to me, baby. This has nothing to do with your loving me. I love you, Tee. I—I didn't realize how much until I struggled with my decision to go with them. It's just something I have to do. I really don't expect you to agree with me, but I want you to understand it's something I have to do."

Trisha suddenly felt...naked. She jerked her robe closed, got off his lap, and stood over him.

He slowly looked up at her, not wanting to see the hurt he knew was etched on her pretty face. She genuinely loved him, he knew that.

David inhaled slowly, as his eyes met a mournful wet pair looking at him, and wondered how he could possibly hurt her. Her head was leaning to one side, and her bottom lip was trembling as she bravely fought back the tears. He had touched a vein of pride that battled to hold back the wave of pleading and crying that lay just beyond that quivering lip. He sensed she was surviving only on her anger.

"I don't know how long I'll be gone, Trisha, but I'll be back, even if you no longer want me."

She didn't say anything. She just stared down at him, holding her robe tightly closed as if it was the fragile dam holding in her emotions.

David stood up, and, as he did, she took two steps back. It was the confused look on his face that saved the situation. She could see that he wasn't completely sold on the idea of going with them.

Trisha shook her head, turned around, and abruptly walked into her bedroom, slamming, and then locking, the door behind her. David sat down on the couch. She needed some time to come to grips with what was happening, he thought. Besides, he couldn't leave anyway. His clothes were scattered around on the floor in the bedroom.

It soon became apparent she wasn't coming out anytime soon. The bearer of bad tidings sat alone on the couch, weighing his decision. He was clear about one thing, in the confusion that had given him a headache, his feeling for the sick duo was unquestionable. Their well-being was as necessary to him as breathing. Then there was the other side of the coin. That side was behind a locked door doing who-knows-what.

David wasn't as sure about his relationship with Trisha as he was the other side of the coin, but they had become very close. They weathered their earlier disagreements and found a closeness he came to rely on. After their trip down to Atlanta, they became very compatible. She kept her promise when they returned and surprised him by never using the trip to underline their relationship. As she learned to trust him, she opened up, and the woman he found inside was as exciting and fun loving as he could have ever imagined. Every time they were together, love—as well as laughter—flowed freely from them. They could be hot and passionate, warm and funny, quiet and tender, playful and innocent, all in the same evening.

Trisha was going to art school for fashion design and illustration. She had drawn three different facial portraits of him that were impressive and meticulously detailed. After convincing him to model in the buff for her, she rewarded him as promised but destroyed the sketch afterward, jealously stating it was too revealing to show anyone. She was very talented, he had to admit. Her intellect, and the depth of her personality, kept him interested.

David thought he heard Trisha moving around and stood up, but her bedroom door remained closed. He debated what to do next. He could knock on her door and apologize, but that wasn't him. Not that he was above doing that, but his hurting her wasn't intentional, and there were no options, in his opinion. Resigned, he sat down back on the couch and quickly washed down the remainder of his now diluted drink.

Resigned she wasn't coming out any time soon, his mind drifted back to the first time they were intimate on New Year's Eve. It was one of those special moments that stuck in your mind for reasons easily understood. He had assumed that the brazen young woman, who dropped her beautiful silver gown at her feet and was wearing only a smile, would be as aggressive in bed as was that act. Boy, was he wrong. But her inexperience made her gift to him more precious. He smiled as visions of their early awkwardness together flashed in his mind, mistakes they laughed about now. Then there were a few toes stepped on, but quickly they learned to dance fluidly and in-step, as if they could read the other's mind and know the other's thoughts, fantasies, wants, and needs.

Trisha's personality began to blossom as her confidence in him deepened. He took her to places and did things with her she never imagined she would like, and she loved them. From an elegant evening in one of the exclusive restaurants above the city in Mt. Washington, to toasting her as they watched the sun set from Schenley Park, or dragging a very reluctant young woman onto one of those crazy rides at Kennywood Park—no matter how nervous or frightened she was, he was always there, holding her hand.

She quickly developed her own audaciousness and came up with ideas of places and things she wanted to see and do, like making him sing with her at a karaoke bar, to seeing the breathtakingly clear view of the thousands of stars in the night sky high up in the mountains of West Virginia.

Her usual hair style and loose, comfortable-fitting clothes soon gave way to form-fitting fashions that accentuated her assets and gave her a look that was meant to captivate him wherever they went and around anyone they met. She held on to being classy—that was just who she was—but added a little sassy.

A good example of that was the dress she wore when he told her he wanted to take her out to dinner at one of the most elegant restaurants in town. He had thought her New Year's Eve gown was the most breathtaking outfit he had seen on her. That beautiful gown was floor length with a long split down one side and revealed just enough cleavage to be a pleasant distraction.

When David pulled up to her house for their dinner date, he checked himself in his car mirror before climbing out of his car. Nothing bothered him more than a slightly off-center tie knot. He rarely wore a tie but, when he did, it had to be straight and tight. Wearing a black suit, white shirt, gray/black striped tie, with black polished shoes, he felt well dressed for where he was taking Trisha for dinner.

When he rang her door bell, and the door opened, his mouth froze in the open, gawking position. The lady standing in the doorway looked stunning. "Wow, Trish, you look amazing, girl."

She did. Trisha stood in the doorway in a shimmering white mid-thigh-length dress that clung tightly to her body, outlining all of her amazing curves.

"Thank you, kind sir. You look kind of spiffy yourself. Would you rather stay home and rip this dress off me?" She chuckled when she noticed the blank look on his face as he started thinking about it, and then she shook her head and pushed him out the door. "Never gonna happen, buddy. Took me forever to look like this."

She took his arm and they walked to his car. David opened her door for her and waited until she was seated. Opening doors for her was what he always did, not just today when she looked hot.

"Where are we eating?"

"What did we say as kids? That's for me to know and for you to find out."

Trisha crossed her legs and tugged at the hem of her skirt. "Eyes on the road, please, smart mouth."

"Busted, you caught me," David said to the smiling young woman. "It's Christopher's—like I told you on the phone, a very exclusive restaurant on Mt. Washington. Have you ever eaten there?"

"I've heard of it, but, no."

"I think you will love it. The view alone is worth eating there. You get a breathtaking look at the city at night, but I'll be staring at another beautiful sight." He looked away from the road for a moment to see her bubbling from the compliments. *That's great*, he thought, *you deserve to be treated as royalty, pretty girl.*

When they pulled up in front of the restaurant, the valet opened Trisha's door for her.

"Thank you," Trisha said to the valet.

"You're welcome, miss. Welcome to Christopher's."

"Can I help you, sir?" the hostess asked when they walked into the restaurant.

"Reservations for Mr. Jackson."

"Yes, sir, this way please." She smiled that all-business smile and directed them to follow her.

"This is so beautiful, David," Trisha said after they were seated at their table and she looked around the restaurant. "What a view."

"It is magnificent."

Trisha started blushing when she turned and noticed he was staring at her.

That was how that wonderful evening went, David recalled as he sat on the couch with Trisha locked in her bedroom. Their surf and turf dinner was delicious and the wine he selected complimented the meal. The lady sitting across from him seemed to be enjoying the ambiance.

"What a wonderful dinner, Davey, thank you," Trish said when they got into his car and started driving off.

"Oh, we have one more stop."

"Really, where?"

"What did we say as kids? It's for me to—"

"Do you know what women say to our dates?" Trisha cut him off. "Oh, yes, if you ever want what's in this little dress you—"

"Right, right, ah, sorry. Well, it's a surprise." David said.

It didn't change the pouting look on her face, but he didn't care. He drove into downtown Pittsburgh and turned left onto Seventh Street. He pulled over in front of the Benedum Theater. "Here we are."

Trisha looked at the theater's marquee and then her grinning date. It read, *The Lion King*.

"Yes, two tickets to the last show in about...twenty minutes," David said as he caught the time on the car digital readout. "Here, take these and wait for me in the theater lobby while I park the car."

"No, Davey, I'll come with you."

"Sweetheart, you look too good to be walking in a dirty garage."

David remembered her reluctance, but she did as he asked. The picture of that stunning woman standing in front of the theater waiting for him was something he would never forget. She was the center of attention of guys walking and driving past.

"You should be waiting inside, Trish."

"I wanted to wait out here for you, in case another woman catches your attention and steals you away."

David shook his head at the teasing woman looking up and down the street as if that might be a possibility. "Only if you have an identical twin sister," he announced, "that looks better than you do."

She absolutely loved the play. She couldn't stop talking about it as he drove her home.

"Aren't you coming in?" Trisha asked when she opened her door and found him standing outside.

"I would love to. babe, but I've got to be at work in a couple of hours."

"Ah, nuts." She had forgotten how early he had to report to work each morning as the reason why they rarely stayed out this late on weekdays. "I wanted to thank you for this amazing evening, Davey," she said as she brushed up against him.

"Trish, being my date was reward enough…almost." He kissed the grinning woman on her forehead. "It was great just being seen with you."

"Trust me, you'll want this reward. Are you sure you can't spare a few minutes?"

David smiled at her and then pulled her to him and kissed her hard on the mouth. "There is no way I would want only a few minutes with you, lady. How about a rain check, beautiful?"

Trisha pouted and sighed but nodded okay.

A change had come over that reserved girl he had first met, David realized. That was evident in her new bravado. Ms. Closed-Mouth-Basic-Kiss-On-The-Lips had transformed into an adventurous tongue dancing, passionately open-mouthed lover, who now roamed all over his body with wet kisses, leaving no spot untouched, much to his delight.

Now, as David sat back on the couch, he savored the young woman who was Trisha Bey Tipton. He paused in reflection for a moment as a question tickled his thoughts. "When did that beautiful lady on the other side of that door become the aggressor in this relationship?"

After the furor of their first intimacy, when he was the one who carried her to bed and into places she never experienced, so much so that she willingly relinquished the authority over her body to him, allowing him whatever act, and in whatever way he desired, as she feasted on the toe-curling results. At some point, that changed. And David was okay with that change. She didn't have the tattooed yellow stripes all over her body like that man in that old phone commercial, but she was a tiger now!

Trisha was no longer just a reclined, satiated, willing recipient of his lovemaking until almost too weak to reciprocate. The girl was now a creatively gifted artist in the bedroom, he pleasantly discovered. Her lush accompaniments alone were enough to garner a spark of life from a dead man found after a hundred years frozen stiff under the ice at the North Pole. Now, no matter what, when, or why, she never left him wanting.

In the excruciating time he sat alone in her living room, debating the many reasons why he would be an idiot for leaving a woman like her, he changed his mind several times. But after the stirring memory of her standing in front of him, gownless, faded, he always came back to the same tough decision. The picture of Mike and Toni dying alone was stronger than the future of love and happiness he foresaw with Trisha.

He had read the books on that terrible disease and clearly foresaw the horror of their tomorrows. Their future was a cruel series of trips into the pits of hell and back. Hope was the mirage that danced just out of the reach of AIDS sufferers—until one after another of the many viruses and diseases, most humans resisted every day, slammed them down to reality.

They would need someone to be there, he resolved—maybe not tomorrow, but soon. How could he deny them, he thought, debating the facts as he saw them, when he had the rest of his life and they only have a few years? He had hoped to explain that fact to the beautiful, angry woman just beyond her bedroom door.

When David finally heard the door to the bedroom unlock, and he turned to see his lady emerge. Trisha was wearing jean shorts covered by one of his shirts. Her hair was combed back off her face in a ponytail, and she was made up as if she was going out. She looked fantastic, all but the look in her eyes.

"Tee, are you all right?" David asked, standing as she approached. "I was sitting here, trying to find the right words to—"

"That's not necessary, honey," she said, cutting off his apology. "I've gotten most of that hurt out of my system."

David tried to speak, but she motioned for him to wait.

"I don't pretend to understand why you would leave me, but I'm convinced you think you're doing the right thing by your friends, and I hate—but respect that. I've come to realize you are a good person, David Jackson. Wanting you all to myself, while others are suffering, I realize is selfish. When I was in there, packing my clothes to leave town, I realized you are the kind of man I would want to care that much about me if I got sick. After all, we've shared the last year, I know you love me. When I walked down the steps in my parent's house and saw you in their kitchen, I knew that what we have is special. I believe in you, David Jackson, but I'm just hurt you could toss that away so easily."

"Wait—"

"Let me finish," she said, walking up to him and cutting him off with a hand to his lips. "Like most women, I figured, if I could make enough passionate love to my man, he couldn't bear to leave me. Stupid, yes, desperate to keep you—yes. Looking back, honey, I'm kind of glad all the sex didn't change your mind because it would be the only thing keeping you here, and you can get that from any woman. When you return—" Trisha lowered her head and then walked over and looked out the window. "I'm going to try and wait for you, David," she said and then turned around and faced him. "Don't think I've come to understand you. I haven't. But like you said earlier, what choice do I have? I like the way I feel around you, and I don't want that to end. I've never felt this way about anyone. I thought I loved a couple of men before, but no one has ever reached this far into my heart."

The look on her face told him more than her words ever could. Again, her tale-tale bottom lip began to tremble noticeably, and those big brown eyes started to water. He could see she was trying to be strong.

The words he knew she wanted to hear made it to his lips but—

"Trisha, I didn't come to this decision easily. I know I'm risking losing your love, and that scares the hell out of me. But I'm sure of one thing. It would always haunt me, haunt our relationship, if I didn't try to help them. It would be like another love standing between us. And don't blame them because they fought me for days on this. They only agreed when I vowed to find them wherever they went. Don't ask me why. I don't know the why myself, I just sense this is the right thing for me to do." David sat down on the couch and placed his head in his hands.

Trisha walked over and sat down beside him. "Then that's enough for me," she said.

She pulled his hands down from his face and gently kissed him. There was none of the fire in her kiss that he was accustomed to. She had become the best kisser he had ever known. This time, there wasn't any message in their lip exchange, unless the fact that there wasn't a message was a message. David wasn't sure anymore.

He stayed the night as they talked more about what his plans were. They didn't make love again, neither was in the mood with what was between them. It was difficult for Trisha, but she started to feel a part of what he was trying to accomplish as he opened up to her about his fears. There was a real taste of sincerity in the concerns he expressed. Had that been her sister, she would have done the same thing, she thought, but she didn't acknowledge it to David.

Trisha felt a twinge of jealously as he elaborated in detail his love and concern for them, but the depth of his feelings for his friends impressed her. She could see that having his love was something special. He was something very special.

Trisha understood what drove David, but she felt no particular affection for Toni or Mike. She still blamed them somewhat for David leaving. But it was obvious to her that David cared deeply for them, and she cared deeply for him. Caring for someone that much was a strong emotion, she was learning, that could sometimes be very painful to understand and live with. But the wonderful rewards made it worth every moment.

He promised, with a frown on his face when she asked, to not leave without seeing her first. "Never!"

CHAPTER 35

W ould you like me to drive?"

"No, I'm good." Mike politely refused David's offer to drive the long, bus-looking motorhome. "I'm feeling great," Mike told him, "and I want to get used to the handling of this bulky vehicle."

David watched Mike closely as he turned onto the Parkway West, heading for the Pennsylvania Turnpike. He was pleasantly surprised with the ease that Mike maneuvered the bulky vehicle down some of the narrow Pittsburgh streets and on to the ramp leading to the Parkway. He was good, David had to admit. What David didn't know was Mike had driven the vehicle around town every day for the last week to get use to how it handled. Within a few days, he was operating it like a pro. Convinced Mike could handle it, David relaxed in the co-pilot's seat. Toni was seated at the table in the middle of the motorhome. She appeared content to let them drive and was talking on the phone to someone. From the apologetic look on her face they guessed it was Brenda.

David looked out at the homes that whistled by as the recreational vehicle got up to speed. There was an undeniable sadness in the mission he had chosen. He felt as if he was splitting apart as the distance away from Trisha increased. It was something he had to do, he reaffirmed almost every mile they traveled. Fate had dictated that he join his friends on this haphazard adventure. *Who knows?* he pondered as Mike swerved to pass a slow-moving little red car. *We may be back long before we planned.*

Try as he might, David felt little or no reassurance that would happen. The truth was, he accepted the distinctly frightening possibility that his relationship with Trisha could be over. That morbid thought prompted another look out the window as the last of

Pittsburgh's neighborhoods raced past. When he looked up, he saw the Edgewood exit approaching.

Toni put the phone down and looked over at David. She knew he was going along reluctantly, and there was something occupying his thoughts, other than this trip. It had to be either Brenda or that new girl tugging at him. His perpetual smile had disappeared the moment they climbed into the motorhome. Toni closed her eyes for a moment. The journey they had chosen was difficult on everyone. The momentary respite, as she heard them up front laughing, was comforting.

She again looked over at David. They had to do something to give him back his life. She had told Mike that last night. He had agreed, but couldn't think of how to accomplish that. Toni did feel a sense of comfort as she watched Mike and David talking. She had to admit it felt great having both of them along. David's argument, about them needing him should they get sick, was an invalid reason for him to accompany them. But she was glad to have him here because he was a delight to be around, and she loved him so much.

"What did your parents say about your leaving, Mike?"

It was still a touchy subject with Mike, but he answered him. "I called them three days ago and haven't heard from them since. They were cold about it when I told them about our plans, but voiced no reservations," he said, looking quickly over at his friend as he drove, "to the eccentric journey we are about to undertake. They did wish me well but said nothing about how they felt about our trip or my leaving. I couldn't sleep much last night thinking about them," he revealed, shaking his head.

"If you're tired, Mike, I'll drive."

"No, I'm fine," Mike answered his friend. "I finally got to sleep around three and slept till ten. So you see," he grinned, "I probably got more sleep than you did."

David just shrugged his shoulders at his taunting and then quietly looked out the window at the traffic slowing in front of them. Mike was right about one thing. He had gotten little sleep last night. Trisha had made "goodbye" love to him on three different occasions, each occurring only minutes after he had won an hour long struggle to finally get back to asleep while holding her in his arms. For some reason, he wasn't sleepy now. Drained, yes, he thought, recalling her creative imagination in bed and the strength of their enthusiasm, but not sleepy.

David told her he loved her as they hugged, and then he walked out her door. She handled everything just great, he proudly recalled. When he turned around to get a last look at her, she was standing in her doorway waving at him. The wind blew her thin, white nightshirt pressing it against her lithe figure. Trisha's hair danced around her head as if it was caressing and soothing her, knowing the pain his departure was causing and wanting to comfort her. He recalled that she looked stunning standing in that doorway and it was a picture he feared, as he got into the cab, that might plague his dreams forever.

As they drove along the highway, Toni shared with them how tough it was to say goodbye to Brenda and how much they all cried and the promise to stay in touch. Brenda's great idea to install a computer in the motorhome and get on the Internet with the mobile phone line would offer them the chance to email messages when they couldn't reach each other by phone. David found the last minute installation in the motorhome was easier than they thought. When they stopped for the night, they would test the "Net."

The discussion never approached the subject of Toni's father. The pain on her face, the last time she had shared the problems she was having with her dad, guaranteed neither David or Mike was going to bring up the subject again.

Anthony DiNardo wanted his daughter to stay home and undergo treatment. Her desire to shirk responsibility, he told her, and drive around the country like a bum with these two losers was totally unacceptable to him. They argued for hours before he finally gave her his blessing. It was a small act by her father, but it was deeply appreciated by his daughter.

Toni and Mike were teasing David about the sleeping arrangements—which hand would he be sleeping with now that he was alone—when he turned on the radio to drown them out.

"Hold it, knuckleheads. Is that...yeah, that's my song," he said as he turned up the radio to listen to "The First Time Ever I Saw Your Face" by Roberta Flack.

The song seemed to lift David's spirits, Toni and Mike both noticed, as his hands played out the words, and he performed in his seat as if he was on stage singing. He continued singing the song, and quite well, long after it was over. It was clear it meant a lot to him, and some of the words touched her. She made a mental note to buy that song. She tried in vain to remember the artist, but she would never forget the title.

Mike pulled the motor coach over to the side of the road as they approached the Pennsylvania Turnpike entrance.

"Well, guys, decision number two, which way do we go, east or west?"

"East," Toni said.

"West," David countered, of course, just to pull her chain.

Toni mumbled something.

"East it is then," Mike laughingly said.

The turnpike east went through Harrisburg and on toward Philadelphia and the East Coast. The turnpike west carried you toward Pittsburgh, Cleveland, and points west. They had planned to travel west, eventually. The only question was whether to go directly there or see some of the rest of the country on the way. They had opted earlier to see as much of the country as they could. David knew that, but just had to disagree with whatever opinion Toni had. He also voiced a mild objection to delaying their opportunity for treatment on the West Coast. He quickly capitulated as they ignored him and enthusiastically planed the sights they wanted to see along the way. It was decided they would head east to visit New York City, and maybe Boston, and then work their way south to Washington DC. Toni only had one place they would *have* to stop at to return an item to someone special.

It was a couple of hours on the turnpike when Toni shouted from the rear of the motorhome where she was laying down reading. "Hey, guys, I'm starving for a hamburger." She had gotten a little carsick and had taken refuge on the bed shortly after they entered the PA turnpike.

"Poor timing, sweets," Mike volunteered, "we just passed the New Stanton exit. If you can hold off, we'll be at the Somerset exit soon. They have every restaurant you can imagine there."

"That will be fine with me, Mike. I don't want to be a bother."

"Since when?" someone shouted.

"Up yours, Jackson," the hungry woman said to the smart

mouthed commentator and went back to her novel.

Toni awoke as the slowing motion of her chariot tossed her forward. She found her paperback on the floor where it fell when she dozed off. A toll booth appeared in the front window of the motorhome. Good, she thought while sitting up. Finally, she could get something to eat.

"Toni, we're here," she heard David calling to her.

"Yes, I see that. Thank God. I'm hungry enough to eat a horse." She heard words and then laughter passing between the two front riders. "Okay, smart asses, what are you laughing about now?"

"Nut-in, honey," Mike answered, still giggling, "David just called me Secretariat."

Toni shook her head. "You wish," she whispered, making a mental note to watch what she said when riding with boys.

Mike drove the motorhome up to a McDonald's. He knew this was Toni's favorite fast-food restaurant. At least their fries were her favorite.

"Is this okay, sweetheart?"

"You know I love their French Fries. But I'll eat wherever you guys want."

David read his cue. "Oh, this is fine with me. Junk food is junk food." He reached above his head and took a tablet down from behind the sun visor. "I'll take the orders."

Toni didn't wait for them to offer for her to be first. She knew that they would have insisted anyway. "I'll have a Big Mac, a large order of fries with ketchup, and a chocolate milk shake."

David looked up at her with a snide look on his face. Toni braced for the expected commentary.

"There goes your girlie figure."

"Davey, you know where you can put the hottest of those fries, don't you?"

"Sssssh, Mike will hear you. He doesn't know yet how kinky you are."

The same Mike was ignoring them as he turned into the back parking lot, circled, and skillfully backed the large vehicle into a space, taking up four or five parking spaces. He had nothing to say to either of them, having grown accustomed to the usually playful verbal battles between his lover and best friend. The truth was he would have been surprised if they didn't pick on each other. This time, however, his mind was somewhere else. He was busy thinking about another more important and difficult decision he had to make. What to eat was easy. Voices of doubt were condemning him before he sinned. He found the last few miles to be very disturbing. David's unexpected transformation from sullen and morose to happy and outgoing again made what he was thinking more damnable.

"Mike."

"Huh?"

"Mike, what do you want to eat?" David asked him. "Are you all right, buddy?"

"Yeah, I'm fine. I'll have what Toni ordered, okay?"

"That's fine with me. I'll probably get the same only with a strawberry shake."

When Mike reached into his pocket for the money, he heard a door opening and looked back to see David frowning at him as he exited the motorhome.

Toni came up and took David's seat in the front of the motorhome. Silently, they sat and watched as David walked toward the restaurant. When Toni looked away, she found Mike staring at her. Unspoken words passed between them until she closed her eyes. Other than the person seated next to them, there wasn't anyone the two of them loved more than the black man going to get their orders. The time they had spent together with him had been the most rewarding and fulfilling period of their lives. Each understood that only their love for the other rivaled what they felt for him, and just his being here spoke volumes about what he thought of them.

"Are you ready, Toni?"

She looked at her best friend and lover but couldn't say the words. When Mike first suggested this as an option, her guilt was almost more than she could bear, but it was their only choice. Toni closed her eyes and then nodded her head in the affirmative.

CHAPTER 36

David walked into the fast food restaurant, hoping it wasn't as crowed as the lot full of cars indicated. The three lines of hungry people, extending almost to the door, dashed his hopes.

He turned to leave and almost bumped into a woman entering.

"Excuse me," he said to the lovely woman blocking the door.

"Boy, I didn't think it would be this crowed."

David turned and looked from the young woman to the people in the crowded restaurant. "Yes, I didn't think so either. I was going to leave, but I guess I'll stay."

"Well, what line should we get in?"

"What?" For a moment he forgot the question as he looked into her eyes. *I know her*, he immediately thought. He waited for her to show some indications she knew him. Only the suddenly odd look on her face prompted him into action. "Ah, how about that one?" he said, pointing to the middle line. "I think it's the shortest."

"I guess we should get in that line then," she told him. "I sure hope you're right. I'm starving."

He smiled stupidly at her and then took another inventory on the shortest line. He wasn't hitting on her, he reluctantly admitted, just stating a fact.

When she stood there looking at him, David finally realized what she wanted. He stepped aside and offered her to lead the way. She nodded thank you.

"Where are you headed?" she asked, after realizing none of the lines of hungry people were moving very quickly.

"Excuse me?" David said when he turned from looking around the restaurant at the people eating.

"I asked, where are you headed?" she repeated, seemingly determined to get an answer. "I'm guessing just about everyone in here is just passing through."

He looked around again at the variety of people in the restaurant. They appeared to encompass all the races and age groups. Two cute young women, seated at a corner table in the rear, made eye contact with him and smiled every time he looked in their direction. She was probably right, David figured, about him passing through, anyway.

"Where am I headed? My friends and I are planning on seeing the country for the next year in a motorhome." He knew that would stir her interest.

She turned around as if to allow that bit of information to percolate, and it took her longer than he had expected for a woman's curiosity to ferment.

As she moved forward in line, he gave her a quick once over. She was a lady of color standing about five-foot-seven, he figured, and maybe 130 pounds. She was full figured and very shapely with long straight black hair that reached past her shoulders. She wore a blue jeans skirt and jacket with a white blouse underneath. *She is a nice-looking woman*, he decided as he moved up in line behind her.

"I'm on my way to Pittsburgh," she said proudly as they moved closer to the counter. "I got a gig at The Comedy Club there,"

"What a small world. We're from Pittsburgh. Wait, did you say you're a comedian?" The unbelieving tone of his voice was obvious.

Her feathers ruffled, she turned around and faced him with her hands on her hips, her head tilted to one side. The frown on her face was self-explanatory.

"Don't get me wrong," he quickly interjected, "I'm surprised because you are too good looking to be funny. No, that's not what I meant. I—I meant most guys would be too busy putting their tongues back in their mouths to laugh." He hoped that he had given her ego enough praise to hold back the verbal beating he expected she was about to unleash on him for his chauvinism.

"I'm also very humorous," she said, accepting his apology and his flattering commentary.

"I bet you are. Even if you're not, with your looks, and

brains," he added for insurance, "you'll be successful at whatever endeavor you undertake."

The wide grin on her face indicated to him he was out of her doghouse. David watched the smiling woman turn around wondering to himself how he could have gotten into trouble so quickly with a woman he just met.

They were close to being waited on when she grew tired of the boredom and started talking again with the handsome guy behind her.

"Are you with that motorhome that was parked out back?" she asked. "You did say you were riding in a motorhome, right?"

"Were you talking to me?" David asked her after looking down from the overhead menu and wondering if he wanted to change his order.

"Yes, I thought you might have been with the couple I saw in that blue motorhome parked outside, but you couldn't have been."

"No, you were right the first time. I'm traveling with two of my close friends in that big blue and white motorhome parked behind this building." David pointed toward the back of the restaurant. He smiled proudly at her and was puzzled by the confused look on her face.

"I might be wrong, but there was only one of those recreational vehicles in the parking lot when I pulled up. It drove right past me as I was walking toward the building. It might seem strange, but the woman sitting in the passenger seat waved as they drove past. I thought maybe I knew them, so I turned and watched them drive out the rear of the parking lot and turn left, heading for the turnpike ramp, I'm guessing."

David looked at her for a moment before her words sank in. The "it can't be them," thoughts delayed his response for a couple of heartbeats. Finally, when the truth reached out and touched him, he was suddenly overcome by a horrible feeling that this crazy woman might be telling the truth.

"Excuse me," he said, getting out of the line.

"Sure," she answered as she watched him rush out the side door, bumping into the people trying to enter. The look on his face gave her chills. She had a feeling that it was his friends she saw leaving, and, for some crazy reason, they had tricked him so they could slip away. Why would they do that to him? she wondered. Where they playing some kind of joke on him? He didn't look like he was dangerous or anything. *Well, he did look kind of—stop it, girl*, she admonished the thoughts she was thinking about that cute guy.

છ૭છ૭

The sour taste in David's mouth was nothing compared to the way his stomach was tossing and turning. The run along the side of the building was suddenly happening in slow motion. His feet felt like they weighed a ton, and he could hear himself breathing as he ran. Fear overwhelmed him, and he'd already lost faith that they would be there when he finally reached the back of the building.

The expanse of cars in the large back parking lot spread out in his view. As David got his bearings, he knew it was gone. He stopped running and took a slower assessment of the vehicles in the parking lot. The fact that the huge motor home would have been immediately visible was momentarily forgotten in the panic he was enduring.

David turned in a circle then ran around to the other side of the building in search of his friends. He wasn't frightened for himself—one way or another he would make it home—he was hurting for another reason. Two people he loved and trusted had lied to him. No, he told himself, that couldn't be it. They went to get gas or something. That had to be it. Or—or they decided they wanted something else to eat, yeah. He ran to the front of the building and searched up and down the streets for his friends.

છ૭છ૭

Monica Tresivant paid for her food and found a small table near a window. She was putting sugar in her coffee when she looked outside and spotted the guy who was in line behind her standing on the sidewalk in front of the restaurant looking around for something. Caught up in his predicament, she accidentally spilled some of her hot coffee on her skirt. "Shit! That's hot," she said, without taking her eyes off him. When he stopped pacing and stood there with his head down, she took that moment to put the cream in her coffee.

Just as the young girl behind the counter asked, she changed her mind about the hamburger, fries, warm apple pie, and cold soft drink she wanted. Vivid memories of her battle to put on a pair of jeans she wanted to purchase before she lost those twelve pounds dieting flashed in her mind. Now she was glad she didn't have all that food to eat. The soap opera happening in front of her was far more exciting.

e⁄ɔe⁄ɔ

David checked out every truck-looking vehicle he could see. The restaurant was set on a hill and offered an excellent view of all the main streets in this small way-stop off the turnpike. Various other fast food restaurants, two gas stations, and a mini mall were all spread out before him as he stood on the sidewalk and looked desperately for his friends.

"We've got to go back and get him," Mike said after seeing his friend's frantic search for them.

Toni turned around and looked up at him. The pangs of regret were chiseled on his distraught face. His eyes were locked on the man pacing in front of the distant restaurant. It was Mike's idea, when they noticed they could see the restaurant from the ramp, to stop and make sure he was okay.

Mike started to move toward the motorhome when Toni placed both hands on his chest. "Mike, we can't. David will never get on with his life as long as we're all together. You know he won't. He loves us too much to let us go, and we have to love him too much to let him stay."

Mike gently removed her hands and walked closer to the edge of the road. From their vantage point along the highway ramp, they could look across the small valley below them and see the parking lot on the far hill where they'd snookered David. They were sadly watching when he ran out of the restaurant and around the back of the building looking for them. Mike recalled hearing a shaken Toni say, "Oh, my God."

"Sweetheart, I know you're right. What we're doing is the best thing for him. I don't want him to see us when this cursed disease reduces us to skin and bones. But I can't hurt him like this Toni, *I can't,*" he groaned. Mike put his fingers in his mouth and bit down hard on them—the pain a kind of spanking for abandoning his closest friend, his only brother.

"Mike." Toni moved in front of the man looking across at their friend. "Remember how we both jumped the gun and turned on each other. Our actions hurt the person we loved the most. We let those emotions almost ruin our lives and waste some of the precious time we have remaining. We can't let our love for David drag him into the mess we made for ourselves and waste his life. He's no Mother Teresa. He didn't receive a Divine call to nurse us when we get sick. He has his own life to screw up."

When Mike took another few steps toward valley below, Toni walked up behind Mike and hugged him as he watched David pacing along the sidewalk. He couldn't read David's face at that distance, but the frantic way he was looking up and down the street was a map easily read.

✌✍✌

Toni, how could you let Mike do this to me? David questioned. There was an emptiness in his heart so deep that it seemed unfillable. He felt betrayed by the two people he would have given his life for. *Mike,* he questioned as he continued to search the street for them, *how could you drive off like that?*

They must have left through the alley behind the parking lot because he would have seen them leaving he figured. That meant their departure was intentional. They could have come into McDonald's and told him if they changed their minds about their food choice. He felt he at least deserved the chance to say good-bye to them. If they didn't want him to come along, they could have just said so.

David walked to the edge of the sidewalk and looked down the road again. He had been pacing the sidewalk for the last ten minutes and saw no sign of them. If they were going for gas or something, he knew they would have returned by now. They were gone. One slow walk around the building confirmed it.

The space the motorhome was parked in when he last saw it, looked like a cold and barren grave. The empty space reflecting how he felt inside. David walked over and stood where he last saw his friends.

A sadness, that wracked his spirit, rose up, threatening to crush him. He took some slow, deep breaths but it didn't work. His eyes started to water. He felt abandoned and unloved. He had a strange thought, as cars, trucks, and people moved past him unnoticed. The ground where they parked should be marked in white chalk because that's where their friendship was murdered.

"Sir, excuse me. Excuse me."

David turned around and tried to find the source of the nagging voice when it was repeated. It took a moment before he saw the opened window of a station wagon. It was parked three spaces over from where the motorhome had been parked. It was the arm waving a white envelope in the air that first caught his attention. He walked over toward the car.

"Hello, ah, the woman in the camper that was parked beside us asked me to give this to you when you came out," the female driver explained as he walked up to her car window. He looked in the car and saw a middle-aged woman and two young kids in the back seat. "Are you David Jackson," she asked? "That's the name on the envelope."

David looked around again before he nodded yes.

"My kids said they thought it was you running around the building, but I wasn't sure." She handed the envelope to him. "The nice lady paid for our lunch and asked me to put it in the mail if we couldn't wait for you." David looked at the envelope and saw it also had his address written on it.

"Thank you for waiting," he told her as sincerely as he could.

She smiled up at him. "No problem. I guess they noticed that we were eating in the car and figured we would still be here because these rug-rats would take forever to finish."

He could see the questions written on her face. He wanted to tell her what his *friends* had done but didn't. "Thank you again."

"No problem."

David stepped back when he heard their car start up. The two small kids looked up at him as the car drove past. Stoned faced, he returned their wave goodbye and watched as their car rounded the building. It only stopped a moment before pulling out into traffic.

David looked at the envelope in his hands as he walked around to the front of the restaurant. He knew what was written inside, but their sorry apologies carried no weight with him anymore. In anger, he ripped the envelope in half and threw it in the air.

He hated Mike for loving the woman he loved and choosing her over him. He hated Toni, he decided, for inducing him to care so much for her and then coldly sneaking away. Sure, he was angry, he thought to himself as he watched the wind blow the halves of the envelope around the parking lot, very angry. But even in the throes of that anger, he knew he could never really hate them.

"Take care of yourselves," he whispered into that swirling wind. "All I wanted to do was just take care of you." He looked up at the sky and, ignoring those walking past, screamed at the top of his voice, *"That's all I wanted to do!"*

The pain returned, and he wanted to feel the rage of hate again, but couldn't. There's no way he could ever hate Mike or Toni. Yes, they had dropped him off without even saying good-bye, but he knew there was nothing they could do to make him hate them, nothing!

⁋ʒ⁋ʒ

One of the people looking out the restaurant windows finished the last of her coffee, stood up, and readied herself for the final drive to Pittsburgh and her interview at the Comedy Club. If everything went as planned, she would be one of the new comedians that they featured the first Friday of every month. She also had a possible gig in Cleveland in two weeks, so either way she was stuck in the "Burg" for a while.

Just then, out of the corner of her eye, she caught that handsome guy who was in line with her walking past the window momentarily derailing her train of thought. Monica felt a strange curiosity as she observed him. She sat down again and watched as he picked up a piece of paper, no an envelope and opened it. She observed as he read what looked like a letter. He was standing only a few feet away from her on the other side of the tinted glass as she looked out the window, but he never seemed to notice he was being watched. If he did, he gave no indications of caring one way or another.

☙❧

There it is, David thought when he spotted the second half of the envelope on the grass. He picked it up and removed the other torn section of the letter from the envelope. The wave of emotions had waned, and he was ready to read the excuses his friends would give for treating him so cruelly. He put the two pieces together and read the letter.

> *Dear David,*
> *First of all, please forgive us for what we did. I know you, and I'm sure you're upset with us.*

David recognized Toni's fluid script right away.

> *What we did was done because of how much we love you. I know you can't see that now, but you will. Every time you see the pitiful stories of people dying of AIDS, you will understand that two people that love you very much didn't want that burden put on you. Sure, you would have taken great care of us. We don't doubt that for a second. But, David, that's not what we want for our best friend. Mike is hurting about it, but he agrees with me. I'm writing this because if you're going to hate someone, I don't want it to be Mike. I'm positive we are doing the right thing, Mike's not as sure.*
> *David, I'm responsible for both of us getting infected. I don't know who gave it to me or when, but I'm convinced now that I gave it to Mike. What a joke, huh? I left him when it was I who was the immoral slut. I'm getting off the subject again, huh? It's getting tough to write between the tears.*
> *David, take care of yourself, baby, and don't waste your life trying to find us. If I find out you are, trust me, we will disappear forever. We know how you feel about*

us, Davey. We thank God every day for your love. Our prayers are that you will learn from our mistakes and live a full life. Never forget us and know we won't forget you. Neither will we forget what we meant to each other. Be as happy for us as we are for you.

We can be reached through our email, don't forget that. Mike told me more about your feelings for Trisha. I always thought Brenda was the perfect woman for you, but I could be wrong. (You know I'll never admit that).

Find out, Davey. I'm sure you will enjoy trying. (Smile).

Goodbye, my love. We left something under your pillow, take it and enjoy your life. You will never know how much I do love you or how hard it was to do what we did.

David, Mike wants me to tell you, he loves you, man.(Smile) That is all he can say, David, I think he's hurting too much. Well, until we meet again, see ya.

With more love than you will ever know,
Toni and Mike.

David read it again. He started to put it away and stopped to read it again. Then he shook his head, folded it up, and put it into his pocket. It was everything he would have expected from them. He started to feel a little guilty about his anger. He knew his insistence on going with them was the spark that prompted this radical move on their part.

David bowed his head and said goodbye to his friends.

ɕ∕ɔɕ∕ɔ

Monica watched him re-read the letter and put it in his pocket. Whatever it said, she gathered, had caused him to lower his head when he was finished. She felt some empathy for the handsome stranger. How he must be hurting. For the first time, she took a minute to scrutinize him. She had already established that he was a very handsome guy, she had noticed that, and was the reason she spoke to him while standing in line. And he's built like he could really take care of a woman. she had also noticed that while standing with him in that line.

He was dressed in nice khaki shorts that displayed his muscular legs and wore a form-fitting white Steelers football jersey with what she gathered was his name on the back. He had a khaki baseball cap on his head that matched his shorts. Powerfully chiseled arms added to her estimate of the man standing outside the window. He looked very athletic and she so loved that in a man. She liked them to be sweet, but look dangerous, she used to tell her girlfriends.

He had light tan-colored features and sparkling brown eyes. The guy looked both masculine and intelligent. But was that reason enough to possibly risk offering him a ride back to Pittsburgh if he really was stranded? Naw, she thought, not quite enough to risk my life giving rides to strangers. *He could really be dangerous*, she tried convincing the growing urge to get involved, *maybe that's why they left him. No, I'm staying out of other people's problems this time.*

There were a few of her own difficulties that the great opportunity to perform at The Comedy Club caused her to leave behind. One was a possessive boyfriend who couldn't handle a strongly opinionated woman. Numerous arguments and his attempt to slap her around ended her stay in the nation's capital and almost ended his chauvinistic life. He did, however, get her point when she put the same gun that was in her purse in his mouth. The tears he cried for her not to kill him she felt were sincere, as was her threat to end him if he ever touched her again.

⌘⌘⌘

David looked up at the late afternoon sky and took a deep cleansing breath. *Okay*, he thought, *let's get on with life. Life without Toni and Mike, maybe Trisha or Brenda can fill the void*, he wondered as he looked around for a bus station. It was only a blur when he saw it, but something on the far hill caught his attention. David squeezed his eyes tightly shut and looked again. Between the trees on a distant hill was something white. Then he felt his knees go weak, and he would have fallen had he moved. The dizziness lasted for only a moment. His legs fought the wave of nausea that gripped them, and they held him upright, but barely.

It was them. David knew it. He could just make out two people standing beside what looked like the motorhome. He was ecstatic. They'd come back for him. The weakness he felt turned quickly into exhilaration. They came back for him, he repeated as he walked across the street without looking out for traffic, toward the distant hillside.

David tried to find a road that led up to the top of that hill. He found one but decided, however, that his best bet was to just walk directly across a mall parking lot and then climb up that hill. The road he saw would have taken him a mile out of the way. That would be all right by car, but not on foot.

He'd known they would come back for him, David told the voices of doubt and started running toward the hill that he hoped had a path that would lead up to where his friends were waiting. There was a long mall parking lot at the base of the hill that separated him from that overlook.

The two people on that hill watched in shock as he ran down the road toward the mall below.

℮⁓℮⁓

Monica picked up her purse and shrugged her shoulders. Those days of dealing with stupid men behind her, she vowed. But after breaking it off and nearly shooting her asshole of a former boyfriend, Monica questioned if maybe that made her negative, and she was making a mistake not using this opportunity to get to know a good-looking brother. "No, Monica, enough with men. It's time for you to concentrate on your career," she whispered.

She put her empty cup on her tray and took one last look out the window at the stranded traveler. That's when she noticed something strange. The handsome guy was staring attentively at something on the distant hillside. She put down the tray, moved closer to the window, and searched for the object of his attention. It took a minute, but she was able to make out what she thought was a camper, or whatever they were called, parked on the top of a distant hill. Two people appeared to be standing beside it looking in this direction. She watched as the "brother" walked across the street and continued staring in the direction of the camper. Was that them, and if it was, what were they up to? Surely they weren't cruel enough to toy with him like that.

Monica could feel herself becoming protective of the poor guy. She watched in shock as he started to run toward the camper. "Don't," she shouted in the crowded restaurant. Monica swore. She noticed, as she picked up her purse, that she was the object of some of the patrons' attention. She rolled her eyes at them and hurried toward the door.

↶↷↶

"My God, Toni, he's running this way. David's coming after us."

Toni spun around and felt her heart about to explode in her chest when she spotted him. She took a step backward, and her hands formed a shield over all of her face except her eyes. David's response had caught her off-guard. She fought the rising need to run down the hill and jump into his strong arms and beg him to forgive them. "No, this isn't right. Come on, Mike," Toni pleaded as she grabbed his arm, "we've got to leave."

"*What*? No way!" Mike shouted as he watched his friend's frantic race to catch up with them. David would be very angry with them, but he would quickly get over it, Mike told himself. "We can't leave him, not again. I can't hurt him again. You can go, Toni, but I'm staying."

"Mike, listen to what you're saying," she scolded him as she grabbed him by the shirt. "You're going to commit David to a life of serving you as your nurse. Wiping your ass. Is that what you want for him, really? Huh? Ask yourself that. Because when he gets here, I won't be able to say no to him either. I love him as much as you do. I don't want that sweet man to spend maybe the next five or ten years of his life changing my diaper. He would gladly do it to because that's that type of person he is."

Mike looked at Toni and knew in his heart that she was telling him the truth. He looked sadly down at David. He had run half way across the parking lot.

"Mike," Toni softly called to him.

Mike was torn between duty and the man who had stuck by him through everything. David was the only other human being to ever love him unconditionally. Toni had left him, his parents had set him adrift, but David—the man racing between parked cars to reach him—had never once let him down.

"Please, Mike, please!" Toni begged, her heart breaking.

Tears ran down his face as he knew what he must do, what he had to do. He felt Toni tugging at him and now crying hysterically. "It's okay, baby, you're right," he said as he grabbed her trembling hands in his. "Come on, get aboard. We don't have much time. He will be up here in a couple of minutes."

❧❧❧

When Monica got outside, she ran to the curb and spotted the good looking brother running across the parking lot of a strip mall. She debated going to her car or watching him and seeing what transpired. Her curiosity about what the good looking brother was doing won out.

"No! You bastards. Don't you leave him again! That's not funny!" Monica raised a clinched fist and shouted toward the hillside.

She saw that as David reached the base of the hill, located at the end of the strip mall, he couldn't see the two running for the camper. She knew why and cursed them for the carrot they hung out to the poor fool now climbing blindly up the hill. She wanted to shoot them or something. "How could you treat your friend like that?" she shouted again. "How could you?" Monica turned and walked to her car, cursing them.

❧❧❧

David was out of breath but couldn't stop. Salvation was at the crest of this darn hill. He grabbed hold to branches and weeds, anything he could to pull himself up the hill. He was only about thirty feet from reaching the top, he figured, when he stopped and doubled over as a sharp pain pierced his side. He had to rest for a moment. He grabbed hold of a tree and steadied himself. He wouldn't be mad at them, he decided between breaths.

He understood why they did it this way. Who knows? Maybe he should have let them go and live their life like they wanted. That was what he'd do, he resolved as the pain subsided. Just stick around for a while until they were comfortable.

David felt he had gotten his second wind as he started climbing again a few moments later. After getting his bearings, he moved a little to his right and saw an opening in the trees. The sound of passing traffic gave him the strength to push on. He broke through the tree line and saw that the road was another ten-foot climb up another hill.

David ran through some tall grass, tripped over something, and fell to the ground. He groaned as his knee hit something hard. Ignoring the pain, he was quickly up and running again. As he cleared the hill, he saw the motorhome a hundred feet farther up the road than he figured it would be.

Mike drove slowly. His reason being he needed to make sure David was all right. All right to him meant seeing David reach the roadside. Mike didn't consider the pain it would cause his buddy to see them driving away. He just wanted to know David was safe.

Toni searched the woods in her mirror for David. As far away as they were, he would have to be exhausted by the time he reached the road. "Come on, David, where are you?"

"There he is!" Mike shouted.

He almost swerved onto the shoulder of the road as he watched David run into view in his mirror. Mike heard Toni sigh with relief as he appeared all right from that long run. She turned around in her seat, put her face in her lap, and cried.

Mike watched painfully as his friend waved at him to come back. What he saw next would forever be one of his most painful regrets. "No, David, stop!" Mike screamed at the haunting reflection in the mirror, "Don't do that."

Toni heard Mike shout David's name and sat up. "What's—the—matter, Mike?"

He didn't answer her but kept looking from the road to his mirror. When she looked herself, what she saw took the last of her strength. David was running after them. The only thing that stopped her from jumping out the motorhome was Mike had picked up speed as he raced away from the image in his mirror. "Stop, Mike!"

"No, honey, it's too late for that now."

ℰ⁄ↄℰ⁄ↄ

David spotted the motorhome and suddenly realized that it was moving away from him. "Mike, wait! I'm over here. Mike, Toni, wait!" he shouted at the top of his voice. He ran out into the middle of the road and started frantically waving his hands. "Mike," he shouted again, "look back, buddy, I'm here."

He realized they couldn't hear him and, in a few minutes, they would reach the crest of the road and be gone forever. He started running faster. There was little left in his legs after his run and climb, but he ran anyway. The old pain returned after a few steps, but he ignored it. His friends were moments away from entering the *Twilight Zone.*

The run up the hill had taken what little breath he had remaining and prevented him from calling out above a whisper now, but still, he called out. He saw the motorhome reach the blue horizon at the top of the hill. For an instant, it was a valued painting, as it rested atop the hill, highlighted by green trees on each side and a blue sky with puffy white clouds above. David stopped running and watched as the *Twilight Zone* swallowed up his friends. Only the blue sky and trees remained at the crest of the road—and silence. It was if nature, stunned by the cruelness of the act playing out before it, inhaled the sounds and stopped the wind in shock.

ℰ⁄ↄℰ⁄ↄ

Sorrow held them in a vise-like grip as they watched their friend disappear behind the summit of the hill they had driven over. Toni heard Mike say goodbye to David as they drove down toward the turnpike tollbooths. She just stared out the window, hoping the last image they saw would someday fade away.

A pair of brown eyes and blue eyes looked solemnly forward as their lives took a new turn. They watched quietly as the miles ran past, and they neared whatever fate had laid out for them. Tomorrow was already drawn out in the sands of time, and they approached it with a new confidence. It was as if they owed it to someone other than themselves to make the best of what was left of their lives. They didn't need any other reason to live every moment as if it were their last. They were their last. The cruel image of their friend running after them was a lasting icon of where they were, and a powerful reminder of where they were going.

They took strength in the life they had left for him back in Pittsburgh. When he returned home, he would find out that he could do whatever he wanted with his future. The quarter million dollars they had deposited in a bank account in his name would take care of him for a long time. It was half of the money Mike's grandfather had given him as his inheritance. Mike thought it apropos that David got the money because his grandfather hated Black people with a zealous passion.

"He'll be okay," Mike said as Toni got up from her seat.

She leaned over and kissed his cheek as he drove and then made her way to the table. Mike took a quick look back and saw Toni was sitting at the computer. He didn't have to see the screen to know to whom she was writing.

໒ৎ৩

David's chest was heaving as he struggled to catch his breath. It seemed like every muscle in his body ached. He stood in the middle of the road until he heard the loud whine of an approaching truck climbing the hill. He stared at the crest of the hill, half expecting to see the motorhome reappear. The first blast of the truck horn prompted him to give up his dream and walk over to the side of the road. He sat down on the guard rail, put his head in his hands, and rested. There was no reason to move. Life had passed him by. Life was racing along at fifty-five miles per hour in the other direction. Two cars drove past, and one blew its horns at him as he sat, but he ignored it. As another one approached, he didn't bother to look up. The questions that troubled him were a far greater a distraction than any approaching vehicles.

David was sitting on the guard rail, feeling sorry for himself, when he heard music playing. Louder and louder it became until he could just make out the words. It was a Roberta Flack favorite of his. Her words spoke to him this time just like they had in the past, and he couldn't deny their power.

As the music grew louder, he kept his eyes closed and listened as the lyrical words spoke to his hurt. The words were so familiar and powerful, they touched the sadness of his spirit. The coincidence was almost more than he could stand. All of the emotions he felt surged up in his heart. In a burst of enlightenment, he came to understand why the song always moved him so much. Just as he felt the familiar tug of the song's lyrics, it stopped.

"Excuse me, are you all right?"

David was startled. Someone was talking to him. He raised his head and was surprised to see a blue car parked in front of him. He looked up into the eyes of—

"Hi there, remember me? I'm the woman who was standing in front of you back at the McDonald's," the woman in the car said before he could answer. She was taken aback by the hurt she read on his face. The way he just stared, she wasn't sure if he remembered her.

David shook off the funk he was in as her words burnt through the pity. He looked at her and saw it was the lovely comedian from the restaurant. He remembered her. "I'm sorry, yes I do," he said as he stood up and walked to her car. "I was trying to catch my friends." He took a deep breath and pointed up the hill. "And they drove off without seeing me. I was so tired from running I stopped here to…"

Monica began to feel a special bond with this forsaken guy as he talked. Try as she might to resist, she began to sense he was going to become part of her life.

Men who weren't afraid to show their emotions were rare, she thought while she listened to him trying to explain. The redness in his eyes told her far more than words could.

She studied him as she debated revealing that his asshole friends had only stopped to lure him into thinking they were waiting for him. And then drove off only when they noticed their cruel prank worked by taunting him into running in their direction. But what good would that do for him to know that? she questioned.

"Look," she said to the man who was sitting on the guardrail when she pulled up and now was looking in her passenger side window, "my name is Monica, Monica Tresivant. If you want, you can jump in my car, and we probably can catch your friends."

David turned and looked toward the top of the hill. No, he decided to tell her. When he searched the eyes of the kind woman, he wondered why she was getting involved. Was she feeling sorry for him because he was stranded? David knelt down on one knee at the open passenger's side window. "I'm sorry," he apologized. "My name is David Gary Jackson. Glad to meet you Monica Tres..."

"Tresivant, Monica Tresivant."

"Monica Tresivant, sorry for meeting you like this."

"Don't be. I just wanted to offer you some help if you need some."

He began to realize how much this woman risked in stopping to help a stranger. "Thank you for the kind offer. And no, I don't want to chase after my friends. It was wrong for me to try and run their lives. If they ever need me, they'll call. Until then, let them have what time they have left together. But thanks for stopping." He stood up and started walking back down the ramp toward the town of Somerset.

"Where are you going?" she asked, getting out of her car and taking a few steps toward the man limping back down the road. She took a few more steps when he didn't answer or stop. "Hey!"

The guy stopped walking but didn't turn around.

"You're limping, are you all right?"

David turned around and looked back at her standing beside her car. Her concern was welcome and friendly, but he wanted to be alone to think. "I'm okay, Ms. Tresivant. There must be a bus stop back in Somerset that will take me back to Pittsburgh," he said then turned around and starting walking down the road. "I'm going to catch it and go home," he shouted back at her and waved his hand.

Monica watched him walking back the way she had come. "Pittsburgh?" she whispered. "That handsome hunk is headed in the same direction." She shrugged her shoulders and got back into her car. She turned and looked at him again as he limped down the shoulder of the road. *Don't, Monica*, she argued with herself, *what you're thinking of doing is stupid*. She agreed but decided to do it anyway. She suddenly felt a rush of excitement. She always liked to push the envelope a little.

"David Gary Jackson.," She got out of her car again. "Can I offer you a ride? You know I'm headed there."

He took another few steps before stopping. Monica didn't expect what he did next.

David stopped for a minute and then started walking again. He took another few steps and stopped again. He turned around and looked back toward the woman standing beside her car on the side of the road. "Monica, I would love a ride," he shouted above the noise of a passing truck, "but I don't want to be an inconvenience. I could use a ride back down into town to catch my bus if you don't mind. These legs have run out of gas."

"You got it," Monica whispered. She jumped into her car, waited for a vehicle to pass, and then backed down the dangerous road to where he was waiting.

She was driving a late model white and blue Buick regal David noticed. The back seat was full of her clothes, neatly folded. David got in and buckled up. He looked over at the beaming driver. He felt a little better. Maybe things were working out like they were meant to, he thought.

On the long drive back to Pittsburgh, after he was tricked by another driver who claimed with a smile that she took the wrong ramp back to Summerset, David began to understand how hard it had been for Toni and Mike to leave him.

"What is it today?" David looked at the grinning young woman driving. "Can I get anyone to take me where I asked?" he said when she surprised him by entering the ramp west to Pittsburgh.

She just smiled at him. "Hey, it's my good deed for the day. I need all the good vibes I can get when I'm on that stage Friday night."

Her reasoning made little sense to him but he didn't want to do anything to jinx her, so he accepted the ride. They rode without speaking more than a few words for the first few miles. From the way his driver was squirming in her seat, David sensed she might be getting nervous in the silence and having second thoughts about picking him up. He was so deep into thinking about his friends, he knew he was a lousy riding companion.

"Where are you from my Good Samaritan?" he asked, trying

to relax her. When she looked at him, and the sparkle returned to her face, he also relaxed.

His driver looked at him again before speaking. "I'm from DC. Lived there all my life."

"Don't get mad at me again, but what made you decided to go into comedy?"

She smiled at him and then thought about what to say. "Like most kids, I didn't know what I wanted to do with my life. I spent two years in college changing my majors until I finally realized making people laugh is what I enjoyed the most. I would probably be a better as a lawyer or business woman, I realized, but would enjoy it less. Being on stage and getting a feel for your audience is a gift I was told, and now I finally understand that. The same jokes you tell down South might break them up but get you booed in New York City, and vice versa. The trick is to tell some jokes and, hopefully, read their response quick enough before bombing. Figuring out what your different audiences like is the tough part, and then it gets easy. Well, not easy, but when you hear them laughing at your material, it's almost better than sex. Don't look at me like that, I said almost," Monica added, grinning.

"Thank you, I like to laugh but when it—"

She frowned. "I know, I know, you men are all single minded."

"What?" David said, shrugging his shoulders and faking innocence.

"Anyway," she said after rolling her eyes at him, "They had an amateur night in a club near the college. Most got up and sang. I was the only one to try standup comedy. It went over so well I was hooked. I finished the semester my second year at school and then started working at a local comedy club as a waitress. I got to see so many funny people come through there. I stole some of their material and made them mine. I was told that's what everyone does in the industry. The owner of the club's son wanted in my pants so bad he let me do some of my material a few nights. I got what I wanted from him and, no, before you ask—"

"Me? Never."

"Anyway, he never got what he wanted."

David smiled at her when she looked over at him, but he

wasn't buying any of that "no" part. But it was her life, and if she wanted to bury that part, fine with him.

"Were your parents behind your dreams?" David regretted the question when she stared ahead as she drove without answering him. "I never knew mine," he said to the silence. "My grandparents raised me and, unfortunately, they died three months apart during my first year at Pitt. I wanted to finish, but, like you, after my second year, I didn't have the money or the drive to stay in school. I was lucky enough to get a get great-paying job a month after I left school. That was good because I was getting caught up in the bar scene and too many one nighters."

"Been there and done that," Monica added, finally rejoining the conversation. "Look, I knew it wasn't going to be easy. Most comedians quit after a few years or resort to drugs or booze. One very funny girl—and I loved her work—her career sank so low she ended up in LA on drugs and making movies. I don't have to tell you what kind."

David listened as his driver expounded on her difficult pursuit of a career in comedy. He had to admit she was very funny when she tried out her routines on him. They both laughed almost all the way to Pittsburgh. He even tried his hand at telling a joke.

"Okay, David, here's one you probably heard before. A woman was sitting at a bar enjoying an after-work cocktail with her girlfriends when an exceptionally tall, handsome, extremely sexy young man entered. He was so good looking that the woman could not take her eyes off him. The guy noticed her overly attentive stare and walked directly toward her. Before she could offer her apologies for being so rude for staring, the young man said to her, 'I'll do anything, absolutely anything, that you want me to do, no matter how kinky, for one hundred dollars, on one condition.' Flabbergasted, the woman asked what the condition was. The handsome guy replied, 'You have to tell me what you want me to do in just three words.'

"She was so turned on by him, the woman considered his proposition for a moment. Her girlfriends were edging her on with vulgar suggestions, so she opened her purse and slowly counted out five twenty-dollar bills, which she pressed into the young man's hand along with her address. She looked deeply into his eyes then slowly and passionately said, 'Clean—my—house.'"

David laughed. Not from the corny joke, but from how she used her body to imply something totally different. He could see how a woman as nice looking as Monica could captivate an audience, a male audience anyway funny or not.

"See, when a woman adds a hint of sex to a story people listen. Men because they're ah…men…and women because when we get together without men, that's how frank we talk with each other."

"So I've heard."

"Okay, your turn."

"You want me to drive?"

"No, smart ass, tell me a joke."

"Me, wait a minute. I don't have eye catching legs like yours in a short skirt."

"So, you did notice," Monica said with a naughty flair.

"No, I'm blind. Okay, give me a minute. All right, a guy is sitting reading his newspaper when his wife walks up behind him and smacks him on the back of the head with a frying pan. Rubbing his head, he asks, 'What was that for?'

"She says, 'I found a piece of paper in your pocket with Betty Sue written on it.'

"He says, 'Jeez, honey, remember last week when I went to the track? Betty Sue was the name of the horse I went there to bet on.'

"She shrugs unapologetically and walks away. Three days later, he's sitting at the kitchen table reading his paper when she walks up behind him and smacks him on the back of the head again with the frying pan.

"Again he asks, 'What was that for?'

"She answers z , 'Your horse just called.'"

"Now that was funny, David, A laughing Monica admitted. "Could I use that joke?"

"No way," he teased her. "I would consider selling it to you at a price."

She agreed, but they never got around to the obscure question of what that price was.

Monica was just the diversion David needed, he realized. She was humorous, determined, good to look at, and damn sexy. That became a real distraction to him as she drove. The fact that she was playing him didn't go unacknowledged, but he considered her excellent company worth the price. It was funny, he thought, despite meeting this warm and wonderful woman, all he could think about was Trisha.

He had the chance to explain to Monica, on the long drive, all that happened to Toni and Mike over the last few years and why they probably dropped him off. A couple of times, she shook her head at what he was saying but didn't interrupt. He even began to feel comfortable enough with her to tell her about his confused feelings for Toni, Trisha, and Brenda. She listened and was gracious enough to offer no personal advice. He liked that. Most women would have told him precisely what to do, as if they clearly understood the situation.

"So, tell me, which woman wins the affection of David Jackson?" Monica asked when her passenger became quiet.

"I wish I knew. I believe it's…"

"Wait!"

A startled David quickly looked up from staring at her to staring at the road in front of them, thinking something out there provoked her.

"David," she said when he turned toward her, "there is a simple test to determine where your heart is." When he didn't answer, she said. "See, David, when a woman makes you hard, that's a date. When a woman makes you soft—she's the one."

He looked at her, trying to read any hidden meaning to what she said. Being a man, he only read her words one way.

"Any attractive woman can make a guy get hard, that's easy." After saying that, she tugged down on the hem of her skirt. "When a woman makes a man soft—" Monica read his face and added, "that refers to his heart, if you missed my meaning—she's a keeper because you have already let her inside and may not know it. You have to figure out which one of them touches you there."

It wasn't an earth-shaking revelation, David conceded, but there was something moving about how she worded that.

"With Toni, I never expected my relationship to be more than friends, even after they broke up."

"Without benefits?"

"Yes—actually. But with Brenda, I had…ah…amazing benefits. Each one of them could answer both of your equations. But the same could be said about Trisha, thus my dilemma."

"No, only one of them makes you soft. You just haven't realized which one it is yet. You ever watch a beauty contest on TV?"

"A few, but none lately."

"Okay, let's try something else. Surely you watch the cheerleaders at a football game. Say the Cowboy Cheerleaders."

"Of course."

"Well, have you ever picked out the one you like? Of course, you have, but why? Are the other girls less pretty? Of course not, they are all pretty and in great shape. There's little difference between them, but there was to you because that one touches something in you. David, if you could put the three ladies in your life together in front of you, it would be easy to see which one touches you the most. It would be nice if life was that easy, right?"

David weighed her words but still wasn't sure which direction his life should now take.

"Well, I see the exit you wanted is coming up. Look, David, I don't want to add to your problems, but you seem like a nice guy. I would be interested in seeing you again, but only after you have resolved your feelings for the other women in your life." She never looked sweeter than when she smiled and added, "I don't want to make it a quartet of Cowboy Cheerleaders."

David laughed. "I don't blame you. You don't need that in your life now."

You are very interested in this guy, aren't you? Monica questioned as she moved over in the exit lane of the highway. The way he freely revealed his painful emotions touched her. Try as she might to ignore it, she had to admit she was turned on by him. Having a guy that really had something to say other than a cheap come-on-line was refreshing.

Monica started to feel a little guilty as they chatted and laughed because, while he was open and vulnerable, she couldn't stop dropping little suggestive hints. She had just begun to warm up to him as they chatted when the *Old Monica* surfaced. Sliding her hand down over legs and repeatedly tugging on the hem of her short skirt was one of the hooks the Old Monica would toss in the water to try and catch male fish. His continued quick glances at her...ah...bait caused her to do what was instinctive for the Old Monica. Hell, when they drove past a few motels she had thoughts of—

Then he surprised her by only looking out the windows the rest of the trip. *Good*, she resolved after her leg-show failed to hook him, *there appears to be more to him than skirt chasing.* That also impressed her.

As they neared Pittsburgh, she had another surprise up her lovely sleeve for him.

"David, where can I drop you off?"

"Where ever is best for you Monica. I can catch a bus or a cab from there."

She nodded as she drove. Some tunnels appeared and, after driving through them, she had an idea. "Where did you say Trisha lives?"

"In the Oakland section."

"Is that far from here?"

"Ah...no, actually, it's the next exit."

"Why don't I drop you off there?"

David looked over at the surprising woman.

"Great." Monica turned at the Bates Street Exit and drove up the hill towards Oakland. "Now let's see. Since you were a jerk for leaving—"

"What jerk?"

"You were a jerk for leaving Trisha. Don't argue with me," she said while waving an accusing finger at him.

David laughed at her but didn't protest.

"Okay, you need to make up for that. Where is there a flower shop around here? Flowers and chocolate always worked on me. Make a note of that for future reference—maybe."

"Make a right at the light, Ms. Reference," David ordered, smiling. "The only local florist shop I know of close is in Squirrel Hill."

When they walked out of the flower shop, she grabbed him by the shirt, pulled him down, and kissed him on the lips.

"And what was that for?"

"Are you complaining?"

"Not at all," David admitted.

"I didn't think so," the brassy young woman said as she walked around her car and winked at him before getting in. "Okay, now that I've solved your problems for you, I have a favor to ask," she said as they drove off. "I want you to promise to come and see my act on Friday."

When he looked at her as she drove, she gave him a coy grin.

"All right, what's up with that demure smile of yours?" he asked.

"If you do come, only come alone."

He laughed. "I promise to come alone and bring fresh flowers and new chocolates if these flowers and chocolates don't work. Thank you for everything, my lady."

"No problem."

He waved to her as she drove away. Monica was an attractive, interesting, and very complex young woman. He wondered if they would ever see each other again. That question was answered a moment later.

"*David*!"

Hearing someone scream his name, David turned around quickly, unsure of what was going on. Before he could say anything, the most wonderful woman he had ever known ran down the walkway toward him. She jumped into his arms, wrapped her legs around his waist and her arms around his neck, and smothered him with hugs and kisses.

"I knew you couldn't leave me. I knew you loved me too much to leave."

With the fervor in which she tightly clung to him, he now understood about becoming "soft." At that tender moment, the joy he felt in holding her in his arms again was worth all the hell he had been through today. This was where he belonged, he acknowledged, looking up into the Heavens. *Thank you, Toni and Mike, and Monica.*

"Yes, baby," he said as he walked to her door while holding Trisha in one hand, the flowers and chocolates in the other, and with her legs and arms still wrapped tightly around him. "There was no way I could ever leave you."

Epilogue

The next three years was a climb up the mountain for everyone involved. Mike and Toni continued on their journey of exploration in their motorhome, stopping first in New York City. They spent almost a month there, visiting all the sights, like the Statue of Liberty, and seeing numerous Broadway plays. They also spent many days just walking around, enjoying the sights, the people, trying the different restaurants, enjoying the feel and smell of that amazing city, and other days stayed in their room, making love all day.

Their health continued to improve. Maybe it was because of the strict diet Toni forced on them or the joy and happiness of being with the person they most loved. They emailed David and Brenda occasionally with the news about their adventures. Finally, they agreed, with David's insistence, to communicate more regularly and promised to on the first of every month.

After New York City, they stopped in the nation's capital for a few days and visited all the memorials there and the White House. Toni woke up one night, sensing a pressing need to visit Carl, so they abandoned plans to see other cities and drove directly to Daytona Beach, Florida. When she walked out on the beach with Mike and spotted Old Carl, they ran into each other's arms and wept. Toni returned his old Cubs hat, and he gave her his new one. Toni learned that his lovely wife Deana had passed away two weeks ago and not a day had passed that he wasn't crying over her. He wanted to die, he told them, and had already sold his beach chair business.

They spent two weeks at Carl's house, cooking and cleaning for him. During that time, Carl opened up to them that he blamed God for his and his wife's infertility, but Deana never did. Her claim was that he was her greatest gift from God, not children.

After her death, he began to realize the truth in that. Children grow up and leave, but your better half is "until death do us part." It was Mike who came up with the idea and asked Carl if he would like to accompany them on their voyage of exploration across the country. It was then Carl revealed he was a retired doctor and would love to spend his last days helping take care of his beautiful "daughter" and new son.

℘℘℘

Brenda did move to Harrisburg with her family and worked in a hospital there. It was her granny that noticed she wasn't happy there or with dating her old boyfriend, Jack Towers. Acknowledging that, Brenda surprised them by announcing she was going to LA and try her hand at acting and modeling. She obviously had the looks, but what the two older women in her life agreed, that wasn't the real reason she chose LA.

Once there, she did get a job at a hospital and began pursuing a career in modeling. As anyone in the City of Angels pursuing a dream could attest, and there were many of those, the nightmares far exceeded the dreams. When she realized what most wanted from her for the chance at maybe getting an opportunity, she quickly became disillusioned. Her saving grace, a year later after fighting the good fight, was a knock on her door.

Katie Thompson walking into Brenda's life again was the answer to her prayers, but more so, a gift from her closest friend. Reading between the lines of their latest emails, Toni sensed Brenda's defeated state of mind and asked Katie to seek her out and help if she could. When her other soulmate from high school walked back into Brenda's life, it was the vitamin she needed. Brenda soon moved in with Katie, and she introduced her to people she knew in the modeling and commercial industry, opening up a lucrative and very successful start of a career for her.

Success brought the beautiful redhead something she didn't expect. Brenda found herself a member of the in-crowd but never found the peace she sought. The annual trip home for the holidays—postponed the last year with hollow excuses—opened her eyes to what really made her happy. When her old boyfriend, Jack, walked back into her life and claimed it was her or nobody for him, she finally saw in his love what she was looking for all along. Despite his vocal objections, she bid ado to her career in the City of Angels and promised to become his better half, making both Toni and Katie happy.

ꙮꙮ

As for David, he asked Trisha two questions. First, to move in with him and second, to marry him. She said yes to both, a,nd six months later, they tied the knot in Atlanta with the large Tipton clan in attendance. It became the reason for that year's Tipton family reunion, and they were swamped with gifts and well wishers. Trisha's father beamed when he walked with her down the aisle and gave her away, and her sister Cheryl was delighted to be her maid-of-honor. David made a man who was too sick to be there his best man.

David moved his new family to Atlanta a year later when Trisha's mother was diagnosed with breast cancer. Thankfully, her mother survived the treatment, and the next year the David Jackson family was enlarged by two beautiful twin girls.

ꙮꙮ

Once a month, Toni kept her word. She emailed David and told him where they were and what they were doing. She refused his inquiries into their health, stating rather how happy they were. She did share with him about Brenda's successful career, and that she surprisingly gave it up and went back home and was now engaged and happy.

That was how the first three years went. The fourth year signaled a change in fortunes with the onslaught of Mike and Toni's disease. Old Carl, getting ill earlier in that year and passing away, didn't help the situation much. A grieving Toni shipped his body back to Florida so he could be buried next to his loving wife. When she learned of their poor health from Katie, a certain redheaded nurse postponed her wedding and moved in with them on the west coast.

Brenda was there when they lost their battle three months apart late that fourth year. First Mike and then a contented Toni.

Seeing her two best girlfriends in the room when she died completed Toni's life cycle, she told them. Brenda kept her word to Toni and didn't tell anyone back home until they both had passed away. David told the crying woman on the phone he understood why she couldn't tell him until afterward. You only had to know Toni.

Brenda did reveal something to David she learned from Toni. Old Carl, determined to be reunited with his Deana, the love of his life, finally went to church as she had desired and he had refused in his anger. She was a born-again Christian, Carl revealed, so, in a desire to be with her again, he accepted Christ as his savior. "It's eternity insurance," the old guy claimed his beloved wife would always tell him. Seeing the remarkable change in him afterward, both Toni and Mike also went to church and got saved. Toni's wish, before taking her last breath, Brenda tearfully revealed to a broken-hearted David, was that her two closest friends would also find Christ.

Toni's father reluctantly agreed for Brenda to cremate her as Toni wished. Year four ended with Brenda, and a surprised David, standing at the rear of a rented boat a mile off the California shores that Toni and Mike loved and visited every chance they could. These two people who loved them the most each held the urn containing their closest friend and, arm in arm, they tearfully scattered their ashes in the breeze. Their other halves, two people who loved them, stood back and tearfully watched.

The End

About the Author

According to author, E. Lessly Taylor, "Looking in the mind of a writer can be a scary place, depending on what he or she has to say." He started writing as a hobby, putting to paper the characters he saw in his mind. A place where he could take his vivid imagination, all the while presenting a calm face that the people around him could be comfortable with.

Working twelve- to fourteen-hours shifts, sometimes every day for three weeks at a clip, when an inspiration strikes, he would scribble notes on any piece of paper he could find. Riding the bus, he would get an idea and, afraid he might later miss the true meaning, scribbled notes on the inside of gum wrappers or on bus schedules.

His over a dozen novels cover a variety of subjects. "It's said great writers steal ideas from other writers," he claims. "My inspirations came from everyday people. The words I've put to paper are meant to reach a variety of intellects and place them in situations they can relate to and with sensitive characters that energize their emotions."

Taylor's wish is that, when reading his novels, readers are taken to a place where the weight of life is lifted for a time, and, once again, that naughty you hiding inside can breathe.